BAPTISM OF FIRE

The American line moved in surges, ten at a time, then twenty, then an entire company, then the entire brigade. They stopped their charge only long enough to raise their rifles to their shoulders to fire. In some cases, they didn't stop at all but merely fired as they moved . . .

As they reached the top of the hill, Todd saw a Spanish soldier suddenly rise up and take aim at Lieutenant Pershing. Pershing didn't see him, and the Spaniard was at point-blank range.

"John, look out!" Todd shouted, firing at the Spaniard at the same time. He saw a puff of dust rise up from the Spaniard's tunic. The Spaniard dropped his unfired rifle, and looked down at the blood spilling through his fingers. Then he looked up at Todd, his eyes pained and confused.

"Muerto?" he gasped.

Todd lowered the still-smoking pistol and watched, in shock, as the man fell forward across the rock wall . . .

IN HONORED
GLORY

Robert Vaughan

St. Martin's Paperbacks

IN HONORED GLORY

ISBN: 0-312-97009-9

Printed in the United States of America

St. Martin's Paperbacks edition/July 1999

St. Martin's Paperbacks are published by St. Martin's Press, 175 Fifth Avenue, New York, N.Y. 10010.

10 9 8 7 6 5 4 3 2 1

IN HONORED
GLORY

CHAPTER 1

New York City, January 23, 1898

Angus Pugh pulled his coat around him and, fighting the cold, walked along the waterfront on Manhattan's Lower East Side. A small bit of bread, wet and sodden, lay along the edge of the dank boards. A rat, its beady eyes alert for danger, darted out to the prize, grabbed it, then bounded back to the comparative safety of one of the numerous warehouses.

Behind Pugh the ships at anchor were representative of the gradual transformation from sail to steam and wood to steel. The masts of the wind ships stabbed into the sky, their rigging free of sail, hanging from the yards and whistling in the wind. The great steamships, their steel hulls rising high above the docks, crowded alongside, haughty in their dominance.

Pugh was a sailor, or at least he called himself one, though he was currently without a berth. He had many voyages under his belt, both as a member of the U.S. Navy and as a seaman aboard vessels of commerce. When his hitch was up three months ago, he had left the U.S. Navy and his ship, the *USS Maine*. He could have shipped over for another voyage, but he refused to do so because a Captain's Mast had divested him of his rating, reducing him from gunner's mate first class to ordinary seaman. Pugh's reduction in rank was the result of an inspecting officer discovering whiskey in his seabag.

The U.S. Navy's ban against all alcoholic beverages on board was asinine, Angus thought. As a merchant seaman he had been perfectly within his rights to keep liquor aboard. But in the navy that was a major infraction. What made Pugh even angrier was his knowledge that several of the officers kept bottles, including Mr. Merritt, the officer who had turned him in.

Now, Pugh was desperately in need of a job, and finding a billet on a merchant ship was proving to be very difficult. More and more the merchant fleets were hiring only those seamen who had union papers, and Pugh had no papers because he didn't have enough money for union dues.

Last week he had been reduced to working on a garbage scow. The indignity of it was almost more than he could take. He was a man who had been a gunner's mate first class in the U.S. Navy, a responsible position that put him in charge of more than thirty men. Before he joined the navy, he had been a bosun's mate on a windjammer that made the China run. Angus Pugh had sailed, as man and boy, for twenty years. Working on a garbage scow was the ultimate indignity, and yet his financial state was such that if he could sign on again today, he would.

He blamed the U.S. Navy for his predicament. The navy and its unreasonable rules and regulations. He also blamed Mr. Merritt, the assistant engineering officer on board the *Maine*. Merritt was the one who had found the liquor in an inspection, and it was Merritt who had put Pugh on report. Of course, Captain Sigsbee was the one who actually took Pugh's rating from him, but Sigsbee was the captain after all, and he had no choice once the matter had been brought to him. Pugh didn't blame Sigsbee, but he did blame Mr. Merritt.

Pugh walked up South Street until he reached Davy Jones' Locker, a cheerless and evilly run bar that catered to the lowest clientele. Here, seamen, and the women who preyed upon them, stayed drunk all the time, or at least when they could afford it. They drank rotgut whiskey, which was bought by the tin cup and drawn directly from the barrel. The customers were what Pugh would have called, in his better days, bilge rats, and yet he found himself coming here more and more often, because the liquor, while raw, was potent and cheap. They also kept a big bowl of boiled eggs on the bar, and for the last three days those boiled eggs had been Angus Pugh's only food.

Inside the bar, the air reeked of unwashed bodies, the sour smell of drunkenness, and the sulphurous fumes of coal from the heating stove. Pugh ambled over to the bar, scooped up three eggs from the bowl, and dropped them into his pocket. Then he picked up another egg, which he began to crack.

"What'll you have?" the bartender asked.

"Wait," Pugh said. He emptied his pocket onto the bar. There was a quarter, two nickels, two pennies, a safety pin, and a small bit of string. "I'll have a whiskey," Pugh said, sliding a nickel toward the bartender.

The bartender picked up the nickel, then filled a tin cup and slid it down to Pugh. He was pretty sure the cup hadn't been washed since the last customer but didn't say anything about it because he didn't want to be thrown out. This was at least a place to get out of the cold and to get something to eat, even if he was tired of boiled eggs.

Pugh walked over to a corner booth and sat down. A moment later Jeremy McTavish sat across the table from him.

"Find any work today?" McTavish asked.

Pugh dipped the end of his egg into the whiskey, then took a bite. He shook his head no but didn't speak.

"I heard tell of a job," McTavish said.

"Garbage scow?" Pugh growled.

"No. I don't know what it is . . . but they are looking for someone who can work with explosives."

Pugh brightened. "Explosives? I can work with explosives."

McTavish nodded. "Aye, I thought as much."

"It's dangerous work," Pugh said.

"The fact that it's dangerous won't stop you, will it? I mean, if you really need the work," McTavish replied.

"I don't know. You make a mistake workin' with explosives, and you could get yourself killed."

"Aye, that's true."

Pugh dunked his egg again. "On the other hand, gettin' blown up might be better than ridin' on that stinkin' garbage scow again. Who is hirin'?"

"I can't tell you that."

"You mean you don't know?"

"Aye, I know all right. But I can't tell you."

"Well, that's a hell of a note," Pugh said. "Who would work for someone like that?"

"Maybe someone who wants to earn $1,000," McTavish answered.

Pugh gasped. "The hell you say! One thousand dollars?"

"Aye. One thousand dollars to you and $100 to me for finding you," McTavish said.

"Wait; hold it. I'm supposed to give you $100 for telling me about this job?"

McTavish shook his head. "No, the 1,000 you get will be all yours. The 100 I get will come out of their pocket as well."

"Whoever this is must want someone pretty bad."

"I think so."

Pugh smiled. "My bet is, they need someone so bad they'd be willing to pay fifteen hundred dollars."

"You're goin' to screw it up," McTavish protested. "The offer was for 1,000. If you insist on fifteen hundred, they'll go somewhere else."

"Where?"

"I don't know."

"All you have to do is tell them that I'm the only one you could find," Pugh said.

McTavish stroked his chin. "What's in it for me?"

"Another fifty," Pugh offered. "If I get the job."

McTavish continued to stroke his chin as he thought about Pugh's offer. Finally, he nodded. "All right," he said. "Be at Pier Nine tomorrow morning at five o'clock."

"How will I know who to look for?" Pugh asked.

"Don't worry about it. They'll find you," McTavish said as he slid out of the booth.

Washington, D.C.

As Maj. Gen. Joseph Daniel Murchison's driver drove him home from his office at the War Department, Joe pulled the lap robe around him to shield him from the cold. The team trotted steadily, the rhythmic clopping of their hooves providing a counterpoint to the ringing of steel-rimmed wheels as the carriage rolled across the paving bricks of Constitution Avenue.

A newspaper, the New York *Daily Banner*, lay face-up on the seat beside him, its headlines blaring:

CONDITIONS OF OPPRESSION IN CUBA

Cubans are daily facing horrors from their Spanish masters that would rival the vilest deeds ever committed by one people against another. Denied even the most basic forms of self-expression, the Cuban must walk his own land with his head bowed and his tongue silent, lest a Spanish soldier take offense.

Attractive Cuban women, even young mothers with children, are often victims of the most debased abusive treatment and physical attacks from the Spanish.

Armed with the knowledge of such brutality against our gentle neighbors to the south, does not every American's spirit rise in indignation against the Spanish? Does obligation to human dignity not demand that our government step in to ease the suffering of the Cubans?

The New York *Daily Banner* finds it heartening to note that thousands of Cubans have joined or helped with the revolution, only because they believe their independence would pave the way to annexation by the United States. If there are some Cubans who oppose this idea, it is because they lack a full knowledge of the American Constitution and of the spirit of American institutions and have been led to believe that annexation would mean only a change of masters.

This newspaper has long expressed an editorial opinion that wresting Cuba from Spain, then annexation, is as much a part of the "Manifest Destiny" of the United States as was the expansion of our great nation to the far Pacific shore. We urge President McKinley to take a more active position in helping the Cubans throw off the yoke of Spanish oppression and in welcoming them into the embracing arms of our protection.

McKinley had given the article to Joe to read this afternoon. The president had stood with his hands behind his back, staring silently out his window while Joe read the article.

"What do you think, General?" McKinley asked without turning around, somehow sensing that Joe had finished the article.

"Mr. President, I think this is just a lot of talk to sell newspapers," Joe replied. "All the papers are jumping on the bandwagon to see who can come up with the most outlandish story, the *World,* the *Journal,* the *Times.* Why should the *Banner* be any different? I wouldn't pay any attention to it."

McKinley turned toward Joe. Tall, clean-shaven, and with a high forehead and gray eyes, the president sighed.

"I know they are just trying to sell newspapers. That's what frightens me, because if they can get us into a war, they will sell even more newspapers. I wish I could ignore it, but it isn't politically possible to do so."

"These newspaper editors can agitate all they want. . . . They don't have the power to declare war. The last I heard, that was still the function of Congress," Joe said.

"That may be true, but the unfortunate fact is the newspapers have put me in a box," McKinley replied. "We have American interests in Cuba and many American citizens who live there. These constant attacks against the Spaniards by our press put those Americans in danger. If I don't act in some way to provide for their protection, I will be accused of neglecting their safety. On the other hand, if I take steps to protect our citizens in Cuba, then Spain might construe it as an act of belligerency. And that is exactly what these unscrupulous publishers want to happen."

"Can't you get the papers to stop printing such stories?"

"How? I have appealed to their patriotism, and they reacted by running editorials that all but waved the American flag, while continuing with their inflammatory stories."

"Order them to stop," Joe suggested. "And if they don't, close them down."

McKinley chuckled. "Now, that really would be a story, wouldn't it, General? The president of the United States suspends the freedom of the press? The American people would hound me out of office."

"Not if the American people knew the truth. If the American people knew that the newspapers were trying to provoke a war, they would understand."

"That's the whole problem, General; they do know it, but they don't care," McKinley said. "They are obviously titillated by the idea of war. Newspaper circulation is at an all-time high. Did you hear about the exchange of telegrams between William Randolph Hearst and the artist Frederic Remington?"

"What exchange is that?"

"Hearst sent Frederic Remington to Cuba to get pictures. I imagine he wanted to make his atrocity stories even more graphic. But when Remington arrived in Cuba he wired back to Hearst: 'Everything is quiet. There is no trouble here. There will be no war. I wish to return.'

"To which, Hearst replied: 'Please remain. You furnish the pictures and I'll furnish the war.' "

"Hearst was that blatant about it?"

"Yes."

"Surely there is something you can do about that," Joe suggested. "Don't you have some authority to prevent such a thing?"

McKinley shook his head. "No. I am a servant of the people, not a king that rules over them. The newspapers are calling the shots. All I can do now is look out for our interests in Cuba. To that end, General Murchison, I have ordered the battleship *Maine* to Havana. And that is where you come in. I want you to go to Havana as well. You will act as my personal emissary to explain to the Spaniards that the *Maine* poses no threat to them. It is making a courtesy call only."

Joe looked confused. "You want me to go to Havana with a battleship? Mr. President, wouldn't a senior naval officer be more appropriate?"

McKinley shook his head. "No. No matter how much he might talk peace, a senior naval officer, with a battleship at his command, could be interpreted as the commander of a naval expeditionary force. But if you go down there, a senior army official with no troops under your command, there would be no implied threat. There is a subtle, but I think important, difference. You will go for me, won't you, General?"

"Yes, Mr. President, of course I will go," Joe answered. "Where is the *Maine* now? Shall I join it?"

"It is already en route," McKinley replied. "I thought it would be better if you went down on a civilian ship. I want some separation between you and the *Maine*."

Joe's meeting with the president had taken place no more than an hour ago. Upon leaving the president's office, he immediately made a telephone call home, informing his wife that he would be sailing, shortly, for Cuba. Tamara, ever the dutiful officer's wife, had asked no questions but told him she would begin packing.

The carriage pulled into the curved driveway under the portico of Joe's house, a large two-story home that was suitable for a general officer but seemed much too large now that Joe's son, Todd, and daughter, Sarah Louise, were gone. Todd was in West Point, soon to graduate. Sarah Louise was away at college.

Joe dismissed his driver, then went inside. The living room of Joe's house was furnished in the style prevalent among his socioeconomic peers, following the theory that "too much is not enough." There were bric-a-brac, vases, lamps, bowls, trays, doilies, and pillows on every table, chair, and sofa back. On the floor there were carpets upon carpets, and the wallpaper—covered with a pattern of huge flower-filled baskets—was liberally decorated with photographs of every size and description, hanging at different heights, suspended by long wires from the picture rail that encircled the room at the top of the wall.

The maid took Joe's coat and hat as Tamara came over to greet him. Tamara was nearly fifty years old, but her hair was still naturally dark, her skin smooth, and her dimpled cheeks rosy. She was as beautiful to him today as she had been the first day he ever saw her, back in Fort Abraham Lincoln, when she had paid a visit to the orderly room of D Troop of the Seventh Cavalry.

"How soon will you have to leave?" Tamara asked. Though Joe's military assignments had taken them all over the country, Tamara still spoke with the trace of a southern accent.

"Tomorrow."

"Oh, tomorrow?" Tamara's voice showed her disappointment. "Todd has the weekend off from school and is coming to Washington for a visit. He will be so disappointed that you aren't here."

"I know; I'll be disappointed too," Joe said. "But Todd is about to embark upon a military career. He will understand such things."

"I am nearly finished packing for you," Tamara informed him. "I put in two extra pairs of long underwear, as well as your other scarf and gloves."

Joe laughed. "Tamara, I am going to Havana," he said. "Cuba is in the tropics. It will be very warm there."

"Oh," Tamara said. "Yes, of course it will, won't it? I don't know what I was thinking."

Joe squeezed her affectionately. "Never mind," he said. "It is the thought that counts."

Havana Harbor, February 15, 1898

The *Maine* was 319 feet long, with large smokestacks amidships and tall masts fore and aft, not for sails but for lookouts. It was painted white, as was traditional for U.S. Navy vessels during peacetime, and would be an impressive sight anywhere. In Havana Harbor, with its heavy armor and turret-mounted large guns, it made a particularly dominating presence.

The *Maine* was not the only American vessel in Cuban waters. There were at least three others, one of which had recently attracted the attention of the harbor police. The 138-foot *Buccaneer* was a private yacht leased by one of the New York newspapers. Even though it was not a military ship, it was fitted with several small pieces of artillery and guarded by the newspaper's private army of armed men.

On board was Julian Hawthorne, a reporter. Hawthorne had already written half a dozen extremely bellicose stories concerning Spanish atrocities and, in the eyes of the Spanish authorities, was fanning the war fever. Hawthorne was very popular in America, not only because of his newspaper stories but also because he was the author of two best-selling novels. In addition, he was the son of another well-known writer, Nathaniel Hawthorne.

Because of the hostile nature of the articles Hawthorne was writing and the belligerency of the New York press, the Spanish decided to seize the *Buccaneer*. They boarded it right under the very guns of the *Maine*. Capt. Charles Sigsbee, of the *Maine*, watched the operation from the deck of his ship but made no effort to interfere with the harbor police. This was a fact that the newspapers in New York regarded as incredible.

One paper expressed its outrage in an article published under a banner headline:

THE SPANISH WAR AGAINST FREEDOM OF THE PRESS

Has war been declared by Spain against America's free press? It would seem so, for the *Buccaneer*, a peaceful vessel that was simply transporting reporters to Cuba, was boarded and seized in an act of outright piracy.

Americans should know that this violation of freedom of the press and private property rights took place under the very guns of the U.S. battleship *Maine*. Despite urgent pleas from the captain and crew of the *Buccaneer* for someone to come to their aid, Captain Sigsbee, the master of the *Maine*, made no effort to render assistance.

This paper has been most outspoken in its effort to expose the American people to the atrocities that are occurring daily in Cuba, not only against the poor, oppressed Cuban people, but also against Americans who, for business or pleasure, have found themselves on that tropic isle. In addition, we take some justifiable pride in helping President McKinley come to the decision of sending the *Maine* to Cuba for the protection of American lives. Thus, we feel that the question can now be legitimately asked: "Where was the *Maine* when we needed it?" The answer is, "It was right there in the harbor, watching impotently as the outlaw Havana Harbor Police made their illegal seizure of American private property."

The seizure of the *Buccaneer* had taken place three days ago, and nothing had happened since. It was toward the end of a long, quiet, hot, and humid day when General Murchison, now in Havana at the president's directive, was piped aboard the *Maine*. It was 6:00 P.M. on the evening of the fifteenth, and Joe was to be the guest of Captain Sigsbee and the wardroom officers for supper. Shortly after the general was piped aboard, the marine bugler on board, Fifer C. H. Newton, sounded Mess Call.

"Well, there, at least, is a ritual I understand," Joe said. "I'm happy to see that the bugle call for Mess Call is the same for the navy as it is for the army."

Captain Sigsbee chuckled. "I guess a hungry man doesn't care what uniform he is wearing." Sigsbee led Joe into the wardroom, which also served as the officers' mess, then pointed toward the head of the table. "Please, General, take the seat at the head of the table."

"No, no," Joe said. "You are the captain of this ship."

"But you are our honored guest. If we had an admiral on board, that would be his position."

The other officers were standing expectantly, and not wanting to make any more of it, Joe expressed his gratitude and took the chair that was offered him. Not until he and the captain were seated did the other officers take their seats.

"General, I understand you are quite a baseball player," Sigsbee said.

"I enjoyed playing when I was younger," Joe answered.

"We have a very good team on board the *Maine*. In fact, our team was champions of the fleet last summer. I have been told that baseball is very popular with the Cubans," Sigsbee said. "Perhaps we could have a game between our team and a local nine."

"Yes," Joe agreed. "That's a good idea, Captain. It might be a very good way to promote good will. I'll see what I can do to make all the arrangements."

"Thank you," Captain Sigsbee said. "So, what are the people ashore saying about the *Maine*?"

"They are saying that this ship is the biggest and most powerful thing they have ever seen," Joe replied with a chuckle.

"Aye, she is a grand ship," Sigsbee said. "Clearly the most impressive vessel I have ever served aboard."

"By the way, Captain, I suppose you have seen all the newspaper accounts of the seizure of the *Buccaneer*?" Joe asked.

"Aye, sir, I have seen them," Sigsbee answered guardedly.

"I want you to know that I immediately sent word to the president that I am entirely in support of your action with regard to that incident. If I had been in your place I would have done the same thing."

"Thank you, General," Sigsbee replied, breathing a sigh of relief. "I'm very pleased that you agree."

"The president agrees as well," Joe said. "I received a return wire from him today."

"Gentlemen," the executive officer, Lt. Comdr. Richard Wainwright, said, lifting his glass. "A toast to our captain!"

"To the captain!" the officers said as one, lifting their water glasses.

Joe joined in the toast.

"I apologize, General Murchison, for the fact that the navy allows no liquor on board," Commander Wainwright said. "What we are actually doing is writing checks, so to speak.

As soon as we are back on shore, we re-drink every toast, in liquor.''

"If we've had enough toasting during our voyage, the first evening on the beach can be quite interesting," Captain Sigsbee added with a little chuckle.

"I can see that it might be," Joe replied. "Captain, I wonder if, after our meal, you would be so kind as to take me on a tour of your ship?"

"It would be an honor, sir," Sigsbee replied.

After a dinner of corned beef and cabbage, Joe followed Captain Sigsbee out onto the deck for a bow-to-stern tour of the ship. They went belowdecks, through the companionways, and into the gun turrets and compartments of the ship as Sigsbee kept up a running commentary.

"Ah, here is Mr. Merritt, our assistant engineering officer," Sigsbee said. "Mr. Merritt, I'll let you give the general the statistics."

"I would be honored to, Captain," Merritt replied as he took over this part of Joe's tour. "The *Maine* is 324 feet long, 70 feet at the beam, with a displacement of 6,650 tons," he explained. "The engines develop 9,200 horsepower, and she can make eighteen knots at flank speed. She has a complement of thirty-one officers and 350 men."

From the engine room they went into the crew's quarters, belowdecks, amidship.

"Attention! Captain on deck!" one of the sailors called as Sigsbee and Joe entered. Here hammocks were hung between stanchions and bulkheads. The compartment was extremely crowded but, Joe noticed, quite clean.

"Carry on, men," Sigsbee said quickly. He then continued his commentary.

"The *Maine* is equipped with four ten-inch guns, two in the forward and two in the after turret. In addition, there are six six-inch breech-loading rifles, seven six-pounder rapid-fire guns, eight one-pounders, and four Gatling machine guns. There are tubes for four torpedoes."

"An impressive bit of firepower," Joe remarked.

"Aye, sir, it is indeed. Had this ship been available to the

Confederacy during the Civil War, it could have destroyed the entire U.S. Navy and laid waste to Washington, D.C.''

"You could do the same thing now, here in Havana," Joe said.

Sigsbee nodded. "That is true, and believe me, it is a responsibility I do not take lightly."

"Oh, I'm aware of that, Captain. As I say, I thought you showed great restraint with regard to the *Buccaneer* matter. But I think it is good that the Spanish understand that we not only have the power but also are able to project it."

An hour later, after saying good-bye to the other officers in the wardroom, Joe and Captain Sigsbee were back up on deck at the the port side gangway. Joe was getting ready to return to shore, where he had a room in a hotel. One hundred yards away from the *Maine* was another ship.

"What ship is that?" Joe asked, pointing. "I didn't notice it when I came aboard earlier."

"No, sir, it wasn't there then," Sigsbee replied. "It arrived while we were at mess. That's the steamer *City of Washington*."

"How do you know that?"

"The OOD brought me a report when it arrived. As captain of the only war vessel in the harbor, it is my duty to keep abreast of such things," Sigsbee explained.

"Yes, of course, I should have realized. The *City of Washington*? Then it is an American ship?"

"Aye, sir."

"I hope it isn't another ship from the newspapers' private navy," Joe said.

"I don't think you have to worry about that, General. This is a merchant steamer, here to trade in tobacco," Sigsbee replied.

"You are probably right. Nevertheless, I think I should call on the captain," Joe said. "If for no other reason than to let him know that I am here, if he should run into any difficulty."

"I'll have my gig run you over there, General," Sigsbee offered.

"Thank you."

* * *

Five minutes after leaving the *Maine*, the captain's gig touched lightly against the side of *City of Washington*. A rope ladder was dropped over for Joe, who, dismissing the gig, climbed aboard. Strong hands helped him negotiate the last few rungs of the ladder.

"I am Captain Stevens. Welcome to the *City of Washington*."

"Thank you, Captain. I am Gen. Joseph Murchison."

"General?" the captain said in alarm. "What is an American general doing here, in Havana? Have we gone to war?"

"No," Joe answered quickly. "On the contrary, I am here to help see that there is no war."

"Well, you can certainly count on my support for that, General," the captain said. "The last thing I want is a war. I have a lucrative business transporting tobacco from Cuba to the U.S., and I wouldn't want to see anything stop that trade."

"The newspapers are all talking war, and if they had their choice, we'd be invading Cuba tomorrow," Joe replied.

"What with the *Maine* here, there are some who might suggest we have already occupied Cuba," Captain Stevens said. "Certainly there is nothing in these waters that can stand up to her. I'm not sure if there is any ship, anywhere in the world, that is her match."

"I had dinner aboard the *Maine* tonight," Joe added. "And I agree, it is a most impressive ship."

"Perhaps you would like to view her from the fantail?" Captain Stevens invited. "I know you were aboard her tonight, but this will give you a totally different perspective."

"Thank you, yes, I believe I would enjoy that," Joe replied.

Joe and Captain Stevens went to the fantail, where, as Stevens promised, the view was extraordinary, especially as the *Maine* was strung with hundreds of glistening electric lights. Shortly after they reached the fantail, they were joined by two more of the ship's officers.

Joe told them about the *Maine*, how its presence in Havana Harbor and, indeed, his own presence as a personal emissary of the president of the United States were meant to have a steadying influence on the situation.

"Well, regardless of why it is here, I must confess that it does make one feel protected," one of the officers stated.

"Like the *Buccaneer* was protected?" the other officer replied.

"You've heard about the *Buccaneer* already?" Joe asked.

"How can we not hear about it? It was front-page news when we left," Captain Stevens said. "The *Journal* is playing it up very big."

"I'm sure they are," Joe replied. "But they can yell all they want. Under the circumstances, Captain Sigsbee's restraint was exactly what was called for."

"I don't know if I would have had Captain Sigsbee's restraint," one of the two officers said.

"Of course you would," Stevens replied. "One does what one must do, when in command."

"It sure is hot," the other young officer said, pulling his collar away from his neck. "It's February, but it feels more like July."

"Yes. I've been here for several days now, and I'm still not used to the heat," Joe replied. He was looking toward the *Maine* when, suddenly, the bow seemed to rise from the water. Even as he was wondering about that strange sight, he heard a rumbling sound, then a thunderous explosion, accompanied by a wave of concussion. A tremendous mass of fire and smoke erupted from the center of the ship.

"My God! What's happening?" Stevens shouted.

As the *Maine* exploded, Joe was horrified to see that, along with the fire and debris, scores of bodies were tossed high into the night sky, like straws in a windstorm. The air around him became oppressively hot and thick with smoke. Joe had to hang onto the railing to keep the concussion wave from knocking him down.

Chunks of metal and flaming debris began falling on the *City of Washington.* As they were standing on the fantail, they had to get under shelter quickly to avoid being hit.

"The *Maine* has been attacked!" one of the officers shouted. "We're being fired on by shore batteries!"

"Sound the alarm!" Captain Stevens ordered. "General, are we at war? What do we do?"

"Look ashore," Joe said. "There are no guns firing at us. What we are being hit by is debris from the *Maine*. Get all of your boats over, Captain. We must save as many as we can."

CHAPTER 2

Aboard USS Mangrove, *Havana Harbor, February 21, 1898*

The blast aboard the *Maine* killed 250 sailors and two officers. The officers killed were Lt. Friend W. Jenkins and Assistant Engineer Darwin R. Merritt, neither of whom were in their quarters, but on duty amidships when the explosion occurred.

Not wanting to waste any time, the court of inquiry was convened on board the *USS Mangrove* on the same day it arrived. Although the proceedings were held in secret session, Joe was present. He had two reasons for being there, the first being that he was the president's personal envoy to Cuba and the second that he was the last one to leave the ship before it exploded.

The board of inquiry consisted of Capt. William T. Sampson, CaptainO Arnold Chadwick, Lt. Comdr. William Potter, and Lt. Comdr. Adolph Marix. The senior member of the board was Captain Sampson, a man Joe knew was about to be promoted to admiral.

Joe sat in a chair in the wardroom to one side of the table around which the board was sitting. His eyes were drawn toward the president of the board. Captain Sampson had a high forehead, intense eyes, heavy brows, a thin face, and a narrow beard with a drooping mustache.

"Gentlemen," Sampson began. "We are met on a matter of great import. The recent disaster is one of the most terrible in the annals of naval history. Is this the result of Spanish sabotage or an onboard accident?'' Sampson continued, ''Upon our findings rests the course of our country's future action. We have a grave responsibility. We should not rush to judgment, for if we erroneously declare this to be an act of sabotage, we may well go to war, at the cost of many more lives. On the other hand, if this is an act of hostile intent, then we must report it as such, for the honor of our nation is at stake. Are there any questions?''

There were none.

''I call the board's attention to the presence of Maj. Gen. Joseph Daniel Murchison. General Murchison is President McKinley's personal envoy to Cuba and, as such, is also the president's personal observer for these proceedings. He will take no part in the deliberation, though he will appear as a witness.''

''What role did he play as a witness?'' one of the other board members asked. ''Meaning no disrespect, sir,'' he added quickly.

''Good question,'' Sampson answered. ''General Murchison was Captain Sigsbee's guest for dinner on the evening of the explosion. He was the last man to leave the *Maine* before the explosion. General, your presence is welcome.''

''Thank you, sir,'' Joe replied.

''Call the first witness,'' Sampson ordered.

An orderly left the wardroom, then returned with Captain Sigsbee. Sigsbee saluted the board, then, at Sampson's invitation, took his seat, a simple wooden chair that had been placed in front of the table.

''Captain Sigsbee, did you maintain a full watch while in port?'' Sampson began.

''I did, sir.''

''And you saw no activity of divers, small boats, or anything else of a suspicious nature?''

''We did not, sir.''

''Assuming that it was a mine, is there any way a mine could have been placed on your vessel without being detected?''

''I don't believe it could've been put on the ship, sir,''

Sigsbee replied. "But it might have been put on the anchor buoy, prior to our arrival."

"Oh?" Sampson replied, his heavy brows lifting at Sigsbee's suggestion. "Would you care to elaborate?"

"When I arrived, I pointed to the buoy to which I wanted my ship anchored," Sigsbee said. "I chose the buoy because it would keep the ship some distance from all the other vessels in the harbor . . . and thus afford us greater security. The pilot refused, however, saying that the harbor authorities insisted that we be anchored at another buoy. I have since spoken with Captain Stevens, of the *City of Washington.* As you know, the *City of Washington* is a freighter and has made numerous trips to Havana. Captain Stevens knows the harbor very well. He informs me that he has never known a man-of-war to be anchored at that buoy and only rarely have merchant vessels anchored there."

"So it is your belief that a mine was placed on the buoy before your arrival?"

"I am suggesting that as a possibility, since we saw no suspicious activity around our ship after we arrived," Sigsbee replied.

"There is, of course, the very strong possibility that the explosion was the result of spontaneous combustion of coal, paint, or some other flammable," Sampson suggested.

"There is that possibility of course," Sigsbee replied. "But I don't think that is the case."

"Did you ever receive any report from the chief engineer of your ship that any coal had been too long in any bunker?"

"None that I can recollect," Sigsbee replied.

"Did the fire alarms in the bunkers work?"

"They worked quite well, sir. In fact, they were overly sensitive and would work in those times when there was no undue heat in the bunkers. Even so, we always examined the bunkers to get a report."

The next witness was Chief Engineer Charles Howell. Howell testified that the bunkers had been cool and well ventilated.

"What about Bunker A-16?" one of the board officers asked. The questioner was Lieutenant Commander Marix.

Marix had once been an executive officer on board the *Maine* and knew the ship well. "I recall that it was a difficult bunker to work with, because of its location."

"Yes, sir, but A-16 couldn't have been the cause. It was cool."

"How do you know it was cool?" Captain Sampson asked.

Howell looked over at Joe. "Why, Captain, you can ask the general there. He took a tour of the ship not more than two hours before the explosion, and while I was telling him about the operation of the ship's engines he was leaning against the A-16 bulkhead. If it had been smoldering, the general would've felt it."

Sampson looked over at Joe. "You felt no unusual heat?" he asked.

"I did not," Joe replied.

"What about A-15, on the port side? It's just as difficult," Marix suggested.

"A-15 was empty, sir. We used that bunker first," Howell replied.

After Howell, the engineering officer on watch was interviewed. He stated that he had personally inspected the coal bunkers less than twelve hours before the explosion and found them in good condition.

After discounting the coal bunkers as the source of the problem, the board investigated, then discarded, the possibility of an electrical short. There had been no electrical malfunction; indeed, all witnesses, even those from ashore, testified that the ship was brightly lit, with no flickering lights or any other indication of electrical trouble.

The boilers were also cleared when they learned that only the two aftermost boilers were fired off and both were operating at below one hundred pounds of steam, well below the safety limit. Engineer Frederic Bowers testified that he had checked the fires and the water in the glass less than two hours before the explosion. "The boilers were, in all respects, in a normal condition," Bowers said.

After clearing the most obvious reasons for an accidental explosion, the board questioned Lt. George Holman. Holman was a particularly good witness not only because he was a member of the crew and present for the explosion but also because he was a specialist in explosives.

"The incident was precisely similar to many other submarine explosions I have heard, except that it was on a much larger scale," Holman said. "A submarine explosion always gives two shocks, one transmitted through the water, the other, the atmospheric shock, immediately following. If you are asking my opinion, gentlemen, there is no doubt in my mind but that this explosion was a submarine explosion of external origin."

When Joe was called to the witness stand, he testified that he had seen the *Maine* rise several feet out of the water, followed by the shock of the explosion.

"You saw the ship lift out of the water?" Sampson asked. "Yes."

"You are certain of that? That is a very important observation, General, for if the ship was lifted from the water, it almost has to be the result of an external explosion."

"I'm certain. I saw the bow lift from the water," Joe repeated.

Sampson nodded. "That concurs with the eyewitness reports we have gathered from others who weren't on board the ship when it exploded. Gentlemen," Sampson said to the others. "All we need now is the report of our divers to complete the investigation, but I am already convinced that their report will validate what we have learned. I am convinced that the explosion was from outside the hull."

"Then our report will say that the Spanish caused the explosion?" Commander Marix asked.

Sampson shook his head. "It is not our task to discover who did it . . . only what was done," Sampson said. "If examination of the keel shows the ruptured plates turning in, then our finding is validated. The witnesses are excused . . . and this court is adjourned."

The divers spent another week investigating the sunken ship. They found that the metal plates had been blown inward, as well as a large hole in the bottom of the bay, as if the excavation had been blasted by a mine placed under the ship.

New York City, March 2, 1898

Angus Pugh sat in a corner booth of Davy Jones' Locker with his hands wrapped around a half-empty mug of beer as if he feared someone might try to take it from him. There were few who would challenge him, though. A broken nose, a puffy mass of scar tissue on his forehead, and the purple lightning flash of a scar that started under his left eye and hooked around the corner of his mouth indicated that he was a man accustomed to violence.

Although it was quite warm in the bar, Pugh still wore his heavy sea coat and his stocking cap. Only recently returned to New York from warmer climes, he was having a difficult time readjusting to the cold.

He was also having a difficult time coping with the fact that so many of his former shipmates had died in the explosion of the *Maine*. Of the thirty men who had once been on his watch, twenty-eight were killed. All but one of the members of the baseball team were now dead, and although Pugh had not been a ballplayer, he had often wagered on the outcome of their games and had known all of them personally. On the other hand, Mr. Merritt was also dead, which, as far as Pugh was concerned, was proof that every cloud had a silver lining.

Pugh's personal fortunes had improved considerably since the last time he had visited Davy Jones' Locker. He had agreed to perform a dangerous job, and he had completed it successfully. He was here now to collect the money that was due him.

McTavish, who had set up the job for Pugh, had told him to wait here and he would bring Pugh's employer to him. Half an hour later, Pugh saw the man who had hired him. He recognized him the moment he stepped through the door, even though it had been more than a month since Pugh had seen him last. The man was very easy to pick out. In his wool overcoat, expensive bowler hat, and well-polished shoes, he stood out like a rose in a cabbage patch.

From the moment the well-dressed man entered the bar, all eyes were upon him. Aware that he was the center of attention, he stood in the door for a moment, stroking his cheek nervously, as he looked around the bar. When he saw Pugh sitting in the corner booth, some of his tension eased and he went over to join him.

"Did we have to meet in such a place?" he asked as he sat across the table from Pugh.

"What's wrong with this place? These are my people," Pugh replied, taking them in with a short wave of his hand. "I like being around my people. I didn't know you were going to be wearing fancy party clothes."

"These are my working clothes," the well-dressed man replied.

Pugh snorted what might have been a laugh. "Yeah, well, there's workin' clothes and workin' clothes, I suppose. You got the money?"

The well-dressed man reached into his inside pocket and started to pull out an envelope. "Fifteen hundred dollars, as agreed," he said. "Right here."

"Shh!" Pugh hissed. He stuck his hand out and pushed the well-dressed man's arm back. "Be quiet about it and don't be flashing it around. People see you giving me that money, we might not either one of us get out of here alive."

"Yes, well, as they are your people, I guess you would know that better than I," the well-dressed man said.

"Slip it to me under the table," Pugh directed.

Moving as stealthily as he could, the well-dressed man slipped the envelope from his pocket, then passed it under the table to Pugh.

"I really don't feel I should give you any money at all," the well-dressed man said.

"What are you talking about? I did the job for you, didn't I?" Pugh replied.

"You bungled it badly. You were supposed to make a demonstration. Do you not understand the term *demonstration*? We wanted a show . . . something we could rally around. Instead of a demonstration, you gave us a catastrophe."

"It was an accident."

"An accident?"

"The charge was a little heavier than it should have been. The hull plates ruptured and the powder magazine exploded. Anyhow, what are you worried about? Ever'one thinks the Spanish done it, and they are all screaming for war now. That is what you wanted, isn't it? To get a war started?"

"Yes. But . . . not at the expense of so many lives. American lives at that."

"Did you know any of them? The men that was killed, I mean."

"No, of course not."

"Well, I *did* know them. I know'd damn near ever' one of them. They was my mates. So don't you be talkin' to me about American lives bein' lost. Besides, you are a damned hypocrite," Pugh charged. "You and all the other newspapers been tryin' your best to get this war started. Did you think maybe there wouldn't be anyone killed in the war?"

"Getting killed heroically in a war is one thing. Being murdered while sleeping in your bunk is quite another. It wasn't supposed to be like this."

Pugh looked up with an angry glare on his face. "I told you, they was all my mates. What happened was an accident. I don't like the word *murder*."

"Perhaps if you had done your job properly, there wouldn't have been an accident."

"You think doing somethin' like this is like diggin' a few fence-post holes?" Pugh asked. "When you are working with underwater explosives you never know for sure what's goin' to happen. I coulda even gotten killed myself. Anyway, I warned that something like this could happen. You remember that I did warn you?"

The well-dressed man took out a handkerchief and wiped his face. "I know, but I never dreamed it could end up so badly."

"What's done can't be undone. Besides, your newspaper is playing it up as big as all the other newspapers."

"Yes, well, we have to play it up, don't we?" the well-dressed man replied. "We can't separate ourselves from everyone else. If we did, people might get suspicious and trace the explosion back to us. Besides, we've let the genie out. We can't very well get him back in the bottle now.''

As the well-dressed man was talking, Pugh was counting the money, keeping it down beside him in the seat so that no one else in the bar could see what he was doing. "Good, good, it's all here," Pugh said. "Well, it was nice doing business with you. If you have anything else you would like done, just let me know."

"No, no!" the well-dressed man replied. He slid out of the booth, then stood. "I think it would be best if we never see each other again or communicate in any way."

"All right," Pugh said easily. "As long as we part friends." He stuck his hand up toward the well-dressed man.

The well-dressed man started to reach for Pugh's hand, then jerked his own back. With a pained expression on his face, he turned and began walking away. Pugh's laughter followed him all the way to the door.

Once in the street, the well-dressed man felt a wave of nausea overcome him. He hurried to the corner of the nearest alley, then leaned against the brick wall and began throwing up. He heard someone laughing from behind, and he whirled around quickly, thinking that Pugh may have followed him. It wasn't Pugh. It was a street derelict, sitting in the alley, leaning back against the wall. His torn and battered coat was pulled around him. With bare fingers protruding from worn gloves, he clutched a nearly empty bottle of whiskey.

"Ain't no wonder you're sick, sonny," the derelict said in a whiskey-scarred voice. "A high-toned fella like you more'n likely don't know the best places to drink down here. Now, iffen you was to hire me, I'd be glad to show you around." The derelict laughed again, a high-pitched, insane cackle.

The well-dressed man left the alley and flagged down a passing hack. After giving the driver the address, he climbed into the back seat and closed his eyes. Closing his eyes, however, did nothing to blot out the images of bodies, floating in the water.

The cab passed a newspaper vendor selling his papers from

a street corner. When the well-dressed man looked over, he saw that it was his own paper.

"America mourns the brave lads killed on board the *Maine*!" the boy was shouting. "Get your paper here!"

On March 21, 1898, the board released its final report:

It is our finding that the *Maine* was destroyed by the explosion of a submarine mine that caused a partial explosion of two or more forward magazines. The evidence, however, is insufficient to place blame for the disaster on any person or persons.

CHAPTER 3

One of the few female reporters in the city, Martha McGuire, or Marty, as she preferred to be called, was very popular with both women and men readers. In fact, there were many men who had been fooled, both by her name and by her writing style, into thinking that the stories they read were written by a man.

Marty asked no quarter and often dived into the thickest part of a story, even if it was dangerous. She had covered fires, floods, and riots. It seemed only natural to her, then, that if there was going to be a war, she should be allowed to cover it. So far her editor, Charles Talbot, didn't agree with her. But she wasn't ready to give up on him yet. She went to his office to plead her case one more time.

"Ah, Miss McGuire, good; you are here," Talbot said, looking up from his desk. "I was about to send for you."

"Oh?"

"Theodore Roosevelt is in town today. He has resigned his position as assistant secretary of the navy to accept an appointment to the rank of colonel in the volunteers. He is going to Texas tomorrow to join his regiment."

"Yes?" Marty said. If Talbot was talking to her about military matters, then maybe his resolve against using her as a military reporter was weakening.

"There is going to be a ball tonight, at the Crestview Country Club. It is actually to honor all the volunteers from New York, but Roosevelt will be the most interesting person there. I want you to cover it.'' He wrote the address on a piece of paper and handed it to her.

"All right," Marty said, looking at the address.

"I want you to cover the ball for our female readers. You know . . . tell them about the dresses the women are wearing, the flowers and decorations, what they served, that sort of thing."

"What about Mr. Roosevelt? You want me to interview him?"

"No, no. It's *Colonel* Roosevelt now. And Art Chambers will handle that. He is our military reporter, after all."

"Mr. Chambers is our military reporter?" Marty asked. "When did that happen?"

"I appointed him to that position today. Tomorrow he'll go to Washington to get accreditation from the War Department. When we send our army to Cuba, he's going along."

"Oh, Mr. Talbot, don't you think two of us would be—" Marty started, but Talbot interrupted.

"Don't ask. I'm not even going to talk about sending a woman to cover a war."

"Good, good; I'm glad you aren't saying no yet. You'll come around; you'll see," Marty said, skipping out of the office before Talbot could respond.

Although Marty was almost masculine in her aggressiveness in covering a story, she could be extremely feminine when she wanted to be or, more importanty, needed to be. Tonight, as she attended the ball, she was very much a woman, and a beautiful woman at that. Her blue-black hair was perfectly coiffed, and her dark eyes needed no augmentation to flash provocatively. She was also blessed with a peaches-and-cream complexion.

The ballroom was gaily decorated with bunting and flags and brightly glowing electric chandeliers. The dance floor was bursting with life, full of young women who floated about wearing butterfly-bright dresses and golden ear bobs that sparkled and flashed from beneath saucily curled black, brown, and yellow hair. The men were just as colorful, resplendent in their bright uniforms, as yet unstained by battle.

There were flowers in abundance, too: tucked behind a delicate ear or demurely placed in the tiny amount of cleavage that showed above the bodices of the dresses. Some of the flowers had already found their way into the pockets of the uniformed men, to be saved as souvenirs of this night. There was a rattle of sabers and the jingle of spurs on highly polished boots as the brightly bedecked officers flashed and spun. And, beyond everything else, there was dancing, laughter, conversation, gaiety, and the tinkling of glasses as the officers and men—nearly all of them Guardsmen, the result of President McKinley's call for volunteers—socialized on a basis of equality that wouldn't be possible in the regular army.

Marty danced several times before she began taking notes. After all, she was going to have to write about this party. Maybe the whole city wasn't invited, but through her story she would make them feel as if they had missed nothing.

Marty jotted down descriptions of the various dresses of the debutantes as well as the colorful uniforms. Then she made a thorough check of the hors d'oeuvre table, where she examined a beautiful swan-shaped ice sculpture. Finally, she stepped back from the ballroom into a darkened anteroom to one side and squinted her eyes slightly to allow the movement and color to swirl about like a rapidly turning kaleidoscope. Yes, she decided, her readers would get the full benefit of her observations.

"If you are a spy, I must say you are a very attractive one," a quiet but resonant voice said.

Marty was startled by the unexpected voice, and she turned to look back into the shadows to see who had spoken. She saw a tall, handsome young lieutenant, sitting quite casually on one of the chairs near the wall.

"A spy?"

"It looks as if you might be, the way you are taking notes on everything," the lieutenant said.

Marty laughed. "I'm a newspaper reporter," she informed him.

The young man looked confused. "A reporter? I don't understand. What is there to report?"

"This party," Marty replied. "It is only the most gala affair in all of New York."

The music suddenly stopped, and the band played "Ruffles and Flourishes." "Ladies and gentlemen! His Excellency, Col. Theodore Roosevelt!"

There was a round of applause for the man who strode briskly into the room, his teeth prominent beneath the brush mustache as he smiled and waved at everyone. His glasses flashed brightly due to the banks of electric lights.

"Do you see what I mean?" Marty asked. "This is where everyone in New York would be, if they could."

"I wouldn't be here if I didn't have to be," the young lieutenant said.

"Is that why you are hiding back here?"

"Yes. Well, no, I mean, I'm not hiding, exactly."

"Then what, exactly, are you doing?"

"I'm watching. Just as you are."

"Ah, but I have an excuse for it. I am responsible to my readers. With tomorrow's edition of the *Banner*, all of New York will attend this party. Or, at least, they will feel as if they have, if I can write the story well enough."

"Do you have a lot of readers?"

"I like to think so. My name is Marty McGuire. Have you never read my column?"

The young man shook his head. "I just graduated from West Point," he said. "I haven't had much time, of late, to read anything but textbooks and military manuals." He came to attention. "Second Lt. Todd Murchison at your service, ma'am."

"I'm very glad to meet you, Lieutenant. Wait a minute. Murchison, you say? Are you related to Gen. Joseph Murchison?"

"He is my father."

"I read about him. He was in Cuba as the president's personal envoy when the *Maine* was sunk, wasn't he?"

"Yes."

"Now, there is someone I would like to interview. I don't suppose you could arrange that for me, could you?"

Todd chuckled. "Miss McGuire, he may be my father, but

he is also a general. Generals are not easily approachable by second lieutenants, whether they are fathers or not.''

The smoke from scores of cigars, pipes, and cigarettes drifted into the room, and Marty coughed.

''It *is* getting a little close in here,'' Todd said. He pointed toward the door. ''Would you care to step outside for a few moments? I'm told that the garden here is very pretty. Or do your duties keep you in here?''

''Well, I should stay in here, but you are right; it *is* a little close. Thank you, yes, I believe I would like to get a little air,'' Marty replied.

Marty took Todd's arm and they walked out through the back door into the formal garden. The garden was strung with brightly colored paper lanterns, and in the far corner, water splashed from a fountain adorned with a green mermaid.

''It *is* beautiful, isn't it?'' Marty said.

''Yes.''

''It's a shame that real estate has become so valuable in the city. There aren't many gardens such as this remaining.''

''It's odd to think of land at such a premium here, when out west there is so much of it that is unoccupied,'' Todd said.

''Yes, but who would want it? All desert and mountains. Of what use is it?''

''I don't know,'' Todd replied. ''Of what use is the sunset, when the clouds are underlit so that they are all pink and orange and lavender? What use is the desert in the Arizona and New Mexico territories, when it is carpeted with spring flowers or turned gold by the morning sun? Of what use are the purple mountains of Colorado, with their peaks crowned in snow, or the great timberlands of California and Oregon?''

Marty laughed softly and raised her hands. ''All right, all right,'' she said. ''I give up. I can't argue against someone who defends his position so eloquently. You must really love the West.''

''I do,'' Todd replied. ''My father spent most of his career in the West, and I grew up there. And I'll be going back there tomorrow, to Texas, to join the First Volunteer Cavalry of the Fifth Corps.''

"To Texas? That's where Mr. Roosevelt is going, too, isn't it?"

"Yes."

"Oh, how exciting all this must be for you. I imagine you are looking forward to going to war."

"Miss McGuire, as my father is a career army officer, I have had some exposure to the Indian Wars. I've seen men brought back from patrols who were spitting up blood from bullet-punctured lungs and turning gangrenous from mangled limbs. I'm afraid I find nothing glorious or exciting about dying in battle."

"And yet you chose the military as a career," Marty said.

"It would be more accurate to say that the military chose me."

"I don't understand," Marty said.

"No, ma'am. I don't expect you would," Todd replied, without elaboration.

A sergeant stepped outside. "Lieutenant Murchison!" the sergeant called from the door. "Are you out here?"

"Yes, I'm right here," Todd replied.

"You'd better come inside, Mr. Murchison," the sergeant said. "Colonel Roosevelt has called a meeting for all those who will be going with him to join the Rough Riders."

"Rough Riders?" Todd replied. "What are the Rough Riders?"

"Why, that'll be us, Lieutenant. From now on, the First Volunteer Cavalry is going to be known as the Rough Riders."

Todd turned to Marty. "If you would excuse me?" he said with a slight bow.

"Of course," Marty replied. "You have your duty."

Marty watched as the tall, handsome young officer returned to the swirl of light, color, and noise that was inside. She had been strangely affected by their brief meeting. He was a just-commissioned lieutenant from West Point and the son of a famous general. From such a person she would expect bravado and hubris. Instead she got modesty and introspection.

*   *   *

A few days later, Marty was sitting at her desk when she heard a woman's voice speaking in Spanish. For Marty, the language was not only familiar but also sweetly poignant, and she wandered up to the front of the large newsroom to hear what was going on.

The speaker was a handsome woman in her thirties, dressed in a manner that indicated she was from a fine old family. Her accent was Cuban rather than Spanish.

"Please, is there no one here who can understand me?" the woman asked. Her voice was near the edge of desperation.

Marty looked into the faces of all the men present, including Mr. Talbot. It was obvious they didn't understand a word the woman was saying.

"Yes, I understand. May I help you?" Marty asked, speaking the language with an easy, comfortable command.

"You understand this lingo?" Talbot asked.

"Yes," Marty answered in English. Then, returning to Spanish, she said to the woman, "What seems to be your problem?"

"Thank God, at last I have found someone who can speak my language. It is a frightening thing to be suddenly struck deaf and dumb," the woman replied. She smiled. "My name is Francesca Alvarez Mendoza. My brother is Col. Juan Alvarez, commanding officer of the First Free Cuba Brigade." Francesca held up an envelope. "My brother has sent proof of Spanish atrocities against our people. Here are photographs of a dozen young men who were murdered and dismembered by the Spaniards. Their only crime was to distribute broadsides for free elections in Cuba."

Francesca showed the photographs to Marty. She looked at the first one, then blanched and turned away.

"I know," Francesca said softly. "It is difficult to look at the photographs. But one must look at them and stories must be published if the American people are to learn the truth about what is happening in my country."

"What is it?" Talbot asked. "What is she showing you?"

Wordlessly Marty handed the packet of photographs to Talbot.

"My God," Talbot said. "This is fantastic! Who are these people? What is she saying to you?"

Quickly Marty interpreted what Francesca had told her.

"Fred!" Talbot shouted, handing the photographs to one of the men. "Get Art. I want cuts of these pictures at once." Talbot smiled and rubbed his hands together, rolling his unlit cigar from side to side in his mouth. "How much does she want for these pictures?" he asked.

"I don't think she wants anything for them," Marty said. "I think her only purpose is to see that the news is printed so that the readers will be alert to what the Spanish are doing down there."

"Yeah, yeah, well, that's great," Talbot replied. "Tell her we'll print the pictures and run the story, but she is not to go to Hearst or Pulitzer with any of this."

Marty relayed the information, and Francesca nodded in agreement.

"I don't care which paper gets them," she said, "as long as the public is made aware. I will honor Senor Talbot's request."

"Does she agree?" Talbot asked.

"Yes."

"That's great!" Talbot said. "Now, you interpret for her, and I'll get Johnny to write the story."

"Why can't I write the story?"

Talbot took his cigar from his mouth and looked at Marty. "You're a good writer, kid; you've proved that to me more than once. But I saw the way you reacted when you looked at those photos. This story is going to have to be composed of some hard stuff, some blood and guts, gory detail. I don't think you have it in you."

"Mr. Talbot, if the story needs to be gory, I'll make it gory."

Talbot studied her for a long, silent moment; then he sighed. "All right," he said. "Tell the woman you'll be doing the story."

Speaking in Spanish, Marty identified herself and explained that she would be writing the story.

"I think it will be wonderful to work with you," Francesca

said, laying her hand lightly on Marty's arm. "You speak our language so beautifully, and with a Cuban accent as well. Why is this?"

"My mother is Cuban," Marty replied. "And I have many relatives there, so I have visited Cuba many times."

"How would you like to visit Cuba tomorrow night?" Francesca asked.

"Tomorrow night? I don't understand."

Francesca laughed. "Of course, I don't mean actually go to Cuba. But the Free Cuba Legation is holding a dinner party tomorrow night, just as if we were home. There will be our native food, drink, music, and costumes. It would be as if you were visiting Cuba. Would you like to come?"

"Yes, of course I would. I would be delighted."

"What's all the jabbering about?" Talbot asked.

"She's invited me to attend a dinner at the Free Cuba Legation," Marty explained.

"What did you tell her?"

"I told her I would go."

"Good idea, good idea," Talbot replied enthusiastically. "The closer you can get to these people, the more exclusive stories we'll be able to come up with. Ha! Don't think the other papers won't sit up and take notice of us now."

The headline that spread across the entire top of the paper the next day read:

POSITIVE PROOF OF SPANISH ATROCITIES

Woodcuts of the photographs gave the story even more impact. A notarized statement by a judge, a clergyman, and a college professor attested to the fact that they had viewed the actual photographs and that the woodcuts were factual, undoctored representations of them. This was particularly significant because many of the papers had been accused of faking stories and pictures to build up their circulation.

Marty managed the delicate balance of making her story forceful without having to resort to sensationalism. It received front-page, lead-story treatment, and the street sales of the

Banner that day were the highest in the paper's history.

Francesca greeted Marty warmly when she arrived at the legation for dinner that evening. She introduced Marty to her husband, Ricardo Mendoza, who was chief of the legation.

"My wife told me of your command of our language," Ricardo said as he bowed to Marty. "I can see that she didn't exaggerate. But none of us had any idea of the power of your writing. I translated your article today so that the non-English-speaking members of our delegation could read it. It is magnificent."

"Thank you, Senor Mendoza," Marty replied, beaming under his praise.

"My wife and I must greet our arriving guests, but please allow my secretary to introduce you to the others."

Marty followed the young man Ricardo identified as his secretary, and soon she was receiving the accolades of everyone present. Not only her story but also her Latin beauty and her command of the language made her an instant hit. After several minutes of polite conversation, Marty excused herself and went to the punch bowl. It was quite warm in the building, and she had grown thirsty.

A tall, handsome man came over to pour a cup of punch for her. When Marty looked up to thank him, she saw that he was in the uniform of an American general.

"You seem to be making quite a hit tonight," the general said.

"I think they are just happy to be able to speak with an American who knows their language," Marty replied.

"No, it's more than that," the general said. "Oh, forgive me; I haven't introduced myself. I'm—"

"General Murchison," Marty said. "I would recognize you anywhere."

Joe chuckled. "Surely the few woodcut pictures that have run in the papers aren't that accurate. If so, I must look worse than I thought."

Marty laughed. "No, it isn't that. Before I came tonight, I managed to get a guest list and I saw your name. Also, I met your son. The resemblance is quite striking. I must say, I was most impressed with him."

"You must've made an impression on him as well," Joe told her.

"Why do you say that?"

"Because he recommended that I begin reading your articles. He has never recommended a columnist to me before." Joe took a drink and smiled at Marty over the rim of the cup. "I can see why he was taken with you. He was right; you are very attractive."

"I thank you for the compliment," Marty said. "But I would rather be judged by my writing."

"Please don't misunderstand. The fact that you are a beautiful woman does not detract from your writing," Joe told her. "And I took Todd's advice. I have been reading you, and I especially enjoyed your most recent story. I was impressed by the fact that your story was supported by verifiable evidence. I find that refreshing, since truth is too often the first casualty in any war."

Someone walked through the rooms ringing a chime, and dinner was announced. There were name cards at the dinner table, and Marty was a little disappointed to see that she would be sitting at the opposite end of the table from General Murchison. She would have enjoyed talking more with him.

Marty's dinner companion turned out to be none other than William Randolph Hearst. Evidently the people who planned the seating arrangement thought it would be good to put everyone from the press in the same place. When Hearst was introduced to her, he registered the greatest surprise of all.

"You?" he said. "You are Marty McGuire?"

"Yes."

"But surely, madam, you aren't the author of those wonderful stories I have been seeing in the *Banner*?"

"I work for Mr. Talbot, yes," Marty said.

"How would you like to work for me?"

Hearst's offer surprised Marty and she laughed, a small, lilting laugh. "Well, I must confess, Mr. Hearst, I am most flattered by your offer. But I am already employed."

"I'll double the salary he's paying you," Hearst said, and at that all other dinner conversation stopped. Marty suddenly found that she was the center of attention, and that situation made her uncomfortable.

"How can you make such an offer?" she asked. "You don't even know what my salary is."

"I don't care what your salary is, Miss McGuire. Whatever Talbot is paying you I will double."

Hearst's offer was translated into Spanish for those guests who didn't understand.

"What . . . what exactly would you have me doing for you?" Marty asked, stunned by the sudden opportunity.

"Why, the same thing you are doing for Talbot, of course."

"I'm also writing women's news for Mr. Talbot. I would prefer to be used just for straight news."

"You should be and you shall, Miss McGuire," Hearst said. "Anyone with your ability to turn a phrase would be wasted writing only of tea parties and the like. No, I would have you writing just such articles as your report published today. Perhaps as many as three a week, exposing the tyranny of the Spanish in Cuba."

Marty gasped. "Are you receiving that much documented evidence about war atrocities?"

"Documented evidence? What documented evidence?" Hearst asked. "Someone who can write the way you do needs no documented evidence. No, Miss McGuire, you'll write your stories from here," Hearst said, touching his finger to his head. "And from here." He put his hand over his heart. "Especially from here."

"I . . . I don't understand," Marty said.

"Allow me to interpret for you, Miss McGuire," Joe spoke from his end of the table. He, like everyone else, had interrupted his own conversation to follow the drama of Hearst's offer. "I believe he is giving you *carte blanche* to create atrocities in case you can't find any supporting evidence."

"What?" Marty gasped. "You can't be serious! Mr Hearst, I'm a journalist. If you want fiction, hire a novelist."

Hearst laughed aloud. "Ah, you mean like Stephen Crane, the novelist Pulitzer hired? As you can see, that isn't an original idea. But if you would turn your flair for writing to more, let us say, creative endeavors, I could make you a star.''

"Mr. Hearst, I consider my stories to be a sacred bond between me and my readers," Marty replied. "They have the right to expect nothing but the truth, or, at the very least, the truth as far as I can ascertain it.''

Hearst chuckled and shook his head. "My dear young lady," he said. "I am most impressed with your sense of responsibility to your readers, but I suggest that you have yet to learn the difference between what is true and what is factual.''

"What? I don't understand what you are talking about.''

"Very well. Let's consider your story that appeared today. It is a true story, is it not? It is an accurate reflection of the Spanish treatment of the Cubans?''

"I believe so.''

"Do you have any supporting evidence for this belief? Other than what was supplied by the Free Cuba Legation?''

"As a matter of fact, I do," Marty said. "My mother is Cuban. I have lived and traveled in Cuba, and though I have never witnessed atrocities such as these, I have witnessed Spanish oppression.''

"Good, good; then the story is true," Hearst said. "You also have photographs and an eyewitness account of this massacre, so that makes the story factual. Without the supporting evidence, however, *it would still be true, would it not?*''

"Well, yes," Marty told him. "That is, I suppose so.''

"Then am I asking any more of you, Miss McGuire? I only want you to write several stories like the one you wrote today. They will be true stories, as this is a true story. They may not be factual, however. Now, what do you say, Miss McGuire? Have I hired myself a new journalist?''

Marty shook her head. "I'm sorry, Mr. Hearst. I am honored by your offer; truly I am. But I cannot accept.''

Hearst laughed. "Too bad," he said. "Well, come see me when it gets too heavy, will you?''

"I beg your pardon? When what gets too heavy?''

"Why, the halo of journalistic integrity, of course," Hearst said, laughing.

CHAPTER 4

A few days after the Free Cuba Legation dinner, Mr. Talbot called Marty into his office. He offered her a seat across from his desk; then he leaned back in his chair with the ever-present, but never-lit, cigar sticking out of the side of his mouth.

"I just got a wire from Mr. Chambers," he said. "He is being detained in Washington for a bit longer than expected."

"Is something wrong?" Marty asked.

"No, nothing is wrong," Talbot assured her. "It's just that the paperwork for accreditation is taking longer than we thought. And that leaves us with a slight problem."

"Oh? Is there something I can do to help?"

Talbot removed his cigar and leaned forward, bringing his elbows to his desk.

"I don't know," Talbot said. He rubbed his chin and studied Marty for a moment. "McGuire, I may be a fool for suggesting this, but how would you like to go to Texas to send back a series of stories about the Rough Riders?"

"What?" Marty gasped. "Mr. Talbot, are you serious? You would let me do that?"

"Would you like to?"

"Yes, of course!" Marty answered enthusiastically. "I'd love to do it. I'll do a good job for you, Mr. Talbot."

Talbot chuckled. "Oh, I have no doubt about that," he said. "You've done an outstanding job on every other assignment I've given you, so I know I will have no problem with this one. And after all, covering an army in training isn't the same thing as covering an army in battle."

"You won't be sorry, Mr. Talbot; I promise you!" Marty said. Then, because she didn't want to give him time for second thoughts, she left the office and hurried home to pack for her trip.

With her suitcase in her lap, Marty rode the electric trolley through the streets of Manhattan to the train station. There were at least half a dozen other electric trolleys in view, plus as many horse-drawn omnibuses and carriages. There were also great, bustling crowds of people hurrying along the sidewalks and across the brick-paved streets: men in their derbies and women in their feathered bonnets, all under the watchful eyes of busy traffic police.

At Grand Central Station she left the trolley and, carrying her small valise, hurried through the main lobby, out under the huge glass-roofed train shed. There were a dozen trains standing inside the great shed, and the hiss of steam and the chug of the engines that were working the lines of cars in and out caused Marty to feel a sense of excitement.

She was not the only one going to San Antonio. As she boarded the train, she saw a group of young men who were also going there. She knew their destination because several pretty young women, wearing bright gingham dresses and flower-bedecked straw hats, had gathered to tell them goodbye.

"Now, there's a fine-looking lot of lads," a man standing near Marty said. "When the Spanish soldiers see the likes of them, they'll be having second thoughts about getting into a war with the good old U.S. of A."

The group of boisterous young men and the women who were there to see the soldiers off began singing a song that had become extremely popular over the last few weeks:

"On to Cuba! On to Cuba!
Sound the war note high and shrill
Rescue from the vulture tyrant
City, village, plain, and hill

As ye charge across the plain
Smite to earth the Spanish Coyote
Slay, in vengeance for the Maine!''

"They seem eager enough for battle," Marty said.

"Why, you know who those boys are, don't you, miss?"

"Volunteers for the army, I suppose."

"No, ma'am, not for the army. For the Rough Riders. And they aren't your average volunteer. They're somethin' special," the other passenger said. He began to point. "Those two fellas there are Bob Wrenn and Bill Larned. They are the best two tennis players in the country. And the wiry one is Stanley Hollister, maybe the fastest half-miler in the world. And that big fella is Dudley Dean. I reckon you've heard of Dudley Dean?"

Marty shook her head. "No, I'm afraid I haven't," she said.

"Why, ma'am, where've you been? He's the quarterback for Harvard. Harvard is just the best football team in the country, that's all."

"I'm sorry. I've never been much of a sports enthusiast."

"Too bad. If you were, you'd be honored to be on the same train with them."

"I'm honored to be on the same train as anyone who would volunteer to serve his country," Marty replied.

"Yes, ma'am," the passenger said. Marty's remark mollified the passenger, who had been somewhat disquieted by her lack of sports awareness.

The going-away party continued, even after Marty had already boarded the train and taken her seat. She watched through the window as the four young men kissed the girls good-bye, shook hands with dozens of well-wishers, then waved at the rest. They didn't board the train themselves until it had already picked up enough speed to require that they run to catch up.

They came into Marty's car, then collapsed in the rearmost two seats, laughing and breathing hard from having to run to catch the train.

"First thing I'm going to do is get myself a box of Cuban cigars," Dudley Dean said.

"Not me. I'm going to look around until I find some se-norita being oppressed by a Spanish soldier; then I am going to come to her rescue," Hollister said.

"Oh, Stanley, my hero!" one of the others said in falsetto, and they all laughed again. Even Marty laughed, though she didn't let them see her.

When Marty went in to breakfast the next morning, the dining car was empty except for the four young athletes. They had finished their breakfast and were having a conversation over coffee.

"We're foolish; you know that, don't you?" one of the young men said.

"What do you mean, we're foolish?"

"Why, they've discovered gold up in the Klondike. We could be going after gold. Instead, we are rushing off to war."

"Ah, but you can look for gold anytime. How many times can you go to war?"

"That's true."

"Besides, why do you need gold? Banks sometimes bounce drafts that are drawn against insufficient funds. . . . You could write a draft that would bounce the bank."

The others laughed.

"I wonder if I might ask a question?" Marty said.

The four young men stood quickly.

"No, please, sit down. If the train went around a curve and you were thrown down and injured, I would not want to have to answer to your officers."

The four young men retook their seats.

"My name is Marty McGuire, and I—"

"Marty McGuire? The writer?" Dudley Dean asked.

"Yes," Marty replied, surprised and unexpectedly pleased that he had recognized her name.

"What are you doing here, Miss McGuire? Shouldn't you be back in New York, writing your stories?"

Marty smiled. "Well, you must admit that the biggest story now is what is happening with Cuba. I'm doing the same thing you gentlemen are doing. I'm going to San Antonio."

"You're going to write about us?" Bill Larned asked.

"Yes, Mr. Larned. You, Mr. Wrenn, Mr. Hollister, and Mr. Dean," Marty replied, looking at each of them in turn as she called his name.

"You know who we are," Wrenn said. It was an observation, not a question.

"I do."

"And you are going to write about us?" Dean asked.

"Yes, but not just you. I'll be writing stories about anything that piques my interest. And what I'm wondering now is, why would you men join the First Volunteer Cavalry as privates when you could join the regular army as commissioned officers?"

The four laughed. "We aren't cut out for the regular army," Larned said.

"There is no telling what kind of person you might be asked to serve with," Hollister added.

"On the other hand, everyone in the First Volunteer Cavalry is a gentleman, from the colonel down to the lowest-ranking private," Dean said.

"That's us ... the lowest-ranking privates, I mean," Wrenn noted, and again, all laughed.

"And as I am sure we shall prove, an outfit composed entirely of gentlemen can't help but be the finest fighting outfit in the entire army," Dean insisted.

Marty smiled. "I'm sure the First Volunteer Cavalry will be an outstanding unit," she said.

The trip to San Antonio was long and tiring. Marty and the others who were going on to San Antonio changed trains in Chicago, again in Saint Louis, and one final time in Kansas City. As Marty traveled across the country, she bought copies of the local newspapers, not only to keep abreast of what was happening nationally but also to see how each part of the country was reacting to the situation.

She learned, through her reading, that there were all sorts of schemes being proposed to create volunteer units. Buffalo Bill Cody had offered to round up thirty thousand Indian braves to kick the Spaniards out of Cuba. Frank James proposed to lead a regiment composed of men who, like himself, had once ridden the outlaw's trail. And a woman from Denver, Colorado, Mrs. Martha A. Shute, took out an advertisement recruiting women who could "ride and shoot like men" to form an all-female regiment.

But the volunteer outfit that was receiving the most publicity was the First United States Volunteer Cavalry Regiment. This was the Rough Riders, the unit that Marty was going to San Antonio to cover.

Mobilization and Training Camp, San Antonio, Texas

Marty McGuire's first day in camp with the Rough Riders was almost her last day. While watching some artillery maneuvers, she got too close to the action, and a team of horses, drawing a large gun caisson, broke loose from the handler and began running wild. Marty was caught in the open, terrified and mesmerized as the runaway team thundered toward her.

Then, seemingly out of nowhere, a mounted second lieutenant galloped to her rescue. Bending down from the saddle, he swept Marty up, not too ceremoniously, and carried her back to safety as the heavy caisson rumbled by.

He set her down, then dismounted. "Are you all right?" he asked anxiously.

"Yes, thank you," Marty said, brushing an errant strand of hair back from her face. That was when she recognized her rescuer as the same young officer she had met back in New York. "You are Lieutenant Murchison, aren't you?"

"At your service, ma'am," Murchison said.

Marty chuckled. "In this case, you really were at my service. I don't know how to thank you. You risked your life, saving mine."

"It wasn't that much of a risk for me," Todd said. "And I couldn't very well let you be run down, now, could I?"

"It was very foolish of me to get in the way."

Todd shook his head. "It wasn't your fault," he said.

"The team was a runaway. They could've gone anywhere."

"Yes, well, I promise you, I will be more careful from now on."

Todd smiled, then remounted. "I'll hold you to that," he said.

New York City

The woman's staccato barks were synchronized with the squeaking of the springs and the thumping of the bedposts against the wall. As Pugh huffed and wheezed and pumped over her, he looked down at her face. It was covered by a light patina of sweat, and a ringlet of her auburn hair was stuck to her forehead. Her eyes were closed and her mouth was slightly open. The smell of liquor was on her breath.

He felt it starting then, in the soles of his feet, behind his knees, in the middle of his back and the back of his neck, all bunching up to an intense accumulation of energy that burst forth in a white-hot spewing emission. He spent himself, then stopped and, breathing in gasps, fell forward, heavily, on Daisy.

At least, that was the name she had told him.

Daisy lay quietly for a few moments allowing Pugh to regain his breath; then she pushed on him.

"Get off, honey; you're so heavy you are mashin' my titties flat," Daisy said.

Pugh rolled to one side, then lay on his back with one arm folded over his head. The bedsprings creaked as Daisy sat up.

"Where you goin'?" Pugh asked.

"I'm going back to work," Daisy said. "The fleet's comin' in, and I don't want those boys to feel like they aren't welcome. Especially since they are all about to go to war."

"What makes you think they're about to go to war?"

"Why, honey, haven't you been readin' the newspapers? The whole country is down on Spain for sinkin' the *Maine* like they done."

"Oh."

Daisy began getting dressed. "Ain't it just awful about all

those boys that was killed on the *Maine*, though? It's enough to just break your heart.''

''Shut up about the *Maine*. You're a whore. You got nothin' to do with the *Maine*.''

''Just because I'm a whore don't mean I didn't cry when I read about all those poor boys getting killed,'' Daisy said. ''Why, I'll just bet I was with a dozen or more of 'em at one time or another. Just think; none of them boys'll ever be with a woman again, or have another drink, or ever see their families.''

''I said shut the fuck up about the *Maine!*'' Pugh yelled, throwing a water glass at her. The glass hit the wall and shattered.

''OK, honey, OK, take it easy!'' Daisy said, holding her hands up. ''Look, if you don't want me talkin' about it, I won't. I know how it is with you sailor boys. You keep thinkin' it coulda been you.''

Pugh lay back on the bed, with his arm over his eyes. ''Yeah,'' he mumbled. ''Yeah, that's what I keep thinkin'.''

''What you should do is just thank your lucky stars that it wasn't.'' When she was finished dressing, she reached over and patted Pugh on the shoulder. ''Well, I must be on my way. You was good, honey. You was real good. I hope you look me up again, sometime.''

''Two months ago you wouldn't have anything to do with me,'' Pugh said.

Daisy laughed. ''Honey, two months ago you didn't have any money. I don't know where you got it, but you got plenty now, and as long as you do have it, why, you're welcome to share a bed with me any time you want. Bye now.'' Daisy blew a kiss, then shut the door.

As Pugh lay in the bed, which was redolent with the essence of sex and alcohol, he began thinking. Although all America was convinced that the Spanish were responsible for the mining of the *Maine*, there were still a few who suggested that it wasn't an absolute that Spain was responsible. Pugh worried that if people began to seriously investigate other possibilities they might discover that he once had served on board the *Maine*. They might also learn that he had left with a personal grudge against Assistant Engineer Darwin Merritt, one of the officers who had been killed in the explosion.

It wouldn't take a great amount of research to discover that Pugh was an expert in artillery and oceanic mine warfare, information that would be interesting to anyone who was investigating the destruction of the *Maine*. And from there it was an easy step to determine that Pugh, who had been unemployed and unemployable in New York, had somehow managed to get a berth on a private schooner and was in Havana at the time the *Maine* was destroyed.

Daisy was not the only one surprised by Angus Pugh's recent reversal of fortunes. Pugh, who had always tried to cadge a few drinks, was now generously buying drinks, and he had even been seen at a few of New York's better restaurants, ordering the most expensive meals without a second thought. And Daisy wasn't the only woman he was spending his money on. If Daisy wasn't available, as she often wasn't, Pugh would turn to the nearest warm female body.

Several had wondered aloud how Pugh had gotten the money he was spending so lavishly, and a few even voiced the opinion that he may have stolen it.

Only Jeremy McTavish knew where Pugh had gotten the money, but not even he knew what service Pugh had performed for it. Or so he claimed. In truth, Pugh believed that McTavish did know but pretended ignorance to avoid any confrontation.

Pugh felt compelled to spend the money as fast as he could, his reasoning being that once all the money was gone, he would be out of any danger of being discovered. As a result, he had already gone through just about every cent of the $1,500 he had been paid.

With the Rough Riders in San Antonio

"Lieutenant, are you serious about taking us out for a night ride?" one of the recruits in Todd's platoon asked.

"Yes," Todd answered. "But it isn't a ride; it is a nighttime maneuver."

"Why? It isn't as if none of us have ever ridden at night."

"I'm sure you've ridden at night," Todd said. "But I doubt that many of you have maneuvered as a body at night."

"Lieutenant, I have, most definitely, maneuvered a body at night . . . if you catch my drift," one of the Ivy League men said.

His comment garnered several laughs.

"I doubt if he does understand your meaning, Ross," another of the Ivy League crowd commented. "The lieutenant is a West Point man. I heard they lock those West Point men up and don't let them see any women for four years."

"No talking in the ranks," Todd said sternly. The men fell silent, and Todd continued with an exercise that was listed on the schedule as Dismounted Drill.

"Right shoulder, arms," he ordered in a crisp, military voice. "No, no, no!" Todd said, reaching out to take the rifle from the private nearest him. "When the command 'right shoulder arms' is given, you don't just pick the rifle up and put it on your shoulder any old way. You must do it properly, like this."

Smoothly and quickly, Todd demonstrated. Holding the rifle by the stacking swivel, he brought it up at a forty-five-degree angle across his chest.

"One," he counted.

With his left hand, he grasped it in the middle.

"Two!" he boomed.

Putting his right hand on the butt of the rifle, he used both hands to guide it to his right shoulder.

"Three!" he called.

After that, he brought his left hand down sharply.

"Four!" he said as he finished the maneuver. He returned the rifle to the man he had taken it from. "Now, let's try it again."

"Lieutenant, why do we have to do all that?" one of the cowboys asked. "I mean if you want us to put our gun up there on our right shoulder, what difference does it make how we put it up there?"

Todd sighed in frustration. He had been told, over and over again, what a lucky break it was for a regular army officer to be assigned to the Rough Riders, but the advantage of the assignment wasn't readily apparent to him. He knew that Theodore Roosevelt had actually been offered command of the regiment but turned it down because he lacked military experience and didn't consider himself qualified. Instead, Roosevelt had recommended that Leonard Wood, who was currently the president's personal physician but did have some military experience, be given the top position. Roosevelt would act as the executive officer.

Todd respected Roosevelt for recognizing his own short-coming but, all things considered, wished he had been assigned to a regular army unit. In the meantime, as Todd had told his father in his last letter, he would do the best he could in trying to mold the disparate personalities of the Rough Riders into something that resembled a military unit.

There were some advantages to being assigned to the Rough Riders. Both Lieutenant Colonel Roosevelt and Col. Leonard Wood had numerous connections in Washington, and they were not above shamelessly using those connections to the benefit of the regiment. Thus the Rough Riders were given preferential treatment as far as equipment was concerned. Even as the regiment was still forming, it was receiving the best of everything. Trainloads of supplies arrived at the training camp on a daily basis. There were plenty of horses, all of the finest quality. And the soldiers were issued the much cooler cotton uniforms, instead of the regular-issue sweat-inducing wool suits. They were the first to wear the new army color known as khaki. The khaki uniforms had the traditional yellow piping to represent the cavalry.

In addition to the best food, horses, and uniforms, the men were equipped with the new Krag rifle, a bolt-action rifle that was far superior to the Springfield rifle that was the standard issue of all the other volunteer units. In addition, Colt machine guns, capable of shooting 500 bullets per minute and costing $10,000 apiece, had been brought in and donated by three of the wealthier volunteers, Woodbury Dane, Joseph Sampson Stevens, and William Tiffany Jr.

The diversity of background of the men of the regiment made training a challenge to the few regular army officers and non-commissioned officers who had been brought in for the task. Roosevelt announced that he wanted his regiment to represent the best elements in American life, and to that end he drew volunteers from both ends of the social spectrum.

He had men who were wealthy and well-educated, men whose names were recorded in the Social Register. They were graduates of Harvard and other Ivy League schools, bankers, stockbrokers, and lawyers.

Roosevelt told these men that, even though they were wealthy, with servants at home, they were now privates and would be expected to act like soldiers. They'd have to take orders and do hard, dirty work without complaint.

In addition to these men, whom Todd called the gilded gang, there were also men from the other end of the socio-economic spectrum. This second group represented the westerners Roosevelt had known, and admired, during his ranching days. They were hard-riding, quick-tempered, hard-drinking men to whom guns were a natural extension of their own bodies. They came from the Rockies and the Dakota Badlands. There were Texans, New Mexicans, Oklahomans, and Coloradans. One of them was Robert Brown, a genuine gunfighter who had killed five men in shootouts. There were active lawmen on temporary leave and outlaws on the run. In a few cases, some of the lawmen had been actively looking for the very outlaws who were bunking right next to them. And though no formal agreement had been reached, the lawmen and the outlaws were recognizing an uneasy truce.

A just-arrived recruit was walking across the parade grounds toward Todd's platoon when one of the cowboys saw him.

"Hey! Hey, look at that dude!" the cowboy shouted from the ranks.

"Ain't he the pretty one, though?" another replied.

"You are at attention!" Todd said. "No talking in ranks."

A ripple of laughter passed through the formation as all looked toward the young recruit. He was wearing a three-piece suit, a bowler hat, highly polished shoes, and spats. A gold watch chain stretched across his vest. He was a relatively small man, but there was something about him that seemed familiar to Todd. Then, as the young man drew closer, Todd realized where he had seen him before, and smiled.

"Hey, fella, you sure you come to the right place?" the taunting cowboy called from the ranks.

The young man stopped and pulled a piece of paper from his inside jacket pocket. "I'm not sure," he replied in a cultured voice. "Would this be the assembly area for the First United States Volunteer Cavalry Regiment?"

"You got that right, sonny. 'Specially the part 'bout this here bein' a cavalry regiment," the taunting cowboy said. "It ain't someplace where you come to drink tea and dance with the ladies."

Again there was laughter from the ranks.

"Cavalry. That does mean horses, does it not?" the young man asked.

"Yeah, it means horses."

The young man grinned broadly. "Splendid. I rather like horses."

"He rather likes horses," the cowboy said, mincing his words. "I'll tell you what. I just bet he ain't never seen nothing but the ass end of a horse from some fancy carriage," the cowboy suggested, and again everyone laughed.

"Actually, I—" the young man started to answer, but Todd held up his hand.

"No need to talk about it," Todd said. "If you can ride, why don't you show us what you can do? Bodine?" Todd called.

"Yes, sir?" Bodine was the cowboy who had been making fun of the recruit.

"Get him a horse."

"Any horse, sir?" Bodine asked slyly.

Todd knew what Bodine had in mind. He was going to get the most difficult horse in the stable.

"Yes, any horse," Todd said.

"Yes, sir!" As Bodine started toward the stable, the others began to chortle.

"Hope you don't get them fancy clothes smellin' all horsey!" someone called.

A few minutes later, Bodine returned with a saddled mount. As Todd had suspected, Bodine had chosen the most spirited animal in the string, and even as the horse was being led over, it was fighting, ducking its head, and trying to pull away.

"What would you like me to do?" the young man asked Todd as Bodine brought the horse to him.

The men had been playing a baseball game earlier, and the ball and bat were nearby. Todd walked over to pick the ball and bat up. He brought them back to the young man. "Do you see that tree down there, about 150 yards away?" Todd asked.

"I see it."

"I wonder if you could strike this ball along the ground, using the bat as a club, all the way down to that tree . . . around the tree, then back here."

"Lieutenant, you give that eastern dude somethin' like that to do an' like as not he'll never get the job done. We don't want to stay out here all night."

"He's right; we don't want to stay here all night. So, as a special favor to me, Wadsworth, please do it as quickly as you can," Todd said, speaking the man's name clearly.

Realizing now that Todd knew who he was, Wadsworth smiled and tossed the ball onto the ground. Then, leaping into the saddle, he raced toward the ball, leaned down from the saddle, and, using the bat as a club, drove it another fifty yards.

There was a collective gasp of amazement from everyone who witnessed the young man's performance, and when he reached the tree he turned the horse on a dime and started his return, driving the ball before him. In far less than a minute he had stroked the ball, always under his complete control, to the far end of the field and brought it back. When the ball lay in front of Todd, Wadsworth leaped from his saddle.

The men in formation, who but a few seconds earlier had been teasing him, now cheered.

"Gentlemen," Todd said to them. "Let this be a lesson to you. Never make a snap judgment, but wait until you have all the facts. A snap judgment could cost you your life.

"Most of you saw the way this man was dressed and considered him to be some dude from the East who had never ridden before. In fact, this is Craig Wadsworth, who happens to be the finest polo player in the U.S. and, many say, in the world.''

"Well, hell, Lieutenant, if he is the best in the U.S. of A., then that means he *is* the best in the whole world," Bodine said. "Wadsworth, hope you don't have no hard feelin's toward me for bein' such an ass," he added, extending his hand.

Smiling, Wadsworth accepted Bodine's offer of a handshake.

"Let's hear it for Wadsworth!" someone shouted.

"Hip, hip."

"Hooray!"

"Hip, hip."

"Hooray!"

"Hip, hip."

"Hooray!"

After the cheer, the formation broke ranks and all the men gathered around Wadsworth, patting him on the back and congratulating him for his fine riding.

Todd, realizing that no further training would be possible this afternoon, dismissed the men.

Attracted by the cheering, Roosevelt came over to join the men.

"What's going on?" Roosevelt asked.

"Colonel, this here little fella, Wadsworth, just put on the damnedest show of horse ridin' I ever seen," Bodine replied.

Like Todd, Roosevelt recognized Wadsworth, and he extended his hand. "Mr. Craig Wadsworth, I believe. Welcome to the Rough Riders," Roosevelt said. "I'm sorry I missed your demonstration, but I'm sure you will have the opportunity to show me again." Roosevelt then turned to the men who, though no longer in ranks, were still assembled. "Men, I've told the bartender at Boots and Saddles that all drinks are on me tonight. You've been working hard; suppose you take an evening off and have a good time? But . . . no fights and no trouble!" Roosevelt added, holding his finger aloft.

"Hooray for the colonel!" someone shouted, and the men broke into a run, headed for a saloon in town that, in order to take advantage of the arrival of the cavalry, had changed its name from Lucky Chance to Boots and Saddles.

Todd had started toward the remuda when he heard Roosevelt make the offer to buy free drinks for all. Startled, he looked back over his shoulder in dismay as he watched his platoon break and run. He sighed. There would be no night maneuvers tonight.

Shaking his head slowly, Todd continued on toward the saloon. He was met by the stable sergeant, who, like Todd, was regular army.

"I've rounded up some really good mounts for your night maneuver, sir," the sergeant said. "I have to tell you, I been in the army for over twenty years, and I've never seen horseflesh this good."

"They *are* good mounts," Todd agreed. "But we won't be using them tonight."

"You canceled the training?"

Todd looked over toward his platoon. By now they were small figures in the distance, already halfway to the saloon. "Yes," Todd said, without elaboration. "I canceled it."

"Wish you woulda told me that earlier, Lieutenant. It woulda saved me the trouble of roundin' up the mounts."

"My apologies, Sergeant."

"I'd better go turn 'em out with the others," the sergeant said.

Todd walked over to the fence and laid his arms across the top rail, leaning into it.

"You didn't cancel the exercise, did you, Lieutenant?" a voice said from behind him. Turning, Todd saw Colonel Wood approaching.

Todd came to attention and saluted. Wood returned his salute.

"I, uh, thought it might be better to reschedule, sir," Todd said.

Wood chuckled. "You don't have to cover up for T. R.," he stated. "I saw what happened. When he said he was buying drinks for the entire platoon, it was over for the day."

"Yes, sir."

"I know Colonel Roosevelt is hard to take, sometimes,"

Wood said. "And I respect you for trying to cover up for him."

"The men are crazy about him," Todd stated. "Everyone likes Colonel Roosevelt. *I* like Colonel Roosevelt."

Wood chuckled. "Of course everyone likes him. He is a politician, and that's what politicians do best . . . get people to like them. And though you may not believe so, I am certain T. R. is going to be a fine officer. He certainly has the drive and stamina for it."

"Yes, sir," Todd said.

"I intend to speak to him tonight," Wood added.

"Colonel, please don't do so on my account," Todd said.

"Your name won't even be mentioned," Wood replied. Hè started to walk away from the stable but after a few steps stopped and turned back. "Lieutenant, I want you to know that I appreciate what you have been doing for the regiment. I know you want to go to a regular army unit, and I can't say that I blame you. But if you'll just stick it out long enough to help me get these boys organized, I'll do everything I can to get you a billet in a regular army unit."

"Thank you, sir," Todd said.

Wood left the stable and returned to the Sibley tent that served as his office. A few moments later, Roosevelt strode in and, turning a chair around, sat in it backward. He tossed his campaign hat onto the corner of Wood's desk, then leaned forward against the chair back.

"I tell you, Leonard, this is absolutely a bully operation," he said enthusiastically. "Why, there isn't a man jack here who doesn't want to be here, and I'll wager that, when the chips are down, we can count on all of them to do their duty."

"I'm sure of it, Theodore," Wood said. "I only hope we have them adequately trained by then."

"Why, of course we will. Why shouldn't we?" Roosevelt asked.

"Oh, no particular reason," Wood replied. "But young Lieutenant Murchison did have a mounted maneuvering exercise scheduled for tonight."

"And?"

"Well, he won't be able to conduct it now, will he?" Wood said. "Not with every man of his platoon down at Boots and Saddles."

Roosevelt slapped his hand against his forehead. "Oh," he said. "Oh, my."

"Colonel Roosevelt, if we are to truly make this a military unit and not just a social club, you must never do anything like that again. Do you understand me?"

Roosevelt nodded but said nothing. Instead he just stood and quietly withdrew.

Later that same night, under a full moon, the San Antonio River was a stream of molten silver winding its way through the low hills. The camp was like a painting in soft shades of silver and black, with the tents, all in neat rows, shining brilliantly white in the moonlight.

Out on the quadrangle a twelve-pounder signal cannon and a flagpole, with its banner struck for the night, gleamed softly. The night held the long high-pitched trills and low viola-like thrums of the frogs. For counter-melody there were crickets in the distance; the long mournful howls of the coyotes; and from the stable, a mule braying and a horse blowing.

From the Sibley tent, that housed not only Colonel Wood's office but also his quarters came the gleam of a kerosene lantern. Roosevelt walked through the darkness until he reached the tent. The flap was open to take advantage of the breeze. Wood was sitting at a field table, writing a letter. Standing just outside the tent, Roosevelt called out, "Colonel, may I speak with you?"

Wood put his pen down. "Yes, T. R., of course. Come in," he said. Wood made a motion with his hand, pointing to the same chair Roosevelt had sat in earlier. It was still reversed, just as Roosevelt had left it. "Have a seat."

"No, thank you, sir," Roosevelt said. "What I have to say won't take long. About my buying the men drinks this afternoon and messing up Lieutenant Murchison's training schedule?" Roosevelt cleared his throat. "Well, I wish to say, sir, that such a thing will never happen again. Also, I want you to know that I consider myself the damnedest ass within ten miles of this camp. Good night, sir."

CHAPTER 5

Todd had taken it upon himself to be responsible for Marty. He told himself that it was because he had saved her life and, in the custom of the Indians, a body of people Todd had learned to know quite well during his boyhood on the army posts of the West, one was eternally responsible for the life one saved.

To that end, Todd had detailed a couple of men to pitch an officer's tent for the female reporter. The tent was large enough for a small cot and a writing table. A keg of water was also kept close by and filled, and Marty found that, thanks to Todd Murchison's thoughtfulness and the soldiers' efforts, her stay was quite comfortable.

She was, however, excluded from the club of journalists who were also in San Antonio. To be honest, she didn't miss their company. They were a boisterous lot, given mostly to complaining. They complained about the food, they complained about the weather, and they complained about having to sleep in tents, even though they had officers' tents just as Marty did. When they weren't complaining, they were drinking or playing cards. Marty often wondered when any of them found the time to write their stories.

Marty filed her own stories every day, but she wasn't certain she was writing about what she was supposed to be writing about. Maybe she should have been discussing military strategy or the progress of the men's training or explaining Colonel Wood's concept of tactics. If so, she was remiss, because she didn't write about any of that. Instead, she filed stories in which she tried to portray the tone and tint of a large army in the field.

Marty's tent was pitched very near a stone fence, and one night she sat with her back leaning against the stones as she looked out over the valley where a thousand men were camped. There were scores of campfires glowing on the valley floor, and the smell of smoke blended with the fragrance of the wildflowers. Behind her, undisturbed by the army, she could hear the serenade of frogs and crickets. All across the valley and into the woods beyond, thousands of flashes of golden lights winked at her. They were fireflies and they looked like tiny stars descended from the firmament.

From some distant campfire came the sound of a group of soldiers beginning to sing, and the haunting beauty of their song moved Marty deeply:

> "The years creep slowly by, Lorena;
> The snow is on the grass again;
> The sun's low down the sky, Lorena,
> And frost gleams where the flowers have been."

As Marty leaned her head back and listened to the singing, she saw a figure walking toward her tent. When the shadowy figure got closer, she saw that it was Todd Murchison.

"Miss McGuire?" he called quietly into the tent. He had not seen her sitting up by the stone fence.

"I'm over here!" she called back to him. "Is there anything wrong?"

"Anything wrong?"

"Did Colonel Wood or Colonel Roosevelt send you?"

"No, nothing is wrong. I just thought I would stop by to see how you are getting along," Todd said. "You haven't gotten in the way of any more runaway caissons?"

Marty laughed. "No, nothing like that," she replied.

"Are you comfortable?"

"Yes, I'm very comfortable, thank you."

"I wish you would share with the other journalists your secret as to how you are staying comfortable. They have badgered Colonel Wood to no end about the privations they are suffering.''

Marty sighed. "I'm afraid the other journalists and I don't speak that much. I'm not even sure they know I'm here." Marty's comment was matter-of-fact. There was no rancor in her voice.

"Oh, believe me, they know you are here. You make them aware of that with every story you write."

"I haven't written anything of real military significance yet," Marty said. "Just a few observations."

"Well, those . . . observations, as you call them, have resulted in some very good stories. Did you know that many of the men have cut out some of your stories and are carrying them around in their wallets as if they were poems?"

"No," Marty said. "No, I didn't know that."

Todd cleared his throat: " 'In the quiet of the night, deep in their souls, each man can hear the distant rattle of musketry, and he must ask himself if he can measure up to the test,' " Todd quoted, saying the words as if they were a line of poetry.

"You've been reading my work," Marty said.

"Yes, I have," Todd answered. He was quiet for a moment, and from the distant campfire the song continued:

"We loved each other then, Lorena,
More than we ever dared to tell,
And what might have been, Lorena,
Had but our loving prospered well.
But then, 'tis past, the years have flown;
I'll not call up their shadowy forms.
I'll say to them, 'Lost years, sleep on.
Sleep on, nor heed life's pelting storms.' "

"That song the soldiers are singing," Marty said. "What is it?"

"It's called 'Lorena,' " Todd answered. "It was a song of the Confederate soldiers during the Civil War, but like all good songs, it was picked up by both sides."

"Surely there aren't any veterans of that war in the Rough Riders," Marty said.

"You'd be surprised. We do have a couple of sergeants who fought in the Civil War, though one of them was a drummer boy. Anyway, a good song never dies, and 'Lorena' is a good song."

"It's a love song, and love songs are good songs," Marty commented.

"Unrequited love," Todd said. "Of course, that's the only kind for the soldier. Or at least it should be."

"That's a strange thing to say."

"It isn't strange at all," Todd replied. "Unrequited love is the army's due. Love fulfilled means marriage, and marriage is incompatible with a military career."

"Your father was married, and he has had a brilliant military career."

"Have you ever read the book *Tenting on the Plains*?"

"No, I don't think I have."

"It's a very good book. You should read it sometime. It was written by Elizabeth Custer, but it could have been written by my mother. Almost literally, as my father was with Custer on his last scout."

"What? But that's impossible. Everyone was killed!"

Todd chuckled. "Only those who were with Custer's element were killed. Reno and Benteen, and most of the men with them, survived the battle. But that does bring up the point I'm trying to make. Elizabeth Custer is a widow now."

"Surely you aren't suggesting that if Custer hadn't been married he would not have been massacred?"

"No, I was just commenting, that's all."

"Your father was married; General Grant was married; George Washington was married—all the great soldiers of our country's past were married. Now, you may have some personal reason for not wanting to marry, but you can't use the military as your excuse."

Todd laughed out loud. "My, Miss McGuire, the way you are defending the institution of marriage, one might think you were applying for the position."

"I most definitely am not!" Marty replied sharply, much

more sharply than she intended. Her cheeks were flaming now, and she was glad that it was too dark for him to see her embarrassment.

"I'm sorry," Todd said good-naturedly. "I had no right to say such a thing. Would you forgive me?"

Todd's apology was so sincere that Marty was able to laugh with him.

"All right," she said. "You're forgiven."

"Good; I'm glad I'm forgiven," Todd replied. "I would not want us to part company tonight with you thinking ill of me."

Marty smiled warmly. "In addition to having saved my life, Mr. Murchison, you have also bent over backward to provide for my every need and comfort. How could I think ill of you?"

"On that note, I will leave while I am ahead," Todd said. He touched the brim of his hat. "Good night."

"Good night, Lieutenant."

As Todd walked back to his own tent, he passed a soldier holding a trumpet.

"Good evenin', sir," the soldier said, saluting.

"Good evening," Todd replied, returning the salute. Todd stopped and leaned against the signal cannon to watch as the trumpeter raised the instrument to his lips. The trumpeter blew air through it a couple of times to clear it; then he began to play "Taps." Todd listened to the mournful notes as they filled the night air, calling the soldiers to bed. They rolled out across the flat open parade ground, hitting the low hills beyond the encampment, then rolling back a second later in a haunting repeat.

Of all the army rituals, "Taps" was the most meaningful to Todd. It was the last thing soldiers heard at night and the final honor accorded them when they died. It was part of the fabric of the warrior's soul.

On dusty army posts with his father, Todd had heard the call, even as he suckled at his mother's breast. And though it was a soothing, comforting tune, there was also a touch of sadness about it, and he could never hear it without thinking of those soldiers who had given their last full measure of devotion. He sometimes envied those to whom "Taps" was just another bugle call and wished that, like them, he could let it pass with little note. But he could not do that. He could no more deny the hold it had over him than he could deny his own existence.

As the last echo of "Taps" died in the distance, Todd went into his small tent, then crawled into the canvas cot that was his bed.

At Sea with the U.S. Navy

Angus Pugh had rejoined the navy, correctly guessing that with the war approaching he would be accepted. He knew that he wouldn't get his old rating back, but that didn't matter. What did matter was that he find a way to get out of New York. Not that anyone was looking for him, but if they started, he wanted to make it harder for them to find him.

When he was sworn in as an able-bodied seaman, he said nothing about his former rate. He didn't even protest when he learned that he was to be a stoker, one of the men who shoveled coal into the furnaces.

The job of a stoker was, without a doubt, the worst job on board any coal-fired ship. Wearing only their undershorts, these men would shovel coal, their bodies bathed in sweat from the 170-degree heat. It was no accident that many artists chose this particular operation as a means of illustrating Dante's Inferno.

Though anyone in the engine room might be referred to as belonging to "the Black Gang," the name actually referred to the stokers themselves. That was because coal dust plugged the pores until their very skin turned black. Within forty-eight hours no one could tell one stoker from another, and as Pugh looked around at the others who were working with him he realized that these were the same type of men who had been killed when the *Maine* exploded.

Angus Pugh had been paid by one of the New York newspapers to place a torpedo on Buoy Number Four. The purpose of the torpedo was to make a demonstration. It was neither the newspaper's nor Angus Pugh's intent to hurt anyone. Unfortunately, good intentions weren't enough. Something had gone terribly wrong, and good men, sailors, men like him, had been killed. As he thought of his involvement in the deaths of so many men, an overwhelming sense of remorse overtook him, and he stood, leaning on his shovel, for a long moment.

"You, sailor!" the engineering officer shouted to Pugh. "You aren't getting anything done by standing there with your thumb in your arse! Get to work!"

"Aye, aye, sir," Pugh replied, tossing a shovel full of coal through the open door into the flames of Boiler Number One. He would have to live with the pain of what he had done. It wasn't something he could share with anyone else.

Shortly after Pugh enlisted, the Navy Department received a cable message informing them that a Spanish task force under the command of Adm. Pascual Cervera had set sail for the Caribbean. The newspapers picked up the story immediately and began fanning the flames of sensationalism by implying that the "enemy was at the gates."

The entire East Coast started seeing ghost ships. Someone reported that they had "on good authority" the information that Cervera planned to sneak into New York Harbor in the middle of the night and destroy the Statue of Liberty. Deepwater fishermen fishing off the coast of Maine swore that they had heard the distant thunder of naval gunfire. Oyster men in Virginia were positive they had passed the enemy task force at sea but, because of a rain squall, managed to sneak by without being seen themselves. Beach walkers in Georgia reported they had seen the Spanish fleet outlined against the horizon.

The Navy Department was besieged with demands to do something to protect citizens from this menace from the sea. Shore defense guns, little more than static displays and memorials of the Civil War, were hastily put back into service. Merchant ships were fitted with deck guns, then sent to sea to form a shield of armed vessels. The navy knew that the

Civil War coastal artillery would be ineffective against a modern warship and that one enemy cruiser could sink the entire armada of armed merchant ships . . . but it made the public feel better to think that something was being done.

With the public somewhat placated, the navy then set about doing something real, and to this end they formed something called the Flying Squadron. The Flying Squadron was commanded by Rear Adm. Winfield Scott Schley, and its mission was to find Cervera and pin him down until a second, more powerful squadron could deal with him.

The ship to which Pugh was assigned was a part of the Flying Squadron. Schley and his squadron of ships dashed around the Caribbean like a pack of hunting dogs. They peeked into Havana Harbor, but Cervera wasn't there. They swung down to San Juan, Puerto Rico, but he wasn't there, either.

Not until Schley neared Santiago de Cuba, on Cuba's southern coast, was there any direct contact with the enemy. There, anchored in the harbor's mouth, was the Spanish cruiser *Cristóbal Colón.*

Schley couldn't go in after the Spanish ship because the harbor defenses were too strong. El Morro, a fortress bristling with cannons, overlooked the narrow entrance from a high bluff. In addition to the fort, powerful shore batteries guarded the entrance.

Schley pulled back from the mouth of the harbor, then arranged his ships in a semicircle. At night he ordered the ships to keep their searchlights focused on the harbor entrance, to make certain the Spanish didn't try to sneak out.

"If only there was some way we could plug the harbor entrance," Schley lamented during a meeting with his officers.

"There is a way," Lieutenant Hobson suggested.

"And what way would that be, Lieutenant?"

"We would have to sacrifice one of our ships," Hobson said.

"What do you mean, sacrifice a ship?" Schley asked. "You mean conduct a suicide mission?"

"Well, I would hope it wouldn't be a suicide mission,"

Hobson replied. "If the plan works, no one will be injured.

"I know this harbor, Admiral. I know it very well," Hobson said. "At its narrowest point, the navigable channel is only 350 feet wide. It just so happens that the coal carrier we have with us, the *Merrimac,* is 330 feet long. What if, during the middle of the night, we slipped the *Merrimac* past the fort and into the channel at its narrowest point? We could swing the vessel around breech to, then sink it. If we did it properly, there would be no more than ten feet of clearance on either side. That would create such a bottleneck that no ship could get by."

"What about the crew of the *Merrimac*?" one of the officers asked. "We can't ask them to do something like that."

"You wouldn't have to. We would take everyone off beforehand, then crew it with only the minimum number of volunteers needed to do the job," Hobson said. "I will, of course, be the first volunteer."

"How many men would you need?" Schley asked.

"No more than six or seven. But in addition to the crew needed to operate the ship, I'll also need one or two who are expert with explosives. I intend to rig several mines to be exploded electrically."

Schley nodded. "All right, send the word through the fleet that we are looking for volunteers."

Angus Pugh had just come off a four-hour stretch of keeping the furnaces stoked when Mr. Bailey, the engineering officer, called for their attention.

"I don't expect this to have anything to do with any of you," Bailey said. "But we have orders to ask in every department. The admiral is looking for volunteers for a very dangerous mission."

"What sort of mission, sir?" one of the men asked.

"How am I supposed to know that?" Bailey replied. "The admiral doesn't discuss his plans with engineering officers. Whatever it is, it is dangerous, and whoever volunteers must be experienced in working with explosives. Since none of you have ever done anything but shovel coal, that lets you out."

"I'll go," Pugh said.

The others looked at him.

"Did you hear what I said, Pugh?" Bailey asked. "The volunteers have to be experienced with explosives."

"I heard you, sir," Pugh said. "I've worked with explosives."

"What kind of explosives?"

"Both surface and submarine explosions, timed and untimed, electrical, fuse, and impact detonation. I've worked with black and smokeless powder, dynamite, TNT, and nitroglycerin. I've armed mines and disarmed impact-damaged shells."

The others in the engine room, most of whom were considerably younger than Pugh, looked at him in a newfound light.

"How did a stoker come by such experience?" Bailey asked skeptically.

"I haven't always been a stoker. On my previous enlistment I was a gunner's mate first class."

"Heavens, man, why didn't you say something when you re-enlisted? You wouldn't have had to serve as a stoker."

"I chose to keep all information regarding my previous service to myself," Pugh said. "And I would have continued to do so, had there not been a fleetwide request for people of my experience."

"On what ship did you serve during your last appointment?" Bailey asked.

"I served aboard the *Maine*, sir."

Again, there were several gasps of surprise. Not only was Pugh much more experienced than anyone had imagined, but also they were now hearing that he had been on the *Maine*.

"Who was your engineering officer?" Bailey asked. From the expression on his face, it seemed obvious that he still didn't believe Pugh. This question was putting Pugh to the test.

Recognizing the engineering officer's intent, Pugh smiled. "Why, that would be Darwin Merritt, sir," Pugh said. "He was sort of a smallish fella, with sandy hair and freckles."

"Yes, you have described him well. I knew Darwin Merritt,'' Baily replied, somewhat taken aback by Pugh's correct answer.

"I understand Mr. Merritt was killed when the *Maine* went down," Pugh said.

"Yes, that's true," Bailey answered. He stared at Pugh for a long moment. "Sailor, I don't understand you. Why is it that you chose not to speak of this?"

"Because I lost my rating, sir," Pugh explained. "And I didn't want anyone to hold that against me. What about it, sir? I really would like to volunteer for this mission, whatever it is."

"All right, Pugh," Bailey said. "Since you once served on board the *Maine,* it seems to me that you have more right than anyone to get some action. Report to Lieutenant Hobson. He is to be the leader of the volunteers."

"Aye, aye, sir," Pugh said. "And thank you."

At 2:00 A.M. the *Merrimac,* manned by a crew of one officer and seven sailors, set out for its last voyage. Except for a few flashes of lightning on the ridge just beyond Santiago, the night was pitch-black.

Slowly and quietly, the *Merrimac* neared the mouth of the channel. Nothing stirred onshore and Pugh was beginning to think they might sneak through completely unnoticed.

But that wasn't to be.

Suddenly the long finger of a searchlight beam stabbed through the darkness. It caught and illuminated the *Merrimac.* From ashore there were shouts of alarm, rendered in Spanish. That was followed almost immediately by orange flashes and red balls of flame. A small patrol boat came after them. Shots from the patrol boat alerted the shore batteries, and a moment later the heavy guns roared into action.

Shells tore into the *Merrimac,* but Hobson kept them moving forward. Then, all of a sudden, small-arms fire opened up, and the bullets started pinging all around them with the rapidity of hailstones. Two Spanish infantry regiments, one on either side of the waterway, had joined into the fracas and were blazing away at the intruding vessel with over two thousand rifles. Pugh and the others had no choice but to lie prone on the deck and pray that the ship wouldn't be blown from the water before they could reach their destination.

When they arrived at the narrowest part of the channel, Hobson shouted orders to the helmsman: "Breech to, hard a port!"

The helmsman spun the wheel, but the ship failed to answer. The rudder had been shot away, and the *Merrimac* was out of control.

"Lieutenant, she won't answer the helm! What'll we do, Lieutenant? What'll we do?"

Hobson rose up from the deck to have a look around. Ripples of light flashed up and down the shoreline as the Spanish continued to fire. "Detonate the torpedoes!" Hobson shouted.

"Sir, that won't do no good! We aren't breeched!" Pugh said.

"It doesn't matter! We have no choice! Detonate them! Do it now!"

Pugh pushed down on the plunger, but only two of the torpedoes exploded.

"Shit!" Pugh shouted.

"What happened?" Hobson asked. "Why didn't the others go?"

"The wires to the others must have been cut," Pugh explained. "They can't be fired electrically."

"Is there any other way to set them off?"

"I don't know. I'll try, sir," Pugh said.

With part of her left side blown away, the *Merrimac* now began taking on water. She started listing to port, but still she refused to turn or slow down. She sped on through the channel into the inner harbor.

Pugh leaned out over the side of the ship and looked at the four unexploded torpedoes. Although all four of them had been wired for electrical detonation, Pugh saw that at least two of them had impact detonators as well. Hurrying back to the toolbox, he took out a ballpeen hammer.

"What are you going to do?" Hobson asked.

"I'm going to set off the impact detonator," Pugh said as he started back toward the port side.

"How in blazes do you plan to do that?"

"By hitting them," Pugh said.

"What?" Hobson asked, not sure he had understood what Pugh said. Then, shocked, he saw Pugh strike one of the detonators. Hobson heard a solid ring, but the charge didn't explode.

"Pugh! Get back here! What the hell do you think you are doing? I'm ordering you to get back here!"

Pugh looked at Hobson, then grinned broadly. "Remember the *Maine*!" he shouted, bringing the hammer down sharply against the impact fuse.

Almost instantly there was a flash of light, a loud explosion, and a billowing puff of smoke. This time, the explosion set off the other torpedoes as well. Pugh disappeared, and the *Merrimac* went down, instantly. Unfortunately, she still had not turned, nor had she passed through the channel. Instead she was lying inside the harbor, which meant there was plenty of room remaining for the Spanish fleet to maneuver. With a feeling of anguished frustration, Hobson realized that his mission had been a complete failure.

The men were shaken by the explosion but unhurt. Their lifeboat had been blown apart, but they managed to climb aboard a raft that was floating nearby. Exhausted, they lay on the raft, knowing that they would have to surrender, if, in fact, the Spaniards didn't shoot them on sight.

"Keep a sharp lookout for Seaman Pugh," Hobson ordered. "If you see him, pull him aboard."

"Sir, there won't be nothin' of Pugh left to see, let alone pull aboard," one of the others said quietly.

"Keep a sharp eye nevertheless," Hobson ordered.

"Aye, aye, sir."

All through the night, the men clung to the bobbing raft. Shortly before sunrise Hobson, totally exhausted, fell asleep.

"Mr. Hobson! Mr. Hobson, you better wake up, sir," one of the men said, shaking him. "Boat's comin'."

Hobson sat up and looked in the direction the man was pointing. With the just-risen sun providing illumination, he saw a patrol boat chugging across the water. Spanish soldiers were standing at the rail, aiming their rifles at them.

"Oh, Lord, they goin' to shoot us, ain't they, Mr. Hobson?"

"Yes," Hobson replied grimly. "It looks that way."

As Hobson prepared himself to die, a bearded officer in a white uniform stepped up to the rail and ordered his men to hold their fire.

"They ain't goin' to shoot, Lieutenant!" one of the other men said. "That fella stopped them! They ain't goin' to shoot!"

The patrol boat drew alongside, and the Americans were helped aboard. Hobson, his teeth chattering after a night in the water, saluted the officer who was in charge.

"Sir, I am Lieutenant Hobson of the U.S. Navy."

"I am Admiral Cervera," the bearded Spanish officer replied as he returned Hobson's salute. The admiral took in Hobson and his men with a wave of his hand. "*Valiente*," he said. Then, because he didn't know if Hobson could speak Spanish, he repeated it in English. "Valiant. You and your men are very brave."

CHAPTER 6

IN THE FIELD WITH THE ROUGH RIDERS
by
Marty McGuire

A cavalry unit is like a beehive; it is a living thing that takes on an identity greater than the sum of its parts. At first it is difficult to see this, because there seems to be utter confusion. Horses run back and forth, sabers flash in the sunlight, caissons bearing heavy cannons rumble into position, sergeants shout, and then, miraculously, what was confusion becomes order. Great blocks of horses and men stand in perfect formation, with bits of red and white cloth flapping proudly in the breeze from the tips of long staffs held in front of each group. These little red and white flags are called guidons, and the men who hold them are called guidon bearers. A member of a particular unit is as proud of his unit's guidon as the average person is of the Stars and Stripes.

Back in San Antonio, flags were flying from every pinnacle and post. Young boys rode bicycles with red, white, and blue bunting strung through the spokes. Pretty young women dressed in red, white, and blue waved tiny flags and cheered as the First Volunteer Cavalry rode by, four abreast, ramrod straight in their saddles, with their eyes straight ahead.

Their destination was the Southern Pacific Rail Depot, where a long train sat waiting on the track, the engine's relief valve sighing as it vented steam. This was the first of the seven trains it would take to move the regiment.

Marty was standing on the depot platform along with the other reporters who had come to San Antonio to cover the events. Shortly after the soldiers arrived, the clarion call of a bugle sounded four notes. This, Marty knew, was the call for attention.

All movement among the soldiers stopped; then they faced right as the guidon bearers took their positions. Col. Leonard Wood rode to the center of the formation; then Roosevelt rode out to the middle as well. Roosevelt turned toward the men.

"Report!" Roosevelt barked. Though he tried to sound military, his voice was rather high-pitched, and Marty heard a few of the men around her chortle. She knew that the soldiers liked Roosevelt, and she had to check the impulse to turn toward these men who were now making fun of Roosevelt's high-pitched voice and remind them that at least *he* was serving his country.

"First Battalion all present and accounted for, sir!" the First Battalion commander called, and his call was repeated down the line until all three battalions had reported. Roosevelt took each of their reports; then he turned to Wood and saluted him. She could hear Roosevelt's voice, strangely high-pitched but carrying strong.

"Sir! The regiment is formed."

Wood returned the salute; then he and Roosevelt rode to the far end of the formation and started a slow parade of the line, coming toward the end nearest Marty. This was to be the last review before the men began boarding the trains for transportation to Tampa, Florida, and Marty watched very carefully. She wanted to capture the excitement she was feeling so she could convey some of it, in writing, to her readers.

She still had not convinced Talbot to send her to Cuba to cover the battle when it came, even though, by Talbot's own admission, the *Banner* had never received more letters of praise from its readers than it was receiving now for the articles she had been writing. He had agreed, however, to let her ride with the troop train as far as Montgomery, Alabama. From there, the troop train would head south, while Marty would board a northbound train, back to New York.

The last car on the train was reserved for journalists. Here the natural enmity and competition of the reporters who were working for different papers manifested itself in a sharp-tongued but not bitter banter. The banter was among the men reporters only, however. Most of the men tended to ignore Marty, and she rode in unmolested silence for hours, sitting by a window, listening to the wheels clack on the rail joints as she watched the countryside pass by. The other reporters played cards in jovial camaraderie. Marty didn't really want to play cards, but she would have appreciated a word from them, anything that would let her know that they recognized her presence.

Finally, Phil Block, a gray-haired old reporter who worked for *Harper's Weekly,* came over to sit beside her. Grateful for his company, Marty smiled sweetly at him. Then she noticed that the other reporters were glaring at him.

Phil chuckled. "They are upset with me for consorting with the enemy," he said.

"The enemy? I am the enemy?"

"In their eyes you are," Phil answered her.

"Why? Just because I am a woman?"

"Oh, it isn't just because you are a woman, my dear. It's because you are a woman . . . and you are very good. They are all hearing from their editors about the articles you are filing. 'Send me something like what Marty McGuire writes,' the editors are saying, and because they can't do it, they resent you."

"I'm sorry," Marty said. She looked at the others, but they had gone back to their card games and individual conversations, so none of them seemed to be paying attention to her. "I was just trying to do the best I could do, that's all."

"And that's exactly what you should do," Phil declared. "Pay no attention to them. They'll come around. They won't have any choice. Especially when we get to Cuba and you really start to shine."

"Oh, I wish that were true," Marty said. "But I won't be

going to Cuba. I'm not even going to Tampa. I will leave the train when we reach Montgomery.''

"Why? Don't you want to go with us?"

"Oh, yes, I want to go more than anything else in the world. But no matter how many times I ask Mr. Talbot, he keeps saying no.''

Block chuckled. "Don't you worry about that. I've known Charles Talbot for a long, long time. He may be obstinate . . . but he's not stupid. With the following you have now, he is not going to make you sit out the war in New York. Trust me; he will have no choice but to send you to Cuba.''

"Oh, I pray that you are right," Marty said.

That afternoon, Marty filed what would be her last article before returning to New York:

HEROIC PASSAGE
Special to the *Banner*
by Marty McGuire

As the train carrying the Rough Riders proceeds to Tampa, Florida, it is met at every stop and crossing by cheering throngs. The depot platforms are crowded with men and women, flags fly, and banners hang from every place of advantage. Although the regiment has its own staff of cooks and bakers, these men can scarcely perform their tasks, for food of all sorts—great roasts of beef, baskets of fried chicken, fruit, bread, cookies, pies, and cakes—is heaped upon us at every stop.

Patriotism abounds, and the nation's heart and well-wishes are extended to our brave young men.

But the trains carrying the men, horses, and equipment of the Rough Riders were not the only special trains crossing the United States. Another troop-carrying train was making the same transit, though with much less attention.

Special Train Number Twenty-seven received no priority routing and, in fact, was shunted aside for every other passenger train. On several occasions, Special Twenty-seven sat on a sidetrack for better than two hours, waiting for a local to pass. There were even a few times when local traffic managers assigned a higher priority to freight trains, so that Special Twenty-seven sat, baking in the hot sun, as a long, slow freight rattled by.

During the times Special Twenty-seven was sidetracked, the passengers weren't allowed off. In some places, they were ordered to keep the shades drawn so that their presence wouldn't disturb the citizens of the town through which they were passing.

This train, too, was taking American soldiers to war, but there was no special press car on this train, and there were no advance announcements. Any flags, banners, or patriotic symbols the passengers of this train saw were incidental and had nothing to do with their passage.

The passengers of Special Twenty-seven were the men of the Tenth Colored Cavalry. For thirty years black soldiers had served in the West in the two Regiments of Colored Cavalry and the two Divisions of Colored Infantry. The distinction with which they had served through all the Indian campaigns was manifest by the eighteen Medals of Honor they had won.

While members of the Rough Riders feasted on the viands provided them by the patriotic public, the Buffalo Soldiers ate Canned Willy, as the tinned beef was called, and hardtack. Most of them had endured years of prejudice and racial hatred from the very people they protected, and yet there were few of them who would have exchanged places with anyone else in America. The desertion rate was lower and disciplinary problems fewer than in any other unit in the army. They were a band of brothers, as close-knit as the Praetorian Guard, with an esprit de corps that was unmatched anywhere in the army. And if the outside world shunned them, so be it. These men were complete, in and of themselves.

On the second day of the Rough Riders' eastward transit, Colonel Wood called Todd into the car that had been specially fitted to serve as the regimental headquarters. Both Wood and Roosevelt had their jackets on, but unbuttoned. Roosevelt was drinking a cup of coffee.

Todd saluted. "Lieutenant Murchison reporting to the regimental commander as directed, sir."

Wood returned a halfhearted salute, and Roosevelt, because he wasn't sure whether one was expected of him or not, did the same.

"I picked up several telegrams at our last stop, Todd," Wood said. "One of them concerns you."

"Me, sir?"

"You wanted to be reassigned to a regular army unit? Well, your assignment has come through."

"Good, sir," Todd said, grinning broadly. Then, because he thought his delight in the assignment might be misunderstood, he hastened to explain himself. "Uh, not that I wouldn't be glad to serve with you, sir. With both of you. I think you and Colonel Roosevelt are fine officers, and you have every right to be proud of the First Volunteer Cavalry."

Wood chuckled. "Stop digging a hole for yourself, Lieutenant; I know what you are saying. You are a West Point graduate and a regular army officer. Of course you would want to serve with a regular army unit." Wood cleared his throat. "The question is, do you want to serve with this particular unit?"

"Is the unit not going to Cuba?"

"Oh, yes, it's going to Cuba, all right. But three of your classmates have already declined the assignment, even though it carries with it an immediate promotion to first lieutenant," Colonel Wood said. "No one will hold it against you if you turn it down as well. And if you do refuse this assignment, I won't give up trying to get you another one."

"What is the assignment?"

"It is to the Tenth Colored Cavalry Regiment," Colonel Wood said.

A broad grin spread across Todd's face. "I'll take it."

"Lieutenant, did you hear what I said? It is a Colored Cavalry Regiment," Wood repeated.

"Yes, sir, I heard," Todd said. "My father once commanded the Tenth Cavalry. I know them to be very good soldiers, and I am looking forward to the assignment."

"Very well, Todd, I'll have your orders drawn immediately,'' Colonel Wood said. ''When we pass through Jackson, Mississippi, you can get off the train and wait for them. I understand that their train will be passing through not too long afterward.''

Like the people of every other town they had passed through, the citizens of Jackson turned out in full to greet the Rough Riders. An editorial in the local newspaper explained the immense popularity of the Rough Riders:

> It has been 30 years since the Civil War ended, a full generation since young men took up arms in defense of hearth and home. The Civil War was an important national experience and continues to be a major topic of conversation, but many young men are tired of hearing about the exploits of their fathers and grandfathers. They are ready for glory of their own, and the war in Cuba offers them that opportunity.
>
> It is also worth noting that the First Volunteer Cavalry Regiment is made up of a mixture of Yankees and Southerners, reuniting, at last, the fighting spirit of America under a common banner.
>
> All hail to Old Glory. Hooray for the red, white and blue.

It wasn't only the Rough Riders who were honored. The reporters who had been filing their stories from San Antonio were also being feted, for many of their articles had been picked up by the local newspapers. The result was enough recognition to go around, thus easing, somewhat, the other reporters' animosity toward Marty McGuire.

When the prolonged stop in Jackson was over, Marty retook her seat in the press car and waved good-bye to the well-wishers as the train left the station. She was surprised to see that one of the people still standing on the platform was Lt. Todd Murchison.

Since their brief meeting at the military ball in New York, Marty and Todd had maintained only a casual acquaintance. He had not been rude to her. On the contrary, he had been most gracious every time they came into contact. But he had also been very busy. In fact, she once had suggested to Colonel Wood that Lieutenant Murchison seemed to be the busiest man in the entire regiment, and Wood hadn't disputed her.

"He is a regular army officer in an organization of volunteers," Wood had explained. "He has a few weeks to teach 1,200 men what it took him four years to learn at West Point."

"Why, that's impossible," Marty said.

Wood shook his head. "Impossible? I'm not sure that is a word that Lieutenant Murchison even recognizes."

Marty recalled that conversation with Colonel Wood as she stared through the window at the young lieutenant. He was obviously not missing the train, for he could easily catch it, even now, if he wished. He was purposefully being left behind, though for what reason Marty had not the slightest idea.

As her train pulled away, Marty wondered if she would ever meet Todd Murchison again. She realized then that she was attracted to him, and she allowed herself a moment of contemplation. What if they had met under different circumstances? What if the world had not been moving with such lightning speed? Would anything romantic develop between them?

"Stop this foolish fantasizing, Marty," she said under her breath. "You are a grown woman; you aren't a giddy schoolgirl."

Special Train Number Twenty-seven passed through Jackson at two o'clock in the morning. This was in accordance with a schedule that was carefully arranged in order to prevent any kind of demonstration against the black soldiers.

When the train stopped to take on water, Todd, his luggage in hand, started to board it. The conductor stepped down from the train and held up his hand to stop Todd.

"You don't want to get on this train, soldier boy," he said.

"Why not? Isn't this Special Train Twenty-seven?" Todd asked.

The conductor's eyes narrowed. "Yes," he said. "Yes, it

is. You sure you're supposed to be on Special Twenty-seven?"

Todd showed the conductor his orders. "I am Lt. Todd Murchison. I am joining the Tenth Cavalry."

"Well, then I'm sorry for you, Lieutenant, but I guess this is your train."

A gray-haired black soldier stepped out onto the vestibule then and stared hard at Todd in the dim light of the platform.

"Beg pardon, sir, but would you be young Todd Murchison, the son of Colonel Murchison?"

Todd smiled as he looked up at the dark face. "Why, if it isn't Corp. Fielding Dakota. How are you doing, Corporal Dakota?" he asked, recognizing one of the men from his father's old command.

"It *is* you! And look at you! An officer now." Dakota came to attention and saluted. "Sir, First Sergeant Dakota reporting, sir."

"First Sergeant Dakota, is it? Well, of course you would be," Todd said. "As I recall, you were an exceptional soldier. And, like they say, you can't keep a good man down."

"Did I hear you right, Lieutenant? You'll be joinin' the regiment?"

"You heard right, Sergeant. I now belong to the Tenth Cavalry."

"Praise the Lord, sir. That is the most wonderfullest thing I've heard yet," Dakota said.

CHAPTER 7

On Board Special Twenty-seven

U nlike the train carrying the Rough Riders, there were no berths in Special Twenty-seven. As a result, the soldiers, who had already been on board for several days and nights, were forced to rest any way they could. Most were in cramped positions in their seats, some were lying in the aisle, and a few had even climbed up into the overhead baggage rack.

"Doesn't look very comfortable," Todd said as he began picking his way around, over, and through the strewn bodies in the car.

"Yes, sir, but we've had it worse," Dakota replied. "Our troop officers is in the next car back, between this car and the car carryin' B Troop. You'll be comfortable there. Want me to go with you?"

"Thanks, but there's no need for you to go to the trouble. If it's just the next car, I'm sure I can find it," Todd said. He started toward the rear of the car; then he stopped and looked back at Dakota. "It's good to see you again, First Sergeant Dakota. I'll look forward to a visit in the morning."

"Thank you, sir. I'll be lookin' forward to that m'self."

The accommodations for the Tenth were one troop per car. Each troop car was separated by a baggage car that not only carried that troop's equipment but also served as a rolling orderly room for the troop in the preceding car. Though this car was not a passenger car, there was enough room among the troop's weapons and field equipment to put up canvas cots for the troop officers. At present, there were only two canvas cots erected, and both of them were occupied.

Not knowing where another canvas cot might be, or even if there was one, Todd started to stretch out on the floor.

"Wouldn't you be more comfortable in a cot?" one of the officers asked.

"Oh," Todd replied, unaware that his entrance had even been noticed. "Yes, sir, I'm sure I would be, but I didn't see one."

"Look behind the first rifle rack. You'd be Lt. Todd Murchison?"

"Yes, sir."

"We got word today you'd be joining us. I'm Capt. John Bigelow, commanding officer of A Troop. Welcome to the outfit."

"Pleased to meet you, sir."

"Todd Murchison, the last time I saw you, you were just a boy," a sleepy voice said from the other cot.

"I beg your pardon, sir?"

The officer sat up. "I'm John J. Pershing. I once served with your father."

"Yes, sir, I remember you!" Todd said, extending his hand.

"You don't have to say 'sir' to me. I was a lieutenant then; I'm a lieutenant now," Pershing replied. "If I stay twenty more years I'll probably still be a lieutenant."

"You two fellas carry on your old home week tomorrow, will you?" Bigelow grumbled good-naturedly as he lay back down. "It's two o'clock in the morning. I'd like to get back to sleep."

"Yes, sir. I'll be as quiet as I can," Todd said.

Bigelow chuckled. "Well, that's good, Lieutenant. You can start now," he said.

There was no dining car on Special Twenty-seven. Instead, at sunrise, a detail of soldiers was selected from each troop to act as servers. The servers would get containers of food from the kitchen car, then return to their individual troop car to serve the men at their seats. Breakfast consisted of coffee, bread, butter, and jam, and First Sergeant Dakota had just received his. He took a swallow of his coffee as he watched the Alabama countryside slide by under the early-morning sun.

"Say, Top Soldier, was I dreamin', or did we pick up a new officer last night?" Corporal Cobb asked. Cobb was sitting in the opposite seat, facing Dakota.

"You wasn't dreamin'. He come in when we was stopped in Jackson."

"I wonder what trouble he be in."

"Trouble?"

"Well, he must be in some kind of trouble," Cobb said. He took a drink of his coffee, slurping it between lips extended to cool it. "White officers don't serve with colored troops 'lessen they gots to."

Dakota shook his head. "Not this officer. I 'specs he's here 'cause he wants to be. Don't you know who it is?"

"No, didn't hear no name."

"It's young Todd Murchison," Dakota said. "Only he's full grow'd now, an' he's a lieutenant in the U.S. Army."

"Murchison?" Cobb asked.

"Sure is."

"Well, glory be," Cobb said. "Who woulda thought that?"

"Who is Murchison?" Private Bates asked.

"Yeah, what makes him so special?" Private English added.

"You mean you boys never heard of what happened at Mule Pass?" Cobb asked.

"Mule Pass? No, I don't think so. Who'd we fight there? Apache or Sioux?"

"A white-trash cracker and a no-'count sheriff," Cobb answered. Cobb and Dakota both laughed.

"What you talkin' about?"

"Tell 'em, Top," Cobb said.

"All right," Dakota started. "Gather round, boys, and listen to a story 'bout the best officer there ever was."

Not only Bates and English but at least a dozen others

drew close to Dakota, crowding the aisle and leaning over the seat backs to hear the story.

"It all started when the white-trash cracker, a man named Clay, shot one of our troopers in the leg," Cobb put in.

"Now, who's tellin' the story, Cobb? Me or you?" Dakota asked.

"Sorry, Top. You go ahead," Cobb replied contritely.

"Cobb's right," Dakota said. "Trooper Whitehead gettin' shot was what started it. He was shot for no reason at all by the fella named Clay. Then, to make matters worse, the no-'count sheriff come in and arrested the troopers who just happened to be with Whitehead, so's, he said, there wouldn't be no trouble. By the way, it helps the tellin' of the story if you was to know that the sheriff was named Pike and the saloon where all this happened was called Pike's Palace. The saloon belonged to Sheriff Pike."

"Just like that? I mean, one of our men gets shot and the sheriff don't do nothin' to the one who did the shootin' but arrest the other troopers?" Bates said. "That ain't right!"

"No, sir, it ain't right a'tall," Dakota agreed. He chuckled. "And Colonel Murchison, he didn't figure it was right, either."

"So, what did he do?" Bates asked.

Dakota looked at Bates but said nothing.

"Bates, will you shut up and let the man tell his story?" Cobb complained.

"Yeah, go ahead," Bates said.

"Me an' Cobb was at a place called Fort Canfield. Colonel Murchison was CO at the time," Dakota continued. "Well, as it turned out, the northern border of the Fort Canfield reservation cut right through the south end of the town of Mule Pass, Mule Pass bein' the name of the town where Whitehead was shot. In fact, the saloon where Trooper Whitehead was shot, Pike's Palace, was actually on military property. So Colonel Murchison figured we had ole Pike right where we wanted him. Colonel Murchison, he went to General Miles and asked the general to put the town under martial law."

Bates smiled. "Yeah, that's good," he said. "Bet that

sheriff didn't like havin' his town bein' run by colored soldiers.''

"It woulda been good, but General Miles turned Colonel Murchison down," Dakota stated.

"Turn' him down? So you mean nothin' happened? This fella Clay and the sheriff, Pike, they both just got away with it?'' Bates asked.

Again Dakota stopped telling his story. He stared silently at Bates until half a dozen of the other soldiers, who had been listening intently, demanded that Bates be quiet and stay quiet until First Sergeant Dakota could continue.

" 'Cause if you open your mouth again, I'm goin' to put my sock in it,'' English said.

"Lord, and you know you don't want English's sock in your mouth. He been wearin' it ever since we left Nebraska,'' one of the others said, and everyone laughed.

When the men had settled down again, First Sergeant Dakota continued with his story.

"After General Miles turned Colonel Murchison down, the colonel, he went back to studyin' the map, all the while strokin' his chin like so.'' Dakota demonstrated, assuming a thoughtful pose and stroking his chin as Colonel Murchison had done. "Then the colonel, he looks around and he says, 'How often do we let our artillery crews fire their guns?'

"We tell him, 'Colonel, we don't get to fire these guns no more than once or twice a year.'

"So the colonel, he nods and says, 'Notify G Troop.' ''

"That was Trooper Whitehead's troop,'' Cobb explained quickly. "It was also the troop me an' Dakota was in at the time.''

First Sergeant Dakota nodded, then continued with his story. " 'G Troop is goin' to have a practice firing exercise tonight,' the colonel says.

"Now, most of us figure he's plannin' to take our minds off what happen' by givin' G Troop somethin' to do. But no sir, that ain't what he's got in mind a'tall. Instead, what he done was, he took us out to the extreme north end of the reservation; then he had Lieutenant Spooner unlimber the guns and set them up, Lieutenant Spooner being the artillery commander at the time.

" 'Lieutenant Spooner,' Colonel Murchison says. 'Do you know what artillery is?'

" 'Well, sir, I s'pose I do,' Lieutenant Spooner says back. 'It's to provide support for infantry and cavalry troops.'

" 'Wrong, Lieutenant,' Colonel Murchison says. 'Artillery is to lend dignity to what would otherwise be an uncouth brawl. So, let's lend a little dignity to the situation.'

" 'Beg pardon, sir?' Lieutenant Spooner says.

" 'Bring your guns on line, Lieutenant,' Colonel Murchison says. 'Your target is that white building.' "

Dakota paused then, and leaned forward to emphasize what he was about to say. It had the desired effect, for now the only sound that could be heard in the car was the rhythmic clicking of steel wheels over rail joints.

"Gents," Dakota said pointedly, "that white building was none other than Pike's Palace."

"The saloon?" English asked.

"The same," First Sergeant Dakota replied, nodding. "Well, Spooner was some shocked that he was bein' told to fire on a civilian buildin', but Colonel Murchison told him that since it was on government land, it must be a government buildin'. And if we wanted to use it for target practice, there was nothin' to stop us from doin' it. So what he done was, he moved two platoons into town and set up a skirmish line. Then he woke up ever' one in town who lived south of that line and had them move north of it. He told us not to let any of them come back across, and when all the folks was woke up and moved out, he commenced firin'."

"What? You mean he wasn't bluffin'?" one of the other soldiers asked. "He really started shootin'?"

"You damn right, he did," Dakota said with a chuckle. "And let me tell you, I never seen them artillery boys shoot so good. It didn't take no time a'tall till that saloon was turned into nothin' more'n kindlin' wood."

"What did Sheriff Pike do?"

Cobb laughed as he enjoyed the memory. "Ole Pike, he come a'screamin' and yellin' that we had destroyed private property. But Colonel Murchison told him that property was on government land and he was going to charge Pike $50,000 rent for havin' built his saloon there in the first place.

"Well, Sheriff Pike, he got so mad he damn near choked. 'Fifty thousand dollars!' he shouts. 'Where'd you come up with a figure like that? Why, there ain't that much money in the entire territory!'

"And Colonel Murchison says, 'That's where you're wrong, Mr. Pike. There is that much money every payday, at Fort Canfield.'

"So Sheriff Pike says, 'Well, you can just take that money somewhere else. I ain't goin' to let none of your niggers come into my town anymore.' " First Sergeant Dakota laughed again.

"What is it? What's so funny about that?" Private Bates asked.

"What's funny is what the rest of the town done," Dakota said. "When they heard there was $50,000 in payroll that come into Fort Canfield ever' month, they told Pike that we Buffalo Soldiers was welcome any time we ever wanted to come around. Then they said it was about time they got 'em a new sheriff. So ole Pike? He was run out of town. And from then on, our troopers was treated decent."

"Damn!" Bates said. "I guess we showed them a thing or two, huh?"

"We did at that," Dakota agreed. He nodded in the direction of the officers' car. "And the new lieutenant who come on board last night? His name is Todd Murchison, and he is the son of that selfsame colonel. I'm tellin' you right now, anybody who don't treat him right will have me to answer to."

"And me," Cobb said.

"And me," Bates added.

Offices of the Daily Banner, *New York City*

When Marty returned to the newspaper office, she found a huge pile of letters on her desk.

"What is this?" she asked Talbot. "What are all these letters?"

Talbot smiled broadly. "They are letters from your many admirers, Marty," he said. "In case you don't realize it, you have thousands of readers out there, and they all love you. Many of them write letters."

"How nice," Marty said.

"I thought you might enjoy them. Oh, and you got one official letter from the embassy of the Republic of Cuba."

"The Republic of Cuba?"

"Yes. The United States government has now recognized Cuba as a free and independent republic. And the Free Cuba Legation you went to is their new consulate in New York. You, my dear, are an honorary citizen of their new country."

"Well, my mother will be proud of that," Marty said. "It's too bad, though."

"Too bad?"

"It's too bad that I am a citizen of Cuba, that I speak the language, and yet I won't be going there."

"Yes, well, uh . . ." Talbot cleared his throat. "I, uh, wanted to talk to you about that." Talbot ran his hand through his hair and looked at Marty with a long, intense stare.

"What is it?"

Talbot sighed.

"It's Mr. Chambers," Talbot finally said. "He has stabbed me in the back."

"Mr. Chambers? You mean your military writer?"

"I mean my *ex*-military writer," Talbot said. "He resigned two days ago and accepted an offer from Hearst."

"You had better watch out for Mr. Hearst," Marty warned Talbot. "Just before I went to San Antonio, he tried to recruit me as well. He may be after all your journalists."

"No, just my good ones," Talbot said.

Realizing that was a compliment, Marty smiled. "What are you going to do about a new military writer?"

"Marty, my girl," Talbot said. "If anyone had suggested this to me a month ago, I would have told him he was crazy. But how would you like to be my military writer?"

"Me?" Marty asked excitedly. "Mr. Talbot, do you mean

it? You would let me represent this paper in Cuba?"

"Yeah," Talbot said. "Sure, why not? You know how to go after a story, you certainly have the talent, and God knows you now have a following. If you want to go to Cuba, the job is yours."

"What about my accreditation?"

"Well, we got a break there," Talbot said. "The accreditation Mr. Chambers got for us belongs to the paper and not to him. Therefore, if he isn't going to use it, I can use it for someone else. In this case, you."

"Oh, Mr. Talbot, thank you; thank you!" Marty said, throwing her arms around his neck in delight.

"Here, here!" Talbot replied with feigned gruffness. "We can't be having any of this," he added. "What if all my reporters acted so?"

Marty laughed happily. "Oh, my, I guess I'd better get back down to the depot. I want to get to Tampa as quickly as I can."

"Uh-uh," Talbot said, shaking his head. "You aren't going by train."

"I'm not? How am I going?"

"You are going by sea. It seems that there are a few high-ranking naval officers who are jealous of all the coverage you have been giving the army. They want equal treatment, so you will be going as a special guest on board the *Conqueror*."

"The *Conqueror*? Is that a battleship?"

Talbot laughed. "Hardly. It's a private ship belonging to Commodore Vanderbilt. He has turned it over to the U.S. Navy for the duration of the emergency. It is leaving early tomorrow morning to take some more volunteers down to Tampa."

On Board the Conqueror

Marty was transferred, bag and baggage, to the *Conqueror* at five o'clock the next morning. The ship Vanderbilt had made available was a steam vessel weighing 6,000 tons and normally assigned to the Atlantic route as a cargo ship. A couple of the cargo holds had been converted to troop holds by the simple expedient of fitting hammocks. In that way the *Conqueror* would be able to transport a regiment of the New York militia to Tampa, where they would join the expeditionary force already gathering there. The regiment being transferred was a volunteer cavalry regiment with the rather grandiose name of Lightning Cavalry.

As soon as Marty came aboard, she was shown to her cabin, which, making allowances for her sex, had been equipped with a private bath. Once she was moved in she found a spot on deck where she would be able to watch the loading of the men and equipment without being in the way.

Crowds of New Yorkers began collecting on the pier even before sunrise, and by 6:00 A.M. there were hundreds of spectators present. A band was playing martial music.

"Here they come!" someone shouted.

From her position on deck Marty had a better view than anyone else, and she saw the Lightning Cavalry arriving, not on horseback, but marching as on parade. They wheeled off West 51st, then continued down to Pier Ninety. The spectators cheered and applauded as the men arrived. The officers and non-commissioned officers went right to work, loading the men quickly and efficiently. By eight o'clock the whistles began blowing as stewards walked up and down the docks urging all ashore who were going ashore.

In the meantime, Marty was sitting on a small canvas chair. She had taken up a position between two large ventilator horns. These were great scoops that forced fresh air below. From her vantage point she watched as the tugboats came up, attached their lines, then started working the ship out of its berth through a process known as walking.

The band onshore continued to play music, but the ship's horn, the shouting of the men, and the sound of the engines quickly drowned out the music. Marty watched as the figures on shore grew smaller until, finally, the ship was well away and headed toward the Statue of Liberty under its own power.

Marty noticed that the loud, boisterous behavior of the men quieted somewhat as they passed the great statue. She looked at it as they did, experiencing a tremendous sense of awe at its great size. The statue was only twelve years old, but already it had moved into the hearts of Americans until it occupied as strong a position as the Liberty Bell or the Capitol Building itself. The statue was a symbol of America, the last thing voyagers saw when they left, and the first thing they saw when they came back.

Marty wondered how many of these men were seeing the statue for the last time. She shivered and put the thought out of her mind.

For the first three days out, Marty began to think she might have made a big mistake. The Bermuda Stream was running exceptionally high, and the ship rolled and tossed in the heavy swells, resulting in a bout of seasickness for the young reporter. Marty discovered that as long as she lay in bed she could fight off the nausea, but once she stood up it would overtake her.

Finally, toward evening of the third day, the sea calmed somewhat, and Marty gained her sea legs to the extent that she began to feel good again. She took a bath, put on something fresh and colorful, then ventured out of her cabin. She felt almost invigorated, an especially pleasant feeling since she had begun to think she would never feel good again.

The ship had seemed monstrously large when it was tied alongside the pier in New York. It had towered over the people on the pier and had stretched for what seemed to be a city block. But now, in the middle of the ocean, with nothing but horizon all around, the ship seemed infinitesimally small.

They were heading south. That was easy for Marty to calculate, because the setting sun was to the right of the ship. Marty smiled. "Starboard," she said quietly. "The right side is the starboard. I must remember that."

As the sun descended into the sea, a long finger of red began to stab toward the ship from a distant horizon. The finger got longer as the sun got lower until, when the disk was half-submerged, the finger of fire came all the way to the ship. The clouds flamed in brilliant golds close to the sun, then changed into pinks, reds, and purples as the distance from the sun increased. Finally the red ball completely disappeared, and Marty watched until the light began to dim.

"Miss?" a voice said from behind her.

Marty had thought she was alone and the voice startled her a little, but she recovered quickly. When she turned, she saw a young man in an officer's uniform.

"Yes?"

"I am Ensign Hayes, miss," the young man said. "The captain extends his welcome. He has noticed that you haven't taken any meals. Is anything wrong?"

"I've yet to take a meal because I've been seasick," Marty told him. She touched her stomach. "Though I am feeling much better, and I must confess that I am quite hungry now. But I don't know where to go or even if I'm too late."

"They'll be serving in the wardroom at four bells," Hayes said.

"Four bells?"

"That's eight o'clock. If you would like to attend, I'll be happy to escort you."

"Why, thank you, Mr. Hayes."

Marty followed Hayes along the deck for a short way. He stopped at a metal door, which he called a hatch, turned the two levers that held it closed, then opened it and bid her to step inside. She stepped over the sill, which was about twelve inches high, then found herself on a floor that was quite different from the deck she had grown used to. Outside, the deck was of gray, weathered wood. But this could have been the floor of a fine home, for it gleamed in a rich, glossy brown. The floor branched out into a hallway. Hayes led the way until they stepped through another door.

"This is the wardroom," Hayes said.

The wardroom was a large room with one enormous table. The table was set with china, crystal, and silver. Around the table stood several young men in crisp white uniforms, waiting to serve. The ship's captain and his officers, as well as Col. Nelson Pickett, the commander of the Lightning Cavalry, and his officers, stood respectfully as Marty entered.

"Gentlemen," Marty said. "I thank you for allowing me to join you on board this ship."

"It was the navy who made the request that you be allowed to accompany us," one of the naval officers said.

"Then I thank the navy."·

"You can thank us best by writing about us the way you wrote about the Rough Riders," the naval officer said.

"Oh, you may rest assured, sir, that as soon as I have something to write about the navy, I will do so."

One of the National Guard officers laughed.

"Do you find that amusing, Lieutenant?" the captain asked.

"Well, sir, it's just the thought of 'if the navy ever does anything.' I found that funny," the lieutenant said.

"Perhaps the lieutenant would like to swim to Tampa," the ship's captain suggested. At his suggestion, all the others in the wardroom, including Colonel Pickett, the young lieutenant's commanding officer, laughed.

"No, sir," the lieutenant replied quickly. "I think the navy is doing a wonderful job, transporting us there."

"I thought you might see it that way," the captain said as he broke a piece of bread.

Early the next morning, the ship was put on alert and all hands were ordered to battle stations. The ship's guns, consisting of two small pieces of artillery and two Gatling guns, were manned. The armament seemed pitifully inadequate to the task of defense, and Marty commented on it.

"I wouldn't be unduly alarmed, miss," Ensign Hayes said to comfort her. "This is a very fast ship. We'll outrun any enemy ship long before she ever gets into range."

Despite the young ensign's assurances, the fact that Marty might actually get close enough to the action to be shot at caused a little thrill to pass across her body, and she shivered.

"Don't be frightened," Hayes said, misunderstanding her reaction. "We're in no real danger, honest."

"Thank you," Marty replied. "I won't be afraid."

Marty could see two columns of smoke rising high into the sky, but she couldn't see the ships themselves because they were hull-down.

"How does the captain know those are Spanish ships?"

Marty asked. "They are so far away you can't even see them."

"Because when we first raised them, they fired at us," Hayes replied.

"What?" Marty gasped. "You mean I slept through my first taste of battle?"

Hayes laughed. "Well, ma'am, I wouldn't call it much of a battle," he said.

True to Ensign Hayes's word, the Spanish warships were soon outdistanced so that even the smoke from their stacks was no longer visible. Then, shortly after they were secured from battle stations, Colonel Pickett approached Marty with a request.

"Miss McGuire, I wonder if you would do me the favor of going below decks to meet with the men?"

"You want me to go down into the troop holds?"

"Yes, if you wouldn't mind. I know it's hot and unpleasant down there, but it would mean so much to the men that—"

"Of course I'll go," Marty interrupted. "You don't have to talk me into it. I would like to go."

Colonel Pickett escorted Marty to the hatch that led down into the troop hold.

"Maybe you'd better wait topside for a moment," he suggested. "It's awfully hot down there, and several of the men have undressed to try and get cool. Let me go down and make certain everyone is decent."

Marty waited topside for a few moments; then Pickett came back to get her. "All right," he said. "You can come down now."

Marty followed Pickett down the metal stairs to the first hold. He held the door open for her, and she stepped inside. The heat struck her with a blow that was almost physical, and suddenly her heart went out to all the young men who had to spend the entire voyage down here. She looked around at the hundreds of pairs of eyes that were looking back at her, and as she thought of their overheated and overcrowded conditions she was doubly thankful for her spacious and well-ventilated cabin.

"Miss McGuire, you goin' to write about the Lightning Cavalry the way you wrote about the Rough Riders?" one of the soldiers asked.

"Yes, of course I am. That's why I am here," she answered.

"Just us? Or are you going to write about all the other units as well?"

"Well, I don't know," Marty quipped. "I suppose it all depends on how much you give me to write about."

"We'll give you plenty to write about," one of the men said, and the others laughed.

"I'm goin' to show it to her," a soldier said.

"No, don't do that; it's embarrassing," another replied.

"It ain't embarrassin'; it's good. And I'm goin' to show it to her."

Marty looked toward the two men who were arguing, and one of them shoved a sheet of paper toward her. There was a drawing on the paper.

"Look at this, Miss McGuire. What do you think of this?"

Marty looked at the drawing, then gasped. It was a picture of her, sitting between the large ventilator horns. She had never seen her own likeness more perfectly drawn.

"Who did this?" she asked.

"Oh, it was Eddie Stone," the young man said, pointing to his friend. "He's all the time drawin', first one thing, then the other."

"Mr. Stone, that is a beautiful drawing."

"I coulda done better," Eddie said shyly, "but I had to do it from memory. I just got that one glimpse of you sittin' there as we come aboard."

"That you were able to do this with such a brief glimpse makes it all the more amazing," she said. Suddenly she got an idea. "Mr. Stone, will you be making drawings while we are in Cuba?"

"I reckon I will," Eddie replied. "Seems like I'm always doin' it."

"Would you mind if, from time to time, I sent some of your drawings back to be published in the paper? We would pay you, of course."

"Whooee! Eddie, think about that! You're going to be as famous as Miss McGuire!"

"As famous, maybe," one of the others said. "But he sure ain't as pretty!"

Later that day, Marty wrote her first article since coming on board the *Conqueror*. She felt a little guilty about it, because it was obvious that she had been invited by the navy to write about them. And she would write about the navy; of that she was certain. But when she visited the troop holds, she had been so moved by the young men who were accepting, without complaint, the miserable conditions of their transit that she knew what her first story had to be:

> The men of the Lightning Cavalry stay in something called a troop hold. The troop hold is a big, square room, dimly lit by yellow-shaded electric lamps. Along all four walls of the hold, and on long poles placed in the middle of the hold, there are rows of hammocks, sometimes stretching eight or nine, one over the other. The men who sleep on the very top hammock must climb up to their beds, using the lower hammocks as steps in the ladder.
>
> In the center of the hold there is a roped-off area, and there the men store their rucksacks. There, too, they congregate, for it is the only spot in the hold that is not dominated by hammocks. The men gather there to sing, spin yarns, talk, or just write letters. The talk is mostly of the war and what they are going to do to the Spanish, though after the braggadocio dies down, the talk turns to the ones they left at home.

CHAPTER 8

Washington, D.C.

The electric fan on the desk hummed as it blew a column of air toward Gen. Joseph Murchison. Joe was reading a letter from his son when Captain Dawes, Joe's adjutant, knocked on the office door and stepped inside.

"General Murchison, I just got a telephone call from the office of the secretary of war. Mr. Alger sends his compliments, sir, and asks that you please step over to visit with him for a few moments."

"All right," Joe said. Because it was hot in Washington, he had not only resorted to the electric fan but also been sitting at his desk without his jacket. He now took it from its rack and put it on. The jacket, like the entire uniform, was wool. It was fine in the winter and fall, but exceptionally uncomfortable for the summer.

Joe thought of the men who were down in Tampa, Florida, soon to go to Cuba. It was much hotter there than it was here, and though some of the men had the new canvas khaki, he knew that at least half of the troops that were assembled there were still wearing the old wool uniform. Joe could relate to them, for he had fought against Geronimo in southern Arizona in the summer and knew how hot the uniforms could be.

Joe's office was on the second floor of the War Department Building. Secretary of War Russell Alger's office was on the first. It took Joe less than a minute to go down the single flight of stairs, then up the hall to Alger's office.

Colonel Smith, the secretary's military aide, stood respectfully when Joe stepped into the outer office.

"General Murchison, go right in, sir," General Miles's adjutant said. "Secretary Alger is expecting you."

"Thank you, Artie," Joe replied. He started toward the door to the secretary's office, then turned back toward the colonel. "Oh, how is your son doing with his baseball?"

"He's doing fine, sir; he made the team," the colonel answered. "Thank you for the pointers. They were very helpful."

Joe had been a particularly skilled baseball player in his younger days and at one time had even considered playing professionally. He never regretted giving up baseball for his military career, but he still loved the game.

"I'll have to come watch him play sometime," Joe said as he opened the door to Alger's office.

"Hello, Joe," Alger said, coming out from behind his desk to greet Joe. "Thanks for coming down."

Joe laughed. "You are the secretary of war, Mr. Alger," he replied. "When you issue an invitation, it isn't exactly an invitation."

Alger laughed. "I must confess, I still can't get used to having generals respond to my bidding," Alger said.

There was a small seating area in the secretary's office, consisting of a leather chair and a leather sofa. Alger directed them to that area, then settled into the chair, leaving the sofa for Joe. "Would you like something cold to drink, Joe? Lemonade, perhaps? Water?"

"No, thank you, sir."

"What have you heard from your son?"

"I got a letter from him today."

"How is he getting along? He is with Col. Leonard Wood and the First Volunteer Cavalry, I believe?"

"He was. He is with Lt. Col. T. A. Baldwin and the Tenth now."

"The Tenth?" Alger said in surprise. "Joe, why didn't you say something? We can do better than the Tenth for him. The Seventh is in Tampa. Why don't we move him to the Seventh?"

"No, no," Joe declared, raising his hand and shaking his head. "The Tenth is fine. They are damn fine soldiers, and I feel that they will look out for him."

Alger stroked his chin and nodded. "That's right; you served with colored soldiers once, didn't you?"

"I commanded the Tenth Colored Cavalry Regiment," Joe said.

"Well, if your son is happy where he is, we'll leave him there. Now, tell me what else has he got to say? Has he made any comments or observations about how things are going?"

"He's showing the usual frustrations a young officer has with his first assignment. Especially with supplies."

"Yes," Alger said. "That's what I'm interested in. What has he said about supplies arriving in Tampa?"

Joe realized now that Alger was seriously trying to get to the bottom of what he had already perceived as a problem.

"It is a real boondoggle, Mr. Secretary," Joe said. "As many as thirty trains are arriving every day, nearly a third of which aren't military at all but are civilian tourists who are clogging up the system. The military trains arrive unscheduled and without bills of lading. That means the men have to go through all the cars, almost as if they were committing grand larceny, just to find food, clothing, ammunition, and equipment."

Alger nodded. "Yes," he said. "Yes, I'm afraid that just about squares with what I've been hearing from General Shafter."

"I expect all that is causing Shafter quite a headache," Joe remarked.

"It is indeed," Alger agreed. "That's why I want you to go down there and do what you can to straighten it out."

"You want me to join the expeditionary force?" Joe asked. "Yes, sir, I would be honored to."

"No, not really," Alger said. "That is, I don't want you to become a part of the force itself. I'd rather have you be just outside the chain of command, so that you are responsible directly to me, and only to me. That way, you'll be free to take whatever action you deem necessary to get the job done."

"What is the scope of my responsibility?" Joe asked.

"You will be in charge of all aspects of logistics and transportation," Secretary Alger said. "Not only the troops and supplies that are coming into Tampa, but I also want you in charge of getting the army from Tampa to Cuba."

"Mr. Secretary, such a job is certain to bring me into contact, and perhaps conflict, with the senior naval officer present," Joe said.

"That is true," Alger agreed. "But the senior naval officer on the scene is Admiral Sampson. You met him, I believe, when he conducted the court of inquiry into the events leading to the sinking of the *Maine*. Did you have any difficulty with him?"

"No, none at all. I found him to be a very competent officer."

"Based upon the relationship the two of you established during the court of inquiry," Alger said, "and the fact that you outrank him," he added with a twinkle in his eye, "I don't think you will have any difficulty with the navy. In any case, I will smooth things over for you here with the secretary of navy."

"Thank you, sir. And I'm sure there won't be any problems with Admiral Sampson," Joe replied. "I'll leave right away."

On Board the Conqueror at Key West

Marty had never seen anything like what she was witnessing at Key West. It was as if all the excitement of the war was swirling around like a hurricane and Key West was the hurricane's eye. She filed a story immediately after she arrived, using all the descriptive terminology she could come up with to provide the atmosphere that would bring her readers here. And in this story she did talk about the navy:

The first impression is of brilliant color. There are flashes of red and yellow from the signal flags that wave from the halyards, shiny white and brass from the spruced-up ships, and, of course, there is the blue of the water and the sky.

The blue surface of the water is streaked with the white wakes of all sorts of boats and ships as they move back and forth on one errand or another. From the bridges of these ships the captains exchange their messages, either by flashing lights or by signalmen who wigwag their colorful flags in some mysterious language understood only by them and then translated for the captains they serve.

It is from here that Admiral Sampson will send his squadron to sweep from the sea any Spanish warships that may threaten our soldiers when the invasion of Cuba begins.

There are many ships here, but the real queen of the bay is the battleship *Oregon*. She made the voyage from Bremerton, Washington, around the Horn, and up through the storm-tossed seas of the South Atlantic, arriving here just 68 days after she left. Everyone is talking about that particular feat of seamanship in tones of awe and respect.

The *Oregon* is a mighty ship of steel and iron, bristling with weapons at every point. There are special turrets that mount cannons as long as trees on her decks and ports in the hull that mount even more of the heavy guns. When our invasion armada proceeds to Cuba, it will be because the *Oregon* and her sister warships have swept the seas clear of all enemy vessels for us.

Two days later, Marty filed another dispatch:

TAMPA, FLORIDA. The *Conqueror* has brought its gallant cargo of volunteers to Tampa, Florida. In this place thousands of soldiers are waiting to be transported to Cuba, and the drumrolls and cadence counting of their drilling rolls unceasingly across the bay. Although Key West or even Miami is closer to Cuba, Tampa has been chosen because it is the southernmost city served by rail.

Preparation for the invasion is now in full swing. Even as I write these words, I see another train arriving to join the many that have already arrived. What is on this train? More soldiers? Ammunition? Cannons, horses, uniforms? I think the average person has little idea of all the preparations necessary to ready an army for battle. To those generals and admirals to whom such responsibility falls we owe a salute of thanks.

On the very train Marty had just observed, in a roomette of the third car, Joe Murchison was nursing a mint julep and studying a file of papers. There was a knock on his door.

"Yes?" Joe asked, looking up from the papers he was reading.

The door opened and the porter stuck his head in. "Mr. General, suh, we'll be in the station in 'bout fifteen more minutes."

"Thank you," Joe said. He held up his glass. "And thank you for the mint julep. They aren't easy to prepare, but you, my friend, have mastered the art. It is excellent."

The porter smiled. "You mighty welcome. It's a privilege to make mint juleps for them that truly appreciates them."

The door closed and Joe went back to his drink and the papers he was studying. Before leaving Washington, Joe had asked Captain Dawes to prepare brief biographies on Generals Miles, Shafter, and Wheeler and Admirals Sampson and Schley. Although Joe had already read Captain Dawes's reports, he decided to look through them one last time before meeting the officers involved. He knew that he would be dealing with high-ranking men with sensitive egos. Such an assignment would require a great deal of diplomacy, and the more he knew about the men he would be dealing with, the more likely he would be to pull it off.

He had already met Shafter and Sampson, though he couldn't honestly say that he knew a whole lot about them. And he had never met Wheeler or Schley, so any information his adjutant might come up with for them would be new.

Report on army and navy high command

Sir:

I have taken the liberty of including information on General Miles in this report, realizing full well that you and he know each other quite well, having served together in the past. However, I thought that if you had information on all the officers at hand, it would help you in making your decisions, especially if decisions brought the personalities of one officer into direct conflict with the personalities of another. To that end, I will start with General Miles, whom the president has appointed as chief of the army command staff.

Like you, Miles is a recipient of the Medal of Honor. But while you won yours for Custer's 1876 (and final) campaign, General Miles won his medal during the Civil War.

Despite this early recognition, however, Miles seems to have made his reputation during the more recent Indian Wars, having done battle with such Indian notables as Sitting Bull of the Sioux, Joseph of the Nez Percé, and Geronimo of the Apache.

The actual field commander of the campaign will be Gen. William R. Shafter. General Shafter is a man of enormous talent, appetite, and girth. His exact weight is unknown, although there are those who say he exceeds, by some degree, three hundred pounds. As one might imagine, General Shafter's prodigious size has rendered him less than agile, and he walks with the lumbering gait of a grizzly bear. He cannot mount a horse without assistance and has been known to use a block and tackle to accomplish this task.

However, despite these physical limitations, General Shafter is recognized by nearly everyone as a person with an exceptionally keen military mind. By coincidence, General Shafter also happens to be one of the best marksmen in the army.

General Shafter's deputy commander is Maj. Gen. Joseph P. Wheeler. Wheeler, known as "Fightin' Joe Wheeler," was one of the leading cavalry officers of the Confederacy during the late war.

Physically, General Wheeler is a very small man, barely over one hundred pounds. However, he is said to be absolutely fearless, bold, and audacious. In battle he achieves a great deal of success because of his willingness to seize the initiative. The officers and men who served under him stated that he was totally oblivious of enemy bullets.

President McKinley, who as you know, sir, is himself a veteran of the Civil War, personally appointed General Wheeler to the position he now occupies. In replying to General Wheeler's question as to why the president chose to appoint a former Confederate General to such a high rank in the U.S. Army, President McKinley justified it by saying, "There must be a high-ranking officer from the South. There must be a symbol that the old days are gone. I need you."

There are also two officers of the navy with whom you should be familiar, these being Adms. William T. Sampson and Winfield Scott Schley.

Adm. William T. Sampson is a graduate of the U.S. Naval Academy, with a long and distinguished career in the navy. He is an electrical engineer and for many years served as chief of the Bureau of Ordnance. He has played an important role in modernizing the navy, to include the use of telescopic sights for long-range artillery.

Adm. Winfield Scott Schley is second in command to Admiral Sampson. Until very recently, he was head of the Department of Modern Languages at the Naval Academy. It might be of some importance for you to know that although Admiral Schley was superior in rank to Admiral Sampson, the Navy Department saw fit to pass over him to select Sampson as commander of the North Atlantic Fleet. There seems to be no particular reason for this, especially as Admiral Schley's performance of duty had always been exceptional.

These are some of the officers with whom you will be working, General. If I can be of any further assistance, please do not hesitate to contact me by telegraph.

Yours sincerely,
Lawrence Dawes
Captain, Adjutant

Tampa was a city with two distinct personalities. To the troops camped just outside the city it was a depressing assembly of swamp, palmetto, sand, mosquitoes, and land crabs. But an entrepreneur by the name of Henry Bradley Plant had developed the port of Tampa Bay, nine miles south of the city of Tampa. Here he built a mile-long wharf from which he operated a fleet of steamships. Tampa Bay, which was connected to the city of Tampa by a railroad, featured an amusement park and several hotels. The crown jewel of the hotels was the Tampa Bay Hotel.

Like many of the other officers in Tampa, including Generals Shafter and Wheeler and Colonels Wood and Roosevelt, Joe took a room at the Tampa Bay Hotel shortly after he arrived. The Tampa Bay Hotel, a dark red structure of Moorish architecture, was an exceptionally beautiful and ornate building. It stood five stories high and spread over six acres. A very large hotel, it boasted 500 rooms and porches that resembled streets. Mosque-like curves topped its numerous windows, and towering above it all were huge silver domes and minarets. The minarets were set off with crescent moons to represent the months of the Muslim year.

Furniture of ebony and gold, rich tapestries, oil paintings that were once owned by crowned heads, huge porcelain vases, carpets, and statuary from European sources made the hotel seem more like a palace than an inn.

There was a T-shaped casino on the hotel grounds, in which there were club rooms, an auditorium, and a swimming pool that was revealed by operating a movable floor. Experts from Scotland had developed the hotel's golf course. Exotic plants covered the entire six acres, and colorful peacocks strutted about. An elaborate German pipe organ provided music.

For many of the officers, some of whom had lived in very sparse quarters on the far-flung posts of the West, the Tampa Bay Hotel was the most glamorous accommodations they had ever known. Several of the higher-ranking officers brought their wives down to be with them, and their preparation for war was accomplished under the most luxurious conditions imaginable.

This would be the largest military expedition ever to leave the United States. For the invasion to take place Joe was going to have to gather enough ships to transport them, and in order to mount an effective invasion the entire army would have to be transported in one shipment. Finding this many ships taxed every ounce of Joe's ingenuity.

No such operation had ever been performed before, and there were not enough vessels in the entire U.S. Navy and Coast Guard to fill the need. That meant that the private sector would have to be used. Some vessels, like Vanderbilt's *Conqueror,* were made available by the generous donations of the owners. Other owners demanded compensation, and in some cases exorbitant amounts, for ships that were barely seaworthy. However, by persuasion, coercion, and diplomacy Joe managed to put together the transport fleet.

It wasn't a fleet that would stir the heart of the purist. It consisted of a mishmash of ships, from the most modern screw-driven, steel-hulled leviathans, to those, much smaller, still powered by paddle wheels, all the way down to a few that weren't powered at all but would have to be towed. The fleet was, however, most impressive in its total size.

Even as the vessels continued to arrive, gradually filling the harbor, there were still details to be worked out. To discuss these details, Admiral Sampson came up from his normal station of duty at Key West, and he and Joe had lunch together on the balcony of Joe's room at the Tampa Bay Hotel.

Sampson stepped up to the rail of the balcony and looked out over the bay at the troop- and cargo ships that were being assembled there; then he shook his head and chuckled. "Never in the history of the sea has such an unglamorous collection of ships, dinghies, rafts, barges, and garbage scows been referred to as a fleet," he said.

"Well, you are right about that. I doubt that there will be any stirring paintings of the transport fleet to commemorate our action," Joe agreed.

Room service brought a fruit compote for dessert, and Sampson sat down to finish his meal. He sprinkled red pepper on a piece of fresh pineapple, then forked it to his mouth.

"Do you remember the *Sultana*?" Sampson asked.

"The *Sultana*?"

"It was a riverboat, large, fast, and, by the standards of the day, well-equipped," Sampson said. "After the Civil War, our government chartered it to take soldiers up the Mississippi River for discharge. Most of the soldiers were former prisoners of war from Andersonville. God bless them, they were nothing but skin and bones, barely breathing. We crowded them all onto the *Sultana* under the most miserable conditions imaginable, but they were so happy to be going home that not a one of them complained. Then, just north of Helena, Arkansas, the boilers exploded; the boat burned, then went down. More than two thousand of our men were lost."

"Yes," Joe replied. "I was still at West Point then, but I do remember." He shook his head. "Why do you bring that up, Admiral?"

"That could happen again," Sampson said.

"I certainly pray that it does not happen," Joe said.

"You do understand, don't you, that this fleet, as it is now constituted, would be easy prey to Admiral Cervera's squadron?" Admiral Sampson warned. "One cruiser could sink four or five of our largest transports, killing thousands of our men, before we ever reached Cuba's shores."

"Understand it? Admiral, I've been having nightmares about it," Joe replied. "That's why I'm depending on you to provide an escort with your ships."

Sampson looked back out over the bay.

"Well, I'll do all I can," he said. "But by the time we get this fleet under way it will be stretched out for some twenty miles. It is impossible to provide an escort screen that long. There would be plenty of opportunities for one of Cervera's fast cruisers or destroyers to slip through an open gap, sink a couple of our transports, then get away. Our first indication that anything might be wrong would be smoke on the horizon."

"Then you must destroy Cervera's squadron before we set sail," Joe insisted.

"Aye," Sampson agreed, nodding his head. "Destroying it is no problem. But finding it is."

"What about Admiral Schley? He made a bold dash into the harbor at Santiago. Has he had any luck in locating the Spanish squadron?"

Admiral Sampson lit a cigar. "A bold dash, yes," he said between puffs as he lit it. Then, squinting through the smoke, he stared at Joe for a moment. "You were with Custer at the Battle of Little Big Horn, weren't you?"

"Yes," Joe replied. "I was with Reno, actually."

"Custer was a courageous and popular military man," Sampson continued. "He made a bold dash into the Indian camps at Little Big Horn. Did he do exactly what General Terry wanted him to do?"

"No, I wouldn't say that," Joe replied.

"What is remembered about that battle today? General Terry's orders? Or Custer's boldness?"

Joe cleared his throat. "Admiral, are you comparing Admiral Schley with General Custer?"

"Like Custer, Admiral Schley feels that he was unfairly passed over for command. And like Custer, the admiral believes, no doubt, that a bold stroke would show the powers that be that they made a mistake. Therefore, he has his own goals to accomplish, and locating and reporting Cervera's whereabouts aren't in his schedule."

"I see," Joe said. "And his action at Santiago, while foolish, has been reported by all the newspapers with such enthusiasm that you can neither replace nor discipline him."

"That is my cross to bear," Sampson agreed.

"And mine," Joe said. "For until I am confident that none of the transports will be sunk en route, I can't, in all good conscience, dispatch them."

CHAPTER 9

A few days after his lunch with General Murchison, and before returning to Key West, Admiral Sampson held a dinner reception for all naval officers currently in the Tampa area, both aboard ship and ashore. He also invited the reporters who were covering the military operation, and that invitation included Marty.

By now Marty's name was well-known, so when she arrived at the hotel dining room for the dinner party the maître d' admitted her without question. Gradually, the other reporters had come to accept her as well, and many of them made a point of greeting her.

"Marty McGuire. I've read some of your stuff," one of the other reporters said. "It's good. It's more than good, actually; it's *quite* good." He was a particularly handsome man, and Marty was very flattered by his compliment, not because he was handsome but because of who he was.

"Thank you."

"I'm Richard Harding Davis, by the way," the man said, extending his hand.

"Yes, Mr. Davis, I know who you are," Marty replied, shaking his hand. "And I have long been an admirer of your work."

Davis smiled. "Have you now? Well, perhaps we could start our own mutual admiration society," he joked.

Richard Harding Davis was, perhaps, America's best-known journalist. Americans trusted him implicitly and considered him to be an expert about whatever he wrote. Once, when President McKinley was discussing a subject upon which he was expected to act, he asked his cabinet what they thought Richard Harding Davis would say about it.

Stephen Crane was nearly as popular, but he was still known more for his novel, *The Red Badge of Courage,* than for his journalistic efforts. Therefore, though he had a great following, he was not able to mold public opinion, as Davis was.

"You know, Marty, I don't know how you did it," one of the other reporters said a few moments later. This was one of the men who had ignored her when they were in San Antonio and even on the train that came east. It was quite a change for her to be treated as "one of the boys."

"How I did what?"

"How you managed to find anything interesting to write about from Texas. Do you know what I remember about that dreadful place? I remember early mornings, hot days, sand, scorpions, and the long, long periods of boredom. Yet all I heard from my editor—all any of us heard, in fact—was how wonderful your stories were and how exciting it must be in Texas. Well, let me tell you, I've been on a dozen other such expeditions, and that one was as boring as all the others."

Marty laughed. "Well, there you have it," she explained. "That was my very first experience, and it was all quite exciting to me. Perhaps that was the difference."

"I guess so," the reporter said. He looked down at the floor. "Oh, uh, I'd like to apologize for the way we treated you back there. That was no way to treat a lady, and we certainly weren't gentlemen."

"I didn't want to be treated like a lady then, and I don't want to be treated like a lady now," Marty surprised him by saying.

"You don't? Well, just how do you want to be treated?" he sputtered.

"I want to be treated like a reporter," she replied. "Just like any other reporter. I'm here to do a job. I happen to be a woman, but I do my job just the same as the rest of you."

Having overheard the conversation, Davis laughed. "I

wouldn't say you were the same as the rest of us," he said. "From what I've read, I'd say you are considerably better than the rest of us. Most of us, anyway."

Marty was now totally accepted by her peers, and it was a wonderful feeling.

When the dinner was over, the reporters and officers gathered for drinks and cigars. Marty thought about whether or not she should join them. As a reporter, she felt that she had every right to do so. On the other hand, drinks and cigars were an institution particular to men, and she was reasonably certain they weren't doing this just to exclude her.

After a short debate with herself, Marty decided that she would leave the men to that pleasure. She was content with the gains she had made and would not push the boundaries of propriety. Instead, she extended her thanks and farewell to Admiral Sampson, then left the hotel and took a walk around the grounds.

She had to admit that the Tampa Bay Hotel was the most luxurious inn she had ever seen. On the side of the hotel away from the water, there was a landscaped garden and a great expanse of lawn with banks of white blossoms scattered through the dark mass of oleander trees. As she walked through the garden and looked back toward the hotel, the setting sun turned the domes, Moorish arches, and minarets to gold.

There were long rows of rocking chairs on the porches, and here officers and their wives sat together under the whirling overhead fans to enjoy the serenity of the hotel. Dozens of romances had sprung up between the dashing young warriors and the beautiful young maidens of Tampa who had been caught up in the excitement of the moment. And they, too, were enjoying the romantic setting of the hotel.

Marty walked under a magnolia tree, from which she picked a white blossom. She felt a little guilty about picking it, but the tree was heavy with the huge ivory flowers and she knew that one wouldn't matter. Holding the flower to her nose and sniffing it appreciatively, she walked down the sidewalk, then crossed a short expanse of lawn to the water.

The western sky was spread with glowing hues as the sun

settled into the gulf. Vibrant bands of brilliant colors, from gold to orange and red, then magenta and finally royal purple, put their beauty on display.

The water itself was tinted by the sunset so that the breakers, gentler here in the bay than in the open gulf, rolled in from a lavender sea. They spilled themselves on the shore, then retreated, leaving a smear of iridescent bubbles shimmering on the sand. The gracefully arched palm trees blazed with a glowing halo of gold, and they shone as if making one final effort to hold onto the exquisite beauty of the moment.

Marty was not the only one taking in the beauty of the scene. That same evening, Lt. Todd Murchison had been his father's guest for dinner. After dinner General Murchison's aide came in with a message about some difficulty with the next day's train schedules, and Joe apologized to his son, explaining that he would have to take care of it.

Todd thanked his father for the dinner, then decided to take a walk around the hotel grounds. Todd, who was bivouacked with his men, wasn't a resident of the hotel. As a result, this was his first opportunity to look it over. His meandering took him down to the edge of the water.

That was when he saw Marty. She was sniffing a magnolia blossom as she came down the sidewalk, then across the lawn, and down to the beach. Todd stared unabashedly at her for a long moment, just drinking in her beauty. Then, growing self-conscious over the intensity of his gaze, especially as he had not yet been seen, he spoke to her.

"Good evening, Miss McGuire," he said.

Marty had obviously been absorbed in the beauty of the moment, for she jumped, as if startled, at the sound of his voice.

Todd chuckled. "I'm sorry," he said. "I didn't mean to startle you."

"Well, if it isn't my own personal hero," Marty said smiling sweetly at him.

"Hero?" Todd asked, the expression on his face indicating that he didn't know what she meant.

"I was about to be run down by a caisson when a shining knight on horseback swept me from danger. You were that shining knight. Surely you remember? Or have you rescued so many ladies that you forget?''

Todd laughed. ''No. So far you are the only damsel in distress I have rescued,'' he said. ''Though getting you out of the way of a caisson isn't exactly like slaying a dragon.''

''Perhaps not, but I've no doubt you would slay a dragon if one presented itself,'' she teased. Easily and un-self-consciously, Marty put her arm through Todd's, then turned to look back out at the sea.

''Isn't this the most beautiful thing you have ever seen?'' she asked.

''Yes,'' Todd answered. He wasn't looking at the sea. He was looking directly at Marty.

Marty sensed that he was looking at her when he said that, and she looked back at him. A tendril of hair fell across her forehead, and she brushed it back.

''My room has a view of the bay,'' Marty said. ''But I think there is something much more intimate about coming right down to the shore, don't you?''

''Yes, the view is very nice,'' Todd replied. He still had not looked away from Marty.

Marty tilted her head. ''Are you all right, Lieutenant?''

''Todd.''

''What?''

''I wish you would call me Todd.''

''All right, if you wish,'' she said. She leaned into him. ''Does your room have a nice view, Todd?''

Todd laughed. ''My room is a Sibley tent,'' he told her. ''And the only view I have is of a low, scrubby palmetto bush.''

Marty looked back at him in surprise. ''You mean you aren't staying in the hotel?''

''No, I'm staying back in Tampa or, rather, at a bivouac just outside of Tampa, with my men.''

''Why, that's just awful, you having to stay in a tent when the hotel has so many lovely rooms. I would think you would want to stay here, at least for as long as your father is here.''

''Colonel Baldwin, our regimental commander, is bivou-acking with the troops; my troop commander, Captain Bigelow, is bivouacking with the men; and so is Lieutenant Pershing, our executive officer. What would it look like if I used my father as an excuse to stay at the hotel?''

''If your colonel stays in the field, then you should, too, I suppose. But most of the other regimental commanders are staying in the hotel. I just don't know why he doesn't.''

''We are staying with our men to make sure nothing unpleasant happens. With the Tenth, there is always the possibility of some difficulty between the local citizens and our men.''

''My word, what sort of difficulty could possibly arise between your men and the townspeople? Why, I thought everyone was treating all the soldiers like heroes.''

''My soldiers are different.''

''Different? How are they different? Oh, wait a minute; you aren't with the Rough Riders anymore, are you? Now that I think about it, I saw you standing on the platform at the depot in Jackson, Mississippi, as our train pulled out. For a moment I thought you had missed the train; then I realized that you hadn't. You had obviously left for some reason.''

''I left so I could join up with the Tenth Cavalry.''

''The Tenth?''

''Buffalo Soldiers.''

''What are Buffalo Soldiers?''

''Colored troops,'' Todd said.

''Why are they called Buffalo Soldiers?''

''The Indians call them that because they think their hair is like the fur of a buffalo,'' Todd explained. ''It is also a tribute. There is nothing more sacred to an Indian than the buffalo. The Buffalo Soldiers realize that, and they take pride in their name. That is how they refer to themselves now.''

''But colored soldiers in the South! I can see why you might expect some trouble with the local population.'' Marty smiled brightly. ''I have an idea. Why don't I do a story about them?''

''No, I'd rather you didn't,'' Todd said.

''But why not? They are going to war just like everyone else. They will be taking the same risks as everyone else. Shouldn't their stories be told?''

"Who would read them?" Todd asked.

"Who would read them? Why, the American public would read them. Their families and loved ones would read them."

Todd shook his head. "The American public doesn't care about the colored soldier. And as for 'families and loved ones,' they are their own family and loved ones."

"That's an odd statement. What do you mean by that?"

"Marty, it is very difficult for a Negro man to find work in civilian life. And any work they do find is so demeaning and so low-paying that they can barely support themselves, let alone a family. As a result, a lot of young Negro men leave whatever homes they might have known as soon as they can, sometimes as early as twelve years old. They do this so as not to be a burden on anyone else. They drift about, barely avoiding starvation, from menial job to menial job, and, all too often, from jail to jail.

"Some of them find the army, and for the first time in their lives they have a sense of belonging and a sense of identity. They are Buffalo Soldiers, members of the Tenth Cavalry Regiment. The regiment is their home, their family, their nation, and their God.

"That's not something you can explain in one of your articles. And it isn't something that they need validated. Their sense of self-worth has already been validated by the eighteen Medals of Honor they have won over the last thirty years. The average American knows nothing of this, but all those Medal of Honor winners live on in the hearts of these men.

"You think there is a spirit to the Rough Riders? Well, let me tell you, there are no military units anywhere in the world that can match the Buffalo Soldiers for esprit de corps; not the Black Watch of Great Britain, the Foreign Legion of France, not even the Praetorian Guard in the days of Caesar."

"I must say, for having just joined the regiment you certainly have developed a deep sense of feeling for them."

"In a way, I didn't just join them; I have always been with them," Todd said. "When I was very young, my father commanded the Tenth Cavalry Regiment. I learned, then, what kind of men they are."

"Then I don't understand why you don't want me to write

about them so that others can see them for what they are! I think the public should be aware that these men, too, are fighting for our country.''

"You don't understand," Todd said. "Even General Sherman once said, 'If I were going into battle, I would not want to do so with Negro soldiers.' I'm afraid if too many people become aware of the fact that Negro soldiers are being used in this campaign, they would agitate to have them left out. Marty, my men can handle second-class treatment, they can excel with the poorest equipment, and they can survive on the worst rations. But were they not allowed to participate in this war, why, it would be tantamount to the murder of their souls.''

"Yes, I can see that," Marty replied. "Especially after what you have told me about them. All right, I won't write about them.''

"Thanks," Todd said.

"Would you like to walk with me for a bit?" Marty invited.

"Sure," Todd said, and, arm in arm, they began walking.

"Do you remember the song we heard the soldiers singing back in San Antonio?" Marty asked.

"It was 'Lorena'; yes, I remember.''

"Such a beautiful, haunting melody. I've thought of that song often, since then. And of what you said about it, how unrequited love was the only kind of love for a soldier.''

"Did I really say such a thing?"

"You did indeed.''

"I was very young then.''

Marty laughed. "You were young then? That was just a little over a month ago.''

"I was a second lieutenant," Todd said. "And it is a known fact that second lieutenants and army mules are two of God's dumbest creatures.''

Marty laughed again, and they continued their walk. It grew dark, but their way was well lighted by several lampposts. Many of the ships in the bay were equipped with electric lights, and they were brightly lit tonight.

They heard the chording of a guitar, and the words and

melody of a song, in four-part harmony, drifted toward them. From the hotel they heard the crashing of a glass, then loud laughter.

"It's all very much like a great party, isn't it?" Marty asked.

"It is now," Todd said. "Though it may be different when we get to Cuba."

"Oh," Marty said. She shivered and leaned closer to him so that she could feel his body heat.

"What is it?" he asked.

"I must confess that I have been caught up in the swirl of things just like everyone else. I was beginning to regard this whole thing as no more than one big party. But it isn't a party, is it? It's preparation for war. And in war, people get killed."

"Yes."

"Somehow, that thought makes all this"—she waved her hand, taking in the gaiety that was going on back at the hotel—"seem unwholesome."

"Unwholesome? No. It's just the opposite," Todd said. "What they are exhibiting now is a very wholesome attitude. In fact, it is the most wholesome attitude they could possibly have."

"But didn't you tell me, back in New York, that one shouldn't look forward to war?"

"I did tell you that."

"And yet you approve of everyone acting as if this were all one big party. Isn't that a suspension of reality?"

"I suppose, in a way, it *is* a suspension of reality. But men who are preparing to go to war must have the ability to suspend reality in order to preserve reason. It's like a vaccination. It takes a tiny bit of insanity to maintain sanity."

Marty chuckled. "It takes a bit of insanity to maintain sanity. So, you are a philosopher as well as a soldier."

"I'm soldier, scholar . . ." Todd paused for a moment before he said the last word. "Lover."

Marty laughed. "What?"

"It's how we used to refer to ourselves when we were cadets at the academy," Todd said. "Soldier, scholar, lover.

It was a joke. Though obviously not a very funny one,'' he added.

"I see."

Marty's face was radiantly beautiful, glowing as if lit by some inner light. Todd brought his lips to hers.

At first his kiss was hesitant, a cautious testing of the waters. But Marty didn't resist him. In fact, her lips were soft and receptive; more than receptive, they were eager. She opened her mouth on his, then put her arms around him and pulled him to her.

Todd could feel her body pressing against his. Through the silk of her dress, every curve and mound was made known to him by their close contact. Finally they separated, and Todd looked into her face.

"I . . . I'm sorry," he sputtered. "I had no right to force myself upon you in such a fashion. Please forgive me."

"Todd," Marty said quietly. "You didn't force yourself on me. If I had not wanted you to kiss me, you wouldn't have done it."

"You wanted me to kiss you?"

"Yes," Marty replied. "I think at that moment, more than anything in the world, I wanted you to kiss me."

Todd grinned broadly and squeezed her tightly. "Well," he said. "Well, all right. How about that?"

CHAPTER 10

In Bivouac with the Tenth Cavalry

Marty wanted to see for herself these Buffalo Soldiers who had so won Todd's respect and admiration. So, with the promise that she would write nothing that might jeopardize their status, she accepted an invitation from Todd to witness a Saturday-morning parade.

The soldiers were in full uniform, including their black-felt helmets with yellow mohair tassels and shining brass shields. Marty had been exposed to the military for several weeks now, and she thought she had seen them at their best and their worst. But she had never seen anything like this.

When the order to form up was given, they became four rows of improvised statues. Their formation could have been a photograph by Brady or a painting by Remington. The eyes did not blink; the cheeks did not twitch. Even the horses were at attention, with not one swish of tail, lifting of the foot, or tossing of the head. Only the red and white guidons showed movement as they snapped and popped in the early-morning breeze.

"Pass in review!" Colonel Baldwin shouted, his command rolling back across the open field. After issuing his order, Colonel Baldwin rode over to dismount and stand where Marty was standing. Marty felt a little sense of thrill that she would be able to enjoy such a vantage point.

In one precise military movement, the regiment faced to the right, then began riding out by columns of four. Two left turns brought them in line with where they would be reviewed. As each troop passed in front of Marty and the regimental commander, their commander gave the order.

"Eyes, right!"

With that order, the officers, who had their sabers drawn, brought them up in a salute, with the handles of the sabers against their chins and the blades sticking up at forty-five-degree angles. The riders who made up the right file continued to stare straight ahead, but every other soldier snapped his head forty-five degrees to the right, staring directly at Marty and their commander. She found it all thrilling, especially when Todd passed by with his troop.

After the parade, Colonel Baldwin invited Marty to dine with the officers, the first sergeants, and the regimental sergeant major. The sergeants were all in dress blues, their uniforms ablaze with yellow chevrons and braid. They made quite an impressive display.

Todd introduced Marty to Captain Bigelow and Lieutenant Pershing, both of whom stood and, as etiquette decreed, waited for her to extend her hand before they shook it. Then, Todd introduced her to two of the NCOs.

"Miss McGuire, allow me to introduce Sgt. Maj. Edward Baker. As the regimental sergeant major, he is the highest-ranking enlisted man in the entire regiment."

"Very pleased to meet you, ma'am," Baker said with a slight nod of his head.

"And this is 1st Sgt. Fielding Dakota," Todd continued. "Sergeant Dakota and I go back a long way. I can remember when he served with my father."

"A finer man never breathed, ma'am, than the lieutenant's father," Dakota said quickly.

Marty pointed to the medal on Dakota's chest. "I see you have won the Medal of Honor."

"I like to say the Tenth won it," Dakota replied. "I'm just lucky enough to be chosen as the one to wear it."

"That's very admirable of you, Sergeant."

Their conversation was interrupted by the sound of a spoon being tapped against the side of a glass, and everyone looked around to see Colonel Baldwin standing at the head of the table.

"Miss McGuire," Baldwin began. ."Officers and non-commissioned officers of the Tenth. Charge your glasses, please."

Soldiers in white mess jackets stepped forward with bottles of wine to fill the glasses of all those present. When the glasses were filled, Colonel Baldwin held his out over the table.

"To absent comrades," he said.

"To absent comrades," the officers and men repeated. They drank their wine, then, when Colonel Baldwin was seated, took their seats as well.

The table was covered with a white cloth and protected from the sun by a canopy. The same soldiers who had poured the wine now began serving the meal.

"What did he mean, 'to absent comrades'?" Marty whispered to Todd.

"It is a salute to the men of the Tenth who have been killed in battle," Todd said.

"Oh," Marty said. She felt a chill pass over her as she looked at these men, black and white, who were dining at the same table, connected not only physically but also spiritually with this shared bond.

After the dinner Dakota and one of the other sergeants excused themselves. Marty thought it was to attend to some duty, but when a chorus arrived a few minutes later to sing for them, she saw that Dakota and the other first sergeant were among their number.

The chorus sang half a dozen songs, all of which Marty enjoyed. But it was their rendition of "The Battle Hymn of the Republic" that she found particularly moving. It actually brought her to tears, and she would have been somewhat embarrassed by it had she not noticed that more than one of the other diners, including Colonel Baldwin, were wiping their own eyes.

The chorus was dismissed after singing half a dozen numbers. Three of the members of the chorus, First Sergeant Dakota, Corporal Cobb, and Private Bates, had passes to go into town. This was the first time anyone had been allowed to leave the bivouac area, and the men were bantering back and forth happily as they got ready.

"Yes, sir, we are goin' to have us a mighty fine time," Cobb said.

"As long as we remember we in the South," Bates reminded them.

Cobb laughed. "'Course we in the South. That's what's so good about it."

"Good? What's good about it? I mean, with people hatin' us like they do?"

"Well, there's some bad, yes. But there's lots of good, too," Cobb insisted. "Maybe the white folks down here don't care too much for us, but there is somethin' here that we didn't have back at Fort Robinson, Nebraska."

"What would that be?" Bates asked.

"What do you mean, what would that be?" Cobb replied. "Somethin' wrong with your eyes, boy? You didn't see all them good-lookin' young chocolate gals standin' back of the depot when the train come in?"

"Yeah, I seen 'em."

"Well, how many colored girls did you see back in Nebraska?"

"Not many," Bates agreed.

"Not many?" Cobb replied, laughing. "How 'bout none?"

"So, you think we goin' find some here?" Bates asked.

"You stick with me and First Sergeant Dakota," Cobb said.

Bates laughed. "Top? What's he want with a woman? He so old, he can't do nothin' with his pecker but piss."

"What do you say, Sarge? You ready for some brown sugar?" Cobb asked.

"I think mostly I'd bes' keep you two outta trouble," Dakota replied.

Half an hour later, Dakota, Bates, and Cobb, with passes in hand, were walking through Tampa. Ahead of them, at a place called the Sea Serpent Bar, a dozen or more white soldiers and half as many young women were standing or lounging on the porch in front of the bar.

One of the soldiers had removed his tunic, and he was sitting on the porch rail, drinking a beer. He had taken off his jacket to combat the heat, though he may also have been inclined to show off his physique to the young women, for he was quite muscular, with wide shoulders and powerful arms. Taking a swallow of his beer, he happened to glance toward the three Buffalo Soldiers as they approached.

"Hey, fellas," he said. He pointed with his beer bottle. "Take a look at what's comin' our way."

"What the hell? Where'd them niggers come from?" one of the other soldiers asked.

"I think we better cross the street," First Sergeant Dakota suggested quietly.

"Yeah, I think you right," Cobb replied.

"Shee-it, you two ole men be scared of a few white boys?" Bates asked derisively.

"Just cross the goddamn street like Top say," Cobb hissed. "I come to town to get into bed with a woman, not into a fight with some peckerhead white boys."

Dakota and Cobb started across the street. Bates hesitated for a moment, then reluctantly went with them.

"I thought you say they be some pussy in this town," Bates said when he rejoined them. "I ain' seen jack-shit."

"They's women here," Cobb insisted. "Trust me. They just up ahead a way."

"How we goin' find 'em?"

"Hell, son, I can find a single Indian in a thousand square miles of territory. You tryin' tell me I can't find one little ole colored girl in this whole town?"

"One? You damn well better find more than one," Bates said, laughing.

"Hey, you niggers! What you doin' wearin' army suits?"

The obscene shout came from the soldier with the muscular physique. His challenge was met by a ripple of laughter from the others.

"What? Top, you hear what that sonofabitch call us?" Bates asked.

"Let it go," Dakota said. "We don't want no trouble."

The obscenity came again: "Hey, niggers! I asked you what are you doin' wearin' army suits?"

"Just keep walkin'," Dakota ordered.

"Damn it, Top, we just goin' do nothin'?" Bates asked. "How you win that Medal of Honor you wearin'? You didn't win it by doin' nothin'."

"Bates, you jus' keep your mouth shut an' do what the Top Soldier say," Cobb added. Like Dakota, Cobb had been around long enough to have dealt with this sort of thing before. He knew that if they were going to get through this, they would have to keep the younger, more excitable Bates calm.

"Niggers, I'm talkin' to you! You answer when a white man talks to you!"

"Keep goin'," Dakota said.

"Hey, Eugene, I don't think them niggers wants to talk to you," one of the other soldiers said.

To back up his challenge, Eugene, and several of the others, including some of the women, crossed the street. Hurrying his pace, Eugene stepped in front of Dakota, Cobb, and Bates, blocking their passage down the street.

"Hey, look at the white hair on this here Uncle Tom," Eugene said. "Boy, you too old to be in the army, let alone that you a nigger. What outfit are you in, anyway?"

"The Tenth United States Cavalry," Dakota replied. It was the first time he had responded to any of the taunts or questions, and this time he did so proudly.

"You mean the Tenth Cavalry lets niggers in?"

"Our entire regiment is colored, which you would know if you was regular army," Cobb said. "But seein' as ever' one of you peckerheads is reserves who ain't never done nothin' but sashay around at fancy balls and the like, I reckon they's no way you could know 'bout real soldierin'."

"You makin' fun of the Ohio Militia, nigger?" Eugene asked angrily, and the others voiced their support.

"What my friend is sayin' is the Ohio Militia, the Tenth Cavalry, the infantry, the artillery, we all be on the same side in this war," Dakota said, still trying to defuse the moment.

"We got no call to be fightin' with one another."

"Hey, look at that, Eugene," one of the other men said, pointing to Dakota's Medal of Honor. "What is that gewgaw he's wearin'?"

"Damned if I know. I never seen nothin' like it," Eugene said.

"It's the Medal of Honor," Cobb explained.

"The Medal of Honor?"

"The Medal of Honor is the highest honor any soldier can get," Cobb said.

"Yeah, I've heard of it. Never seen one, though. How'd this nigger come by it?"

"First Sergeant Dakota got it for bravery in action during a fight against the Apache at Salt River, Arizona," Cobb said proudly. "That was March 7, 1890. I was with him. You was probably back in Ohio someplace then, drinkin' beer and piss-in' foam."

"Yeah, well, I don't believe the U.S. Army would give a nigger a Medal of Honor, no matter what he done. So I reckon I'll just take it back," Eugene said.

As Eugene reached for the medal, he suddenly and unex-pectedly felt something hard jab into his abdomen. Surprised, he looked down to see that Dakota had pulled his pistol and was pushing the end of the barrel painfully into his stomach.

"Eugene, if you touch that medal, I'm góin' pull this trig-ger and blow half your backbone away," Dakota said. His voice was low and icy calm.

"You goin' to do somethin' like that, right here in the middle of town, in front of all these witnesses?" Eugene asked. He grinned confidently and shook his head. "No, I'm bettin' you won't."

"Well, now, that would be a losin' bet . . . Eugene. You see, killin's what I do for a livin'," Dakota said.

The fact that a black man had not only addressed him by his first name . . . twice . . . but had done so in a manner that was anything but obsequious wasn't lost on Eugene. For the first time since the confrontation had started, he began to get a little nervous.

"Are you crazy? There's ten of us and only three of you,"

he said in one final effort to regain control. "You can't kill us all."

"Well now . . . Eugene . . . what difference will it make to you how many we kill? You'll be dead."

"He's bluffin', Eugene," one of the other soldiers said.

The laughing and taunting had stopped now, and when Dakota thumbed the hammer back on his pistol, the sound of its double metallic click seemed exceptionally loud.

Eugene began perspiring heavily. His pupils enlarged, and his lower lip started quivering.

"No," Eugene said. "No, I don't think he is bluffing." He held his hands up and took a couple of steps back. "Look, we was just funnin' with you boys. We didn't mean nothin' by it, and I didn't really have no intention of takin' your medal."

By now, Bates and Cobb had their pistols drawn as well.

"So, what do we do now?" one of the white soldiers asked, obviously bewildered by the sudden and unexpected turn things had taken.

"Hell, Top, what you say we just commence killin'?" Cobb suggested coldly. "We ain't none of us goin' to get out of this alive anyway. Seem to me like the best thing we can do is kill as many these white sonsofbitches as we can, startin' with Eugene here."

"Oh, God, no!" Eugene sobbed, shaking his head and waving his hands. Losing control of his bladder, he wet his pants.

"We didn't none of us have nothin' to do with all this," one of the others said in a frightened voice. "It was all Eugene's doin'. We was just watchin', that's all. You boys got no call to start shootin'."

"Skedaddle," Dakota ordered.

The men of the Ohio Militia, and the women who had followed them, turned and ran back across the street.

Bates started laughing.

"Let's get outta here before they round up a few guns and a lot of courage," Dakota suggested.

"We can go between these buildings and down the alley," Cobb replied, having already worked out an escape route.

*   *   *

Five minutes later the three men were in East Tampa. Emerging from the alley, they saw several dozen black men, women, and children.

"Glory be!" Cobb said. "Would you look at this!"

A young, very attractive girl sidled up to the three soldiers. She was wearing a red turban on her head and a yellow and green dress that clung to her shapely figure. She arched her back proudly, seductively, and smiled at them.

"You be colored soldier boys?" the girl asked.

"That we are, miss," Dakota said. "We are with the Tenth Cavalry."

"Colored soldiers!" one of the men shouted. "Hey, ever'one! Look! Colored soldiers!" Within moments the three Buffalo Soldiers were surrounded by scores of Tampa's black residents, and had lemonade, tea, and cold water thrust toward them.

"You got 'ny whiskey?" Cobb asked.

"Cobb, where are your manners?" Dakota asked critically.

"Sorry, Top," Cobb responded contritely. "This lemonade be real good," he said, taking a swallow and smacking his lips appreciatively. Several of the children laughed at his antics.

For the next several minutes the three men were the heroes of the hour, answering dozens of questions shouted at them.

"Yes, there are coloreds in the army. We got two regiments of cavalry and two divisions of infantry."

The girl who saw them first had, by now, adopted a proprietary attitude toward them, pushing away any of the other young women who were trying to stake their own claim.

"These men be mine," she hissed, pushing one young woman away. "Get your own."

"Easy, now, easy," Bates said. "They enough of us to go aroun'."

"No, they ain't," the girl said. "Not where I'm takin' you."

"What your name, girl?"

The girl leaned into Bates and looked up at him. "Tulip," she said.

"My name is Bates."

"Bates, you think I be pretty?"

"I think you 'bout the prettiest thing I ever did see," Bates said.

"Come on, Top," Cobb suggested. "Let's me 'n you leave Bates to Tulip. We'll look around a bit."

"No, don't go," Tulip said.

"Let 'em go," Bates said. "We don' need them."

"Yeah, honey," Cobb said. "You a pretty girl, but Bates done lay his claim on you. Me 'n' the first sergeant need to find us someone of our own."

"Don' worry. You come with me."

"Where we goin'?"

Tulip smiled, thrust out her hip, then crooked her finger. "You come with me," she said again.

Cobb looked at her, then at Dakota. "We may as well go with her," he stated. "If they ain't nothin' there, we can always come back. The pickin' looks pretty good from what I can see."

"You boys be hungry?" Tulip asked. "You like fried chicken?"

"Fried chicken?" Dakota replied, perking up at the suggestion. "My God, the last time I had any fried chicken, my mama cooked it for me. Girl, where we goin' get 'ny fried chicken?"

"My mama be the best cook in the world when it come to fried chicken," the girl said. She started pulling on Cobb. "Come to my house. I show you."

"Wait a minute. You takin' us to see you' mama?" Cobb asked. He shook his head. "Come on, Top; let's see what else we can find."

"Hold on there, Cobb," Dakota said. "Ain' no sense in us bein' rude, now, is they? She talkin' fried chicken! When the last time you had fried chicken?"

"I don't rightly remember," Cobb replied.

"What would it hurt to go eat a little?" Dakota asked.

"You know damn well we ain't goin' to get it for free," Cobb said.

"You ain't goin' get what you after for free, either," Dakota reminded him.

Cobb laughed. "All right," he said. He looked over at Bates, who already had his arms around Tulip. "Bates, you one lucky sonofabitch. You got you a woman and goin' get some fried chicken, too."

"Lucky? Hell, I ain't lucky, Corporal. I jus' be good-lookin', tha's all."

Dakota and Cobb laughed.

"All right, Tulip girl," Cobb said. "Lead the way. We come with you."

"My house jus' over there," Tulip replied, pointing.

Dakota was a little self-conscious as the three soldiers accompanied the bubbly young girl down the street. Children ran from every house and from behind every nook and cranny to walk with them. They reached out to touch the uniforms. Several of them saluted and one or two, overcome with curiosity and eagerness, even tried to touch the men's pistols.

"Uh-uh!" Cobb said, pushing them away from his gun. "Don' you kids be tryin' to touch my pistol, now."

"You goin' fight in the war?" one of the older boys asked.

"Yes."

"You mean colored soldiers is fightin' in the war?"

"That's right."

"I want to fight in the war, too."

Dakota figured the boy was between twelve and fourteen. Although Dakota was in his early fifties, he could still remember when he was the boy's age. Knowing, and appreciating, the boy's deep hunger for something more than he had known for his entire life, Dakota reached out and put his hand on the boy's head.

"Jus' a couple more years, son," he said. "Couple more years, you go down to the army recruiter and tell 'em you want to be a Buffalo Soldier."

"Buffalo Soldier," the boy said.

"That's what we are," Dakota said.

"Buffalo Soldier, yes, suh, tha's what I tell the man. I wants to be a Buffalo Soldier." The boy walked away, saying the words "Buffalo Soldier" over and over to himself.

"That's my house," Tulip said.

The house was a long, narrow structure built of unpainted wood and roofed with woven palm fronds. A woman came out onto the porch as they approached. Like Tulip, she was dressed in a bright, form-revealing dress. She was, Dakota decided, not much older than Tulip.

"Woowee!" Cobb said. "Top, would you look at that? Lord, that be the mos' beautiful woman I done ever seen!"

"Tulip, who you got there?" the woman asked.

"I gots me some colored soldiers, Aunt Belle. Goin' off to fight in the war!" Tulip said.

"Colored soldiers? You don' say. You boys come to eat some of Doney's fried chicken?" she asked.

"Fried chicken? I hope that ain't all we gets here," Cobb replied.

Belle laughed. "Boy, what you talk?" she asked.

"Cobb, I done tol' you, mind your manners," Dakota scolded.

"Mind my manners? Yes sir, Top Soldier, I'm goin' do that," Cobb said. "I'm goin' do whatever it takes to ride this filly."

First Sergeant Dakota watched as Doney Montjoy forked the golden brown pieces of fried chicken out of the heavy black skillet. She was cooking over a clay stove on the back porch of the four-room house that she shared with her sister, grown daughter, and three young children.

Dakota wasn't sure which of the young children, two boys and a girl, belonged to who, but it didn't seem to matter. The children were well behaved, and no matter which adult gave them orders, they obeyed.

Bates was in one of the bedrooms with Tulip. Cobb was in another bedroom with Belle.

From the moment they arrived it seemed as if Bates and Tulip, and then Cobb and Belle, were in worlds of their own. They had paired off, talked quietly, laughed often, then disappeared, first Bates and Tulip, then Cobb and Belle.

That left Dakota with Doney, and Doney had not quit frying chicken since they arrived.

Doney looked to be in her mid- to late forties. Her skin, which was the color of cinnamon, was still smooth, though there was a rather bad three-corner scar under her right eye. A flash of white blazed through otherwise dark hair. Although he knew that the other two men figured they had stuck Dakota with the older woman, he was actually much more attracted to her mature beauty than he was to the youthful pulchritude of her daughter and younger sister.

Doney had spread newspaper out on a scarred old table, and as she took the chicken from the skillet she put the pieces down on the paper. The just-cooked pieces would be immediately surrounded by a halo of dampness from the grease the newspaper leached from the fried chicken.

"Sergeant, you sure you want to be hangin' roun' here? 'Cause I don' want you bein' disappointed by thinkin' you goin' get somethin' you ain' goin' get," Doney said as she floured more pieces of chicken and dropped them into the bubbling oil of the skillet.

"You mean I ain' goin' get no chicken?" Dakota asked.

Doney laughed and nodded. "Chicken I can sell you," she said. She looked at him. "But tha's all you can buy from me, if you get my meanin'."

"I'm a tired old man, Doney," Dakota said. "Could be that fried chicken is all I can handle at my age."

Doney smiled at Dakota in a way that, despite her previous words, was almost flirtatious. "I don' know," she said. "I think a handsome man like you has been roun' more'n you lettin' on." Quickly and deftly she turned the chicken in the pan.

"You sure know your way round a stove," Dakota said.

"I get lots a practice," Doney replied as she continued turning the pieces.

"What you do with all this chicken you cook?" Dakota asked.

"I cook 'em for Mista Herald. He own a café over on Third Street, and ever' since all the soldier boys come to Tampa his business be real good. I been cookin' maybe fifteen or twenty chickens ever' day," Doney answered.

Doney picked up a fried chicken liver and brought it to

him. "I gets a dime for ever' chicken I cook. And I gets to keep all the livers, gizzards, backs, and scrags for myself," she added. "Mista Herald, he can't sell them 'cause the white folks don' like them parts."

"What's a scrag?" Dakota asked as he put the liver in his mouth.

Doney laughed. "Where you from, you don't know the scrag? The scrag be the neck 'n' ribs."

"I'm from Maryland. Uhm, uhm, this here liver be the best thing I done ever tasted," Dakota said. "Anybody don't like this got to be crazy."

"Fire's gettin' down," Doney remarked. She started toward the wood box, but Dakota put his hand out.

"I'll get it," he offered.

Dakota got several pieces of wood, then tossed them onto the fire through an opening in the back of the stove.

"Reach up on that shelf behind you," Doney said. "Get down a couple of glasses."

Dakota did as he was asked, and when he turned around he saw that Doney was holding a bottle of rum. She poured some rum into each glass, then put the bottle away. She handed one glass to him, then held hers out to bump against it.

"Here's to good luck to you while you be in Cuba," Doney said.

"Thanks." Dakota tossed the drink down, then wiped his mouth with the back of his hand. "Doney," he said. "How you ever come by a name like Doney?"

Doney laughed. "It s'posed to be Doña."

"Doña?"

"It's what you call titled Spanish ladies. A doña visit the plantation where my mama was, just before I was born. My mama say this doña be the nicest an' mos' beautiful white lady she ever see, and she see the way ever' one be all a'scrapin' and a'bowin' and a'makin' up to her. So, when I come along a couple months later, she figure Doña would be a good name for me. So, that what she name me, only she can't say it right, so I grow up bein' called Doney."

"It's a good name," Dakota said. "And it fits. You are a beautiful and gracious lady."

Doney smiled, then clucked her tongue and shook her head slowly. "I tol' you, Sergeant, you wastin' that silver tongue on me."

"It wasn't no waste," Dakota said. "It made you smile."

CHAPTER 11

The first of the many newspaper reporters to see action was not Richard Harding Davis, as everyone supposed it would be, but the novelist Stephen Crane. His opportunity came when Lt. Col. Robert Huntington invited Crane to accompany his battalion of U.S. Marines in establishing the first U.S. base on Cuban soil. From their impromptu base the marines protected the blockading U.S. Naval vessels as they shuttled from their station off Santiago.

When the Americans' presence was discovered, the Spanish troops made a few nighttime sorties against them. In retaliation, the marines attacked the Spanish camp, destroying their only fresh-water well.

After one particularly sharp engagement between the marines and the Spanish soldiers, Crane sent a dispatch back to Pulitzer. Crane's story read more like a passage from his novel, *The Red Badge of Courage,* than a newspaper article. Though the article was written for the *New York World,* it was picked up by the Associated Press and carried in several newspapers across the country. Soon Marty and the other correspondents still in Tampa were reading it:

As I lay flat, feeling the hot hiss of bullets trying to cut my hair, I heard someone dying near me. He was dying hard. Hard. It took him a long time to die. He breathed as all noble machinery breathes when it is making its gallant strife against breaking.

Breaking.

But he was going to break.

The darkness was impenetrable. The man was lying in some depression within seven feet of me. Every wave, vibration, of his anguish beat upon my senses. He was long past groaning. There was only the bitter strife for air which pulsed out into the night in a clear penetrating whistle with intervals of terrible silence in which I held my own breath in the common unconscious aspiration to help.

I thought this man would never die. I wanted him to die. Ultimately he died. At that moment the adjutant came bustling along erect amid the spitting bullets.

"Where's the doctor? Where's the doctor?"

A man answered briskly: "Just died this minute, sir."

The story was also read by President McKinley, and he was just finishing it when Maj. Gen. Joe Murchison, recently returned to Washington from his mission to Tampa, was shown into the president's office. Joe had been summoned to the White House to give the president a firsthand report on the state of readiness of the U.S. Army.

"Ah, General Murchison, welcome back to Washington," McKinley said, laying his newspaper aside.

"Thank you, Mr. President."

"Mr. Simpson, would you bring us coffee?" McKinley asked his appointments secretary.

"Yes, Mr. President. General, how do you take yours?"

"Black," Joe answered.

McKinley pointed toward the leather couch and chair that formed a little conversational area, away from his desk. "Have a seat, General," he invited as he settled in the chair.

Joe sat on the end of the couch, out toward the edge so he wouldn't be tempted to lean back.

"I just read Mr. Crane's story about the marine incursion into Cuba," McKinley said. "Did you read it?"

"Yes, sir, I did."

"Very powerful story. Very powerful," the president

added. "And sad. But I welcome it. Right now the newspapers have the entire country whipped up into a fever pitch. They are looking at this upcoming war as if it were a football game between two college elevens. Maybe Crane's story will provide them with some perspective."

Simpson brought the coffee in, served it, then withdrew quietly.

"So, tell me, General, how goes the effort to assemble a fleet to transport the soldiers to Cuba?" McKinley asked.

"It has been an extremely difficult task. We are a nation of sea power, but we have never made any provisions for transporting a large army, by sea, onto foreign shores to do battle. As a result, all the vessels of our navy, Coast Guard, and merchant marine put together are insufficient for the task. Of course, I'm sure it is not something our forefathers would have ever considered."

"But you have succeeded in putting together a fleet?"

Joe laughed. "If you are generous with your definition of the term *fleet,* yes, we have succeeded."

"General Miles has been talking about what he calls the army's 'striking lack of preparation.' Is it as bad as all that?"

"There are some glaring shortcomings, Mr. President."

"Is it a matter of money? We have $50 million set aside for national defense expenditures, but if need be, we can appropriate more."

Joe shook his head. "No, Mr. President. It isn't a matter of not having enough money. It is a matter of how best to spend the money we already have."

"What are some of the problems?"

"To begin with, the supply system is in shambles," Joe explained. "A light railroad connects Tampa City to Port Tampa, but it was built for local traffic, taking a few hundred people at a time on a leisurely trip to the beach. It was never intended to transport thousands of men and horses and all the equipment that would accompany them.

"In the meantime, supplies continue to pour in from all over the country, with the result that we have literally hundreds of freight cars stalled along the tracks and at spurs off the main lines. Presumably, these cars are filled with supplies we desperately need, only no one really knows what they contain, because there are no packing lists. Supply officers are having to break into each car to learn its contents."

McKinley shook his head. "It sounds like quite a boondoggle."

"Food supplies, especially fresh meat, are rotting in the heat," Joe continued. "And the canned beef we have been given was treated with a chemical to prevent it from spoiling. The result is an abomination so disgusting in both taste and appearance that the soldiers call it 'embalmed beef.' "

McKinley laughed. "Leave it to the soldiers to find humor in the darkest situation. How are the men holding up?"

"That is the one bright spot in this entire episode. The morale of the men is very high. Every man-jack of them wants to go to Cuba."

"I'm afraid if they languish down there much longer, though, their morale might be drawn thin," McKinley suggested. "And at this point, General Miles seems singularly disinterested in allowing General Shafter to mount an invasion. I feel as frustrated with them as President Lincoln was with General McClellan." McKinley laughed. "I recall that Lincoln once sent McClellan a message saying: 'Dear General, if you aren't going to use your army, may I borrow it for a while?' "

Joe laughed with him.

"What about the invasion, General Murchison? You were down there. Where does it stand? Will we be able to mount an invasion?"

"Yes, sir."

"This year?"

"Whenever you give the order, Mr. President, the invasion will take place. Despite whatever difficulties we might have in launching it."

"But will it succeed? As I understand it, Cervera's squadron has not yet been eliminated. He could attack our troopships, sink them, and kill thousands. After that, anyone who manages to land in Cuba will have to face one hundred thousand well-armed Spanish soldiers."

"Yes, sir, but that is one hundred thousand soldiers who

are operating in a country where the people are hostile to them," Joe said. "Don't forget, the Cuban people have been fighting for their own independence for some time now. We will have immediate allies the moment we put troops ashore."

"That's true, isn't it? It's too bad our chief of the army command staff can't show that kind of positive attitude," McKinley said.

"I'm sure General Miles is just being cautious."

"It is far beyond mere caution. A successful military leader must be prepared to take some risks, but Miles wants the guarantee of a sure thing," McKinley said. "That's because he has presidential fever."

"Presidential fever?"

McKinley nodded. "He has a burning desire to occupy the office I now hold," he said. "And he sees this war as a way to do that, provided he makes no missteps. And I fear he is more concerned about not making a mistake than he is about victory."

"I wasn't aware of General Miles's political aspirations."

"Word has gotten back to me that he is seeking support," McKinley said.

"As a Democrat or Republican?"

"As a Democrat. That's why I'm not too worried about him. He already has a powerful opponent for the Democratic nomination."

"That would be William Jennings Bryan?" Joe asked.

"None other," McKinley replied. "By the way, are you aware that William Jennings Bryan has had himself appointed colonel in command of a brigade of the Nebraska National Guard? He calls it the Silver Brigade . . . no doubt in deference to his tired old campaign for a silver standard."

"No, sir, I didn't know he was there. I didn't run across him in the assembly area."

McKinley laughed. "And you won't. At least I won't have to worry about running against Bryan's military record in 1900. For his own purposes, General Miles is seeing to it that Bryan's Silver Brigade will get no farther south than northern Florida. To that degree, Miles is playing right into my hands. He is inflicting the greatest damage to the man who would be the most formidable candidate I could face, thus strengthening my own position."

Joe shook his head. "Well, I'm afraid that's all beyond me. I mean no disrespect, sir, but I am totally disinterested in presidential politics."

"That's too bad, Joe," McKinley said. "The truth is, I think if you were so inclined, you would make a very good president."

Joe laughed and shook his head. "Me as president? I can't even imagine that. I'm a soldier. That's all I've ever been and all I ever want to be."

"What about vice president?"

"I beg your pardon, sir?"

McKinley walked over to the door of his office, opened it and looked around outside, then closed it and returned to the chair. He began speaking very quietly.

"Not many people realize this, Joe, but Vice President Hobart is not in the best of health. We have discussed this issue between us, but it has gone no further. There is a very strong possibility that I may have to select someone else as my vice president in the next election. I have been drawing up a list of people I think would make good running mates, and I would like to put your name on that list."

"Mr. President, I can't tell you how honored I am to even be considered," Joe replied. "But in all sincerity, there are many more who would be much better qualified than I. There are men who have devoted their entire lives to politics."

"A lifetime in politics is not always the best recommendation," McKinley said. "Though a lifetime of public service is. You certainly fit that requirement."

"What about General Miles? Have you thought about asking him? I know you say he is seeking the Democratic nomination, but if Bryan has that party's nomination sewed up, you might convince him to switch parties. He is, as you say, a cautious man."

"Yes, and rather calculating," McKinley said. He shook his head. "You aren't the first to come up with that suggestion, Joe, and it may be that I will ask him. But I'd like to explore every other option first."

"What about Leonard Wood? Or even Theodore Roosevelt? I think Roosevelt would make a very good candidate. He is certainly popular among his men, and they represent all walks of life."

"Roosevelt?" McKinley laughed. "Oh, wouldn't Mark Hanna love to see that cowboy as vice president, though?" he asked sarcastically. "Mr. Hanna had a few choice words to say about it when I appointed T. R. assistant secretary of the navy." McKinley rubbed his cheek. "On the other hand, his Rough Riders have captured the attention of the American public, haven't they? And Cabot Lodge certainly thinks highly of him. All right, I shall put Roosevelt's name on the list . . . along with yours."

Tampa, June 6

Doney smiled when she opened the door and saw Dakota standing there.

"Dakota, what you doin' here?" she asked. "This be the fifth night in a row you come see me. I don' believe anyone like fried chicken that much, not even you. So, what you doin' here?"

"I like bein' with you," Dakota said.

"All right. Come on in." Doney stepped away from the door, enabling Dakota to go into the house. He looked around.

"If you lookin' for Tulip an' Belle, they ain' here," she said. "They down at Sweet Mary's Bar and Dance Club."

"I know. Cobb an' Bates be there, too."

"Well, come on in the kitchen. I'm just cleanin' up afore I start cookin' tomorrow."

Dakota followed Doney into the kitchen. She pointed to the glasses, and he took two of them down. She poured them each a glass of rum.

"Doney, I've got a proposition for you," Dakota said as he took a swallow of his drink.

"What kind of proposition?" she asked.

"A business proposition."

Doney shook her head. "Now you done messed up with

me, Mr. Top Sergeant man," she said. "I tole you, I ain' no whore. You can buy fried chicken from me, an' tha's all. Anythin' else I got I might give to the right man, but I ain't goin' sell it."

"Who is the right man?" Dakota asked.

"It could be you," Doney admitted. "If you'd stop talkin' about tryin' to buy what I ain't goin' sell."

Dakota smiled broadly and held up both his hands. "I ain' lookin' to buy nothin'," he said. "But if you lookin' to give somethin' away, then I'm your man."

Doney smiled back, and her dark eyes flashed brightly. Dakota couldn't get over how deep her eyes were.

"You talk too much," she said. She moved to him, and he knew that she wanted him to kiss her.

Dakota ran his hands lightly over her body. He stopped at her breasts and could feel the heat coming through the shirt she wore, setting fire to the palms of his hands. He began to unfasten her shirt, hesitating for one agonizing moment between each button, as if expecting her to challenge him.

Doney offered no challenge, so Dakota continued to unbutton the shirt until it hung open. Her naked flesh glistened golden brown in the glow of the candles that pushed back the dark. Dakota slipped her shirt off her shoulders and then down her arms until Doney was naked from the waist up. He bent down to kiss her breasts, and as he did so his hands moved down to her hips and thighs. Grabbing the waistband of her skirt, he pushed it down until she stepped out of it. That left her standing before him, completely naked.

"Tell me, Mr. Top Sergeant man. You ever goin' get out of that uniform?" Doney asked seductively.

With a happy little chuckle, Dakota stripped out of his uniform so that, within a moment, he was as naked as she.

Taking him by his hand, Doney led Dakota into her bedroom. Once there, she lay back on her bed with her arms up over her head, looking up at him hungrily. Dakota inhaled sharply as he put his knees on the bed between her legs. Reaching up to him, Doney pulled him down to her.

Dakota could feel Doney's skin, smooth and soft beneath

his muscled body. She helped him make the connection, pushing up against him as he thrust into her.

Dakota moved with her, matching his deep, plunging thrusts with her bucking motions so that they were, for that moment, joined not only physically but spiritually as well.

Beneath him, Dakota could feel Doney's body convulsing in pleasurable shudders as involuntary cries of pleasure escaped from her throat. Unable to hold it in any longer, he let himself go in one explosive orgasm, which pulled and whipped at him until he was completely spent.

Afterward, they lay together for a long moment, floating with the pleasant sensations that stayed with them like the warmth that remains after a fire has died out. Finally, Dakota rolled away from her and lay beside her, inert now, where he had been so powerful but moments before. His breathing came hard for several moments before it stilled.

"Doney," he said after they had lain quietly for a while. "You ever think about goin' into business for yourself?"

"What you mean?"

"I mean, you ever think about openin' your own restaurant? Fry chicken not for Mr. Herald but for your own sweet self?"

"You're funny," Doney said.

"What's so funny about that?"

"How'm I s'posed to start a restaurant? It takes a lot of money to do that."

Dakota raised up on one elbow and looked down at her. "I got money," he said. "I got lots of money."

"What? How you come by lots of money?"

"I been in the army over thirty years," Dakota said. "I didn't have to buy my own food, and I didn't have to pay for a roof over my head. Didn't have nothin' to do with all my pay 'ceptin' maybe drink, an' I ain' never been much for drinkin'. So, all these years, I been savin' my money."

"How much money you have?" Doney asked.

"Over three thousand dollars," Dakota said. "Could we build a restaurant for that?"

Doney's eyes grew wide in excitement. "Lord, honey!"

she exclaimed. "We could build the finest restaurant in all
Florida with that much money."

"Then we'll do it."

Suddenly Doney's eyes narrowed and she grew suspicious.
"What you want from this?" she asked.

"I thought maybe we could be partners," Dakota suggested.

"Partners," Doney said. She scooted over closer to him,
then put his arm under her neck. She rolled onto him, pressing
her naked breasts into his bare chest. "Partners," she repeated.

Sweet Mary's Bar and Dance Club was doing a bigger business than it had at any other time since it opened. The Ninth
and Tenth Cavalry, as well as the twenty-fourth and twenty-
fifth Infantry, had been exceptionally generous with overnight
passes, and hundreds of Buffalo Soldiers were in town,
having a good time.

Because most of the black soldiers were inside Sweet
Mary's Bar, Eugene and several other Ohio volunteers didn't
see them when they wandered up into the Heights.

Still smarting from the run-in he had had with some black
soldiers a couple of weeks earlier, Eugene was determined to
"put the damned niggers in their place." He had been unarmed before, but the three black soldiers he had braced were
carrying pistols, and they had pulled their guns on Eugene.

Eugene had lost face over that incident, and he had no
intention of ever letting that happen again. Tonight he and
the other Ohio volunteers were armed. Let the blacks try
something now.

The woman who had been looking after Tulip's two-year-old
son, Julius, had brought him to Sweet Mary's. It upset Tulip.
If she had wanted Julius at Sweet Mary's, she would have
brought him herself, instead of paying someone else to watch
him. There was nothing to do now but take the boy home,
and that was what she was doing when she saw the white
soldiers. She knew they were going to be trouble from the
moment she saw them. They were loud, boisterous, and

drunk. Some of them were so drunk they could scarcely walk. They were also armed, and they were brandishing their pistols about menacingly.

In order to avoid any trouble, she scooped Julius up into her arms and started across the street.

"Well, now, hey, lookie here; lookie here!" Eugene called. When he saw Tulip crossing the street, he called out to her, "Hey, you, nigger gal, don't you go runnin' 'way now!"

One of the others laughed. "Eugene, I don't think she likes you."

"'Course she does," Eugene said. "All nigger girls would have a white man if they could. Where do you think all the high-yellow babies come from?"

By now Eugene and the others were right in front of Tulip. They spread out around her so that she was trapped. She looked around, her eyes as wide and frightened as the eyes of a doe would be in a similar situation.

"That your boy?" Eugene asked.

Tulip didn't answer. Instead, she pulled the baby closer to her.

"Put the kid down so I can get a better look at you," Eugene said. "You don't look old enough to have a baby. You got titty enough to feed one?"

Still silent, Tulip continued to stare at the men who surrounded her.

"I told you, put the kid down!" Eugene said. He raised his hand menacingly, though he didn't hit her.

Involuntarily Tulip raised one hand to protect herself. When she did, she loosed her grip on her child and Eugene grabbed him.

"Give me my baby!" Tulip screamed.

Eugene tossed the child to one of the other men, who then tossed him to another. Tulip, crying, tried to get her baby back.

"Hold that nigger woman still, John!" Eugene ordered.

John and a second soldier grabbed Tulip and held her.

"Hey, wanna see her titties?" John asked. He put his hand

on the neck of Tulip's dress, then jerked it down, exposing her breasts.

"Don't do that," Eugene said. He looked at Tulip and, for a moment, she thought she could almost see some compassion in his eyes. "Cover yourself back up," he told her.

"Please, give my baby back to me," Tulip pleaded as she pulled the torn bodice of her dress back together.

"Hey, hold the little nigger out," John said. "Let me see how close I can get to it."

The man with the child held him out by one leg, head down. The baby began to scream.

"Bet I can put a bullet through that part of his shirt that's hangin' down without hittin' him," John said. He fired, and Tulip and the baby screamed.

"Missed."

"John, what are you doing?" Eugene asked.

"Wait; I'll do it this time," John said. He fired again, and this time one of the bullets clipped through the loose-fitting sleeve without hitting the baby.

"Hey, son of a bitch, I did it!" John said.

"Let me try," one of the others said.

"No!" Eugene barked, grabbing the baby. He gave the baby back to Tulip. "Here, take the kid and get out of here," he said.

"Damn, Eugene, what you doin', goin' soft on us?" John asked.

The other soldier laughed. "He seen her titties and fell in love with her," he said.

"Roustin' a buck nigger's one thing. Roughin' up a woman and scarin' a kid is somethin' else," Eugene said.

"What the hell difference does it make?" John asked. "To my way of thinkin', a nigger's a nigger."

Shaking his head, Eugene turned around and started walking back in the direction from which they had come.

"Where you goin'?" John shouted to him.

"Back to the camp!" Eugene called back over his shoulder.

*   *.   *

Within half an hour, the black soldiers at Sweet Mary's had learned of Tulip's ordeal. Angry and anxious to punish the whites who would do such a thing, men of the cavalry and the infantry put aside their normal rivalries and became allies in this spirited fight against the injustice perpetrated by the white bigots.

By now, the men who were actually responsible for the degrading and terrifying episode with Tulip had already returned to their camp. The black soldiers didn't know this, but it didn't really matter. They were lashing out against all white bigotry, and, on this particular night, one white target was as good as another.

They ran through the streets of Tampa, shouting curses at the white man, firing their guns into the air, throwing rocks through storefront windows, and terrorizing any white man who happened to get in their way.

CHAPTER 12

"Miss McGuire?" the desk clerk called as he saw Marty passing through the lobby of the hotel.

"Yes?"

"I have a message for you."

Marty walked over to the desk as the clerk turned to pull an envelope from one of the hundreds of little cubbyholes behind him.

"Thank you," Marty said.

At first, Marty thought it might be a letter or a telegram from her editor, but the only thing written on the outside of the envelope was her name. Curious, she opened it, then removed a folded card. On the front was a simple engraving:

Todd Armstrong Murchison
Lieutenant U.S. Cavalry

She opened the card:

Dear Marty,

I would very much like to have a quiet dinner with you. However, as your popularity is too great and the dining room of the hotel is too crowded, a quiet dinner would be impossible unless a bold step is taken.

As a professional military man, I am well aware of strategy. Accordingly, I have taken the bold step called for by securing a suite at the Tampa Bay Hotel. I hasten to add that this suite is for tonight only.

I know this may be forward of me, but these are tumultuous times, and he who hesitates is lost. And, like any tactician, I would rather lose by miscalculation than by inaction.

Sincerely,
Todd

Marty smiled. Perhaps decorum would dictate that she turn him down with a sharp upbraiding for being so presumptuous. Had this been peacetime New York she would have done just that.

But this wasn't peacetime New York. And times were changing, not only with the war fever but also with the fact that the world was on the dawn of the twentieth century. Opening her purse, Marty took out a pencil, as well as one of her own cards. On the back she wrote one word: "Accepted."

Marty returned to the desk. The clerk, who was putting cards in cubby holes, turned toward her.

"Yes, Miss McGuire?"

"Would you summon a bellboy, please?"

"Yes, of course." The clerk struck the small bell on his desk. "Front!" he called.

A moment later a uniformed bellboy appeared. Marty gave him the card and a quarter. "Would you please deliver this to Room 604?"

"Yes, ma'am," the bellboy replied, taking the card and accepting the coin.

Todd stood on the balcony outside his suite, enjoying the view of the bay as he waited for Marty.

"The table is prepared, Lieutenant," a voice said from the room behind him. "When you are ready for your dinner, just telephone the kitchen and they'll bring it up right away."

"Thank you," Todd replied. He came back into the room to show the hotel employee out, then turned to survey the room. Room 604 wasn't just another hotel room; it was a suite. In fact, it was the most elegant suite in the entire hotel. It was called the Penthouse Suite, and it enjoyed the best view of the bay of any room in the building.

It was also beautifully decorated, from the crystal chandelier to the royal blue deep-pile carpet. The table was set for two, and it was laid out with the finest china, silver, and crystal available at the hotel. Nearby, a silver ice bucket held a bottle of champagne. All this had cost Todd a full month's pay, but he could think of nothing he would rather spend his money on than making a favorable impression on this woman who had so captivated him.

Todd checked his image in the mirror. Tonight he had chosen to wear the white mess uniform. It was the most elegant of all the army uniforms, and this was the first time he had worn it since being talked into buying it by the uniform tailor at West Point.

Todd walked over to the champagne bottle and, grabbing the neck between his palms, gave it a twirl. He had no idea where all this was leading, but he had started down the path and had no intention of turning away now.

In her own room on the second floor, Marty was getting ready for the dinner engagement. She, too, was giving some thought as to what she should wear. For the most part, her wardrobe had been designed to allow her to cover an army in the field. Thus she had half a dozen dresses that the fashion magazine *Harper's Bazaar* identified as "Ladies Sportswear," such as the kind women wore while hiking or playing golf. She also had a few ladies' hunting dresses, which were much simpler and easier to handle than the more stylish gowns with all the flounces. She even had two outfits that were called *faire le bicyclette,* or bicycle trousers. *Harper's* had declared that they were quite proper for women, even though they were trousers, because, in the words of the magazine, the Turkish trousers were "long and ample, and made of such fullness that when standing upright, the division is obliterated, thus preserving m'lady's dignity."

Marty had packed one gown, a *demi-saison* gown, which,

by design, was suitable for wear from spring until fall. The gown was of sky blue silk, designed by the Paris designer Felix. It was an unusual dress in that it featured a skirt that fastened at the side. It was elaborately trimmed at the collar and the hem with three rows of dark blue braid. The lowest row of braid was outlined with gold and red velvet. She wasn't sure why it was so important to her to dress so elegantly. She only knew that she wanted to make the best possible impression on this young lieutenant.

Marty stepped out of the bathtub feeling squeaky clean. Her skin was softened and scented with aromatic oils, and her hair was such a shiny deep black that it was nearly blue. For the last several weeks she had insisted that everyone treat her like a reporter. But tonight, all that was behind her. Tonight she was going to enjoy being a woman.

Marty left her room to walk to the elevator that would take her up to the sixth floor. In the hallway, she passed by several of the other reporters. They all spoke and lifted their hats to her, but though they were her working colleagues, not one of them recognized her! Marty could scarcely contain the smile as she stepped onto an elevator and gave the floor number to the operator.

When Todd opened the door, they both laughed.

"Well, I see I didn't surprise you by dressing up, did I?" Todd asked. "How did you know?"

"I didn't know," Marty answered. "It was just something I felt like doing."

Todd took a step back from the open door to invite Marty in. She looked at the suite and the furnishings, then let out a gasp.

"Do you like it?" Todd asked.

"Like it? Todd, it is absolutely the most elegant room I have ever seen. It must be costing you a fortune!"

"It is," Todd agreed. "But I figure it is compensation for all those nights I've spent in bivouac. Besides, I wanted to make an impression on you."

"Oh?"

Todd put his hands on her shoulders and looked at her.

"Yes," he said. He brushed her hair to one side, then kissed her temple.

"Oh," Marty said, turning away from him to maintain control of the situation. "The table looks particularly lovely."

Todd smiled. "I see my flank attack was repelled," he said. "Perhaps a diversionary maneuver?"

"A diversionary maneuver?"

"Our dinner," Todd replied, smiling. "Have a seat while I call down to the kitchen and have them send up our dinner."

"You . . . you have a telephone in this room?"

"All the modern conveniences," Todd said as he turned the crank to call the hotel operator.

They dined on cold shrimp, broiled red snapper, and broccoli, washed down with white wine. For dessert they had ice cream, then afterward an entire bottle of champagne. Marty sat on the sofa, and Todd sat down beside her. He put his arms around her and pulled her to him, pressing his lips to hers. Their mouths opened, and their tongues touched. Marty made a strange little sound deep in her throat.

Todd could feel her body against his, her softness against his hardness. His kiss became more demanding and Marty became more responsive. The tip of her tongue darted across his lips, then dipped into his mouth.

The warmth Todd had been feeling blazed quickly into a roaring inferno. His hands began wandering around her body; then one slipped down into the scoop neck of the dress and pushed under the camisole.

He could feel it now. The soft skin of her breast, incredibly hot, alive, and trembling. And the hard little button of her nipple. It was an exceptionally intimate contact. How wonderful it felt to him.

The knock on the door was loud and unexpected.

"Todd! Todd, are you in there?"

Quickly, and as if caught in the act of doing something he shouldn't be doing, Todd jerked his hand back, pulling it out from the top of Marty's dress. Marty pulled away from him and began making hasty repairs to her appearance, tugging on the dress here, touching her hair there.

"Todd!"

Todd recognized Lieutenant Pershing's voice. Technically, he and Pershing were the same rank. Both were first lieutenants. But Pershing was thirty-seven years old. And Todd had known Pershing from his service with Todd's father, many years earlier, when Todd was still a boy and Pershing was a brand-new second lieutenant.

"I'm here, Jack!" Todd called back. Standing, he pulled at the hem of his uniform jacket.

Marty got up from the sofa and went back to the table as if they had been sitting there when disturbed by the knock. She picked up a glass of water and was taking a sip as Todd opened the door.

"We have to get downtown, right away," Pershing said excitedly.

"What is it? What's wrong?"

"Our men are rioting," Pershing said.

"Rioting?"

"In Tampa. They are on a tear," Pershing said. "If we don't get them reined in quickly, there is going to be hell to pay."

Todd looked back toward Marty, the expression in his face pleading with her to understand that duty was calling him. He didn't have to say a word. She knew.

"Go with him, Todd," she said. "I know what those men mean to you."

"Let's go," Todd said.

It wasn't until that moment that Pershing realized Todd was in his mess dress whites. He chuckled and shook his head. "Good Lord, man, you are in mess dress whites? What in the world would compel you to wear mess dress whites?"

Dakota was sound asleep. Doney was lying beside him, with her head on his shoulder, but their rest was disturbed by someone pounding on the front door, calling Dakota's name.

"Top! First Sergeant Dakota!" Cobb banged on the door so hard that it shook on its hinges. Then he called out again. "Dakota, I know you in there! Wake up, man! Wake up!"

"Cobb?" Dakota said, responding groggily. He sat up and

looked around, confused for just a moment as to where he was.

"What is it, baby? What's wrong?" Doney asked sleepily. She turned over and buried her head in the pillow.

"Dakota! God damn it, man, wake the hell up!" Cobb shouted, his voice reflecting a great deal of stress.

Rubbing his eyes, Dakota got out of bed and padded, in his bare feet, over to the window. He looked outside and, in the silver splash of moonlight, saw Cobb standing just off the front porch.

"Cobb, what the hell you doin' out there, yellin' to wake the dead?" Dakota demanded. "What's goin' on?"

"They riotin' somethin' fierce!" Cobb said in a high state of agitation. "They's a regular war goin' on down there. You gots to come down there 'n' stop it."

"Let me get dressed. I'll be right there."

By now, Doney was also out of bed, and hearing that Dakota was going to willingly put himself in the middle of a riot, she began protesting.

"Baby, please don't go down there where folks is riotin'," she said. "Ain' no call for you to mix into it."

"Yes, there is," Dakota replied. "I'm the first sergeant.

"Cobb, what brought this on?" he called back through the open window.

"You 'member them crackers we had a run-in with, a while back? One of 'em was a big son of a bitch named Eugene?"

"Yes, I remember him."

"Well, he come down to Sweet Mary's with a bunch o' his white friends and they started shootin' at Tulip's baby."

"Oh, my God!" Doney screamed. So frightened and concerned was she that she made no effort to hide her nakedness as she leaned out the window. "Did you say somebody shot Tulip's baby?"

"No, ma'am, the baby, he not hurt!" Cobb said quickly to put her mind at ease.

"We should've killed the son of a bitch when we had the chance," Dakota growled.

"Yeah, only the funny thing is, Tulip say Eugene the one

that stopped 'em. He the one made 'em give the baby back.''

"You sure the baby's not hurt?" Doney asked.

"Yes'm, I be real sure 'bout that. I done held the boy myself. He scared, but he ain't hurt. I figure maybe it's all over now, but when all the colored soldiers hear what happen, why, they come pourin' outta Sweet Mary's figurin' on settin' things right.''

"They catch Eugene?" Dakota asked.

"No. Eugene and all his friends done gone back to camp. But that don' stop our boys. It don' matter none they can't find Eugene. They on a tear. They bustin' out all the window lights; they shootin' guns off in the air. Ain't no tellin' where this is all goin' to lead to. Top, you got to stop 'em if you can. 'Cause iffen you can't, they goin' all be put in jail, and if they's a jail full of colored soldiers when ever'one else starts to Cuba, you can bet ain't none of us goin' to go.''

"We ain't goin' to let that happen," Dakota said. He started fumbling around in the room for his clothes. "Where my socks?''

Doney lit a candle as Dakota began getting dressed.

"Top Sergeant man, if you go down there, somethin' bad's goin' happen," Doney said. "You goin' get either hurt or killed, or you goin' wind up in the white man's jail. And baby, believe me, you don't want to wind up in the white man's jail in Tampa.''

"I have to stop it. Or at least, I have to try," Dakota said. "Don't you understand? I have to try.''

"You a crazy man," Doney replied, shaking her head.

"I reckon I may be at that.''

Doney put her hands to either side of Dakota's face, then leaned down to him. "Don't get yourself killed, crazy man," she said. "I done waited all my life to meet someone like you.'' She kissed him.

"I ain't goin' get myself killed," Dakota said as he stood to leave. He smiled at her. "Not now," he added.

"Fielding, wait! Your pistol!" Doney said, calling him by his first name for the first time and pointing to the pistol and holster on the dresser.

Dakota shook his head. "I won't be needing that," he said.

A moment later Dakota and Cobb were moving quickly down the street toward the center of town. Dakota didn't have to ask where to go. The sounds of occasional gunshots, crashing glass, and loud, boisterous laughter guided them toward the center of the disturbance as surely as any beacon.

"How many are there?" Dakota asked.

"Fifty, maybe sixty," Cobb replied.

"All our men?"

"No. They some from the Ninth and from the infantry, too."

The middle of Tampa was well lit by electric streetlights, which allowed Dakota and Cobb to see, quite clearly, what was going on. A large mob of black soldiers was surging down the street, lunging from side to side, pausing just long enough to break out storefront windows. Two or three of the men were carrying torches, though, as far as Dakota could tell, no fires had been lit.

"Hey, whitey! Come on out, whitey! Come on out and show us how brave you are!" one of the black soldiers shouted. The shout was punctuated with a pistol shot. "Let us take a little target practice with you!" That was followed by loud laughter.

"You think you can handle us, whitey?" one of the others called. "Come on out here. You don't need to go to Cuba. We'll give you all the war you want, right now!"

Running hard, Dakota managed to get into the street, just in front of the mob. He stood there, glaring back at them, and as they surged toward him, he held his hand up.

"Detail, halt!" he shouted.

"Detail, halt!" someone mimicked, then laughed.

"God damn it! I told you sons of bitches to halt! And that's an order!" Dakota shouted in his best parade-ground command voice.

"Who the hell are you, nigger, to be tellin' us to halt?" one of the black infantrymen called back.

"I am 1st Sgt. Fielding Dakota."

"He be the Top Soldier of the Tenth," one of the others answered. Though it was too dark to see, Dakota thought he could recognize English's voice.

"Private English, that be you?" Dakota called.

"Yes, First Sergeant," English replied contritely.

"I don't care whether this son of a bitch be a first sergeant or not; he better get out the way or he goin' be hurt."

"I want a platoon formation, right here, right now!" Dakota said. "Fall in!"

Startled by the unexpected military command, the black soldiers stopped.

"What you say?"

"I said fall in! And do it now, soldier!"

"How we goin' fall in? We ain't even from the same comp'ny. We can't form no platoon!"

"You in the same army, ain't you? Now, fall in! I'm giving you a direct order!" He pointed to some of the noncommissioned officers who were a part of the mob. "You, Sergeant, and you two corporals, take the right guide. Corporal Cobb!"

"Yes, First Sergeant Dakota!" Cobb snapped back.

"You are temporarily promoted to acting platoon sergeant. Post!"

"Yes, First Sergeant Dakota!" Cobb said.

Quickly Cobb moved to position himself in front of the formation. He stood at attention, glaring at the soldiers who were still milling around, surprised and confused by this unexpected turn of events.

"Hey, I outrank that son of a bitch!" one of the sergeants called. "How come you make him platoon sergeant?"

" 'Cause he ain't so goddamn dumb he be rioting," Dakota answered. "You are squad leader for the first squad. You other sergeants, you are squad leaders for the second and third squads. Now, form your squads!"

The sergeants stood for a moment as if trying to decide whether or not to go along with Cobb and Dakota. This, Dakota realized, was the critical moment. If he could win the non-commissioned officers over, then he would have a chance with the rest of the men.

"I be in your squad, Sarge," Bates said to the sergeant who had complained.

"I be in yours," English said to one of the other sergeants.

From somewhere down inside, the non-commissioned officers managed to find a sense of duty and honor. Dakota breathed a prayer of thankfulness for English and Bates as the NCOs assumed their positions. Then, holding their left arms straight out beside them, they called out: "Squad, form on me!"

At first, only one or two joined the formation.

"You crazy?" someone shouted. "What you-all doin'?"

"No talking in the ranks, soldier!" Cobb growled.

"Let's fall in, like the man say, Rogers," one of the men said.

By ones and twos the formation grew until soon there were more men in the formation than there were those still boycotting it.

"Any man not in formation in five seconds I'll put under arrest," Dakota said. "While the rest of us are going to Cuba, you dumb bastards will be sitting out the war in a Tampa jail. I don't think you want to be a colored man in a Tampa jail after tonight."

There was only another moment of hesitation; then the remaining soldiers moved over to stand in formation.

"Report!" Dakota ordered.

The sergeant in charge of the first squad looked down his file and saw that everyone was standing at attention. He saluted Cobb and rendered his report.

"First squad, all present and accounted for, sir!"

The other two sergeants followed suit; then Cobb turned to report to Dakota.

"Platoon all present and accounted for, sir!"

Dakota returned the salute.

"Parade rest!" Dakota ordered.

As one, the men of the composite platoon extended their left legs so that their feet were a shoulder's width apart. They clasped their hands behind their backs and stared straight ahead. For a long moment, there was absolute silence. Somewhere a baby was crying.

From the stores and buildings along each side of the street men and women began to emerge, making a curious but cautious move out into the middle of the street to see what was going on.

"We cannot let this happen," Dakota began, speaking in a quiet but resolute voice. "We will not let this happen. *I* will not let this happen," he added as if, by the power of his will alone, he could stop it. And indeed, so far tonight, he had stopped it.

He was quiet for a moment; then he continued. "For thirty years, men of color have served with distinction, pride, and honor, in the Twenty-fourth and Twenty-fifth Infantry Divisions and in the Ninth and Tenth Cavalry Regiments.

"For thirty years, we have fought Indians, heat and drought, blizzards and cold. And we have done it with . . . *honor.*

"For thirty years, we have fought poor rations, bad equipment, the meanest living conditions. And we have done it with . . . *honor.*" This time, the word "honor" was a little louder than it had been before.

"For thirty years," he continued, building up steam now, "we have fought bigotry and hatred. We have defended people who had no more regard for us than they did for the Indians who were threatening their lives.

"And . . . we . . . have . . . done . . . it . . . with . . . *honor!*" This time the word exploded with the thunder of a cannon blast so that it became a challenge that resonated in the soul of every soldier present.

He was quiet for several seconds, the word "honor" hanging over the soldiers, challenging and reproaching them.

"Is there anything honorable in what you did tonight? Do you take any pride in destroying private property and in terrorizing innocent people?

"By your behavior today you have disgraced those whom you represent. You may think you are representing only the Twenty-fourth or Twenty-fifth Infantry or the Ninth or Tenth Cavalry.

"If that is what you think, you are wrong! We are bound by duty, honor, and a profound love and respect for the army we serve.

"It does not matter that the army we love does not love

us. Just because you love a thing, that don't mean it's goin' to love you back. All we ask for is the privilege to serve. We are brothers to one another and we are brothers to those who served before us, men who died in New Mexico, Arizona, Utah, Montana.

"They didn't die for the U.S. government!" Dakota paused for a moment, for effect.

"They didn't die for the flag!"

Another pause.

"They didn't die for the army!

"They died for their brothers, just as some of us will die when we go to Cuba."

Dakota paused for another moment.

"*If* we go to Cuba," he added as a quiet afterthought.

Dakota spread his arm out. "After tonight, we may not go at all. You know there are people in Congress, there are even people in the army, who don't want us to go. Somethin' like what happened here tonight is just the kind of thing they lookin' for. 'You see what them niggers did in Tampa?' they'll say. 'You really want to send niggers to Cuba?'

"Well, I ain't goin' let that happen. I've spent my whole life to get here, and I'll be goddamn if I'm goin' to let a bunch of drunken bastards like you keep me from goin'. Acting Platoon Sergeant Cobb?"

"Yes, First Sergeant!"

"Have the squad leaders pass the hat. I want every pocket turned out. Collect every cent . . . and that means *every* cent, from every trooper and soldier here. We are going to pay for all the damage we have caused tonight."

Dakota looked out over the platoon. "If any of you question that, I hereby give you permission to break ranks, right now."

Although there were a few quiet groans, no one moved.

"Good. I thought we would all be together on this. Squad leaders, do your duty."

The squad leaders started down the squad.

"Hold it!" Dakota shouted. "Squad leaders, empty your own pockets first!"

That order brought laughter from the men as they saw the squad leaders emptying their own pockets.

A moment later, Cobb brought all the money that had been collected to First Sergeant Dakota. Just as he was handing the hat full of money over to Dakota, a buckboard, pulled by two running horses, slid to a halt in the middle of the street. Lieutenants Murchison and Pershing were in the buckboard.

"Platoon, 'tenhut!" Dakota shouted.

Todd, still in his mess whites, and Lieutenant Pershing climbed down from the buckboard and looked around. They had come to help quell a riot, if possible, but were confronted with something quite different. A platoon of men was standing at attention in the middle of the street. In addition to the soldiers, there were, by now, over two hundred of Tampa's citizens, white and black, looking on in awe at what they had just witnessed.

"Sir, First Sergeant Dakota reporting!" Dakota said, rendering a salute. Todd and Pershing returned Dakota's salute.

"What is this, First Sergeant?" Todd asked. "What is going on?"

"Sir, a few of the men were upset about something that happened earlier tonight," Dakota said. "They made a small demonstration."

"What do you mean, they made a demonstration?" Todd asked.

"Demonstration, hell! It had all the makin's of a full-blown riot," one of the civilians said, coming out of the crowd.

"And who would you be, sir?" Pershing asked.

"I'm Sheriff Pynchon. And I've seen a few riots in my day, but I swear to God, I ain't never seen nothin' like what happened here tonight."

"Exactly what did happen?" Todd asked.

"What happened?" Sheriff Pynchon pointed to Dakota. "That crazy nigger stopped the riot, all by hisself!"

Looking over at Dakota, Todd saw that he was holding a hat filled with money. "First Sergeant, what is that money for?"

"Sir, the men wanted to make up for what happen here tonight," Dakota said. "So, we took up a collection to pay for the damage we caused."

"Hope you collected enough. An awful lot of windows got broke," Pynchon commented.

"We will see to it that it is enough," Pershing replied. "Lieutenant Murchison and I will contribute $100 each to the pot."

Todd looked at Pershing in surprise, then, shaking his head, grinned ruefully. The hotel suite had cost him a lot of money tonight. But if another $100 could prevent this incident from going any further, he was more than willing to participate.

"The lieutenant is right," Todd said, taking the money from his billfold. "We'll help out." Ordinarily he wouldn't have been carrying that much money with him, but because he had wanted this night with Marty to be special, he was carrying every cent he had. The $100 contribution left him with just over $10.

"If more money is needed, we'll collect it from the rest of the officers," Todd said.

"Just a minute," Dakota added. "I haven't made my contribution yet."

First Sergeant Dakota was also carrying more money with him than he normally would, because he had wanted to demonstrate to Doney that he was serious in his suggestion that they go into business together. He took $100 from his own billfold.

"Here's another $100," he said.

The men had been quiet when Todd and Pershing put their money into the hat. The gap between enlisted and commissioned ranks was so great that, though $100 was a lot of money to the men, they had no way of knowing whether or not it was a huge sum for white officers.

But when First Sergeant Dakota, one of their own, and a man who hadn't even been involved in the rioting, added $100 to the kitty, they gasped in surprise and unrestrained admiration.

"Look at the Top Soldier!"

"He got money like that?"

"Ain't no colored man got money like that!"

Dakota handed the money over to the sheriff. "I hope there is enough here," he said.

Sheriff Pynchon looked at the money for a moment, then added some of his own. Then one of the white citizens came over to add money, followed by another, and another, until at least half a dozen had made a contribution.

"I'm sure this will be enough money to cover all the damages," Pynchon said, clearing his throat in surprise and unexpected emotion. "More than enough."

"If there is any money left over, give it to the sheriff's relief fund," Pershing suggested. "I'm sure there is a sheriff's relief fund of some kind, isn't there?"

"Uh . . . yes, there is," Pynchon said, saying the words in a way that made Todd realize that if no such fund existed before now, it soon would exist.

"And, Sheriff? We can assume that this is the end of it?" Pershing asked. "There will be no charges filed, no reports sent to the military?"

The sheriff looked at the citizens who had gathered, those who had contributed to the fund and those who had come only to watch what was going on. Several of them were the owners of the businesses whose windows had been broken.

"I get my window fixed, it's over far as I'm concerned," one of the businessmen said.

"Me, too," another added.

Sheriff Pynchon looked at Todd and Pershing. "This'll be the end of it," he promised.

"First Sergeant!" Pershing barked.

"Yes, sir!" Dakota replied, coming to attention.

"Thank the men for their generous contributions; then dismiss them."

"Yes, sir!" Dakota said. "Platoon, attention!"

As Dakota thanked the men for their generous "donations" to the fund, Lts. John J. Pershing and Todd Armstrong Murchison returned to the buckboard that had brought them out here.

"The other officers call me Black Jack," Pershing said.

"They call me that because they say I am enamored with the colored soldiers under my command. Well, to that charge, sir, I plead guilty. By God, I've never seen more magnificent men."

"Amen," Todd added.

CHAPTER 13

On Board the Battleship Oregon

Three days after Marty applied for permission to visit the battleship *Oregon,* a young naval officer called for her at the hotel with the news that permission had been granted. He took her by carriage from the hotel down to the slip where a destroyer was waiting. The destroyer took her to Key West, where the *Oregon* and other warships in Admiral Sampson's armada lay at anchor.

The admiral, who was on board the *Oregon,* sent his gig over to the destroyer for Marty, and six sailors pulled on the oars as the boat moved swiftly between the two ships. As they approached the *Oregon,* Marty looked up in awe at the steel sides that rose, like a cliff from the water, to tower high above them.

At first, she feared she might have to board the ship by means of a rope ladder, but the gig was steered around to the starboard side, where a portable stairway hung over. With steel steps going up at a forty-five-degree angle, instead of rope rungs going straight up, and a rail to hang onto, boarding the ship was much easier than it might have been.

Marty expected Admiral Sampson to greet her the moment she stepped on board and was a little disappointed when he didn't. However, the ship's captain, Charles Clark, did greet her, then turned her over to a young lieutenant, who conducted her on a very thorough and exciting tour of the ship. The lieutenant allowed her to look inside the gun turrets, go down into the magazines, and even see the boiler room. Here a narrow catwalk stretched between two rows of boilers, four on each side. It was so hot that Marty could barely get her breath.

"This is the heart of the ship," the lieutenant explained.

"Oh, my, it's very hot in here," she said, fanning herself. She was actually beginning to feel dizzy from the heat and wondered how the men who worked here could stand it.

"Yes, ma'am," the lieutenant agreed. "And we have only two boilers lit, just enough to keep the generators going and provide us with maneuvering power. You should come down here when we are under way."

"Heavens! You mean it gets hotter than this?"

"Much hotter."

When they left that part of the ship Marty was relieved. She also felt somewhat guilty for being able to leave the boiler room, knowing that the sailors who were on duty there had to stay.

When the tour was over, Marty was asked if she would like to join Admiral Sampson for lemonade. At that moment nothing in the world sounded better to her than a cool glass of lemonade.

Admiral Sampson was quartered in a beautiful paneled stateroom that stretched all across the beam of the ship. He stood and smiled a greeting as Marty was shown in.

"I hope you enjoyed your little tour of the ship," he said.

"Oh, I did, very much."

He motioned to a chair. "Won't you be seated?"

Marty sat down, and immediately a steward put a glass of iced lemonade before her. "Thank you," Marty said to the steward. "And thank you, Admiral, for allowing me to visit your ship."

Admiral Sampson chuckled. "You really don't know, do you?"

"Know? Know what?"

"My dear, you are the toast of New York. Not only of New York, but of the country. Your stories have been picked up by papers everywhere."

"Well, I'm flattered. But I am just doing my job."

"And you are doing it very well," Sampson said. "Which

brings me to the reason I asked you to stop by for a little visit before you returned. Miss McGuire, we have received orders to proceed to Matanzas. My orders are to destroy any Spanish warships we may find there and to attack the fort. How would you like to go with us?''

"What?" Marty gasped. "Admiral, do you mean it?"

"Yes. You will be my personal guest on the *Oregon*. When I discussed the possibility with the president, I assured him that it would be perfectly safe for you."

"The president? You discussed me with the president?"

"Yes. And he agreed with me. So, if you want to go, it has been approved by the highest authority."

"Oh, I'd love to go!" Marty said, nearly squealing with excitement.

"Then you shall. It's about time the navy got the benefit of your delightful way with words."

The squadron moved out early the next morning, and Marty was given a position on the bridge of the ship, where she had a commanding view of the entire fleet. The ships moved in two columns, with the battleships on the left and the cruisers on the right. Huge wakes rolled out from the two great columns, and the smaller, faster destroyers, including the one that had brought her to Key West, darted up and down among them, bouncing in the wake like corks in the surf.

It was all very exciting for Marty. She had spent two weeks on board the *Conqueror*, but never during that time had she seen any of the operation of the ship. Here she was on the bridge, watching as the captain gave orders to the helmsman or shouted instructions through the speaking tube to the engine room below.

They steamed steadily the whole day, reduced speed considerably during the night, then resumed full speed the next morning.

Midmorning saw a stream of smoke make an arc through the sky, far in front of them.

"What was that?" she asked.

"That was a rocket. The Spaniards have spotted us," Admiral Sampson replied. "Captain Clark, make signals; form in line of battle."

"Aye, aye, sir," Captain Clark replied, and the order was passed on to a young signalman who immediately took his position on the signaling platform and began wigwagging his flags to the next ship in line. A few minutes later, Marty saw the ships all fold into one long line. By the time the battle line was formed, a green mass of land had risen from the ocean and they were within sight of their target.

Suddenly ripples of light flashed from the fort.

"Admiral, the fort has opened fire on us," the captain said, announcing the fact as calmly as if he were pointing out nothing more remarkable than a flock of birds.

"All right," the admiral replied.

A line of geysers erupted in the water nearly a thousand yards away.

"They are way off," Admiral Sampson said.

"They need to elevate about another ten degrees," the captain replied.

The Spanish were firing heavy guns at them, trying to sink the ship, and yet the admiral and the captain were talking about it as if it were a routine task. Indeed, they were calmly discussing what the Spanish could do to correct their error and thus succeed in their attempt.

"Captain, the lookout reports the Spanish fleet," someone said.

"Where, away?"

"To our starboard, sir."

Marty ran to the right side of the bridge and looked across the bright blue water. At first, she saw nothing.

"Where are they?" she asked.

"There, ma'am," a sailor said, pointing.

Marty still saw nothing.

"That's not a low-hanging cloud. It's smoke," Admiral Sampson said. "The ships are hull-down over the horizon."

Marty continued to stare until, almost as if rising from the sea, several ships appeared. She was amazed that the lookout had caught them when he had.

"Captain, we will engage the ships," Admiral Sampson said. "Alter course to meet them."

"Very good, sir. Mr. Crane, to the foremast with the stadiometer."

"Aye, aye, sir," Crane replied. Crane, the young lieutenant who had escorted Marty through the ship, now took an instrument from a felt-lined box. He stepped outside the bridge, then started climbing the mast.

"What is that device he has?" Marty asked.

"It is called a stadiometer," Captain Clark answered. "It's an instrument that can gauge the distance to the target."

At that moment a shell, which had been fired by one of the guns ashore, landed so close to the ship that its explosion threw a sheet of water all the way up to the bridge platform, drenching everyone, Marty included, in salt water.

"Captain Clark, fire one salvo toward the fort, then have the guns reloaded and ready to fire before we come within range of the Spanish ships."

"Aye, aye, sir!" Captain Clark replied, and the order was transmitted to the gun crews. Marty heard a cheer from the sailors, and she hurried over to watch the men in the gun crew nearest the bridge as they worked. There was a lot of shouting back and forth among the men.

"Set fuse, point detonating!" the gun captain yelled.

"Fuse, point detonating, set!"

"Load, two rounds explosive shell!"

Two men picked up a black cone and carried it to the rear of Tube Number One. They set it on a track; then a third man pushed the shell into the gun with a long rod. They did the same thing again, for the second gun tube.

"Shells loaded!"

"Load charge, two bags!"

Two linen bags of gunpowder were placed in behind the shell on Gun Number One; then the breechblock was closed and screwed down. The action was repeated for Gun Number Two.

"Charge loaded."

"Range, one five double-O yards!"

Two men began to turn a crank, and the two gun barrels

of the turret were slowly elevated. The gun captain who had been shouting the orders looked through an aiming device, then stepped back.

"Number One Turret, ready for firing!" he shouted.

Marty could hear the other turrets calling in their own readiness so that, within a moment, every gun on the ship was ready to fire.

"Miss McGuire, I would recommend you cover your ears," Admiral Sampson suggested calmly. Then, to Captain Clark: "You may commence firing at your discretion, Captain."

Captain Clark nodded to the gunnery officer, and the command was passed to fire.

Marty had never heard a noise as loud as the sound of all the guns erupting at the same time. Huge clouds of smoke billowed out from the ends of the barrels, and for a second it was as if a cloud had come down to cover them. Then, just as the cloud rolled away, she saw a series of explosions ashore as the shells fell on their targets. The other ships fired soon afterward, and even from a distance the noise was deafening. By the time the final salvo was shot, there were several fires burning ashore, and the men cheered the success of their shelling.

The fleet left the burning fort behind while they steamed at full speed to meet the Spanish warships. The Spaniards had already moved their ships into a line of battle, and as the American fleet closed, one of the officers loaned Marty his binoculars so she could get a closer look at them.

"Notice," the officer said, "that they have already cleared for battle and they have 'engage the enemy' signals flying from their halyards."

Marty saw figures running around on board one of the Spanish ships, doing much the same thing she had seen the American sailors do a few moments earlier on board the *Oregon*. She saw a group of the Spaniards cheering, and then she saw something that made her suddenly drop the binoculars.

"Oh!" she said.

One of the Spanish sailors, who was separated from the others, was throwing up. In fear?

"What is it?" the officer who had loaned her the glasses asked. "What did you see?"

"I saw the men," Marty said quietly.

"I know," the officer replied in a tone of voice that told her he understood. "It all seems very exciting until you realize that they are men, just like us. Then it isn't a game anymore. Then it is serious."

"Miss McGuire, away from the glass, please!" Captain Clark called.

Marty stepped away from the window, and it was very fortunate that she did, for the first shell fired from the Spanish fleet arrived at that moment, bursting about one hundred feet above them. Shrapnel from the shell rained down onto the ship, and the window where Marty had been standing but a second earlier was shattered. Great shards of glass sprayed out from the broken window. One piece hit the helmsman, but other than inflicting a rather clean cut to his arm, it did no damage.

"You may return fire when ready, Clark."

A moment later the American ships began firing, and Marty could feel the ship rocking with each salvo. The noise of the firing was so loud that it was painful to her ears, and when a sympathetic sailor handed her a couple of cotton balls she thanked him, then stuffed them in her ears to help deaden the awful sound.

The American fleet sailed back and forth in front of the Spanish ships, firing often and accurately. Marty had a ringside seat for the battle, and it all looked like some carefully rehearsed show rather than a real life-and-death struggle. The ships moved in a stately fashion, firing regularly, ceasing their fire only when the smoke became so thick they couldn't see. Marty discovered that she could actually see the shells in their flight, and she followed the black projectiles as they arced out toward the Spanish ships. She saw many of them crash into the vessels and then explode in a flash of fire. After several minutes, at least four of the Spanish ships were burning fiercely.

Marty looked down onto the deck at the American sailors. She was surprised to see how calm and orderly they were. They were handling the guns and ammunition with a mechanical precision that belied the fact that they were in a life-and-death struggle.

Every time the *Oregon* fired a salvo, the ship shook so that Marty had to hold onto something to keep her balance.

"Captain, the engineering officer reports the temperature in the engine room is over 140 degrees. Some of the men are passing out," a man with telephone earphones said.

"Very well. Tell the engineering officer to start a shuttle," Captain Clark commanded. "Send one-third of his men up to the deck for ten minutes; then switch them around."

"Aye, aye, sir."

One hundred and forty degrees! Marty thought of those men who were having to spend the battle in the engine room, battened down without ventilation, baking in the heat of the furnaces and engine boilers, working hard from the physical exertion of shoveling coal. She hurried to the opposite side of the bridge and saw ten of them tumble out onto the deck. They were naked except for shoes and drawers, and they were covered in sweat and soot. They lay near exhaustion, breathing hard, showing neither concern nor any interest whatever in the battle that was still going on.

As the battle continued, Marty was able to discern Admiral Sampson's plan. The American ships would steam by the Spanish fleet at a steady speed of six knots. At the end of the line, the ships would bear around so that they described a long oval, returning to the fray at the beginning. The *Oregon* was leading the racetrack type of formation, and each time it returned to the battle they were a little closer to the Spanish ships. Finally, they were so close that Marty could see the men on board quite clearly with her naked eye. It was soon obvious that they were suffering far more than the Americans. Every Spanish ship had been severely damaged, and two were burning out of control. Many of their guns were out of operation, and she could see those gunners, now without jobs, standing at the railing to watch the battle. They were naked to the waist and black with the residue of spent powder. Many had their heads wrapped in water-soaked towels, and their bodies glistened with sweat.

For the American gun crews there was no respite at all, and the men continued to load shell after shell and charge after charge, each weighing upward to two hundred pounds, into the huge guns. And as if the heat of the battle and their exertion weren't enough, the sun was so hot that it was melting the pitch on the decks.

An hour and a half after the battle started, three of the Spanish ships were entirely out of action and the remaining vessels, badly wounded, broke off the engagement and began limping away.

"Shall we follow them, Admiral?" Captain Clark asked.

Admiral Sampson rubbed his chin and watched as the ships retired; then he shook his head.

"No," he said. "We have inflicted a terrible defeat upon them. To proceed now would take it beyond war and into savagery. Set a course for our return."

"Key West, sir?"

"Tampa Bay," Sampson said.

"Aye, aye, sir."

The *Oregon* flew signals to withdraw from action, then turned away on a return course.

"Secure from quarters," Admiral Sampson said.

A moment later Marty heard a cheer. Battle gratings were lifted then, and grimy men crowded out onto the deck, then rushed to the rail, not only to get some much-needed fresh air but also to cheer their comrades on the other ships.

These men, Marty knew, had fought the worst battle of all. They were trapped below, working under conditions in which the average person would find it hard to survive. Had just one Spanish shell hit the boilers, dozens of them would have been scalded to death. They didn't have the satisfaction of watching their shells hit the Spanish, nor the peace of seeing how badly aimed the Spanish shells were. They were dirty and unsung, but there was no doubt in Marty's mind that they were the real heroes of this engagement.

"Well, Miss McGuire, did you get enough to write a story?" Admiral Sampson asked.

"Oh, indeed I did, Admiral."

"What will you write about? The accuracy of our gunners? The excitement of battle?"

"No, sir," Marty said. She walked over to the windows and looked down on the men who had come up from the engine room. They were all leaning over the railing, letting the spray hit them, feeling the wind blow across them.

"I'm going to write about them," she said.

Admiral Sampson stood beside her and looked down at the men. "You mean the Black Gang?" he asked.

"Yes. I can't imagine what it must have been like down there," Marty said.

Admiral Sampson looked at Marty and smiled. "I knew I was right in asking you to come with us," he stated. "I doubt there's another reporter covering the war who would realize that those men are the real heroes of this battle. You write about them, Miss McGuire, and you'll have a friend in the navy for as long as I'm around."

"Thank you, Admiral," Marty said. "And thank you for letting me come on this voyage."

Admiral Sampson sent a fast destroyer on ahead of them, so that by the time they sailed into Tampa Bay word of their great victory had already arrived. The ships in the harbor blew their whistles, and sailors crowded the rails and hung in the lines and shrouds to cheer. Those soldiers who were bivouacked near the bay ran down to the shore and waved their hats and cheered, and when the gig took Marty and the officers ashore they were treated like heroes.

One reason for the great rejoicing was the fact that their victory now meant the invasion could proceed. The soldiers who had been languishing in the brutal heat, suffering from mosquito bites and growing bored with inactivity, could at last rejoice, for the word had come down. As soon as they could get loaded, they would proceed to Cuba.

Marty's first obligation was to her story, so she went to the telegraph office to file it the moment she returned. After the story was filed, she went back to the hotel, where she took a much-needed bath, then fell into bed to sleep the sleep of the exhausted.

When Marty awakened at about five the next morning, she was aware of a great deal of activity going on in the hallways of the hotel. Wondering if invasion orders had already been given, she dressed quickly and was about to go down into the lobby to find out what was going on when there was a knock on her door.

Opening it, she saw Phil Block, Richard Harding Davis, and three other reporters.

"Ah, Marty, good morning," Richard said. "You should've been with us last night. We had a fine time, and it's a good thing, too, because it was our last night here."

"She couldn't have come with us last night; she's a woman," one of the others said. This was a recently accredited reporter whom Marty had not yet met.

"She's not a woman. She's a reporter," Richard said.

Marty felt a glow of satisfaction at that remark. The same men who had once ostracized her were now taking up for her.

"I'm afraid I was too tired to do anything but sleep last night," Marty remarked.

"That's right, you were on board the *Oregon* during the naval engagement, weren't you?" Phil said.

"Yes."

"My hat is off to you."

"Thank you."

"What do you say we all go down to the dining room and eat a good breakfast?" Richard invited. "I have a feeling that it's going to be a long time before we eat well again."

"Good idea," one of the others replied. "And, Marty, you can tell me what it's like to be under fire. I've never heard shells coming toward me. I'm not sure I won't run. I really admire you for staying there."

"Where could I run? I was on a ship," Marty replied, and the others laughed so loud that one of the hotel patrons, still in pajamas and nightcap, opened his door and glared angrily at them for disturbing his morning.

The reporters took the elevator down to the dining room, then trooped in like a conquering army. The room was already bustling, but they saw a large round table and Richard, the acknowledged leader of the group, dispatched one of the men to secure it before anyone else could claim it.

"Gentlemen," Richard said. "I work for Mr. William Randolph Hearst. Now, I think you will all agree that Mr. Hearst is the wealthiest of any of our employers, right?"

"Right!" the others answered in concert.

"Right. Then it seems only fitting that Mr. Hearst buy breakfast for the lot of us. I shall merely charge it off to expenses. Order what you will."

Marty and the other five reporters sat around the table and continued to laugh and talk among themselves. A moment later a waiter came over to them.

"May I serve you?"

Richard answered for all of them. "We are reporters on a crusade for truth. We need something good and solid to carry us through this day, so bring ham and eggs and coffee for all of us. And keep it coming till we say stop."

"And for the lady?"

Richard looked at Marty and smiled.

"We're all reporters, old sport," he said. "One of us just happens to be a lady, that's all."

By the time breakfast was finished, the lobby of the hotel was jammed with men and luggage. Marty learned that there were nearly one hundred reporters who were certified to cover the invasion, including William Paley, an employee of the Edison Manufacturing Company. Paley would be taking motion pictures of the campaign for a company called Vitagraph.

The reporters were scrambling around to get their transport assignments. As Marty had already drawn the *Conqueror,* she didn't have to participate in the pushing and shoving match that went on among the others. She did stand just outside the crowd and watch, though.

Marty found the dress of the motley assembly particularly interesting. Some were wearing hunting suits, some were dressed in white ducks, and some in the same field uniform that the army was wearing, though without insignia. A few,

Marty noticed, were as immaculately attired as if they were going to a party.

She also laughed at the assortment of equipment the reporters were carrying. They were festooned with dangling canteens, blanket rolls, binoculars, cameras, and leather pouches stuffed with notebooks and pencils. Several of them were actually wearing pistols and crossed belts of ammunition. Many were carrying machetes.

Richard saw Marty standing just outside the crowd watching the others as they shouted and shoved for a ship assignment.

"Are you going to wait for what is left?" he asked.

"I have my assignment. The *Conqueror*."

"Then, if I were you, I would go down to the docks and get aboard," he said. "Pretty soon some of these fellows are going to realize that possession is nine-tenths of the law, and they are just going to forget about the assignments."

"Thanks," Marty replied. "Maybe I'd better do that."

Marty picked up her bag and went outside. Several hacks were drawn up, waiting for the onslaught they knew was about to start. She got in the first one and directed that she be taken to the docks.

When they arrived at the docks, she stood up in the hack and looked out over the scene of excited disorder. There were dozens of regiments waiting to board the transport vessels. Supply wagons were backed up along the roads, and the entire waterfront was swarming with men.

"Here you are, miss," the driver said.

"Thanks," Marty replied, paying her fare and climbing down. She wandered through the area, taking in everything. This was completely different from the embarkation from New York. There the soldiers had arrived at a steady tramp, tramp, tramp, to the stirring music of a military band. Here there was no martial music. There was only grim determination on the face of every commanding officer and every overworked quartermaster to get a particular regiment on board its assigned transport. The docks were piled high with tents, luggage, and commissary supplies. The sweltering, already-exhausted soldiers struggled in long, thin lines to get their own equipment aboard.

Marty recognized Colonel Roosevelt and saw that he was engaged in a rather spirited discussion with another colonel. The other colonel was speaking.

"Colonel, the *Yucatán* has been assigned to the Seventy-first," he said. "That is our ship, and you had no right to board your men."

"Well," Roosevelt replied, smiling broadly. "We seem to have it now."

"But it was assigned to us."

"I had verbal authorization to board," Roosevelt said.

"And who, may I ask, gave you such orders?"

"The assistant secretary of the navy," Roosevelt replied.

Knowing that Roosevelt was, himself, the former assistant secretary of the navy, she smiled, then studied the face of the colonel of the Seventy-first Infantry to see if it would dawn on him that he had been tricked. It did not.

"I'm afraid you'll have to make other arrangements for your men, Colonel," Roosevelt said.

Disgruntled, the commander of the Seventy-first turned away in defeat.

Marty located the quartermaster general, then, with a few well-chosen words of flattery concerning the task before him, managed to pry some significant information from him.

The invasion force would consist of 819 officers, 15,058 enlisted men, thirty civilian clerks, and 272 teamsters. In addition, there would be 2,295 horses and mules, 114 six-mule army wagons, eighty-one escort wagons, sixteen light guns, four seven-inch howitzers, four five-inch siege guns, one Hotchkiss cannon, eight 3.6 mortars, and four Gatling machine guns.

And, Marty thought but did not say, *one female reporter.*

CHAPTER 14

It was no easy task, getting all of the soldiers to the embarkation docks. Depending upon where they were bivouacked, they were anywhere from five to fifteen miles away. It had been supposed that the soldiers would simply be marched to the railhead and there loaded onto trains to be shuttled to the docks, but it didn't work out that way.

On too many occasions the commanders, afraid that their unit would be left behind, commandeered trains. Marty had seen Roosevelt take over the *Yucatán*. What she didn't know was that that was actually the second time he had moved the Rough Riders ahead in line. The first time was when he marched them down to the track, not at the railhead, where he was supposed to take them, but a mile before the railhead. There he waved down a train as it was on its way, then loaded his men aboard. As a result, the train rolled through the station and by the U.S. Sixth Infantry, a regular army unit to whom the train had been assigned.

Colonel Berry, the commander of the Sixth, who had legitimate orders to board, could do nothing but stand by the track and watch in confusion as the train passed through the station without stopping.

"Colonel, what is it? What's going on here?" one of his officers asked.

"I don't know," Berry replied. "That was supposed to be our train."

When the last car passed by, Berry saw Theodore Roosevelt standing out on the rear platform and then realized what had happened.

"The goddamned volunteers stole our train," Berry swore angrily. "Roosevelt!" he shouted. "You son of a bitch! What are you doing on that train? That's my train!"

"Sorry, old man!" Roosevelt replied, waving cheerily. "I'm sure there will be another train along directly."

There was another train, but it was certainly not one Berry would have chosen. However, fearful that they would be left behind if he didn't act, he confiscated it. His men were loaded into cattle cars where they stood, ankle-deep in cow dung, for the four hours it took the train to travel ten miles. Since this was not a scheduled troop train, it had the lowest priority of all the trains and was often sidetracked and jostled about in the midday sun. The men waited in miserable conditions as the other trains, filled with hooting and mocking soldiers, passed them by.

Reaching the pier did not mean the end of their ordeal. There the tired and hungry men had to stand for several more hours before they were put aboard transports.

Back in the Tenth Cavalry's bivouac area, the tents had already been struck, the packs rolled, and the men formed up to move out.

"Wonder how long we goin' stand here before we go?" Bates grumbled.

Dakota looked at him. "Trooper, you best be happy we goin' a'tall after that little fracas you pulled downtown the other night."

"Weren't just me, First Sergeant."

"No, but you was sure goin' along with it."

"Anyhow, it all come out all right," Bates said. "Besides, when you come down there and told ever'one to fall in, if me'n English didn't fall in, you woulda been in one hell of a mess."

Cobb chuckled. "He's got you there, Top."

No more than fifty feet away from the conversation going on among Dakota, Cobb, Bates, English, and the others, Todd and Pershing were sitting on the trunk of a fallen tree. Captain Bigelow had left two hours earlier to try to secure transportation for them.

"Think he'll find anything?" Todd asked.

"He's pretty resourceful," Pershing said as he filled his pipe. "Colonel Baldwin wouldn't have sent him out if he didn't think Captain Bigelow could do it. If there is anything to be had, Bigelow will find it."

"I don't know," Todd remarked. "When I was down at the railhead early this morning it was complete chaos. And I'm not looking for us to have any kind of priority."

"You've got that right," Pershing said. He lit his pipe and looked out over the men as he drew several puffs to get it started. A cloud of smoke soon wreathed his head. "You know, Todd, when this is all over, you'd do well to get yourself another assignment."

"Why do you say that? Haven't you told me yourself what good soldiers these men are?"

"They are wonderful soldiers," Pershing agreed. "A man couldn't ask for a better command, as far as the quality of his troops. But the higher-ups don't see it that way. Do you think I'm still a first lieutenant because I'm a dunce?"

"No, sir. I think you are a fine officer."

Pershing chuckled. "Ordinarily, I wouldn't put that much stock in the opinion of an officer whose commission is less than six months old. But you are from a military family and I know you've been around, so I'll accept your compliment. And, at the risk of being immodest, I will agree with you. I am a fine officer. But I am also an officer who has spent many years with colored troops, and when promotion boards meet we often get overlooked. Take Baldwin, for example. He should be a full colonel instead of a lieutenant colonel. He's filling a colonel's position. And Captain Bigelow should have been promoted to major, or perhaps even lieutenant colonel, long ago."

"I see what you mean," Todd said.

"Lieutenant, rider comin' in!" one of the men called.

"Who is it?"

"It be the cap'n, sir."

Todd and Pershing got up from their seat and, brushing off the backs of their pants, walked out to meet Bigelow as he dismounted.

"Find anything, sir?" Pershing asked.

"Maybe," Bigelow said. He looked at Todd through narrowed eyes. "Lieutenant Murchison. Do you have the guts to make the maximum use of your name?"

"I'm not sure what you mean," Todd replied.

"Evidently, there is a train made up exclusively for the use of Roosevelt's Rough Riders. First-class coaches, complete with padded seats and ice water."

"What do you expect with that bunch of gilded lilies?" Pershing replied. "They've been getting the best of everything, ever since all this started."

Bigelow smiled broadly. "Yeah, but this time we might be able to turn the tables on them."

"What do you mean?" Pershing asked.

"It seems that Teddy-boy got a little anxious and hijacked the train that was supposed to be for the Sixth Infantry. That leaves this train without an assignment."

"Come on, Captain; you don't really think they are going to give it to us, do you?" Pershing asked.

"No. But they would release it to General Murchison, if they thought he ordered it. All Todd has to do is write out the order. If you're game, that is," Bigelow said to Todd.

"You mean you want me to forge my father's name?" Todd asked hesitantly.

Bigelow shook his head. "What do you mean, forge? Murchison is your name, isn't it? Just leave off your first name and omit the rank, that's all."

Todd looked at Bigelow for a moment, then laughed out loud. "I'll be damned," he said. "Captain Bigelow, if you ever get tired of the army, I believe you could make a living as a riverboat gambler."

"I don't know if there is such a thing anymore," Bigelow said. "But I'd sure be willing to give it a try."

Fifteen minutes later, Todd accompanied Captain Bigelow back to the railhead. The train Bigelow spoke of, with its long line of polished cars, sat on a sidetrack. Bigelow pointed to it.

"I need that train for my men," he said to the train master.

"Captain, you and about forty other commanders have asked for that train," the train master replied. "But I'm not giving it to anyone until I get orders from someone a hell of a lot higher in rank than anyone who's asked me for it yet."

"What about orders from Shafter or Murchison? Would that do?"

"You have orders from Shafter?"

"No. But I have orders from Murchison."

Todd noticed that Captain Bigelow had carefully omitted the word *General*.

The train master looked skeptical. "Let me see them."

Bigelow handed him a pre-printed transportation form, upon which was written one paragraph:

To: Any transportation director as may see these orders:

You are hereby directed to provide to the Tenth Colored Cavalry transportation by the first available train or by any train as Captain Bigelow may require. By order of:

                                        Murchison

Todd held his breath as the train master read the orders. He knew that his father's signature was on many sets of orders now and there was a very high probability that the train master had seen General Murchison's signature. Therefore, Todd had signed the name Murchison in the same expansive style as his father, complete with a great looping swirl in the top of the *h*.

The train master pointed to the empty train. "Captain, that there is a first-class train. Are you tellin' me that I'm supposed to turn it over to a bunch of nigger soldiers?"

"I'm not telling you that; Murchison is telling you that," Captain Bigelow replied. "And they aren't niggers. They are soldiers."

The train master sighed. "All right," he said, throwing up

his hands. "Nothin' I can do about it, I suppose. It's your train."

"Get them here fast," Bigelow said as they left the railhead. "Before he starts checking."

"Yes, sir," Todd replied, barely able to restrain his laughter.

A short time later, the Tenth Cavalry arrived in smart marching formation to load onto the train. By now hundreds of other soldiers were milling about, waiting in increasing frustration as their own transportation failed to show. One of the waiting units was the Ohio Militia.

"What the hell?" Eugene said when he saw the Tenth Cavalry getting onto a first-class train. "Would you look at that?"

"Them's niggers," another said. "Them's niggers gettin' on that train."

Eugene took several steps toward the loading platform, then recognized some of the same men he had had his run-in with.

"Look there, Eugene. Ain't that there first sergeant the same fella that backed you down?" one of the other Ohio Militiamen asked.

Eugene glared at him. "He didn't back me down," Eugene insisted. "I was just funnin' him, that's all."

"Yeah, well, I'd sure like to know how come they got that train over us."

As Todd, Pershing, Captain Bigelow, and Colonel Baldwin passed through the cars of the train, they were cheered by their men. The men weren't sure exactly how their officers had secured the train for them, but they knew that it had to be something out of the ordinary.

"Look at the men lining up at the water coolers," Sergeant Major Baker said to them later. "You'd think they'd never drunk water before."

"Well, I'm sure they were thirsty after standing around for so long in the sun, then the march down to the railhead," Todd said.

"Yes, sir, that's true," Baker agreed. "But ice water,

plush parlor chairs for seating . . . these men never had anything like this.'' Baker came to attention and saluted. ''I thank you, Colonel. On behalf of all the men, I thank you.''

''Don't think me,'' Baldwin said. ''Lieutenant Murchison and Captain Bigelow are the ones who pulled it off.'' Baldwin's eyes sparkled with good humor. ''By the way, I want everyone to remember, when they come looking for whoever forged General Murchison's name, that it wasn't me.''

The men laughed. They were almost as giddy as the troopers, who were laughing and joking in high spirits throughout the rest of the train.

There was a letdown in the men's spirits when they reached the docks at Tampa Bay. They had eaten nothing since a 3:00 A.M. breakfast of coffee and hardtack, and there were no mess facilities available at the loading dock for them. Bigelow went into a restaurant on the pier to make arrangements to have his troop eat there, but the woman who ran it refused.

''Why would you refuse?'' Captain Bigelow asked. ''I'm willing to pay you the going rate.''

''Don't you understand?'' the woman replied. ''If I let these colored men eat in my dining room it will ruin my business. No one would ever eat here again.''

''No, I don't understand,'' Bigelow said.

''That's just the way it is. I'd be glad to feed you and the other white officers, though,'' she added.

''No, thank you,'' Bigelow said bitterly.

By three o'clock that afternoon it had been twelve hours since the men last ate. Captain Bigelow assured them that they would be able to eat as soon as they were aboard ship. In the meantime, they would just have to bear it.

''How are the men holding up, First Sergeant?'' Bigelow asked.

Dakota rubbed his stomach. ''I reckon they're about as hungry as I am, Cap'n,'' he said. ''But there ain't nothin' we can do but bear up to it, so that's what we'll do.''

''Yes, I know what you mean. I'm so hungry I could eat a horse.''

"There ain' no need for you and Lieutenants Pershing and Murchison to be goin' hungry," Dakota said. "They's lots of places where you folks could eat."

"You don't really expect us to eat if you can't?" Bigelow said.

"Sir, the fact that you-all aren't eatin' sure don't get us fed."

"First Sergeant, suppose I told you you could eat, but none of your men could; would you?"

Dakota shook his head. "No, sir, I don't reckon I would," he said. "But I'm colored, same as they are."

"And we're members of the Tenth Cavalry, same as they are," Bigelow replied.

Dakota nodded. "Yes, sir," he said. "I didn't really expect you to eat but wanted you to know that none of us would hold it against you if you did."

"Top! Top! Come quick!" someone shouted.

Dakota looked over to see Corporal Cobb running toward him, yelling and laughing.

"Corporal Cobb, what is it?" Dakota asked.

"Yes, Corporal, what's going on?" Bigelow asked.

Cobb came to a halt, then saluted. Bigelow, Pershing, and Todd returned the salute.

"Sorry, sir. It's food."

"Food? What kind of food? From where?" Dakota asked.

"You ain' goin' believe this, Top," Cobb said. "It's Doney."

"Doney?" Bigelow asked, confused. "First Sergeant, what, or who, is Doney?"

"Doney is my . . . uh, friend," Dakota said. "A woman friend I met in Tampa." He turned back to Cobb. "What about Doney?"

"Doney and near 'bout a dozen other women from the Heights," Cobb said. "They done brought a whole wagon-load of fried chicken and biscuits down here. Top, they's enough in that wagon to feed the entire troop!"

By that time a roaring cheer erupted from the throats of the other soldiers, as they had discovered what was in the wagon.

"Sir, permission to let the men mess?" Dakota asked, saluting.

"Permission granted," Bigelow said, returning the salute.

On board the Conqueror

Once again, Marty found herself on board the *Conqueror,* with the Lightning Cavalry. The Fifth New York Volunteers (Lightning Cavalry), the First Volunteer Cavalry (Rough Riders), and the Tenth Colored Cavalry, regulars, formed the First Cavalry Brigade, under the command of Brig. Gen. S. B. Young. Though the three cavalry units were part of the same brigade, they did not share the same ship in transit. The Lightning Cavalry was on the *Conqueror,* the Rough Riders were on the *Yucatán,* and the Tenth Cavalry was on the *USS Gaffey.* The *Gaffey* was part of the U.S. Merchant Marine fleet and much less luxuriously appointed than the *Conqueror.* General Young had made his headquarters on board the *Conqueror.*

As the flotilla got under way, they formed up outside Tampa Bay. The ships were in three long lines. There were thirty-two transports, one of which was towing a barge. Another transport was towing a schooner that was filled with fresh water. Surrounding the flotilla was a fleet of naval vessels, providing protection in the unlikely event the Spanish would attempt to mount an attack at sea. As Admiral Sampson assured Generals Lawton and Shafter, though, the Spanish had no ships left with which to mount an attack.

On board the *Oregon,* Marty had made the voyage to Cuba in just under twenty-four hours. She knew this trip wasn't going to be anywhere near that fast, however, because the entire convoy was creeping along at a snail's pace. Sometimes they moved at a rate of seven miles per hour, sometimes four miles per hour, and sometimes they didn't move at all. The entire convoy, now nearly thirty miles long, would sit for hours at a time on the gulf, which, fortunately, was as calm as a lake. There was no danger in sitting still, though, because there wasn't a Spanish ship in sight. The flotilla had the ocean all to themselves.

Marty had been at sea before. Not only was there the cruise down from New York on board the *Conqueror* and her experience on board the *Oregon* for the quick, slashing attack of Admiral Sampson's task force, but she had also made several trips to her mother's native Cuba over the years.

Never, however, had Marty been involved in a sea operation as large as this. The *Conqueror* was having no trouble keeping up, but Marty was amazed at the amount of difficulty the other transports seemed to be having. Engines broke down, they couldn't keep in line, and they constantly lost one another. That kept the navy's destroyers and torpedo boats busy rounding them up. An officer on one of the naval vessels would shout sharp, precise orders through a megaphone to the crews of the struggling transports, and the transport crews would respond, but an hour or so later one or another of the navy vessels would have to bring them into line again. To Marty it seemed that the swift little navy boats were like keen-eyed, intelligent sheepdogs rounding up lambs that strayed.

Once, the *Oregon* made a slow pass along the line. It was a magnificent sight, and Marty, watching the ship pass, felt a thrill as she realized she had been on board during the vessel's first engagement. The sailors looked so clean and sparkling in their shining white uniforms, and the ship's brass gleamed so brightly, that the soldiers on the transports often cheered and waved as the ship passed.

On the fifth day, the convoy circled north of Cuba, then lingered for a few days along the shore, creating a barely moving target for the Spaniards. They passed a Spanish barracks and saw several soldiers standing in front of the buildings, watching them. Some of the soldiers on the ships waved at the Spaniards, and the Spanish soldiers, who were the enemies of these men, returned the waves as if they were old friends.

The convoy was supposed to be following strict blackout discipline to avoid making themselves targets, and the *Conqueror* was doing so. However, not all the transports made such an effort. Signal lights flashed all night long, and many of the ships were as brightly lit as a floating city. From General Shafter's ship Marty could hear the music of a ragtime band.

Marty wrote of the conditions on board the ship:

The *Conqueror* is temporary home to the Fifth New York Volunteers (the Lightning Cavalry) and the Sixth U.S. Infantry (regulars). As a result of the additional troops, the holds belowdecks are twice as crowded now as they were when we came from New York. But the sea is calm and the portholes are opened, so there is a fair breeze that allows the men to sleep comfortably.

Many men sleep outside on the deck. The sentries pass by, stepping on some of the men and over the rest of them, but there are few complaints.

The food consists mostly of coffee, hardtack, canned beef, and canned tomatoes and beans. Often, some of the more enterprising men will concoct a stew from the rations.

We are within sight of Cuba, and in the morning the rugged mountains of the Sierra Maestra appear to us, wrapped in tendrils of blue mist. They are actually quite a beautiful sight, and the men crowd to the railing to enjoy the view ... and to wait for their chance to go ashore.

Marty was sitting on a stanchion at the ship's stern while she wrote her story. She had just finished it when an army lieutenant approached her.

"Miss McGuire?" he asked, touching the brim of his field cap.

"Yes?"

"General Shafter and Admiral Sampson have come aboard. They send their compliments and ask if you would care to join them in the wardroom."

"Yes, of course," Marty said, pleased by the invitation but curious as to why it had been tendered. She followed the lieutenant back along the now-familiar decks and passageways of the ship until she reached the wardroom. Admiral

Sampson and General Shafter stood graciously as she entered.

"Miss McGuire, may I present General Shafter?" Admiral Sampson said. "General, Miss McGuire stood on the bridge of the *Oregon* during our engagement with the Spanish fleet," Sampson continued. "She was as cool under fire as any of my officers."

"Then you think she would be of service to us?"

"Absolutely," Admiral Sampson said.

"Service?" Marty asked, curious about the remark.

"Miss McGuire, General Shafter, General Young, Colonel Pickett, and I are going ashore tonight to confer with the Cuban patriot general Calixto Garcia. I have been told that you speak Spanish fluently. Is this correct?"

"Yes, I speak the language," Marty answered.

"What we want, Miss McGuire," Shafter said, "is someone who will interpret for us. I know that General Garcia speaks English, but if we encounter any difficulty I would like someone I could depend upon, to interpret not only the words but also all the subtle nuances of the words."

"Yes, of course; I'd be glad to," Marty said, pleased that she was going to be included in this important meeting.

"There's more to it than that," Shafter went on. "We would also like you to keep one ear open for any conversations that might take place around us, even if they aren't directed to us. It is possible that you could hear something that would be of great importance."

"I understand," Marty said.

Admiral Sampson smiled. "I was sure we could count on you."

CHAPTER 15

A fter sunset that evening, Marty climbed down the small access ladder to the gently rocking dinghy that lay alongside the *Conqueror*. One of the sailors helped her into the small boat, and as she sat there waiting for the others to board, she studied the ship from this angle.

The sides of the ship were cream-colored, and the hull curved in at the waterline and then bowed out as it worked its way up. There were four rows of portholes on the hull, and these were all open. A number of heads and shoulders protruded from the portholes as the men watched, with interest, anything that might bear on what they were going to do.

About forty feet behind the gently bouncing dinghy, a bilge pipe began pumping water back into the sea.

When all were aboard the dinghy, it pulled away from the ship and headed toward a beach that was overhung with palm trees. In the dark shadows beneath the trees a light flashed three times.

"There's the signal, Admiral!" one of the sailors called.

"All right," Admiral Sampson answered. "Steer directly for the light."

"Aye, aye, sir."

The little boat cut quickly through the waves, rising and falling with the surf as they moved toward shore. Marty's face was splashed with spray, but she paid no attention to it. Her mind lay on what was in front of them.

As they started through the surf, a dozen Cubans, stripped

to the waist, dashed out into the water to grab the boat and pull it ashore. They dragged it far enough up onto the beach that everyone in the boat was able to get out without so much as wetting the soles of their shoes.

A double line of Cuban officers formed a guard of honor for the visitors, and as they left the boat Marty saw the looks, first of surprise, then of pleasure, as the men saw her.

At the end of the phalanx, a tall, handsome officer stood alone. He saluted the Americans.

"Welcome to Cuba, our friends and liberators. I am Col. Juan Alvarez, chief of staff to His Excellency, Gen. Calixto Garcia. I will take you to him."

The Americans introduced themselves one at a time, and when it came to Marty, Colonel Alvarez looked at her with unabashed interest.

"And you, my beautiful senorita?"

"I am Marty McGuire. I'm a correspondent for the New York *Daily Banner*." Marty said the first part in English; then she continued on in flawless Spanish. "I recently met your sister, Francesca. I am pleased to tell you that she is looking well and her thoughts are with you."

Juan smiled broadly. "What a wonderful surprise," he said. "You not only bring me news of my sister, but you do so in our language, spoken with a Cuban accent. Why is this?"

"My mother is Cuban," Marty explained. Then, to the Americans, Marty said that she had just extended greetings to Colonel Alvarez from his sister.

"Senorita, gentlemen," Juan said, "the general is one mile inland. If you will follow me?"

Marty and the small party of Americans followed Juan as he led them inland from the sea. They followed a small trail that cut through the palmetto and thick growth. About fifteen minutes later they came upon a palm-frond hut where General Garcia, a small man with a white mustache and goatee, met them. He had a deep scar on his forehead, and Marty knew from reading about him that it was the result of a self-inflicted bullet wound. When General Garcia had been a captive of the Spaniards ten years earlier, he had tried to kill himself.

The Spanish doctors had saved him, and now he was fighting against them.

"The people of Cuba welcome you," General Garcia said. "I have maps spread on a table inside. Come; we will discuss the liberation of my people."

For the next several moments Marty was no more than an interested observer as weighty decisions of how the war was to be waged were made around a hand-drawn map spread out on a rough-hewn table in the hut. Marty couldn't help but think that there was something rather ludicrous about all this. Congress had declared war, millions of dollars had been raised, the public was whipped up into a frenzy of support, and the largest invading army the Americans had ever put to sea had all begun without a definite plan of action.

It was Admiral Sampson's proposal that the army land at both sides of the entrance to Santiago and charge up the steep slopes to capture Morro Castle and the artillery emplacements. Then, according to Admiral Sampson, the navy would attack the rest of the Spanish fleet after first sweeping the mines from the harbor.

General Shafter was against that. He had read of a disastrous eighteenth-century British expedition against Santiago. Santiago was perched atop a 230-foot cliff, and he couldn't see trying to storm a position that was as inaccessible and impregnable as Santiago was.

Admiral Sampson then suggested that the army disembark at Guantánamo and march forty miles to attack from the rear, but General Shafter was concerned that yellow fever would then become their biggest enemy.

"Since you seem opposed to all of my suggestions, General, suppose you tell me what the army will do?" Sampson said.

Shafter moved over to the table and pointed to a spot on the map.

"I suggest that we land here at Daiquiri, which is fifteen miles east of Santiago, and at Siboney."

Sampson shook his head. "I'd have to advise against that," he said. "I know those waters. There is a very heavy swell against the beach there."

"Pardon me, Admiral," Juan said. "But the plan is . . ." He looked at Marty. "How do you say *mereciente*?"

"Deserving," Marty answered.

"Si. The plan of General Shafter is deserving. There are only about three hundred Spanish troops at Daiquiri. We can drive them away and make demonstrations elsewhere to distract the Spanish. That will allow the Americans to come ashore without trouble."

Admiral Sampson stroked his chin and studied the map for a long, long moment. "Very well," he said. "Can you drive them away before Wednesday?"

"Si," Juan replied.

"General, will your men be ready to go ashore Wednesday morning?"

"They are ready any time, Admiral," General Shafter replied.

"Then let's return to the ship. We'll land Wednesday morning. What date is that?"

"June 22, Admiral," Marty answered.

"June 22," Admiral Sampson replied. "Perhaps, gentlemen, this is a date that will go down in our history, like July 4, as one of our nation's most glorious days."

The great fleet lolled at anchor just off the northern coast of Cuba near Daiquiri. On board the troopship *Gaffey,* Lieutenant Murchison leaned over the rail and looked toward the lush green forest ashore. The rumor, as yet unconfirmed, was that they would be landing the next day. Earlier, someone had reported that a boat carrying General Shafter and Admiral Sampson had gone ashore from the *Conqueror.*

The *Gaffey* and the *Conqueror* had sailed alongside each other for the entire voyage and were now lying side by side at anchor. Todd had not seen the boat carrying Shafter and Sampson go ashore, but now, as he stood by the rail, he saw it coming back. When the boat got very close, he saw that the general and the admiral weren't the only passengers. Marty McGuire was with them.

Todd's first reaction was one of surprise. He wondered how Marty had managed to get herself onto that boat. His second reaction was one of admiration. He knew there were at least one hundred reporters covering this operation, and yet Marty was the one who was permitted to go ashore with Shafter and Sampson. That was quite a coup. His third reaction was one of delight to discover that Marty, whose whereabouts had been a complete mystery to him up until this moment, was only one ship away from him.

However, as he thought more about that, he concluded that there was as much frustration as joy in such knowledge. The fact that she was only one ship away meant nothing. Each ship was a self-contained world, and a thousand yards' separation kept the ships as remote from each other as those separated by thirty miles. Marty was, as the saying goes, ''so close, yet so far away.''

As Todd watched her climb from the boat to the deck of the *Conqueror,* he felt an aching to talk to her, to touch her and hold her. He was somewhat surprised by the reaction he had to the sight of her. He had wanted to see her again, yes, but he had no idea how intense that longing would be.

It was with sensory pleasure that he recalled that time in his room just after their dinner but before Pershing came to tell him of the impending riot. He had taken her in his arms, and he could still taste her kiss on his lips and feel her against him.

''Damn!'' he said aloud. ''I'm in love with her.''

''Beg pardon, sir?'' Dakota asked.

Startled, Todd looked over to see that First Sergeant Dakota was also leaning over the railing, looking toward the *Conqueror.*

''Uh, nothing, Sergeant,'' Todd replied, embarrassed that he had been heard speaking to himself. ''I was just thinking aloud, that's all.''

''Yes, sir, I know what the lieutenant means,'' Dakota said. ''I 'specs when a man has a lot to think about, it sometimes helps him to think aloud. I got me a lot to think about now, too.''

''And what thoughts have been occupying your mind, First Sergeant?''

''Gettin' out of the army,'' Dakota said.

"What?" Todd asked, shocked to hear that Dakota would even contemplate such a thing. "Why would you do that, First Sergeant? I thought you loved the army."

"Yes, sir, I do love it," Dakota replied. "And I've loved it man an' boy for some thirty years now. But I'm gettin' old, and my time has about come."

"What will you do when you leave?"

"Fry chicken."

Todd chuckled. "What did you say? You would fry chicken?"

"Yes, sir. That chicken we all had before we left Tampa? You think that was good?"

"First Sergeant, I think that was the best chicken I've ever eaten in my life," Todd replied.

"That was my woman that fried that chicken," Dakota said. "Her name is Doney Montjoy, an' when this war is over I'm gettin' out of the army an' me 'n' Doney's goin' get married. Then we goin' open us up a place where folks can buy the best fried chicken they ever tasted."

"Well, I'll be," Todd said. "I figured you would stay in the army till you were sixty-five and they forced you out."

"You ain't goin' hold it against me if I get out, are you, Lieutenant?"

Todd shook his head. "No, I'm not going to hold that against you. In fact, I'm going to wish you all the best. I just hope Doney knows what a fine man she'll be getting."

"Thank you, Lieutenant. And Miss McGuire? She be getting a fine man, too."

"What?" Todd asked. He was surprised that Dakota even knew of Marty's existence, let alone her name or any connection between them.

"She do be the one the lieutenant was thinkin' out loud about, don't she?"

Todd laughed. "It's kind of hard to keep things secret around here, isn't it?" he said.

"That was her climb up out of that boat a while ago, wasn't it?"

"Yes."

"Would the lieutenant like to go over to the *Conqueror* and see her?" Dakota asked.

"Wouldn't I?" Todd replied. "But if I were to ask for the gig just to visit a woman, I'd probably get thrown in the brig."

"No, sir, it ain't no problem if you know how to go about it."

"Oh? And just how would I go about getting over there?"

"General Young be on the *Conqueror*, don't he?"

"Yes, he is."

"And ain't he the commandin' general of the cavalry brigade we be in?"

"That's right," Todd replied, beginning to follow Dakota.

"Well, sir, I heard Colonel Baldwin tell Sergeant Major Baker to prepare a readiness report for General Young. I 'specs if you spoke to the sergeant major, he'd be happy to let you take the report over."

Todd laughed. "That's a great idea, First Sergeant. I don't know why I didn't think of it."

Marty was sleeping a dreamless sleep when she felt a hand on her cheek. She opened her eyes in sudden fear, then saw, with relief, that it was Todd. He was sitting on her bed, looking down at her.

"Todd?" she gasped. She looked around. "Am I dreaming?"

"If it is a dream, we're having the same one," Todd replied.

"I . . . I can't believe you are here! Where did you come from?"

"My ship is the next one over," Todd explained. "And there was a report due, so I volunteered to bring it over."

"I'm glad you did!" Marty said. "But how did you know which stateroom was mine?"

"I asked the duty officer," Todd answered. "I knocked on your door, but you didn't answer. Then, when I tried it, I found that it was unlocked." Todd shook his head in disapproval. "By the way, it was foolish of you to leave your cabin door unlocked," he scolded.

"I . . . I suppose I was thinking about tomorrow," Marty said.

"Tomorrow?"

"Yes. Tomorrow is when all the troops will go ashore. You didn't know that?"

"We've heard strong rumors," Todd said. "But we've heard nothing official yet."

"What time is it?"

"It's about midnight," Todd replied.

"That means General Shafter is going to start moving the men ashore in only four more hours. Have you slept?"

"No."

"You should try and get some sleep. You are going to be exhausted."

"I couldn't sleep," Todd said. "Not until I got the chance to see you again."

"I'm sure we'll see each other ashore," Marty replied.

"Yes, but we'll always be surrounded by other people," Todd said. "We won't have another chance for this." He moved his lips to hers, where they lingered briefly. Then he moved them to the hollow of her throat.

"Todd, I don't think we should . . . ," Marty started nervously, but she was unable to finish her sentence. The sensations she was experiencing were so overwhelming that she had no choice but to surrender to the moment. Her arms encircled his shoulders, and as she gave herself over to him, Todd began to caress her.

Todd slipped his hands under her gown and moved them softly, ever so softly, across her breasts, where they lingered a long moment to fondle her nipples. His fingers moved down her quivering stomach to slender thighs, where they gently parted her legs. They paused there for just a moment, then resumed their work, stroking, caressing, slowly, gently, but most persistently. Then, in one unbroken motion, he pulled her gown over her head. He felt a spinning in his head and a hollowness in his stomach as he examined her beautiful nude body, visible in the ambient glow of the yellow-shaded electric lamp that burned just over the door to her compartment.

Then Marty's hands, as if guided by their own volition, went to Todd's clothes. Todd allowed her to pull at buttons and tug at his belt until, in a few moments, he could feel the air against his own naked skin.

He pushed her down, gently, onto the bed. They came together for one long, probing kiss as they lay against each other, naked and unashamed. Their body heat transferred from one to the other, stoking to a conflagration the flames of desire they were feeling for each other.

Marty felt the muscles of Todd's chest and the iron-hard strength of his thighs. She was extremely cognizant of the eager thrust of his maleness, and then, because she could wait no longer, she raised her legs to pull him into her.

Todd moved with her as their bodies took up the rhythm that would eventually bring them to the desired climax. If either of them harbored any thought of this being wrong, such thoughts were put aside in their quest for each other.

Marty was a creature of flesh and spirit, ignited by a passionate fire. She discovered, to her surprise, that she was possessed of an almost unquenchable erotic thirst. When the first tremor of sensation hit her, it was full and satisfying in its own right, but it was followed almost immediately by an orgasmic fire-burst that licked at her with tongues of flame, igniting and reigniting rapture as wave after wave of pleasure swept over her.

Afterward, they lay together, communicating without words. Todd could hear all the sounds of the ship, the throbbing of the engines, the rattle of chains, and the creaks and groans of load-bearing steel bulkheads under pressure. Already the work parties for disembarkation were preparing the landing boats, and he knew that he would have to return to his own ship.

Todd thought of the morning and what it would bring, and he prayed that Marty would be spared any harm. He wished with all his might that she wouldn't go ashore with the men, and yet he knew that if he tried to prevent her from landing he would be unsuccessful. Any suggestion that she stay behind would do nothing but cause difficulty between them.

Todd reached over to lay his hand on Marty's naked hip.

As he did so, he could feel the sharpness of her hipbone and the soft yielding of her flesh. The contrasting textures were delightful to his touch. He let his hand rest there, enjoying a feeling of possession, until finally, reluctantly, he knew he could stay here no longer.

He sat up.

"You have to go back," she said. It was an observation more than a question.

"Yes," Todd replied. "There are a couple of hours left before everything starts. You should probably go back to sleep."

Marty sat up. "No," she answered. "I want to be in on it from the beginning. If I go to sleep now, I'm afraid I won't wake up in time. It will be easier to try and stay awake."

"I imagine there's coffee in the wardroom," Todd suggested. "That might help you."

"Good idea. And thanks."

"For the coffee? I'm afraid I can't take any credit for that."

"No. I mean thanks for not trying to talk me out of going ashore tomorrow."

Todd wanted to tell her then that he would rather she not go, but he knew it was best to say nothing.

By now Marty was dressing as well, and once, while each of them was reaching for a particular item of clothing, they bumped together. They laughed and kissed.

"I love you, Marty," Todd said.

"I love you, too," Marty replied, putting to voice something that, for some time now, she had known to be true.

"Oh, I almost forgot. Would you marry me?"

"What?"

"I asked—"

"I know what you asked," Marty said. She laughed.

"What is it? Why are you laughing?"

"Well, it's just that all girls dream of the day the right man will ask them to marry them. But, in my wildest dream, I never thought I would be proposed to on board a ship, just prior to the commencement of a war."

"The time and place aren't as important as the substance of the question. Will you marry me?"

"This coming from a man who once told me that unrequited love was the only love for a soldier?" Marty teased.

"I was young and innocent then," Todd said.

Marty smiled at him, then leaned into him, pressing her body against his. "Innocent, were you?" she asked teasingly. "Well, my darling, neither of us is innocent now, are we?"

"No, I . . . I suppose not," Todd said. "Marty, I'm sorry; I didn't think . . . I *couldn't* think. I was so carried away by—"

Marty interrupted him with a laugh. "Darling, do you think either of us were capable of thinking then? Let alone stopping? To answer your question, yes, I'll marry you." She let her finger trace down the side of his cheek. "I suppose I'll have to marry you now, if for no other reason than to make an honest man of you."

CHAPTER 16

Aboard the Command Ship Seguranca

As the sun rose, General Shafter, General Wheeler, and General Lawton stood looking toward the shoreline. The American ships were all anchored as close to the shore as they could get, but there were a couple hundred yards of heavy surf between them and the beach. Beyond the beach, and stretching for twenty miles in each direction, was a limestone bluff that rose 250 feet high. All along this bluff the Spanish had built blockhouses with commanding views of the beach and the approach to it.

"I hope Alvarez was able to draw the Spanish troops away," General Lawton said after he lowered his field glasses. "If General Linares has left enough people in position here, he could throw us back into the sea."

"General Lawton, it seems to me like we are going to have to work with the information Alvarez gave us," General Wheeler replied. "After all, if the Cubans are going to be our allies, then we must be able to depend on them."

"I know," Shafter said. "And he did say that there were only about two hundred Spaniards here. If that's the case, the landing should go easily. But if Linares has managed to sneak his entire army back into position, it will make Custer's little fiasco up in Montana look like a Sunday-afternoon picnic."

"I see smoke," General Lawton said in alarm, pointing ashore.

"And there, too. And there, and there, and over there," a staff officer added.

"Look; the machine shop of the iron company is burning," another pointed out.

"General, I don't like this. It looks as if Linares has done just what you said," Lawton said. "He's sneaked back in during the night, with an entire army."

"Damn!" Shafter said.

"Why would he show himself to us?" Wheeler asked.

"What?"

"If you were Linares and you had four or five thousand men with you, waiting for an army to land, wouldn't you keep your men hidden until the landing army was committed? I mean, think about it. Even if he has his entire army with him, we still outnumber him. Therefore, his two biggest assets would be his defensive position, which is the bluffs, and the element of surprise. Now, he certainly wouldn't have any reason to come down off the bluffs to meet us at the surf, would he?"

Shafter smiled. "No," he said. "Nor would he willingly give away the element of surprise. Good point, General. He's not there."

"Are you sure he's not there?" Lawton asked. "We've come a long way since the Civil War. I don't think the nation is ready to accept casualty figures like we had then."

"Nor do I intend to give them such figures," Shafter said.

"But the smoke? What about the smoke?"

"I can answer that," Wheeler replied. "I used that technique a few times myself, during the war. You Yankees always were a cautious lot. A few campfires spread out made you think I had two or three times more men with me than I really had. They're trying to make it look as if their army is there, with full strength."

"With all due respect, General, this isn't the Confederate army we are dealing with," Lawton said. "What we are looking at might be breakfast fires from an army that is so large and so sure of its defensive position that it doesn't care whether we know they are there are not."

Wheeler chuckled. "They may not be Confederates . . . but you're still a Yankee," he said. "And you're still falling for the same old tricks."

"I think prudence is better than recklessness. As we proved to you during the war," General Lawton said disdainfully.

"Gentlemen, there is no need to argue among ourselves," Shafter interrupted. "General Wheeler, you will be the first ashore. You have no reservations about this?"

"None, General."

"Then we shall proceed as planned. I am in command, and the final decision is mine. We are going ashore." He turned to Admiral Sampson. "Admiral, would you please show signals to the other ships: prepare to land?"

"Aye, General," Admiral Sampson replied.

Approximately five minutes after the signal flags were hoisted, the navy warships began their shore bombardment. All along the shoreline and along the limestone cliffs, explosions erupted from the naval bombardment. The echos of rapid-fire cannons and machine guns rolled back from the cliffs like long drumrolls, while the five-, seven-, and eight-inch guns boomed and thumped like great bass drums. The shells ripped through the trees, smashed the cliffs, uprooted great palms, and tore out large chunks of earth.

No return fire came from the blockhouses or anywhere else on shore. Finally, after at least half an hour of steady bombardment, a Cuban appeared at the end of the iron pier, waving a white cloth to signal that there were no Spaniards present.

On board the *Conqueror,* after the bombardment, the soldiers were gathered on the deck, preparatory to going ashore. When Marty inquired which boat would be hers, she was told that she was not to be in the first wave of boats. She hurried back to the fantail to speak to General Young. Colonel Pickett of the Lightning Cavalry and Colonel Berry of the Sixth Infantry, as well as a couple of naval officers, were with the general. They were looking at a map, orienting it toward features on the shore. General Young was obviously busy, but Marty would not be denied.

"General Young, I've been told that I cannot be in the first wave that goes ashore," Marty said.

General Young looked up from his map. "That is correct, Miss McGuire. I have asked the transportation officer to find a position for you in one of the subsequent waves."

"General, I've asked for no special considerations before, and I don't want any now. I am willing to take the same risks as the men correspondents. I'd like to go ashore as quickly as possible."

"I'm sure you would," General Young replied. "But you aren't the only correspondent affected by the order. General Shafter has issued instructions that no newspeople will be on the first wave. It has nothing to do with your safety. You are a non-combatant, Miss McGuire, and, as I'm sure you can understand, we must be able to bring maximum firepower to bear immediately. That means put as many combatants ashore as quickly as possible."

"Oh," Marty said, a little embarrassed that she had misunderstood the reason for keeping her from the first wave. "Yes, I understand. Of course, I will wait."

General Young smiled. "Good, good," he said. "In the meantime, if you are interested, I can tell you that the Tenth Cavalry will be landing right about there." He pointed to a spot ashore.

"The Tenth Cavalry?"

"You do have a particular interest in the Tenth Cavalry, do you not? To be more specific, in one of its officers? Or is my information wrong?"

There was a long beat of silence, and Marty could feel, or imagined she could feel, the eyes of the others staring at her.

"Your . . . information isn't wrong, General," Marty said hesitantly. "I am curious, though, as to how you came by such knowledge."

"I read the duty officer's log," General Young explained.

"I beg your pardon?"

"The duty officer keeps a log of everything that happens during his tour of duty," General Young explained. "Last night he reported that Lieutenant Murchison, who had come aboard to deliver a report, inquired about directions to your cabin. I surmise that his concern for your whereabouts was more than a passing interest."

Marty wondered just how detailed the duty officer's log was. Did it record that Todd had actually visited her cabin? Did it say how long he stayed? She felt her cheeks flaming.

She cleared her throat and nervously ran her hand through her hair. "It is more than a passing interest," she admitted.

"Ah, I thought as much," Young said with a little chuckle. Marty was pleased to note that there was absolutely no condemnation in his voice. "You've made a good choice, Miss McGuire. Lt. Todd Murchison is a fine young man. He comes from good stock. General Murchison is a close friend of mine and, I believe, one of the finest officers this country has ever produced."

Although Marty didn't like her relationship with Todd being spoken of in the same vein as one would speak of breeding horses, she said only, "Thank you, sir."

On board the *Gaffey* at that precise moment, the subject of Marty and General Young's conversation was supervising the debarkation of his men. Those men who would be in the first wave were climbing down the nets to load themselves and their guns into the small boats that bobbed on the water below.

Todd was going ashore with the first wave and would be the only officer to do so. He waited at the railing, watching the others as they climbed down the cargo netting and into the bobbing boats below.

"Remember, men, grab only the upright strands!" Todd shouted at the others. "If you grab the cross strand, the man above you can step on your hands."

First Sergeant Dakota was also going in with the first wave, but he had not yet climbed down into one of the boats. Like Todd, he was supervising the loading. Corporal Cobb came up to him. Cobb had been assigned as non-commissioned officer in charge of the rear party. That meant he would be one of the last to leave the ship.

"I can't believe you makin' me stay behind, Top," Cobb complained bitterly. "Me 'n' you been together for more'n twenty years now. How can you do this to me?"

"It ain't like you not comin' ashore," Dakota said soothingly. He put his hand on Cobb's shoulder. "It's just I need someone I can count on to keep things together till everyone has landed, that's all."

"And you can't find anyone else? What about all the sergeants we got? Why can't you use one of them? I ain't nothin' but a corporal."

"You may be only a corporal," Dakota said. "But you are the most dependable NCO I've got."

"That's true," Cobb agreed. "Which is why I should be with you when the shootin' starts."

"You will be," Dakota promised. "But they ain't goin' be no shootin' today. You ask me, they ain't no Spanish within twenty miles. That's why we landin' here. By the time we run into the Spaniards, you'll be there."

Cobb sighed. "All right, Top. You want me to stay behind, I'll do it." He pointed to Dakota. "But you owe me for this, an' I'm goin' to find a way to collect." He smiled. "I know what it'll be. You tell Doney she goin' have to fry two chickens, just for me."

"You got yourself a deal," Dakota said.

"Last group, over the side, into the boats!" Todd called, and the last group of men who would be going in with the first wave climbed over.

Todd scrambled down the netting quickly, then waited at the bottom of the net as the ship rolled. Had he let go of the net at that precise moment, he would have had a drop of more than ten feet. After the ship rolled back, however, it was a simple step from the net into the boat.

Just before the boats put away, a fast destroyer sailed between the ships and the shoreline, generating a large cloud of smoke. Then, concealed by the smoke, the boats started ashore.

The boats were longboats. Once the boats rowed away from the ships, they formed into lines where they were towed ashore by steam launches. The idea was for the steam launches to get the boats close to shore, at which time the men would cut themselves loose and paddle through the surf to the beach itself. There they would unload quickly, except for two of the men. The two men would stay in the boats to row back to the launch. The launch would then tow the boats back to the ships to prepare for the next wave to land.

Under the cover of smoke, the boats and launches began to scurry toward the shore. The steam launches rolled and pitched, tugging at the weight behind them. Soon the 500 men of the first convoy were bunched together, racing bow by bow for the shore.

One launch towing a barge turned suddenly and steered for a long pier under the ore docks. When a heavy incoming wave lifted the barge to the level of the pier, six of the men leaped through the air, landing on the pier head, waving their rifles above them. At the same moment, two of the other boats were driven through the surf to the beach itself and the men tumbled out and scrambled to their feet. These were the first to set foot on Cuba itself.

General Shafter had been warned about the heavy surf, but he had overlooked the warning, choosing this location because of the lack of armed resistance. Had he realized how difficult and dangerous landing through the heavy surf would be, he might have had second thoughts. Several boats were tossed into the piers or rocks or slammed ashore with enough force to destroy them. But it wasn't until late afternoon, when the final wave of the first day was coming ashore, that tragedy struck.

Most of the Tenth had already taken up positions on the beach, where they were setting up their Gatling guns, digging hasty rifle pits, and keeping a wary eye on the cliffs. No one really believed that there were any Spanish there, but Colonel Baldwin was operating on the assumption that it was better to be prepared, just in case.

"Lieutenant Murchison, as soon as all our men are ashore, Colonel Baldwin wants us to form up and move off the beach," Captain Bigelow said. "Anyone still on the ship?"

"The last of our supplies are on the way in now," Todd answered, pointing toward a barge being pulled in by a steam launch. "Corporal Cobb and Private English are bringing it in."

Bigelow chuckled. "Cobb wound up with the rear party?

Knowing him, I'll bet he liked that. Well, let me know as soon as everyone has landed.''

"Yes, sir."

Todd started down to the beach where Dakota was standing with hands on his hips, watching the launch and barge as it came toward the shore.

"They're nearly here," Dakota said.

Cobb, seeing Dakota watching him, waved, his face split by a big grin. "That's two chickens, Top!" he shouted, holding up two fingers. "And don't you forget it!"

Dakota laughed, and nodded his head. "Two chickens!" he called back.

The launch made a large sweeping turn as it approached the pier, causing the lighter to swing around behind it. As the barge headed toward the pier, Cobb and English moved forward to stand at the bow.

"What they doin', movin' up there like that?" Dakota asked.

"Maybe they are going to secure the barge to the pier," Todd suggested.

Dakota shook his head. "No, sir, Cobb ain' got nothin' like that in mind. That crazy bastard plannin' on jumpin' and English goin' jump with him."

Dakota started running toward the pier. "Cobb! Cobb, don't do it!" he shouted, waving his arms. But even Dakota's command voice sounded thin above the crashing surf.

Todd saw Cobb and English getting ready to make the jump. In order to do so, however, they would have to time their leap just right, for the lighter was rising and falling as much as ten feet with each wave.

The lighter lifted high on an incoming wave so that it was equal in height to the pier. The two men timed the rise and fall perfectly. But they had not anticipated the wake of the steam launch. When it hit, it caused the barge to roll hard back to port. As a result, the space that had been no more than a step from the barge to the dock became a chasm of twenty feet. It would have been a prodigious jump even if they had been ready for it. They were not, and both men slammed into the side of the pier, then fell into the water. At almost the same time the barge rolled back, smashing them between its several tons of weight and the pilings of the pier.

The closest person to them at that moment was Capt. Bucky O'Niel. O'Niel, who in civilian life had been the mayor of Flagstaff, Arizona, and now was the commander of one of the companies of the Rough Riders. Without so much as a second thought, O'Niel leaped, fully clothed, into the water in an attempt to rescue the two Buffalo Soldiers.

Dakota had a head start on Todd, but Todd, being younger, was able to catch up with him before he reached the pier. As a result they reached the pier at about the same time. O'Niel surfaced from his dive just as Todd and Dakota arrived, took a breath, and went under again. Todd jumped in with him.

It was murky underwater, but Todd could see O'Niel tugging one of the men from beneath the pier. When O'Niel saw Todd, he pointed back beneath the pier, and Todd saw the other one. Both were still.

Todd swam underwater to the other form, then reached for him. When Todd turned the man around he saw that it was Cobb. Cobb's eyes and mouth were open. Todd pulled him out from under the pier, then swam-hauled him up to the surface.

O'Niel was already on the surface with English. By now, several hands had come down to help him get English ashore, while others reached down to relieve Todd of his burden. Todd looked over at O'Niel, and O'Niel shook his head.

"Sorry, Todd," O'Niel said. "I know they were your men."

"Thanks for trying," Todd replied.

Sadly, Todd climbed out of the water, now assisted by Dakota and Pershing.

"Both of them?" Pershing asked.

Todd nodded.

"The dumb shits," Dakota said. When Todd looked at Dakota, he saw that the first sergeant's eyes were red-rimmed and filled with tears. "The dumb shits. Why'd they do a dumb thing like that?" Dakota asked, his voice on the edge of breaking.

Todd put his hand on Dakota's shoulder. "I'm sorry,

Top," he said. Top came from *Top Sergeant* or *Top Soldier*. It was not an official title but was one of respect, used by the men, though seldom by the officers. On this occasion, however, the name came easily from Todd's lips.

When Marty and the other correspondents reached the shore half an hour later, she learned about the two Buffalo Soldiers who had been killed.

"They were the only two casualties from the entire landing. Given the conditions of the surf and the number of men involved, I think we can consider ourselves very lucky," General Young said.

"Yes, and if we had to lose two, it was good that it was a couple of niggers rather than whites," one of the correspondents replied.

Marty glared at the reporter.

"What's wrong with you?" the reporter asked when he saw how Marty was looking at him.

"You," Marty said. "You are what's wrong with me."

"Me?" The reporter looked confused. "What are you angry with me for? What have I done to you?"

"I didn't care for the remark you just passed."

"What? About the niggers that got killed? Would you rather it have been a couple of white soldiers?"

"Jake, why don't you just shut up before you make a bigger ass of yourself than you already have?" Phil Block suggested.

"I don't know what's got into everyone," Jake replied. "I just said aloud what everyone is thinking, that's all."

"The real tragedy is that you don't even know any better," Marty said.

"Look, it's not like I wanted the niggers killed," Jake said. "I'm sorry they were killed. All I'm saying is . . . if it had to happen, then better that it happen to them."

Jake was greeted with silence.

"Well, isn't it?"

Shaking her head sadly, Marty left the group of correspondents, then walked down the beach until she found the

Tenth Cavalry. Seeing her as she approached, Todd came over to her.

"Did you hear?" he asked.

"Yes. It's awful."

"They were good men, both of them," Todd said. He nodded toward Dakota, who was, at the moment, berating a soldier for letting his rifle get full of sand. "First Sergeant Dakota is taking it pretty hard. Cobb was his best friend."

"I wish there was something I could do or say," Marty said.

"Yes. We all feel like that. But Dakota is a veteran. He's lost friends before. That's part of being a soldier."

"Lieutenant, horses are comin' in!" someone called.

"You're getting your horses?" Marty asked. "I thought all the cavalry units had to leave their horses behind."

"We did leave them behind," Todd said. "These are just the horses we'll use to pull wagons and caissons, plus a few for courier duty. Same as everyone else."

The Tenth wasn't the only unit getting horses then. The horses, which were the last things to be brought ashore, were being brought in for all the units. It was proving, however, to be the most difficult part of the entire landing.

The horses were loaded onto large lighters, then pulled close to the shore by steam launches. When they were as close in as they could get, they were shoved, reluctantly, into the sea. There they were caught by men in small boats, then led by their halter shanks to the breakers, where they were turned loose to be washed ashore.

Marty felt sorry for the poor animals, who had no idea why they were being subjected to such treatment. After the horses swam ashore, they were taken to a picket line, where they stood quietly, a picture of dejection and weariness.

"Colonel Baldwin, look at that group!" one of the men shouted. "They're swimming the wrong way! They're going out to sea!"

Marty looked toward the group of horses the man had indicated and saw that at least a dozen of them had become disoriented by the breakers and were, indeed, swimming out to sea. She knew it wouldn't take long for them to tire and drown.

"Oh, Todd! The poor horses!"

Sergeant Major Baker saw them too. "Bugler!" he shouted. "Sound 'To the Post'!"

The bugler ran down to the edge of the water and played the bugle call that civilians hear when horses are called to the post in a horse race, but which also is called when cavalry troops assemble into their proper formations. The horses, well trained to respond to all the bugle calls, wheeled around, as if in formation, and began swimming to shore. Marty squealed and clapped her hands in delight. At the same time, all the men gave a hearty cheer.

"Good job, Sergeant Major! Good job!" Colonel Baldwin called. "You saved the horses."

"Yes, sir," Baker said. "I just wish I could've saved Cobb and English."

By the end of the first day, 6,000 American soldiers had come ashore without a single Spanish shot being fired. Standing on the beach, cranking away on his motion-picture camera, William Paley of Vitagraph and the Edison Manufacturing Company was filming the landing. Within a matter of weeks, through the magic of moving pictures, people all over America would thrill to the sight of "actually being there when the landing took place."

Once, as she came close to the camera, Marty saw that Paley was taking pictures. She stopped.

"No, no, go ahead; walk across in front of the camera!" Paley called, waving her across with his free hand. "This must look as natural as possible."

One of the other reporters laughed. "How natural is it to see a woman on the beach during a military invasion?" he asked.

"By now, millions of American know Miss McGuire by name," Paley replied as he continued to crank the handle. "Perhaps it is time a few of them saw how beautiful a lady she is."

Despite Paley's admonition to "be natural," Marty felt

very self-conscious as she passed in front of the camera, knowing that her moving image would soon be on display all across the country.

Soon after the Tenth Cavalry was assembled, they were ordered to move off the beach. Just beyond the beach, Todd's men found 8,000 rounds of rifle ammunition, plus well-constructed rifle pits and blockhouses running in all directions. They also found an uncompleted letter on a desk in the house of the commandant.

"I'd give a dollar to know what this says," Colonel Baldwin said, holding the letter.

"I can read it for you," Marty told him. "And I won't charge you anything."

Baldwin handed the letter to her, and she looked through it quickly.

"It's a letter from Colonel Diaz to General Linares," she said. "In it, Colonel Diaz is begging to be granted permission to stay here and resist a possible landing. He says that with 3,000 men he could resist any attack at Daiquiri that might be made by sea."

"He's right," Todd said. "He could have. General Linares was a fool to pull him out. Now we have a foothold."

"Colonel, the American flag has just been run up on top of the blockhouse," a soldier said, sticking his head in through the door of the commandant's house. "It was raised by Colonel Roosevelt and the Rough Riders."

Baldwin looked over at Todd and smiled. "Your friend Teddy is trying to get in his bit of glory, I see," he noted.

"Yes, sir," Todd said. "But I imagine the men appreciated seeing it."

"That's true," Baldwin admitted. "I'm just upset I didn't think of it first."

CHAPTER 17

After the successful landing, General Wheeler, who was the highest-ranking general ashore, ordered the expeditionary force to move three miles up the beach to Siboney. They made quite a parade, moving up the beach, mostly afoot, even those who were supposed to be cavalrymen.

Marty found that she was able to keep up with the soldiers quite easily. On two or three occasions firing broke out, and the line of marching soldiers would dash off the beach and look anxiously toward the trees. In every case, though, it turned out to be a false alarm, the firing initiated by a nervous soldier who "thought he saw something." Finally, they reached Siboney, where, still on the beach, they bivouacked for the night.

Marty knew that the majority of newspaper writers who were part of the morning's operation would be writing stories about the landing. She had planned to as well, but the loss of the two Buffalo Soldiers dimmed the luster of the landing for her. Especially as they were men from Todd's command. So, for her first dispatch, which she wrote the next day, she chose to write about Siboney:

Siboney, once a quiet hamlet of no more than a thousand people, has been transformed into a bustling metropolis. General Shafter will be transferring the unloading of the remaining men and supplies here, and here, too, he will set up the headquarters for the ordnance, quartermaster, commissary, and Medical Corps.

By American standards, Siboney is not much of a town. It is a cluster of a few squalid houses, which sit near the beach. The most imposing structures in the entire village are the sawmill and storehouse. The former has been taken over by the engineers, the latter by the commissary. Just west of these buildings flows a sluggish creek, emptying into a stagnant pond. All around this creek are slimy swamps, ideal places for the vapors that seem to cause malaria and yellow fever.

Last night was our first night ashore. No one slept during the night because troops were still being unloaded into the surf until two o'clock this morning. The darkness was no problem, though, as two naval warships were anchored nearby and they played their giant searchlights upon the shore, lighting the area as brightly as the ballroom of a Fifth Avenue hotel.

Behind the ships, the ocean gleamed bright silver from the full moon, while ashore there were hundreds of glowing campfires. The exhausted and half-drowned soldiers congregated around these, drying their uniforms and hoping the smoke would drive away the mosquitoes. (The uniforms dried, but the mosquitoes remained.)

Hundreds of men stood in the surf, helping their comrades ashore. As there was no Spanish resistance, the landing took on, somewhat, the aspects of a great game. The pontoons and other boats charged in through the surf, then were picked up by the breakers and hurled ashore like sleds whipping down a water chute.

It was a most remarkable sight, this landing of a great army on an enemy coast in the dead of night. It was a great feat, perhaps unequaled in the annals of war, to land such a large expeditionary force so quickly. What made it even more unusual was the fact that the landing started early yesterday morning, under the protective bombast of cannon shot and shell, and ended at two o'clock this morning, amid the cheers and shrieks of laughter such as one might hear from the surf bathers at Coney Island.

This morning the smell of coffee, bacon, and beans permeates the air as the men cook their breakfast. For many, it is the first meal in more than twenty-four hours, yesterday being such a busy time that most didn't eat, either for lack of opportunity or because the excitement was so great that it suspended appetite.

The Spanish army is here, as we well know. Why they have, thus far, refused to engage us we do not know. General Wheeler and the other senior officers have stated how fortunate we are that the Spanish didn't resist the landing. But every soldier on the beach realizes that General Linares has something planned for us. We just don't know what.

Col. Carlos Diaz stood in the tree line just behind Siboney and looked down on the massive American army. For two days they had been landing men and equipment ashore, doing it as easily as if they were arriving routinely at a train depot.

Diaz spat angrily. If General Linares had not been such an old woman, he wouldn't have withdrawn all the troops. Diaz could have given him half of his men and still prevented the landing. He knew this area like the back of his hand. He knew where to direct the artillery fire and where to put his riflemen so that the Americans would have been forced to call off their landing. Now they were ashore, and they were in strength far beyond the small demonstration General Linares had expected.

Diaz left his vantage point and walked down toward the Americans. It was easy to do; he hadn't shaved in four days, and he was wearing a peasant's shirt and trousers. He looked like one of the many Cuban refugees who were in the area. He picked his way through the muddy street of the town and walked down onto the beach, right in the middle of the soldiers who were gathered around the several campfires, cooking their breakfast.

"Hey, you!" one of the soldiers suddenly shouted out to him, and Colonel Diaz froze. Had he been recognized? If so, he could be shot, for he was clearly out of uniform and clearly engaged on a spy mission. "You, Pancho!"

"How do you know his name is Pancho?" one of the other soldiers asked.

"All Cubans are called Pancho, didn't you know that? Or is it all Mexicans?" The soldier laughed.

Diaz breathed a little easier. It was obvious the soldier hadn't recognized him. But then he was only an American enlisted man, and how could an enlisted man know the commander of the Spanish troops in this sector?

"You speak our lingo, Pancho?"

"Si, a leetle," Diaz said, making the accent more pronounced than he normally would.

"Listen, you seen any Spaniards around this place? I come here to fight, not slap mosquitoes on the beach."

"I have seen no Spanish troops, senor. I think they have all left."

"Yeah? Well, I wouldn't doubt it. You know who we are? We're the Fifth Volunteers from New York, the Lightning Cavalry. Some folks call us Fighting Lighting. And we're here to kick the Spaniards in the ass and send 'em back to Spain where they belong."

"You are cavalry, senor?" Diaz asked. He looked around. "But where are your horses?"

"Yeah, well we're supposed to be cavalry, but the generals in charge didn't let us bring our horses. That doesn't matter, though. We can lick the Spaniards whether we got horses or not. We're here to free your people, Pancho. You'd like that, wouldn't you? You want to be free?"

"Si, senor," Diaz answered.

"Hey, Pancho, you hungry? You want some bacon and beans?"

"No, senor," Diaz answered. He saw the coffee. "I would drink some coffee."

"Sure. Here, have a cup. I reckon we're on the same side."

Diaz held a cup out while the coffee was poured; then he looked up and down the beach at the equipment that was still being brought ashore. He saw a couple of Hotchkiss guns.

These guns fired two-inch explosive shells at a very rapid rate, making them exceptionally effective. Such firepower, Diaz knew, could have a tremendously demoralizing effect on his men. They were going to be demoralized enough when they realized they were outnumbered nearly three to one. Of course, that ratio would have meant nothing had he been able to resist the landing in the first place. Now that the Americans had landed, though, the numbers were significant.

Diaz finished his coffee, then thanked the soldiers and continued down the beach. He didn't notice that Eddie Stone was busy making a sketch of him.

As Marty continued her sight-seeing stroll, she came upon the Lightning Cavalry.

"Hey! Hey, Miss McGuire! You want to eat breakfast with us?" one of the soldiers called to her.

Marty smiled at the invitation, then recognized Eddie Stone, the young man who was such an accomplished artist. She walked over to them.

"I wouldn't want to take anyone's breakfast," she said.

"Heck, we got lots of food," the soldier who had invited her said. "Why don't you sit on that log there and join us?"

The soldiers quickly found a clean pan and spoon, and they put a generous portion of bacon and beans into the pan, then handed it to her.

"You want a pepper, Miss McGuire? It makes the beans better."

"No, thank you; this'll do just fine," Marty said. It was ironic. She had just written an article about how this was the first meal for many in two days, and now she realized she was in the same situation. She hadn't eaten the day before, either.

The soldiers were all telling her stories of the landing, how their boat turned over and they thought they were going to drown, how one of them lost his rifle and was afraid his sergeant was going to discover it, how they never knew a place could have so many mosquitoes. Then Marty saw Eddie's sketch pad.

"Have you been making a lot of drawings?" she asked.

"No, ma'am," Eddie said shyly. "This is the first one I've made since the landing." He handed the pad over.

Marty studied the drawing. It was of a Cuban peasant, like the many Cuban peasants who had been wandering around the landing site. And yet there was something about this man . . . a fierce sense of pride, almost of defiance, that leaped from his face. It was in the set of his mouth and the gleam in his eyes. There was almost an aristocratic demeanor to the man, even though he was just a peasant. Marty thought it would make a great illustration for her first article.

"Eddie, may I have this drawing to print in the paper?" she asked. "I'll see to it that you are paid and given credit for your work."

"Yes, ma'am," Eddie said, beaming proudly. "Only you don't need to pay me nothin'."

"Don't be silly. Of course you must be paid. Don't you realize this would be a good career for you once the war is finished?"

"Let her print the picture, Eddie," one of the other men said. "Or would you rather drive a beer wagon all your life?"

"All right," Eddie said.

"Thanks," Marty replied. She took the drawing; then, after breakfast, she told the men good-bye and wandered around the area looking at everything, taking it all in for future stories.

She spoke in Spanish to a group of Cuban children, then laughed when they shyly broke into a run. Finally, she found herself at the place where General Wheeler had established his headquarters. Col. Juan Alvarez was there.

"Ah, the beautiful lady with the golden tongue," Juan said, greeting her in Spanish. "Tell me, beautiful lady, why do the Americans let someone as lovely as you come to a war? Don't they realize a war is dangerous for a beautiful woman?"

"Just for beautiful women?" Marty replied. "And here I thought wars were dangerous for everyone."

Juan laughed. "So they are, senorita; so they are. And anyway, who am I to complain? If the Americans have let you come, then it only means I am privileged to enjoy your great beauty.''

"You tell me my tongue is golden, but yours is silver with flattery,'' Marty said.

"When one speaks the truth, one is not engaging in idle flattery,'' Juan replied.

Marty put Eddie's sketch on the table, then walked over to get a drink of water from the Lister bag that hung on a tripod. The Lister bag was a canvas bag filled with water. As water slowly seeped through to the outside, it evaporated, and the evaporation made the water inside the bag pleasantly cool, even though the bag might hang in the hottest sun.

Behind her, Col. Juan Alvarez continued to discuss with General Wheeler, Colonel Wood, Colonel Pickett, and Captain Bigelow the best approach to Santiago. During the discussion, Juan happened to glance over at the drawing; then he gasped.

"Dios Mío!'' he blurted aloud.

His exclamation of surprise didn't mean anything to Wheeler and the other officers, but it did alert Marty, and she turned back toward him.

"*Que?*'' she asked.

"Senorita, where did you get this picture?''

Marty saw that he was holding Eddie's drawing.

"One of the soldiers drew it,'' Marty answered. "Why?''

"This is a picture of Colonel Diaz.''

"That's Colonel Diaz?'' Colonel Wood asked, reaching for the drawing.

"Si. He is the *commandante* of all Spanish troops in this area, under General Linares,'' Juan said.

"You say one of our soldiers drew it, Miss McGuire?'' General Wheeler asked.

"Yes, a private in the Lightning Cavalry. His name is Eddie Stone.'' Marty pointed to Eddie's signature at the bottom right-hand corner of the drawing. "He and his friends said it was a refugee who came down to the beach and had coffee with them.''

"This is no refugee,'' Juan said. "Diaz is here on a spying mission. He is walking on the beach right before our very eyes, seeing everything we have. General, he must have his men very close by. He is going to either attack you on the beach or ambush you when you start your march to Santiago.''

"Lieutenant!" General Wheeler called to a nearby officer. "Get ten men, have them study this drawing, then send them out to look at every Cuban on the beach. If they find him, bring him here at once."

"Yes, sir," the lieutenant answered, taking the drawing with him.

"You won't find him," Juan said. "He's much too clever for that."

"How clever can he be?" Wheeler asked. "He let someone make a drawing of him."

"You'll find out how clever, Colonel, when you start your march to Santiago," Juan said ominously.

They didn't find Colonel Diaz among the Cuban refugees. Diaz had either finished his leisurely exploration of the American soldiers and equipment or realized he was being looked for and simply disappeared. At any rate, the searchers came back empty-handed.

Meanwhile, Marty continued to walk up and down the beach, wandering from one unit to another. She visited the Sixth Infantry, the Ohio Militia, the Alabama Blues, then the Rough Riders.

As she had covered the Rough Riders during their period of encampment in Texas, many of the soldiers recognized her and greeted her warmly.

"Miss McGuire!" one of the soldiers called to her. "Is it true that the commander of all the Spaniards was walkin' around among us?"

"Not of all the Spaniards," Marty answered. "But he is believed to be the commander of the Spaniards who are in this area."

"What Spaniards in this area?" one of the other soldiers asked derisively. "We been here now goin' into the second day, and we ain't seen hide nor hair of a Spaniard."

"No Spaniard better let me see him, or he won't have hide nor hair left," another said bombastically.

Marty chuckled, then moved on. She watched as the men prepared themselves for the battle they were sure was to come. They cleaned their weapons, checked their ammunition, and filled their canteens. Seeing her, one of the men came over with a small packet of pictures, letters, and a locket.

"Miss McGuire, my name is Private Morrison. I'm from Utica, New York, and I wonder if you would hold these for me? If anything should happen to me, I would like you to send them home for me."

Marty wasn't sure what to do. She didn't want to turn the man down in what might seem a callous rejection, but she knew if she accepted such things from him, others would be making the same request of her. She obviously couldn't become a clearinghouse for mementos.

"You know, Private Morrison, I will be going along with you," she finally said. "So leaving those items with me is no guarantee of their safety. On the other hand, I'm sure you'll come through this all right. Besides, wouldn't it comfort you to have the picture with you during battle?"

"Yes, ma'am. Yes, ma'am, you're probably right," Morrison said, surprised to hear that she would be facing the same dangers and a little embarrassed that he had shown fear, even in this way. "It's going to take more than a handful of Spaniards to get me," he added.

When Marty passed back through the Lightning Cavalry area, Colonel Pickett called out to her, "Miss McGuire, I wonder if you would do a little interpreting for me?"

"Certainly, Colonel."

"We've got these Cuban peasants gathered in a group over here. They're confused and angry, and most of them are frightened. I've tried to tell them what's going on, but I can't make them understand."

Marty chuckled. "I can translate for you, Colonel," she said. "But that's no guarantee they'll understand what's happening to them."

"At least they'll have an idea," Pickett said.

Marty followed the Lightning Cavalry commander over to the lumber shed where the refugees, nearly a hundred, had been gathered.

"Good afternoon," she said to them. "How are you getting along?"

"Are you Cuban?" one of the refugees asked, surprised to hear her speaking not only Spanish but Spanish with a Cuban accent.

"I am American."

The Cuban who questioned her looked at her in surprise. "You are an American soldier? The Americans have women in their army?"

Marty chuckled. "I am a newspaper correspondent," she explained. "But because I understand the language, I was asked by the American officers to come over and speak to you."

"Are the Americans going to shoot us?"

"Do they think we are Spanish?"

"Why are we here?"

"You have been brought here for your own protection," Marty said. "The American commander expects a battle will be fought soon, and he doesn't want any of you hurt."

"Since when do the soldiers care whether the peasants are hurt?" someone asked in an angry shout.

"These men aren't Spanish soldiers," Marty said. "They are American soldiers, and they have come here to help throw the Spanish out. After this war, Cuba will be a free country. You won't have to worry about the Spanish soldiers anymore."

"We won't worry about the Spanish soldiers, but we must worry about the American soldiers."

"No, not the American soldiers," Marty said.

"The guns pointed at us are American guns," the protester said. "The men holding the guns are American soldiers."

"I told you, they are merely trying to keep you from being harmed."

"I think they are trying to keep us from going to the Spanish."

Marty was quiet for a moment; then she decided that truth was better than fiction.

"That is also one of the reasons," she admitted. "They know there are some Spanish spies among you. One was seen earlier today. There is a good chance that there are more . . . that one of you may be a Spanish spy. If that is so, they don't want to give you the opportunity to warn the Spanish soldiers that we are coming."

"But we are not spies," someone said. "You can let us go."

"Wait," one of the others said, addressing his own people. "She is right. How do we know that there are none among us who would spy? I want the Spaniards out of Cuba, and if this is what it takes, then I will cooperate with the Americans. And I think we all should."

There were a few nods and grunts of agreement; then the man turned to Marty. "All right, we will stay here until you have moved on. Then, we want to be freed."

Marty turned to Colonel Pickett. "They won't give you any trouble. But they want to be freed after you have left the beach. May I tell them that they will be?"

"Yes, of course," Colonel Pickett agreed.

Marty relayed Colonel Pickett's assurances; then the Cuban who had done most of the speaking shouted out: "*Viva Cuba Libre! Viva los Americanos*!"

The others joined in his shout, then cheered and applauded the Americans. The guards smiled in embarrassment.

"Thanks," Colonel Pickett said as he and Marty walked away from the makeshift prison. "You kept the situation from getting difficult."

CHAPTER 18

Just before nightfall, Captain Bigelow ordered Todd to take two men with him to conduct a thorough scout of the area. Todd asked Dakota to get two volunteers for him.

"You only need one, Lieutenant," Dakota replied.

"I need two men."

"Yes, sir, you need two men, but you only need one volunteer, since I done volunteered."

Todd shook his head. "First Sergeant, this isn't a job for you. Get me a couple of young privates."

"Lieutenant, you tryin' to tell me I ain't as good as a private?"

"No, nothing like that. It's just that, well, you're the first sergeant. It wouldn't be smart for you to put yourself at unnecessary risk."

"You planning on takin' any risk that's unnecessary, Lieutenant?"

Todd started to protest again; then, with a smile and a sigh, he surrendered. "All right, First Sergeant, I give up. If you want to go, you can go."

"Thank you, sir. Bates!" Dakota called.

"Yes, First Sergeant?" Bates replied, hurrying over.

"You just volunteered to go with the lieutenant and me, didn't you?"

"Yes, Top."

"We're ready, Lieutenant," Dakota said.

Todd took his two volunteers back to Captain Bigelow for final instructions.

"This is what I want you to find out for me," Bigelow told them. "Where are the Spanish, and how many of them are there? Also, what type of guns do they have? Artillery? Gatlings?"

"Yes, sir," Todd said. "Captain, if we were mounted, we could cover more area faster."

Bigelow stroked his chin for a moment as he contemplated Todd's request. The horses were strictly rationed, and commanders were told to be very careful about risking them.

"All right, draw three mounts. I'll square it with Colonel Baldwin."

"Yes, sir," Todd said.

Five minutes later Todd, Dakota, and Bates, envied by nearly every other man in the bivouac, rode out of the encampment to begin their patrol.

Though not all the expeditionary force was ashore, more than half of it was. The remaining men would be put ashore at Siboney, where the surf was less severe. General Shafter had agreed to this because they had not yet encountered any Spanish soldiers, even though signs of their presence were all around. However, nearly everyone believed they had pushed their luck about as far as they could. They were sure that a Spanish attack was imminent. As a result, many of the men were very jumpy.

Several times during the night the American sentries, hearing a rustling nearby, would fire into the darkness, only to discover that they were being attacked by land crabs. That would startle other sentries, who would also fire, so that throughout the night there was an almost steady but disconnected rattle of musketry, as if battle were about to break out at any minute. In addition to the crabs, the men had to contend with a ceaseless rain and swarms of biting mosquitoes.

Just a few miles away, scouting along the road to Santiago, Todd, Dakota, and Bates could hear the shooting going on back in Siboney. At first they thought their comrades might be under attack, and they nearly turned back to join in the fight. But the sporadic nature of the firing soon let them know that it was either no more than a probing of the American positions by Spanish scouts . . . or nervous shooting. In neither case would the three have to return.

They rode on through the rain and the steady swarm of mosquitoes until Bates suddenly hissed a warning.

"Lieutenant, I just seen somethin' ahead."

"Dismount," Todd ordered, and the three men dismounted.

"First Sergeant, you hold the horses. Bates, come with me."

Dakota took the reins as Todd and Bates moved ahead on foot. The mud was deep and walking was difficult. Not only was it hard to pull their feet out of the sucking ooze, but the mud also began to ball up on their feet, making it feel as if they had heavy weights attached to their boots. In addition, the rain made visibility even more difficult, and it tended to deaden all sound. Because of that, Todd and Bates nearly blundered right into the Spanish camp.

Todd saw the Spaniards first, and he stuck his hand out to hold Bates back. Looking at Bates, he held his finger over his lips in a "shushing" fashion, then with a waving, pointing motion signaled that Bates should go one way and he would go the other. The idea was to probe along the wood line for as far as there were Spanish troops in order to get an estimate as to how many were there.

So effective a mask was the rain that Todd and Bates were able to examine the entire Spanish camp without ever once putting themselves into danger. That wasn't the case when they returned to their own lines, though. As they approached the beach at Siboney, they were suddenly taken under fire by nervous American sentries. Sergeant Dakota's horse was hit, and it went down with a thud as Dakota leaped clear.

"Dismount!" Todd shouted, and he and Bates slid quickly down from their saddles. The horses, trained to stand under fire, stayed where they were until Todd and Bates were able to get them down on their sides, reducing their exposure.

"Top! You all right?" Todd called anxiously.

"Yes, sir," Dakota replied. "That's the third horse I done had shot from under me, but the first time it was ever done by my own men."

"Hey!" Bates shouted, raising up a bit. "What you fellas shootin' at?"

More shots rang out and Todd could hear the bullets whizzing by them in the darkness.

"Don't call to them anymore, Bates," Todd said. "Because of the rain, they can't hear well enough to understand you. They'll just shoot more, thinking we are Spaniards shouting insults at them."

"I am insulting the dumb bastards!" Bates swore. "Do I *look* like a Spaniard?"

Dakota chuckled. "What do you mean, do you look like a Spaniard? Hell, if they could see us well enough to see what we look like, they wouldn't be shootin'."

"Well, what are we goin' to do? Just stay out here all night?" Bates asked.

"We might have to," Todd replied. "Tomorrow, in the light of day, we can more easily identify ourselves."

"Well, now, ain't this fun?" Bates growled.

The three men lay in the rain for another half hour. The horses grew restless and became more difficult to hold down.

"Lieutenant, I don't know how much longer I can keep this horse down," Bates said.

"Let him go," Todd told him.

"Beg pardon, sir?"

"I don't know why I didn't think of this before. Let him go. We'll let both of them go. If the horses get through, maybe our guys will recognize them."

Todd and Bates let go of the reins, and the horses got up, then galloped toward the American lines. As before, nervous sentries opened fire, but the horses managed to get through, unharmed.

Half an hour later, Todd saw someone crawling toward them from the American lines. It took only a moment longer before he saw that the man coming after them was Lt. John J. Pershing.

"What are you coming out here for, John?" Todd called. "You planning to shoot us, or bring us in?"

"Damn!" Pershing said. "I thought it might be you. Are any of you hurt?"

"Just our feelings," Todd replied. "It really hurts not to be wanted by your own people."

Pershing laughed, then rolled over and shot his pistol into the air in three measured shots.

"Come on," Pershing said, standing. "Let's go in."

"You sure we're welcome now?" Todd teased.

"I don't know," Pershing joked. "I guess it depends on how popular I am."

"Oh, Lord," Bates teased. "Now we are in trouble."

Ten minutes later, after Bigelow apologized to the men for the nervous perimeter guards' shooting at them, Todd gave his report.

"They're out there, Captain," Todd said. "The nearest place I can identify on the map to where they are is Las Guasimas."

"How many men?"

"Well, that's the crazy part of it," Todd answered. "Bates and I took a count, and we didn't come up with any more than five hundred. With no more than fifteen hundred, they could keep us trapped down here on the beach for as long as they wanted to."

"They're well fortified?"

"Yes, sir, that they are," Todd said. "They have trenches dug in at the crest of a pretty high ridge. Also, the approaches are thick and overgrown, and I didn't see any way to go around them. If we intend to get to Santiago, we're going to have to go right through them."

"I don't understand the Spaniards, Cap'n," Dakota commented. "They supposed to have this large army. They coulda denied us the beach, but they didn't. And now they could keep us trapped here on the beach if they would just put a few more men there in Las Guasimas, but they don't. Why?"

"According to Colonel Alvarez, the Spanish figure to make a big fight of it at Santiago," Bigelow said.

"Yes, sir, well, I guess that's what they have in mind, all right," Dakota replied. "I know I'm just a first sergeant without all the schoolin' you need for tactics and strategy and all that. But it sure don't seem to me like the Spaniard has got him all that good a plan.''

Early the next morning, June 24, Gen. Joseph Wheeler began planning an attack against the Spaniards in order to dislodge them from their fortifications at Las Guasimas. However, because General Shafter was still on board the *Seguranca* and had issued no specific orders to attack, some of Wheeler's staff officers advised him against the bold move.

"I fear such rashness could have bitter consequences," one of the officers said.

"Son, there is nothing at all rash about my decision to attack," Wheeler said. "Quite the opposite, for the rash policy would be to do nothing. The Spaniards are very close to the beach, and they are holding a well-fortified strategic gap in the hills through which we must pass. From that ridge, they command a rugged terrain that stretches all the way back to the beach. That allows them to control the road to Santiago, as well as the only fresh water supply in this area. Sooner or later, unless he is a complete fool, General Linares is going to realize that, and he is going to move more troops in. If he does that, we will be trapped on the beach. We have no choice; we must attack."

General Wheeler wrote a report on the situation and ordered it to be taken by the next boat out to the *Seguranca*. He didn't ask for permission to attack; rather, he informed Shafter that he was *going* to attack. He knew full well that by the time Shafter received the report it would be too late for him to countermand it.

To Major Gen'l Shafter Cmndg Expeditionary Force
From Major Gen'l Wheeler

On this day, June 24, I have ordered Brigadier General S. B. Young's brigade of cavalry to attack the Spaniards who have fortified a ridge known as Las Guasimas.

Your obedient servant
J. Wheeler

*　　*　　*

At 5:45 in the morning, Lt. Col. T. A. Baldwin snapped his watch shut. "It is time," he said.

Although most of the reporters were with Colonel Wood and Colonel Roosevelt and the Rough Riders, Marty made the conscious decision to cover the Tenth. Seeing her, Colonel Baldwin sent a corporal over to inform her that she would have to stay behind until the objective was captured.

Marty looked at the steep sides of the hill in front of them. She knew that the Spanish would be shooting down on them and that the Americans would make good targets. If she went along, there was no guarantee that she wouldn't be one of those targets. She wanted to cover the war, but she had no intention of being foolish. She thought staying behind was a good idea.

"Very well, Corporal," she replied.

The corporal let out a sigh of relief and grinned at her.

"What is it?" Marty asked.

"The colonel, he tol' me I was to keep you back even if I had to hold you," the corporal said. "I'm sure glad you ain't goin' make me do that."

Marty laughed with him, then found a big rock that would provide cover against any stray bullets while also affording her a good view of the operation. She watched as the Tenth Cavalry started up the side of the hill. She saw the color-bearer carrying the flag, and right beside him, bending forward at the waist as he made the steep climb, was Todd Murchison.

"Please, God, protect him," Marty prayed; then, feeling a sense of shame that her prayer hadn't included all the men, she amended it. "Please, God, protect all of them."

It was a hard hill to climb, and the men were moving slowly toward the crest. Todd was glad they were all regulars, because every man was in good-enough condition to keep up. Looking over toward some of the volunteers, he saw that the steep hill and the early-morning heat were beginning to take their toll among those citizen-soldiers who were not quite in good-enough shape.

"Bugler!" Captain Bigelow called. "Bring the machine guns to the front."

The bugler raised his bugle and sounded a loud clarion call. Todd felt admiration for the young man that he had breath enough to make the call as clearly as he did.

Looking around, Todd saw the machine-gun crews bringing up their weapons, working through the other men. They were easy to pick out because they had pack mules carrying their guns.

With the weapons at the front, the advancing army stopped and spread out along the hillside. Until now, the Spanish had not fired a shot at them, but when the advancing troops spread out in a battalion front formation, the Spanish suddenly opened fire.

First Lt. Todd Armstrong Murchison, a graduate of West Point and a second-generation professional military man, the son of Maj. Gen. Joseph Daniel Murchison, was getting a baptism of fire in his very first battle.

The Spanish were using the new, smokeless powder. Therefore, unlike the clouds of billowing smoke that rolled up from the American lines when they returned fire, all that could be seen of the Spanish weapons were a few discrete puffs of thin smoke rising from behind a long, low pile of stones. As a result, it was hard for the Americans to pick out targets.

The shooting grew more intense with each passing second. Todd thought of corn popping in a pan, how it starts slowly, then gradually builds to a crescendo where so many kernels pop at once that the individual pops could no longer be discerned.

This battle was like that.

Todd could hear—almost feel—the Spanish bullets as they whizzed by, frying the air by his ear. Then, in the midst of the buzz of bullets, he heard a dull thump and a sharp cry. He looked over just in time to see a pink, misty spray of blood as a bullet plunged into the thigh of a nearby soldier. The soldier went down.

"Stretcher bearers!" Todd shouted. "Stretcher bearers!"

Two men, one of them carrying a rolled-up stretcher, came toward him.

"Take care of him," Todd said, pointing to the wounded trooper.

Without a word, the two men set about their task. Putting the stretcher down on the ground, they opened it up, rolled the wounded man onto it, then picked him up and started back down the ridge with him.

Back at the foot of the hill, Marty was too far away to see any individual action. She had tried to keep her eyes on Todd as he went up the hill at the head of his men, but as they got farther away she lost sight of him.

"Medics, prepare for the wounded!" someone called, and Marty saw two men open a box with medical equipment. A moment later, she saw a man on a stretcher, the first casualty to come down the hill. As he passed by, Marty saw that his right leg was covered with blood. She felt a little sick, but she managed to fight it down.

"Hit in the thigh," someone said, though his information wasn't needed. Everyone who saw the wounded soldier knew where he had been hit, and because he was the first battlefield casualty, there wasn't a man who didn't come over to see him.

A moment later, another wounded soldier was carried down the hill, then another and another still until the casualties started coming down with alarming swiftness. Some of the men were being carried back on stretchers, some were helped down, and some came down on their own.

By now the rear area was crowded with men from all the engaged units. Their natural desire to follow what was going on on the hill caused them all to gather together, so that men of the Tenth Cavalry, Lightning Cavalry, and Rough Riders were in one large, unregulated group.

One of the reserves, unable to contain his curiosity any longer, yelled at one of the walking wounded, a man from the Rough Riders, "Soldier! How are things going up there?"

"I don't know," the soldier answered in an excited, frightened voice. "If you ask me, we're gettin' whupped pretty good. They was men dyin' all around me."

"Dyin'? We ain't seen no one dyin'," one of the soldiers of the reserve battalion said.

"They ain't wastin' their time bringin' the dead ones back down," the wounded soldier replied. "They ain't got 'nuff men to do that. They can only mess with the wounded. The ones what's gettin' killed are just left lyin' up there."

The soldier's frightened report began spreading through the ranks like wildfire. All around her, Marty could hear the soldiers mumbling about the ones who were killed, and many expressed the belief that they were being soundly beaten.

"Hold on, here! Hold on!" a sergeant shouted to the others. "Don't pay him no never-mind. He's just been shot, 'n' he ain't thinkin' right. You can't blame him none, but look up there! Does it look to you like we're gettin' whupped? Can't you see that we're still movin' on up the hill?"

Marty looked up the hill and saw that the Americans, in groups of ten and twenty, were moving up closer to the crest in surges.

"The sergeant's right!" someone shouted. "We are a'whuppin' them!"

"Go get 'em, men! Go get 'em!" another called.

"Save some for us!"

"Thanks, Sergeant," one of the officers said gratefully. "I was afraid for a moment there we might have a panic on our hands."

"I was just a young pup durin' the War between the States, Cap'n," the sergeant replied. "But I seen this before. A man gets wounded, he don't have no idea what's goin' on 'ceptin' he's hurtin' pretty bad, and he gets to panicking. Most of these boys down here ain't never been in battle before, so they don't know how to take it. You just gotta calm 'em down a little, that's all."

Up on the hill, the day dragged on, second by interminable second. The advancing Americans were beginning to pile up casualties; eight men had been killed, while three officers and twenty-five enlisted men had been wounded. And, for all this, there was just one medical officer and one Hospital Corps man to attend to them.

The day became hotter and more oppressive, and the advance slowed, then came to a stop. They were at the most critical point, where they were the most exposed, and tired from the long climb. The defenders behind the rock walls seemed to understand this, and they redoubled their effort, so that the firing became even more intense.

Over in the Rough Riders' sector, Sgt. Hamilton Fish Jr., the son of the former secretary of state under President Grant, had struck up an unlikely but close friendship with a half-breed Cherokee named Ed Culver. At breakfast that morning, Fish and Culver had discussed their personal cache of canned tomatoes. Fish, who came from one of America's wealthiest families, had used his own money to buy two cases of the tomatoes before they left Florida. He loved them, and though he had planned to ration them, he was also generous to his friends. At breakfast he surprised Culver by suggesting that they eat as much as they want.

"We'll run out of them; then we won't be able to get any more," Culver said.

Fish shook his head. "What if we get killed today?" he asked. "Think of the waste of leaving all those tomatoes behind."

Fish and Culver ate the canned tomatoes until they could eat no more.

Now, as they were climbing the hill, Fish had a pair of expensive shoes hanging around his neck. Out of breath and sweating profusely, he suddenly took the shoes from his neck and threw them into the bushes.

"Sergeant Fish, why did you do that?" Culver asked. "You may need those later."

"No," Fish replied soberly. "I have a strange feeling that I won't be needing anything later."

Almost immediately after his remark, Fish gasped, then called out in pain, "Culver, I'm shot! I'm badly wounded!"

"So am I," Culver replied, his voice also strained with pain.

"You, too? The same bullet must've hit both of us," Fish mumbled. He examined his wound. The bullet had gone in his left side, then emerged on his right, before striking Culver in the chest, just above his heart.

Both men sat slowly down. Unable to hold himself up, Fish lay down, then turned on one side and looked over at his friend. "God, I'm thirsty," he said. "I've never been so thirsty. You have any water?"

Culver had also gone to the ground, and now he raised up on one elbow and handed his canteen to Fish. The exertion caused him to pass out. When he came to a few seconds later, Fish was, once again, sitting up. He smiled faintly at Culver.

"Are you all right?" Fish asked the Indian.

"I'll be OK," Culver replied. "Are you hit hard?"

Even as Culver was asking the question, Fish fell forward, the smile gone from his face. Culver reached over and took off Fish's hat to get a closer look.

Hamilton Fish was dead.

General Wheeler didn't realize that one of the most prominent members of his command had just been killed, but he did realize that the fighting had become intense enough for him to commit his reserves. Without hesitation, he ordered nine regiments of infantry into the battle.

From the top of the hill, Todd and the others could hear a faint yelling behind him as the fresh soldiers entered the battle at a run.

"Look at 'em," Dakota said, chuckling. "They tryin' to run up the side of the hill like it's a parade ground. A few more steps and they'll find out they can't do that without gettin' tuckered out."

Dakota's prediction was correct as, a moment later, the reserves dropped back to a walk and, finally, to a slow climb. Eventually they came on line and, with the addition of their firepower, were able to start up the hill again.

Suddenly they began receiving very heavy fire, not from

the hill directly in front of them, but from a ridge to the right.

"Colonel Baldwin! We're being enfiladed!" Captain Bigelow shouted.

Baldwin nodded, then sent a courier to General Young with the news that he would be turning the Tenth Cavalry to the right. Without waiting for a reply from the brigade commander, Baldwin ordered a right oblique, and the well-trained cavalrymen responded immediately. The Spanish were in a very strong defensive line here, firing from small rock forts that had been constructed along the entire length. They were also supported by two machine guns.

When the commander of the Hotchkiss gun battery saw that the Tenth Cavalry was heavily involved, he ordered his guns to turn their firepower toward the little forts. The guns, firing one explosive shell per second, were employed with devastating effect.

Under the terrible fire of the Hotchkiss guns and the relentless press of the Tenth Cavalry, the Spaniards who were on the right flank broke and ran.

Down at the foot of the hill, General Wheeler was given word that the Spaniards in enfilade had been dislodged from their position. He jumped up and whooped, "Hot damn, boys! We've got the Yankees on the run!"

Back near the crest of the ridge, the Tenth, having cleared the flank, now turned its attention back toward the crest of the hill that was the ultimate objective.

"Let's go, men!" Todd shouted.

"We got 'em now!" someone else called.

The American line moved in surges, ten at a time, then twenty, then an entire company, then the entire brigade. They stopped their charge only long enough to raise their rifles to their shoulders to fire. In some cases, they didn't stop at all but merely fired as they moved.

Todd wasn't carrying a rifle, but he did have a pistol in his hand. So far he hadn't fired it, because his job was to lead and not get into personal firefights. Also, he had not yet been in pistol range. Now, however, as they reached the top, he

saw a Spanish soldier suddenly rise up and take aim at Lieutenant Pershing. Pershing didn't see him, and the Spaniard
was at point-blank range.

"John, look out!" Todd shouted, firing at the Spaniard at
the same time he yelled his warning. He saw a puff of dust
rise up from the Spaniard's tunic. The Spaniard dropped his
unfired rifle, then put his hands to his chest. He looked down
at the blood spilling through his fingers as if surprised that
such a thing could be happening to him. Then he looked up
at Todd, his eyes pained and confused.

"*Muerto?*" he gasped.

Todd had fired by reflex. Now he lowered the still-smoking
pistol and watched, in shock, as the man he had just shot fell
forward across the rock wall. The Spaniard's hat fell off and
his arms flopped forward, the tips of his bloody fingers just
reaching the ground. He lay motionless in this grotesque position, and Todd knew that he was dead.

Todd stood there for a long moment. He was scarcely
aware that the shooting had stopped, and not until he heard
a loud cheer from the ranks did he realize that an American
flag was now flying from the same pole where a Spanish flag
had been flying just moments before. Las Guasimas had been
taken.

Todd walked over to the soldier he had killed. While the
others celebrated their victory, Todd just stared.

"Sir, the thing to do is don' let yourself think about it,"
Dakota said, coming over to him. "You just done what had
to be done, that's all."

"The first sergeant is right," Pershing said. "If you hadn't
been Johnny-on-the-spot, I wouldn't be here now."

"I know," Todd stated quietly. He looked at his pistol
almost as if it were something unclean; then he slipped it back
into his holster. "There is a tremendous difference between
talking about battle in the classroom, in the abstract, and actually fighting in one."

Pershing put his hand on Todd's shoulder. "Forget everything you learned in that boys' school on the Hudson," he
said quietly. "You've just had your first real lesson."

*   *   *

Down at the bottom of the hill, Marty was still waiting. For some time after the battle, the casualties had been coming back, the walking wounded hobbling along with the assistance of sticks they had managed to pick up on the way down, or supported by other, less grievously wounded comrades.

The dead were also brought back down. The first dead to return were from the three cavalry units who had spearheaded the attack: the Rough Riders, the Lightning Cavalry, and the Tenth Cavalry.

Marty saw a frenzy of several photographers, shoving one another to get the best angle for a shot of one particular body. Thinking this was certainly odd and a little morbid, she went over to see what had caused the sudden interest. That was when she recognized the body of Hamilton Fish.

Fish was a handsome man, and his face was composed as if he were merely sleeping. It was hard to believe that this man, whom she had seen so many times, laughing and full of life in the dining room of the Tampa Bay Hotel, was now dead. Nearby, she heard someone laughing, and she wondered how anyone could laugh at such a time.

Two men from the Lightning Cavalry were standing over one of the bodies. "Ole Eddie said the Spanish couldn't catch him," the soldier said, "and lookie here; they got him the first one."

Marty looked at the body the two were laughing over; then she gasped. The dead soldier was Eddie Stone, the artist. She whirled away so that she wouldn't have to look at him, as tears stung her eyes.

One of Marty's peers, another war correspondent, was brought down then. His name was Edward Marshall, and when they carried him past her he opened his eyes and looked up at her.

"Miss McGuire, what a pretty thing you are," he said. "Are you here to lay your hand upon my fevered brow?"

"I would be honored to lay my hand upon your brow, Mr. Marshall," Marty replied.

Marty put her hand on his forehead. It was indeed hot, though whether from a fever caused by the wound or the heat of the day she didn't know.

"What a tonic you are," Marshall said. "Lads, you can forget about the surgeon telling me I'm going to die. Miss McGuire has worked her cure upon me. I have no doubt but that I will survive." To the astonishment of everyone there, Marshall began singing "On the Banks of the Wabash."

"Miss McGuire?" one of the soldiers who had carried Marshall down the hill said.

"Yes?"

"Mr. Marshall gave his notebook to me and asked me to give it to someone so his story could be filed. I don't know who to give it to."

"I'll take care of it," Marty offered.

"Thanks." The soldier handed the notebook over to Marty, then, answering a call from his sergeant, left her alone. Curious as to what Marshall had written while he was up on the hill, Marty opened the notebook and began to read:

I saw many men shot. Every one went down in a lump without cries, without jumping in the air, without throwing up hands. They just went down like clods in the grass.

There is much that is awe-inspiring about the death of soldiers on the battlefield . . . the man lives, he is strong, he is vital, every muscle in him is at its fullest tension when, suddenly, "chug" he is dead. That "chug" of the bullets striking flesh is nearly always plainly audible. I did not hear the bullet shriek that killed Hamilton Fish. I did not hear the bullet shriek which hit me.

A bit of steel came diagonally from the left. I was standing in the open, and, from watching our men in front, had turned partially to see Roosevelt and his men on the right. "Chug" came the bullet and I fell into the long grass, as much like a lump as had the other fellows whom I had seen go down. There was no pain, no surprise. The tremendous shock so dulled my sensibilities that it did not occur to me that anything extraordinary had happened.

Finally three soldiers found me and, putting half a shelter-tent under me, carried me to the shade. Here, as I wait to be carried the rest of the way down the hill, I am writing my story. If it is to be filed, it will be filed by the good grace of someone else, for a surgeon has just told me that I am about to die. The news is not pleasant, but, for some reason that I cannot fathom, neither does it particularly interest me.

CHAPTER 19

W ithout specific orders to do so, you had no right to bring on this battle," General Shafter said to General Wheeler.

"General Shafter, I know you are in command, but if I had been in General Wheeler's position I would have done the same thing," General Lawton said. "If he had not acted quickly and decisively, General Linares could have reinforced that ridge and held us off indefinitely. We would have had no choice but to put back to sea and try to effect a landing somewhere else . . . assuming Congress would let us try again."

Shafter thought for a moment; then he nodded. "Of course, you are right," he said. He stuck out his hand. "Congratulations, General. You did exactly what needed to be done."

"Thank you, General," Wheeler replied.

"Now, we must make plans for the attack against Santiago," General Shafter said. He unfolded a map and summoned Colonel Humphrey, his quartermaster general, to give his report.

"We have the reports of the Cubans on the road between Siboney and Santiago," Colonel Humphrey began. "Although one of the most difficult obstacles has been removed now, it is still going to be difficult. The road passes over a range of high ground and through depressions, ravines, watercourses, and small rivers There are no bridges across the water barriers. Much of the road is deeply cut and so narrow that our supply wagons will barely fit through. It seems to me that at any one of a dozen points the Spanish could launch an attack that could completely bottle up our army.

"Which brings us to your cavalry, General Young. Do you think you could go through the road first, secure it, and hold it secure while we pass the rest of the army and supplies through?" Shafter asked.

"Yes, sir, I think so," General Young replied.

"Who will spearhead your operation?"

"The Tenth fought exceptionally well at Las Guasimas," General Young said. "I'll use them."

"The colored troops?" Shafter asked.

"Yes, sir."

"You think they can handle it?"

"Yes, sir. As I said, sir, they fought exceptionally well."

"General Young, I might suggest that you use another unit," General Shafter said.

"Of course, General, I will use any order of battle you wish," Young stated. "But I have the utmost confidence in my colored soldiers. They can do any job I give them."

"I don't doubt that," Shafter said. He stroked his cheek. "But this war is unlike any other war we have ever fought," he explained. "It seems like we have as many correspondents in the field as we do soldiers. The people back home want to read of the glorious accomplishments of our men. I don't think they would care that much about reading of the glorious accomplishments of colored soldiers. What do you think, General Wheeler?"

"Well, as you fellas know, I am from the South," Wheeler said. "So my views of the colored man are well-known. But I must confess that the colored soldiers I have seen are unlike any conception I've ever had. These men are tenacious and bold, and by God, if the Confederacy had used them, this uniform I'm wearing would be gray."

"So you are saying use the colored troops?"

"That would be my recommendation, yes, sir."

"Gentlemen, if I spit on the floor today, a million Americans will read about it tomorrow. We are under a very close scrutiny. We have to give the Americans a unit to glorify, and there is no way we can give them the Tenth Cavalry.''

"What about the Seventh Cavalry?'' General Wheeler suggested.

Lawton snorted. "The Seventh? Custer glorified the Seventh, and look what happened. No, gentlemen, if we choose the Seventh as our fair-haired boys, I'm afraid we would have a lot of ghosts to fight.''

"How about the First, or the Fifth?'' Wheeler suggested. "They are both regular cavalry units. We know we can depend on them in a tough fight.''

Shafter shook his head. "As you said, they are regular army. That means the ranks are filled with drunkards, criminals on the run, all sorts of riffraff. That is scarcely the image we wish to portray. I'm afraid there is only going to be one glory regiment in this war, and the press has already selected them.''

"You would be talking about the Rough Riders?'' General Wheeler asked.

General Shafter nodded. "Colonel Roosevelt is practically a national hero,'' he said. "He's only second in command, but I'll bet if you asked ten Americans who is the commander of all the American forces down here, most would answer Roosevelt.''

"And you want to build him up even more?'' General Lawton asked.

Shafter looked at Young. "You were in the field with them, General; how did the Rough Riders do?''

"In truth, they performed quite admirably, sir,'' Young answered. "I wouldn't have thought so, what with the strange mix of society figures and cowboys that make up their number. But, for all his bombast, Roosevelt seems to be the unifying figure. The society bunch sees him as one of their own, while the cowboys genuinely love him. He truly is the heart and soul of the Rough Riders, and they did prove themselves under fire.''

"Then the Rough Riders it is. General Young, they will be your vanguard.''

"Yes, sir,'' Young replied.

Shafter sighed, then wiped his sweating forehead with a handkerchief. "Gentlemen, the truth is, my health is not up to this campaign. I stayed on board ship as long as I could, but the sun . . . the heat . . . my weight . . . ," he said, letting his voice trail off.

Marty, who was one of the correspondents whose stories were so affecting General Shafter's decisions, was just putting the finishing touches to her latest article:

By now, all the readers of this and other newspapers will know of the outcome of yesterday's battle. The Americans carried the day, though, I'm saddened to say, not without the loss of life to eight of our brave men. The particulars of the battle, its description and so forth, have been filed in a previous dispatch. This dispatch is written to provide the wives and sweethearts, the mothers and fathers, of our brave men with a portrait of how they are doing today.

Let me begin by saying that the men are doing marvelously. They are all quite tired right now, and even as I write this article, seated beneath a shading palm tree, I can look around and see dozens of the men catching up on much-needed sleep while their companions sit, awake by their sides, ready to sound the alarm should anything happen. Nothing seems likely to happen right now, as this is the calm after the storm . . . or, in this case, after the battle.

After we won the battle, the Spaniards were driven off and the way was open for the American Expeditionary Force to pass along the narrow road through the deeply cut draws to the plains beyond Las Guasimas. The critical mission of making certain that the road was indeed clear and not endangered by a hidden Spanish ambush fell to the Rough Riders. The brave young men of this magnificent force, drawn from all walks of life and ably led by Col. Theodore Roosevelt, responded to their task in a way that would make all Americans proud. The road was explored and found to be clear.

Today, the remainder of the army is pouring through.

Mr. Edison's moving picture camera is here, and from time to time I have seen Mr. Edison's camera operator, Mr. William Paley, taking pictures. If the opportunity presents itself to you, do not fail to view this magnificent sight, though neither film nor my words can do true justice to thousands of soldiers marching along with their weapons gleaming in the sun. Behind them come the pack mules, and each of the sturdy little animals is laden down with supplies and matériel for making war.

Behind the mules come the wagons carrying cargo that is just as important, for the wagons are loaded with salt pork, canned beef and beans, coffee, and sugar, the fuel that makes the army run.

From here, we can see Santiago very plainly. It is about seven or eight miles away. The country between here and Santiago appears level for about six miles; then there are some hills that rise just outside the city. Those hills appear to be deserted, and earlier this morning I overheard some of the officers saying that General Shafter intends to move artillery onto the heights, from which point he will commence shelling the city.

If the thought of shelling a city sounds ominous, one must remember that Santiago is our major objective and, though we haven't yet met the brunt of the Spanish army, everyone now believes that Santiago is the place where General Linares will make his decisive stand.

It was not by accident that Marty had chosen her seat under a shading palm in the bivouac area of the Tenth Cavalry. She was quite comfortably fixed in her location with a folded blanket for a cushion and piece of canvas stretched to augment the shading effect of the tree. Those improvements to her position had been provided by First Sergeant Dakota, who also pointed out the fact that Lieutenant Murchison was stretched out, asleep under a small tent, no more than twenty feet away from Marty.

*   *   *

Todd's duties during the previous night had not allowed him to go to sleep until just after sunup. It was for this reason that he was able to sleep so soundly, even in the midst of so much activity. When he opened his eyes he was surprised, but pleased, to see Marty sitting against a nearby tree, working on her article. He crawled out of the little tent and went over to speak to her.

"Good morning," he said. "Or is it good afternoon?"

"I think it is just about noon," Marty told him.

Todd looked out toward the road and saw the wagons rolling along undisturbed.

"It looks as if we are getting through the draw, all right."

"Yes," Marty said.

"Are you hungry?" Todd asked.

"A little," Marty admitted.

"Suppose I cook up a little pork and beans for us?" Todd suggested. "Doesn't that sound good?"

Marty laughed. "It sounds as good as the last meal I had."

"What was that?"

"Pork and beans."

"I thought that had a familiar ring to it," Todd said. He rubbed his hands together. "However, you haven't eaten pork and beans until you've eaten mine."

"Oh? Do you know some special trick of preparation that others don't know?"

"Absolutely," Todd replied. "You forget, I'm an army brat. I've been eating this type of fare for my whole life. I've learned a few tricks over the years."

Todd walked over to his pack and pulled out his cooking utensils and field rations. A short while later, he had a fire going, while canned beans and bacon sizzled in the pan. Into the mixture he added a pepper and several other spices that he took from a small cloth bag.

"I must confess," Marty said, "this concoction does smell better than the other pork and bean dishes I've eaten. When we're married, I'll let you do all the cooking," she teased.

"I'm quite good at it, you know," Todd replied, stirring the mixture.

"Married," Marty said with a sigh. "It seems unreal, doesn't it?"

"Are you having second thoughts?"

"No, not at all," Marty said. "It's just that . . . well, ordinarily when two people decide they are going to get married, they can start to make plans."

"We can't make plans yet," Todd said.

"I know," Marty replied.

"Marty, you knew at the beginning of this relationship that it was going to be different. You knew I was a soldier, and you knew it was my career. Our situation is even more unique, in that you are here with me, rather than waiting at home as so many other soldiers' wives and sweethearts are forced to do."

"I know that, too," Marty said. She laughed. "Sometimes I wonder which of us is the luckier, me or those women who wait at home for their men? I can see you every day, yes, but it's a mixed privilege, because I must always be the proper reporter and keep my distance."

Todd looked up from his pan of beans and smiled. "Would you rather I send you back to General Shafter? Maybe he could find you another assignment, where we wouldn't have to be together."

"Todd! You mean you would actually do that?" Marty gasped.

Todd laughed. "You said you can't stand the sight of me—"

Todd didn't get to finish his statement because Marty, laughing, hit him with her notebook.

Todd reached up and grabbed her arms to stop her; then, suddenly, there they were, in each other's arms, just a kiss away. Todd looked at her for a long, hungry moment; then he pulled her to him and crushed her lips beneath his.

"Lieutenant Murchison, I hope I'm not interrupting anything," a voice said.

Todd and Marty broke off the kiss and looked around into the disapproving eyes of General Young.

Marty felt a sudden surge of embarrassment, then fear. She was afraid of how Todd would react to General Young's obvious disapproval. She was pleased to see that he displayed the same cool courage here that he had shown under fire.

"You aren't interrupting anything that we can't continue later," Todd said easily. "What can I do for you, General?"

"I was looking for Colonel Baldwin."

"I'm sure he is around here somewhere, but as I have been sleeping all morning, I haven't seen him."

"You have been sleeping all morning?"

"Yes, sir," Todd said.

Marty noticed that he did not add that he was on duty last night, which clearly would have excused him. Instead, he just held General Young's eyes with a steady gaze from his own.

General Young sighed, then pulled out his watch and looked at it. "I haven't the time to look for him. Please tell him that there is to be no reconnaissance in force unless specifically authorized by General Shafter, General Wheeler, or myself."

"Yes, sir," Todd said, saluting.

General Young, with another scowling glance toward Marty, returned Todd's salute, then left.

"Oh, Todd, I have gotten you into trouble, haven't I?" Marty asked, after General Young was out of earshot.

Todd laughed. It was a soft, intimate laugh. "You've gotten me into trouble? I thought it was always the man who got the woman into trouble."

At first, Marty didn't understand what he was saying. Then, when she did, she gasped and blushed.

"Todd," she scolded.

"Don't think I wouldn't like to get you into trouble," he said, brushing her lips with his once more. He sighed. "But for now, I'm afraid duty calls. I must see the colonel and tell him of General Young's visit."

The Americans made no effort whatever to observe blackout discipline that night. There were at least one hundred campfires spread out across the flatlands beneath the ridge that had been fought over the day before.

Of course, there was really no need to worry about hiding their position. The Spanish certainly knew the Americans were there, and the Americans were so confident of their strength that they weren't at all cautious.

Marty stood atop a small elevation, looking down upon the encampment and the many campfires, listening to the soft whisper of sound that reached her ears; there was laughter here and there, conflicting songs, and a low buzz of unintelligible conversation.

She was alone up here, cloaked in the soft, dark satin of night. Her tent had been pitched earlier, but she wasn't ready to sleep yet. She was enjoying the sounds of an army at rest too much to give it up just yet.

Marty sensed someone walking up the side of the hill toward her, and almost as soon as the figure emerged from the shadows she could tell it was Todd, just from the way he walked. A moment later he was standing there, right beside her.

"I thought you would be in bed by now," Todd said.

"No," Marty replied. She took in the fire-lit valley with a sweep of her hand. "I was just watching. Oh, Todd, I know it must be evil of someone to be thrilled by something like this. After all, we are fighting a war, and war is evil. But this is so . . . so magnificent!" she said, searching for the right word.

Todd chuckled.

"Be very careful who you say that to," he warned. "This has been a secret known only to men for fifty centuries."

They stood together in silence for a moment longer; then Marty spoke again.

"I'm sorry about what happened earlier, when General Young came by," she said.

"What do you mean?"

"I know it can't be too good for your career to have a general find us kissing in the middle of a battlefield. I don't ever want to embarrass you."

"The only thing I'm sorry about is that the general interrupted us," Todd said. He put his arms around her and pulled her to him. "I don't intend to let that happen again."

"Todd, don't you think . . . ," Marty started to protest, but her protest died in her throat as his lips came to hers. Again, as had happened this afternoon, Marty was engulfed in a rising tide of pleasure.

She felt herself being moved, gently, and the next thing she knew they were slipping into her tent. A minute earlier they had been outside in the soft breeze with a hundred glowing campfires as a backdrop; now they were in the total darkness of her tent. She sensed him moving toward her; then he was poised over her for the final connection. She put her arms around his neck as she took him into her, and she felt the liquid fire consume her as he began.

CHAPTER 20

As night slowly gave way, morning found the great army encamped in the flatlands at the base of the ridge. The night before there had been a hundred glowing campfires. This morning there were but a few.

Thousands of soldiers sitting or lying about were just beginning to wake up to the new day. A thin, diaphanous haze of smoke hung over the campground, and there drifted on the morning air the smell of bacon and coffee from those industrious soldiers who had risen before dawn.

Marty crawled out of her small tent that held the faint, but still discernible, perfume of last night's lovemaking. She smiled as she thought of it. How exciting it had been to share her love with Todd, right here on a battlefield encampment, in the midst of ten thousand men! She had been lifted to the stars last night, yet none of them knew. Or did they know? She thought of it for a moment, then smiled. She didn't care whether they knew or not.

Marty pulled her wash pan from the tent, filled it with water, and began washing her face. She wondered where Todd was, right now.

Todd was six miles away from the encampment. The Tenth had been forbidden to conduct a reconnaissance in force, but the general had not said anything that would prevent Colonel Baldwin from sending out a small scouting expedition to see what lay ahead. Thus Captain Bigelow had sent Todd and Dakota on a mounted patrol.

They had left before dawn, and now they were approaching the hills where General Shafter intended to put his artillery to shell the city of Santiago.

Dakota had received a letter from Doney the day before. In it, she told him she had found the perfect building for them to put their restaurant.

"'Course, none of the white folks will come there to eat," Dakota said. "But they'll all buy her fried chicken an' take it home with 'em. They won't have no trouble with that. . . . Most of Tampa been eatin' Doney's fried chicken all this time anyhow."

"I'm sure it will work out for you, First Sergeant."

"Could I give the lieutenant some advice?" Dakota asked.

"Of course you can," Todd said. "First sergeants have been looking out for lieutenants ever since armies began."

"Yes, sir, well, this don' rightly have anything to do with the army. But, on the other hand, maybe it do. Folks like you an' me . . . professional soldiers . . . has always thought there was no place in our lives for a woman."

"That's what they say," Todd said.

"Yes, sir, an' all these years, I believed that. There was a woman once. . . . She was a laundress back at Fort Larned. Pretty woman. I coulda married her, too. Like as not, I'd have me a couple of kids now. But I passed her by."

"Well, look on the bright side," Todd said. "If you had married her, you wouldn't have met Doney."

"Yes, sir, I guess that be true, all right. But that don't make up for all the loneliness I done had all these years."

"I guess not," Todd said.

"The thing is, Lieutenant, me 'n' you's more alike than we are different. I know, I'm colored, you're white, I'm an enlisted man, you're an officer, but under the skin and under the rank, we be closer brothers than most anyone else."

As Todd looked over at his first sergeant, he realized that there was a fundamental truth in what he was saying . . . at least in so far as their relationship went. He felt a closeness to this man that transcended race, rank, and age.

"So, what I'm sayin' is, don' make the same mistake I done made all these years. Don' try an' deny yourself the love of a good woman, just 'cause you in the army."

"You're talking about Marty McGuire?"

"Yes, sir. She be a good woman. I know, they might be some think that she just be handy and that's all there is between you. But I can tell there is more. I can see it when I look at the way you two look at each other."

Todd laughed. "So, if I told you that Miss McGuire and I were planning on getting married, you would approve?"

"Approve? Yes, sir! I think that would be the most wonderfullest thing in the . . . *ungh!*"

An instant after Dakota let out his strange grunting sound, Todd heard the sound of a rifle shot. He looked in the direction of the sound and saw half a dozen Spanish soldiers running toward him. None of them were mounted, but all were armed, and several were shooting at him. They didn't stop to take aim, and their shots went wild.

"Dakota!" Todd shouted.

Dakota looked down at the spreading stain of blood on his chest.

"I been shot, Todd," Dakota said. In his pain and shock, he had called Todd by his first name. He started weaving, then fell off his horse. He lay flat on his back staring up at the sky, gasping for breath. The six Spanish soldiers were still rushing headlong toward them, screaming threats and challenges.

Todd drew his carbine from his saddle scabbard and raised one leg up and across his saddle. He leaned forward and put his elbow on his knee; then, using that as support, he took a very careful, deliberate aim at a Spanish soldier, picking the one who was ready to fire next. Todd squeezed his trigger. The Spaniard went down. Todd levered another round into the chamber of his carbine, then aimed at the next Spaniard. One more trigger squeeze, one more Spanish soldier down. Calmly and deliberately, Todd operated the cocking lever a third time and dropped one more of the attackers. With three shots in a space of less than five seconds, he had cut by half the size of the attacking force.

The three remaining soldiers looked around and saw the grim efficiency with which the American was decimating their ranks. They stopped their charge, then turned and ran back to the safety of the hills.

Todd could have dropped all three of them quite easily, but he didn't. Instead, he sheathed his rifle and jumped down to see to Dakota.

"Dakota, how bad is it?"

Dakota had been trying to stop the flow of blood from his chest, but the entire front of his blouse was now red and sticky. His face was gray, his pupils clouded, and his eyelids fluttering.

"I've got to stop the bleeding," Todd said. He crushed his campaign hat, then slid it under Dakota's shirt and pressed it up against the wound. Next, he stripped out of his own shirt and wrapped it around Dakota's chest, then tied it tightly over the top of his hat.

Dakota tried to chuckle, and when he did, flecks of blood came out of his mouth. Todd knew that his lungs must be filling with blood, and he knew that was bad. Dakota was drowning in his own blood.

"You know what they say," Dakota said. "A sucking chest wound is God's way of telling you to slow down."

"I've got to get you back to a doctor," Todd said. "I've got to get you up on your horse."

Todd let go of the reins of his horse so he could work with Dakota. He tried to lift him, but Dakota cried out in pain.

"Wait, Lieutenant! Wait!" Dakota said. He lay there and gasped for a moment.

"I've got to get you back," Todd said. "If I don't, the Spanish will come again."

As if to underscore his statement, the Spanish soldiers fired another volley from the protection of a distant group of rocks. One of the bullets slammed into the saddle of Todd's mount, and the horse bolted and ran. Todd whistled for it, but the horse kept going. Dakota's horse would have run as well if Todd hadn't been holding onto the animal's reins.

"Did one of the horses bolt?" Dakota asked.

"It's all right. We'll double up."

"No," Dakota said. "Go on, Lieutenant. Leave me here."

"I'm not leaving you."

"I won't make it."

"Yes, you will."

"Doney," Dakota gasped.

"What?"

"Doney," Dakota gasped again. "Lieutenant, make sure . . . she . . . gets . . . my . . . money," he said, barely able to speak now. "She . . . won't be able to make it . . . if she don't have that money."

"You give it to her yourself. I'm taking you back."

Dakota smiled weakly. "Beggin' your pardon, sir, but I been in a lot more battles than the lieutenant. I know what this wound means. Tell her . . ." Dakota stopped speaking, and his breathing became more labored.

"Dakota! Fielding! Fielding!" Todd called.

Suddenly an easy, peaceful smile spread across Dakota's face.

"Why, we all together," he said.

"What?"

"Here, in Fiddler's Green," Dakota said. "Colored man and white. All the horse soldiers is together, like brothers."

Dakota's facial muscles relaxed, and his breathing stopped.

"Dakota! Dakota!" Todd called.

Todd looked at Dakota in disbelief. Just a moment ago they had been laughing and talking together, and now Dakota was dead.

"Save me a place there, Fielding, my friend," he said, reaching down to close Dakota's eyes. "Save me a place in Fiddler's Green."

Suddenly there was a sound like an angry wasp, then a puff of dust and the retreating whine of a spent bullet as one of the Spanish soldiers shot at him. Todd looked around and saw that the Spanish were running toward him again. This time there were ten soldiers.

Todd reached down and picked Dakota up and threw him belly-down across the front of his saddle. He climbed on behind Dakota's body, then slapped his legs against the horse's flanks. The animal responded immediately, and Todd galloped away from the Spanish, whose shots were now so wild that he couldn't even hear the whine of their bullets.

Todd's riderless horse had galloped into camp a few minutes earlier, and now a dozen or more people were gathered at the edge of camp, looking toward the distant hills. One of the people was Marty.

"It could mean anything, Miss McGuire," Sergeant Major Baker said. "The lieutenant may have gotten off to check somethin', and the horse spooked. I've seen that happen lots of times."

"Sergeant Major!" one of the men called. "This here horse wasn't just spooked. Lookie here, they's a bullet lodged in his saddle. He been shot at."

"Oh!" Marty gasped.

"That still don't prove nothin'," the sergeant major said with an angry glance toward the soldier for upsetting Miss McGuire.

A couple of the men had field glasses, and one of them spotted a rider coming in their direction from a couple of miles away.

"Here comes a ride, but there's only one."

"Who is it?"

"I can't tell," the man said.

"Well, is he white or colored?" Baker asked.

"Still too far away to tell. Wait; they's two people on that horse. One of 'em ridin' 'n' the other belly-down across the saddle."

"Dead?"

"Sure looks like it."

"Well, who is it, man? Who's ridin' 'n' who's belly-down?"

"Ain't really no question 'bout that, is there, Sarge? You seen whose horse come back, didn't you?"

Sergeant Major Baker looked toward Marty, who bit her lower lip and fought hard to keep from crying out. She clenched her fists so tightly that the fingernails dug into her palms.

Please, dear God, she prayed silently. *Please let it not be Todd.* Even as she prayed, she knew that if the man draped across the saddle wasn't Todd, it would have to be First Sergeant Dakota. She didn't want it to be Dakota, either, but, pray God for forgiveness, if it had to be one of them, she would rather it be the first sergeant than Todd.

"The lieutenant's been killed," one of the soldiers said.

Marty felt her knees grow weak; then her head began to spin. Suddenly everything went black.

"Are you all right?" Todd asked. He was bending over her, touching a damp cloth to her forehead.

"Todd? Todd, you're alive! You're all right!" Marty said. She tried to sit up, but her head started to spin again, and she had to lie back down.

"Just lie there for a moment or two," Todd said. "You fainted."

"I know," Marty said. "I thought you . . . what happened? Your horse came back without you; then we saw . . ." Marty gasped and put her hand to her mouth. Oh, Todd, it's First Sergeant Dakota, isn't it? Dakota has been killed."

"Yes," Todd said quietly.

Marty blinked several times, but she couldn't prevent the tears from pooling and sliding down her cheeks.

"What happened?" she asked quietly.

"We were ambushed by the Spanish," Todd said. "We were . . . surprised."

"Oh, poor Sergeant Dakota. Wasn't there a woman, back in Tampa? Doney, I think her name was?"

Todd looked at Marty with a strange and pained expression on his face.

"Yes," Todd said. "Doney."

Marty sat up, and this time her head didn't spin.

"Where is he?" she asked. "Where is Sergeant Dakota?"

"He's back there," Todd said noncommittally. "They're . . ." He was quiet for a moment as if unable to speak; then he went on. "They're putting him in a canvas sack. We'll bury him in a few minutes."

"So . . . so soon?" Marty gasped.

"Yes, the quicker the better. It's not good for morale to leave the dead lying around for long."

"But . . . can't you send him back to Tampa, where someone cares for him? Shouldn't he have the right to a funeral?"

"We care for him," Todd said. "And we will give him a funeral. We are all the family he needs."

"But . . . he was going to marry Doney. Doesn't she have any rights?"

"This is war, Marty. You evacuate your wounded and you bury your dead. That's the way it is. Doney knew there was a chance he might wind up dead and buried on some distant battlefield. Anyone foolish enough to fall in love with, or to marry, a soldier knows that."

Todd walked away before Marty could say anything. His words frightened her. "Anyone foolish enough to marry a soldier," he had said. Did that mean her? And, more important, did that mean he was changing his mind about marrying her?

Marty wanted to run to him right then, to find out exactly what he meant by his strange comment, but she knew this wasn't the time or the place for it. Better to let him suffer in private for a while.

It was less than an hour later when word passed throughout the Tenth Cavalry that 1st Sgt. Fielding Dakota was about to be buried. Several hundred people drifted over to the place where a grave had been dug and a long canvas lump lay. The lump looked almost like a bag of dirty laundry. It was hard to imagine that someone as vital and alive as Dakota had been could now be nothing more than an inert bit of clay, sewn up inside a canvas bag.

Marty looked into the faces of the men. All had long, sad faces, but one, Private Bates, was openly crying. Tears were streaming down his face.

After the regimental chaplain finished the Prayers for the Dead, General Young stepped up to say a few words.

"I didn't know First Sergeant Dakota as well as most of you knew him, but from what I did know, I knew him to be a brave soldier and a good man.

"All cavalrymen, colored and white, take comfort in a

place known as Fiddler's Green. Now, just in case there is anyone who doesn't know about Fiddler's Green, it's a cool spot under the shade trees, near a nice stream of water, where ever'one who's ever responded to the bugle call 'Boots 'n' Saddles' goes after they die. And when you get there, you aren't colored; you aren't white; you aren't an officer, or non-commissioned officer, or enlisted man. You are a cavalryman, each and all equal in spirit.

"Sergeant Dakota is probably already there, having a drink with Cobb and English and the other brave soldiers who have gone before him. General Custer is there, too, along with his men. And I don't mind telling you I have an awful lot of good friends of my own up there, wearing the blue and the gray, just waiting for me.

"Now, I know there are some who may not think this quite squares with the theological teachin's of heaven 'n' all that, but if you stop to think about it for a moment, it's not all that far off. Heaven is the place we're all wantin' to get to, isn't it? And who among us doesn't want to renew acquaintances, long gone, who have made their final roll call?"

After General Young finished speaking, four men lowered Dakota's body gently into the ground. Then the chief bugler stepped up to the grave and raised the instrument to his lips. The notes of "Taps" sounded loud and clear, sending their mournful tones out to the bluffs of the nearby hills, then returning a second later as a haunting echo.

As the last note hung in harmony with its echo, the soldiers who had come to the impromptu funeral turned away. Those who had known Dakota were fighting back lumps in their throat, ashamed of the pressure behind their eyes that might erupt into tears at any moment. Many of them stopped by to comfort Bates, as if he had been a "member of the family," for Bates had been the closest to Dakota and was making no effort to hold back his tears.

"They're all gone," Bates said. "Cobb, English, now Top. All gone."

Those who hadn't known Dakota but were merely drawn to the occasion by a sense of decency or, in some cases, morbid curiosity, turned away with their own thoughts. Everyone there knew that it could well be one of them lying in that shapeless gray canvas bag. They knew that the time might still come when they would lie alongside First Sergeant Dakota, and though none of them said it aloud, each of them wondered about General Young's words. Was there really a Fiddler's Green? Were old friends really there?

Later that day, as the sun began to set and the campfires were relit, Marty tried to find Todd. She wanted to comfort him over the loss of his friend. She saw Sergeant Major Baker.

"Sergeant Major, have you seen Lieutenant Murchison lately?"

"I think he had some business to take care of back in Siboney, ma'am," the sergeant major said. "He won't be back till tomorrow."

"Siboney? Lieutenant Murchison went all the way back to Siboney?"

"Yes, ma'am," the sergeant major said.

"Thank you."

Marty returned to her tent and sat in front of it, watching the sun set. She stayed there until the last vestige of color was gone from the western sky and the shadows of night had come down to claim the distant hills, then the closer trees, and, finally, the entire valley, except for those hundred or so golden campfire lights that flickered in the dark.

The songs started again. Maybe it was just Marty's imagination, but the music seemed much sadder tonight than it had the night before, perhaps in memory of Dakota. That was a foolish thought, of course. There were more than ten thousand men camped out here in the valley, and only those men who were a part of the Tenth Cavalry even so much as knew Dakota's name. Marty finally realized that it was just her own melancholy that gave the music a more somber tone.

Marty watched as the stars popped out, one by one. She looked up at them and saw that they were no different tonight than they were the night before. And yet, last night, Dakota had been on earth to enjoy them.

She thought of Doney back in Tampa. As far as Doney knew, her man was still alive. She would probably go to bed tonight saying a prayer of protection for him. She would be praying to God to keep Dakota alive, and yet all the while she was praying, Dakota was already dead. It might be as long as two weeks before Doney received the news, and for that entire two weeks she would think Dakota was alive.

That was awful.

No, maybe it was better. This way, at least, she would have him a little longer.

Todd Murchison stood on the beach at Siboney and looked out over the moonlit water at the ships of the fleet that were still anchored offshore. Colonel Baldwin had asked Captain Bigelow to send an officer to Siboney to ask General Shafter to authorize a reconnaissance in strength. If there were that many Spanish that far from Santiago, then Colonel Baldwin was convinced there were many more. If General Shafter tried to put his artillery into position on those heights without first clearing them of the enemy, the Spanish were going to have a field day with him.

Actually, Captain Bigelow had asked Pershing to go, but Todd volunteered to go in his place. Todd volunteered so he wouldn't have to face Marty tonight. He knew she would ask him questions, would want to know exactly how Dakota had been killed. And he didn't want to tell her. He didn't want to tell her that Dakota had been killed because the two of them were discussing Todd's love life and his proposal of marriage to Marty instead of paying attention to what they were doing. If Todd had been doing his job properly, if he had been alert as a scout as he should have been, he would have seen the ambush before it was sprung on him. And Dakota would still be alive. Dakota was dead because Todd had failed him.

Tomorrow, when Todd returned to the campsite, he would tell Marty what he should have had the strength to tell her a long time ago. He was a soldier, fighting a war. Thus there was no room in his life for a wife. He could not marry Marty, and he would not marry her.

Todd turned and started walking down the beach, walking along the line between the wet and dry sand. The wet sand glowed softly silver in the reflection of the moon, and even in his depression, Todd couldn't help but notice how beautiful it was. It was beautiful the way Marty was beautiful. She was the most beautiful woman he had ever known, but there was more than beauty. There was also . . . *"No!"* he said aloud.

"Did you say something?" a nearby soldier called to him.

"I just coughed," Todd lied. He hurried on down the beach. He hadn't realized he had spoken out loud, but he had to do something to stop the thoughts.

After Marty completed her morning ablutions, she saw Todd riding back into camp. She smiled happily and waved at him, but he didn't return her wave. Worse, he didn't stop by to see her or even visit her after she knew he had had time enough to take care of any pressing military business.

Marty waited until nearly noon, but Todd never came to see her. Finally she could take it no longer and she gathered her courage to go over to speak to him.

Todd was sitting on a fallen tree trunk talking to the sergeant major when Marty walked up. He looked over at her.

"Yes, Miss McGuire, can I help you?" he asked.

There was a strange tone of detachment in his voice as he spoke. It sounded cold and frightening, and the tiny fears that had been nagging from deep inside Marty's soul grew larger.

"Todd, I want to talk to you. I need to talk to you."

"I'm sorry, I don't have any news for the press," Todd replied.

"What?" Marty asked in a small voice. Her throat grew tight. What was he talking about? Why was he acting this way?

"You want something you can write, don't you? A story about the Tenth Cavalry?"

"Why are you . . . ," Marty started; then she realized that the sergeant major was still there. She looked at him with a pleading expression on her face.

The sergeant major cleared his throat and picked up his campaign hat.

"Lieutenant Murchison, I called a meeting of all first sergeants," he said. "I better go take care of it."

"That meeting isn't until two o'clock this afternoon," Todd said.

"Yes, sir, I know, sir," the sergeant major said. "But I need to ... uh ... make certain they all have the correct time."

"All right," Todd said. "Go ahead."

"Thank you, Sergeant Major," Marty said gratefully.

The sergeant major left; then Marty and Todd were alone.

"Todd, what is it?" Marty finally asked in a weak voice. "Why are you acting like this? You didn't even tell me you were leaving last night; you didn't come to see me when you came back. I don't understand."

"I wasn't aware that I had to report my every movement to you," Todd said coldly.

"Todd, please!" Marty gasped, barely able to hold her tears in check. "What's going on? What have I done?"

Todd ran his hand through his hair, then sighed. "You haven't done anything, Marty," he said in a softer tone of voice. But even though his voice was softer, it was no more comforting. "It was me," he added. There seemed to be a resignation in his voice.

"What?" Marty asked. "What have you done?"

"I got First Sergeant Dakota killed!" Todd suddenly said, almost shouting the words. "Don't you understand, Marty? I got him killed!"

"How? You were scouting, weren't you? Things like that happen on scout missions. The sergeant major explained it to me."

"He did, did he?" Todd replied. "Tell me, Marty, did the sergeant major happen to explain how two battle-experienced men could be riding on a scout with as much vigilance about them as if they were riding through Central Park?"

"No," Marty said. "I mean, I don't know what you are talking about."

"Then I will explain it to you," Todd replied. "Sergeant Dakota and I were talking about our women. He was talking about Doney, and I was talking about you. We had let the two of you come into our lives, to occupy our minds and our senses. Don't you understand? We went out to find the Spanish. . . . Instead we blundered right into an ambush. I should have been paying attention, but I was thinking and talking about you."

"Oh," Marty said in a very quiet, very vulnerable voice. "I'm sorry, Todd."

"Yes," Todd said. "Sorry." He sighed and ran his hand through his hair again. "Well, I'm afraid that has proven the wisdom of my original thinking," he added. "A career soldier has no business getting involved in a serious relationship with a woman, especially if the soldier is in battle."

"I see," Marty said. She fought hard to keep from crying, and though she didn't break down, the tears did slide down her face. She took a deep breath. "I think it would be best if I moved my tent and the focus of my activity somewhere else."

"Under the circumstances," Todd said, "I think that would be the wisest decision you could make. I'll have the sergeant major detail someone to help you with your things."

"That won't be necessary," Marty replied. "I'll take care of myself." She turned and angrily strode away. She didn't see the tears that had formed in Todd's eyes.

CHAPTER 21

Marty had started her military correspondent career with the Rough Riders, so it was easy enough to return to them. In fact, the Rough Riders seemed to be generating all the attention now. Colonel Baldwin had asked to be allowed to conduct a reconnaissance into the hills. General Shafter had approved the mission, but assigned it to the Rough Riders.

Whenever any pronouncement about the conduct of the war was made by Colonel Roosevelt, all the correspondents gathered round and hung on his every word. Marty had no way of knowing, but it seemed almost as if the Rough Riders had been designated by General Shafter to be his "unit in the news."

The Rough Riders' scout of the hills proved that the hills surrounding Santiago weren't deserted. And yet, despite this obvious evidence, General Shafter still seemed ready to ignore it. He kept his army in position, though totally inactive, for several days.

Richard Harding Davis, the most experienced of all the correspondents, made no secret of his feelings about the general's strategy. He expressed his opinions one night around a campfire shared by all the reporters in the field, including Marty.

"I think it's criminal," Davis said without mincing words. "I've been far enough forward that I can see the Spanish in the hills. They just stroll leisurely around through the rifle pits as if they had all the time in the world. And why shouldn't they think that? We are certainly giving them enough time to prepare for us. The network of pits grows longer and more complex. Soon they'll have the positions so well fortified that we won't be able to drive them out of there with ten times the artillery we have now.''

"Surely, Richard, General Shafter knows what he is doing,'' one of the other reporters suggested.

"Does he? Every day now the Spaniards have had a parade through the streets of El Caney. A parade, mind you. I believe they have made Shafter an honorary general in their army.''

The other reporters laughed nervously. Though some of them may have shared Davis's feelings about the general, they would never voice them. For one thing, none of the other reporters considered themselves expert enough in military matters to comment. Davis was immune to that, though, for he had covered a hundred campaigns in a dozen wars around the world.

The other reason the reporters were reluctant to comment on the situation was because they were there at the sufferance of General Shafter. He could send them away simply by withdrawing their authorization. Again, Davis was immune to such fear, because he was a reporter of tremendous popularity and power. If Shafter withdrew his authorization, Davis easily could have it reinstated by the president or even by Congress if necessary.

"The only one doing anything right now,'' Davis went on, "is Col. Juan Alvarez. I tell you, if I could speak Spanish, I'd be with him. That's where the news is being made.''

Shortly after that, the subject changed. But though the reporters began talking about something else, Marty continued to think about Davis's remark with regard to Colonel Alvarez. Well, Marty could speak Spanish. And if her relationship with Todd was irreparably broken, then she should pay all the more attention to her profession. Her profession was journalism, and if doing her best meant going with Colonel Alvarez, then that was where she was going. Innocently, as if she weren't really interested, she managed to find out the location of Alvarez's headquarters. Tomorrow, she would go there.

*   *   *

Marty got up at the break of dawn the next morning and started toward Colonel Alvarez's headquarters. It was about five miles away, but it wasn't toward the hills around Santiago, so Marty felt reasonably safe. Also, she was prepared to pass herself off as a Cuban woman, should any Spanish soldiers happen upon her.

She had been walking for a little over an hour when someone called out to her.

"Tell me, my beautiful one, do the Americans know you have strayed so far from their camp?"

She had not seen anyone, and didn't see anyone now, so the voice shocked her.

"Who is it?" she called into the thick growth of trees. "Who is there?"

"It is I, Colonel Alvarez," Alvarez said, suddenly appearing then. He stood in front of her, his hands on his hips, looking at her through laughing black eyes that were almost mocking.

"I don't know if they know or not," Marty replied. "I didn't ask anyone's permission; I just came to see you."

"You came to see me?" Alvarez preened his mustache. "I am truly flattered."

"No, you don't understand," Marty said. His cavalier attitude disturbed her, and she was beginning to think the whole thing was a mistake. "I came to write a story about you."

"A story?" Alvarez said. "A story about the dashing and handsome *querrero,* yes?"

Marty sighed. If he wanted to call himself a dashing and handsome warrior, who was she to argue? In fact, she had to admit, he was dashing and handsome. "Yes," she said.

"Very well. Come with me; I will take you to my camp."

The Cuban camp was vastly different from the American camp. It wasn't just that the Americans all had uniforms, while the Cubans, except for Alvarez, had none. It wasn't that the American camp had some semblance of order, with tents laid out in neat rows, while the Cubans seemed to pitch them helter-skelter, wherever their mood dictated. It was much more than that. It was the overall mood of the camp.

Although the American soldiers did sing songs and laugh and talk around their campfires at night, by day the soldiers drilled constantly. There was no drilling at all going on in this camp, and the songs weren't quiet, lonesome ballads; they were loud and cheerful and backed up by guitars and bongo drums. It was almost as if the war were nothing but a big party. Marty saw two or three dozen women, many of whom were dancing for the soldiers, while others worked over cooking pots that were suspended above the open fires. To Marty's amazement, there were children darting around, playing games, laughing, and squealing.

"Is this . . . is this a war camp?" Marty asked.

"Yes, of course. What do you think it is?" Juan asked.

"I don't know," Marty said. "There are women and children here. . . . You are singing and dancing."

"You mean it is different in the Americans' camp?"

"Yes. It is very different."

"I know the difference," Juan said. "The Americans have come down here to make war on the Spanish. The Americans are big and rich and they come from the north to save us. Then, when they have saved us, they will tell the rest of the world how powerful they are. For them, it is but a game they play upon the world stage. For us, senorita, it has been a way of life for many years. When I was a child, I was fighting the Spanish. When I was a young man of fifteen, I was fighting the Spanish. And now I am a man of thirty, and still, senorita, I am fighting the Spanish. You think this doesn't look like a war camp? It is, but life must go on. For us there is always the war, but there is also life. Do you blame my men if some have wives and some have girlfriends and some have children? No, you cannot. And look closely, senorita, because when the Spanish have been beaten, if the North Americans do not return soon to their own country, then we will fight them as well!"

The passion of Juan's statement surprised Marty, and when she heard his thinly veiled threat against America she looked at him with a flash of anger. She was quick to respond.

"How can you threaten to fight the Americans when they have come to help you?" she asked. "My mother is Cuban;

I know of the Spanish oppression. You say this is a game for the Americans, but if it is, it is a dangerous game. Already many have been killed, and more will be killed before the Spanish are beaten. But what do you care? You have your guitars and your dancing and your wives and your girlfriends! Why don't you just enjoy yourself and let the Americans win the war for you?"

"Tell me, senorita, if the Americans are fighting so bravely, why have you come here?"

"I was told that I could get a good story if I came here," Marty said. She looked around, then made a scornful clucking sound with her tongue. "The only story I can get from here is how to have fun at an outdoor picnic."

"I see," Juan said. He sighed, then looked at Marty for a long moment. "You say your mother is Cuban. All Cuban women I know can ride a horse. Can you ride a horse?"

"Yes."

"I will find you some clothes. Change into them. Tonight you will get a story, senorita."

"Why must I change my clothes?" Marty asked.

"In those clothes you stand out. I have learned, after twenty years of war, that one's chances of living longer are greater if one doesn't stand out. Go into my tent. I'll find someone who is small and get pants and a shirt from him. Unless, of course, you have no wish to go on a raid."

"A raid? You . . . you are willing to let me go on a raid?" She didn't even try to hide her surprise.

"You did say you wanted to get a story, didn't you?"

"Yes," Marty said.

"Does the idea of going on a raid frighten you?"

Marty paused for a moment; then she answered.

"Yes," she admitted. "It frightens me a great deal. But I want to do it."

Juan laughed. "Good for you," he said. "I'm glad you admitted you were afraid. I think I may not have let you go otherwise."

"Why not?"

"Because you would be either lying or crazy," Juan said. "Now, I will find you some clothes."

A half hour later, Marty had removed her *faire le bicyclette* and replaced it with a man's trousers and shirt. She bunched her hair up under her hat and from a distance could be taken for a slender young boy.

Juan introduced her to a young woman as an American newspaper reporter. Marty made friends with the woman, whose name was Carlotta. Carlotta invited Marty to eat with her that night.

"Are you Colonel Alvarez's wife?" Marty asked.

Carlotta laughed. "No. Colonel Alvarez has no wife . . . though he could have any woman he wanted. I am the girl-friend of Lieutenant Carillo. Someday we will see a priest; then I will be his wife."

"It doesn't bother you to live like this?" Marty asked.

"Live like what?"

"Like this," Marty said, taking in the camp with a wave of her hand. "A camp follower."

"I am not a prostitute, senorita!" Carlotta said sharply.

"No, I didn't mean to imply that you were," Marty said quickly. "I just meant that . . . it must be difficult for you to live in the field like a soldier."

"I am with my man," Carlotta replied simply. "That is enough."

Marty thought of the simple elegance of Carlotta's words. She was with her man. That was enough.

Marty led Carlotta into a conversation and was able to get several stories about camp life with the Cuban patriots. Despite the friendship, stories, food, music, and dancing, there was an awareness in Marty's mind that tonight there was going to be a raid against the Spanish.

Marty was nervous about it, but no one in the camp seemed to share her nervousness. The music and gaiety continued, unabated, until well after nightfall. When it was nearly ten, Marty began to wonder if there really was going to be a raid, or had Colonel Alvarez just told her that?

Juan had disappeared immediately after he introduced Marty to Carlotta. Now, as the music was dying down at last, Juan appeared out of the shadows. He stood in the flickering orange glow of the campfire and smiled at Marty. His eyes, always flashing anyway, now glowed with the reflected light of the fire. It was almost as if she could see . . . in his soul . . . the fires of hell.

"Do you still want to go on the raid?" he asked quietly.

"You mean you are going to have a raid?"

"Of course. Why would you question it?" Juan replied.

"I thought it was too late."

Juan chuckled. "I learned long ago that raids are more successful when the enemy is in bed," he said. "Come."

Marty followed Juan through the darkness to an area lighted by burning cones. There were at least two dozen men there, silently tending to their horses. Marty examined the expressions on the faces of the men. These were the same men she had seen playing guitars, singing, chasing the women, and teasing the children. Now, it was if they were completely different men. Their faces were very serious.

"Here, use this," one of the men said, handing Marty a bowl.

"Use it? Use it for what?" Marty looked into the bowl and saw a little pile of powdered charcoal.

"Put it on your face," Juan said. "Like this." He dipped his fingers into the powder, then began rubbing it on Marty's face.

"Hey, what are you doing?"

"This darkens your face," Juan informed her. "With this, your face won't shine in the moonlight."

Marty saw that all the men either were using the same thing or had already used it. In the cases where it was already used, she could easily tell the difference. Twenty yards into the darkness and they disappeared. Those who hadn't yet used it shone brightly.

"All right," Marty said. "I'll use it." She dipped her fingers into the bowl and began smearing the black stuff liberally all over her face.

"Do you have rowels on your spurs?" Juan asked.

"I'm not wearing spurs."

"Good. You could wear spurs if you wanted; it's the rowels that cause the trouble. Sometimes they jingle, and that can give us away."

The men who were going on the raid tied leather thongs around their trouser legs to keep them from rustling. They tied down loose straps on their saddles, and they emptied their pockets. Soon, they were ready.

"Now," Juan said. "We are real guerrillas."

The little guerrilla army moved out silently, slipping quickly into the shadows, where they were swallowed up by the night. Marty rode along with them. She was frightened, but she managed to hide her fright, because she was excited by the opportunity. She was certain that no other reporter had ever actually gone along on a guerrilla raid, not even Richard Harding Davis.

They stayed off the road, but because every man knew the country so well, they were able to use the gullies, depressions, and streambed as effectively as if they were brick-paved roads. The riders were totally unhampered by the terrain.

Finally, after a ride of about an hour, Juan held up his hand and the others stopped. They were on a little rise, looking down toward Santiago. It was after midnight now, and there were very few lights burning in the city. In fact, the city was only visible because the moon was exceptionally bright, and the buildings loomed like great shadows within shadows.

A dog barked.

A peal of laughter floated up to them, the response to some funny remark passed by someone unseen.

A door slammed.

"Cervera," Juan hissed. "Take three men and create a diversion on the south side. When they have responded to your diversion, we will hit them from the north. Remember to be very careful with the civilians. We want to free our people, not kill them."

"Si," Cervera said, and he counted off three men, then started around to the other side of the town while Marty, Juan, and the others waited. One of the horses shuffled nervously.

"Raids such as these are merely nuisance raids, I know," Juan explained. "But it keeps the Spanish nervous, and when the Americans make their attack at Santiago . . . if they ever do make their attack . . . perhaps it will be easier for them because we will have deprived the Spaniards of their sleep."

"Such raids are very dangerous, aren't they?" Marty asked.

"Yes."

"Do you think the results are worth the risk?"

"We are at war, Senorita McGuire. We do what we must," Juan said.

The sound of gunfire erupted from the other side of the town. From somewhere inside the town there was the sound of a hammer beating against a steel rim, sounding an alarm. Several other dogs joined the one that had been barking steadily, and shouts of alarm floated up to them. The volume of gunfire increased rapidly as the Spaniards began shooting back.

Juan laughed. "Listen to them! They think that, somehow, the Americans have managed to slip around behind them during the night. They have all rushed to the other side of the city!"

Marty could see flashes of fire illuminating the night, and she thought the scene would be very pretty if it weren't for the fact that the flashes all represented potential death.

Juan stood in his stirrups and looked over at his men, then back toward Marty.

"Are you ready, Senorita McGuire?"

Marty felt her heart in her mouth.

"Yes," she said quietly.

"Stay close to me," Juan said. "If I get shot, then find someone else and stay close to him. Bend low over the neck of your horse so that you do not make a good target."

"All right," Marty said.

Juan held his hand up, suspending the drama for an agonizing moment. Then he brought it down sharply, and his line of irregular soldiers swept forward.

Juan's raiders pounded into the city from the north, while all the defenders had rushed to the breastworks to the south. His men started firing and shouting.

Juan rode straight toward a barricade that was manned by a handful of Spanish soldiers. Marty, who had been told to stay by his side, followed. An instant later, she realized that Juan intended to leap the barricade, so she prepared her horse to jump. She urged her horse up and over, and the horse jumped as if it had wings. It was an exhilarating experience.

"This way!" Juan shouted.

Marty followed Juan along the rear of the prepared trench. She heard explosions behind her, and she saw that others in the raiding party were following Juan's lead, but they were throwing lighted bombs into the trenches. She watched one cannon as it was lifted off its carriage by an explosion.

Suddenly Juan turned away from the trench and began riding out of town, and Marty followed. It wasn't until then that she was aware of the angry buzzing sounds that were made by the bullets as they zinged past.

Marty could feel the muscles of the horse working beneath her, and she bent low over its neck, not only remembering Juan's admonition to present a smaller target but also in an effort to urge greater speed from the animal. A moment later, they passed the last structure, and Marty realized they were out of the city and making good their getaway.

One of the riders let out a war cry, and the others joined in. Marty surprised herself by yelling with them. For the first time in her life she could understand the battle cries of men at war. They weren't defiant yells of challenge, as she had often thought. They were spontaneous whoops of joy at still being alive.

CHAPTER 22

The camp turned out to greet Juan and his raiders when they returned. There were shouts and laughter and good-natured bantering between those who had gone and those who had stayed behind.

Marty had been unarmed, of course. She had gone along as an observer only, and yet she felt the same sense of excitement as the men. Never had she been more alive than at this moment! What a thrill it was to ride into the very teeth of the enemy, then ride out again! Her skin was flushed and tingling from her adventure.

"Double the guard!" Juan said as they dismounted amid the laughter and shouts of congratulations. "The Spaniards may try and return the favor."

"Never!" one of the others called. "The Spaniards are frightened old women. They'll go inside and close their doors and shutters."

"Colonel Diaz is not a frightened old woman," Juan said. "We must watch out for him."

One of the men took Marty's horse for her, and she headed for the tent Juan had given her to use. She was met there by a young woman who was holding a basin of water.

"I thought you might want to wash your face before Colonel Alvarez visits your tent," the young woman suggested.

"Thanks," Marty said, taking the basin. "I would like to clean this stuff off, though I was glad I had it tonight." Marty started to walk into her tent; then she stopped and looked back at the young girl who was already walking away.

"Wait!" Marty called.

"Si, senorita?"

"What did you just say? Something about Colonel Alvarez coming to visit me?"

"Si, senorita," the young girl said. "After every raid, he visits one of the women of the camp. Tonight, I think it will be you."

Marty smiled. "I think not," she said.

"Oh, si, senorita. He likes you very much. You are the only woman he has ever let go on a raid. He will come to see you tonight."

"You don't understand," Marty said. "I am a reporter from North America. I came to visit this camp, and I went on the raid so I could get a story. I'm not interested in Juan Alvarez."

"But, senorita, he is El Commandante. No one refuses El Commandante."

"This is one person who can, and will," Marty said resolutely.

Marty went into her tent and lit a small candle. By the candle's wavering light, she stripped out of the man's shirt she had worn on the raid; then, naked from the waist up, she began washing her face, neck, shoulders, hands, and arms in the basin. The water felt good and cool to her flushed skin.

Marty heard the tent flap move, and she looked around to see Juan standing there, smiling at her, with his dark brown eyes flashing brightly from his handsome face.

"What . . . what are you doing here?" she asked, so surprised and angry by his sudden, unannounced appearance that, for the moment, she forgot that she was partially nude.

"The candle," Juan said easily.

"The candle?"

"The candle makes the inside of your tent golden," Juan said. "It projects your shadow on the walls, and I watched from outside as you took off your shirt."

Marty crossed her arms in front of her, covering her breasts.

"Colonel, I have placed myself in your safekeeping," she said. "Are you going to betray that trust?"

Juan made no attempt to approach her, but neither did he leave. Instead, he just stood there looking at her with a bemused smile on his face.

"Did you enjoy the raid?" Juan asked.

"Enjoy? I wouldn't use the word *enjoy*, but I found it interesting," she admitted.

"Exciting?" Juan asked.

"Yes. I found it exciting."

Juan's smile broadened. "I am glad you do not lie to me. I watched you. I knew that you were excited. You were more than just excited. You were excited as if you were with a man."

"What?" Marty gasped.

Juan laughed. "Don't be frightened by the feeling," he said. "As I told you, I have been at war for many years. I know this feeling. It is something that one can't explain, but everyone who engages the enemy experiences."

"I . . . I don't know what you are talking about." Marty wished she could free herself from the penetrating stare of his black eyes.

"I feel it every time," Juan continued. "First there is a feeling of joy at just being alive. Then there is more. There is an excitement at having cheated death, and that excitement makes me want to have a woman. You feel the same thing, only, of course, you want a man."

"What a preposterous statement!"

"You do not want to make love?"

"No, I do not want to make love."

Juan sighed and shook his head. "Very well," he said. "If you say you don't want to make love, then I won't force myself on you. There are many beautiful women in Cuba. I can easily find another who is just as beautiful, and also is willing."

"Thank you," Marty replied.

Juan started to leave, but at the tent flap he turned back toward her. "If you change your mind," he said, smiling at her with flashing white teeth, "I'll be ready."

"Thank you," Marty said. "If I change my mind, you'll be the first to know."

Juan left and, with a sigh of relief, Marty reached for her shirt.

Suddenly she heard rapid, angry firing outside. The firing was as intense as it had been at Santiago during the raid.

The tent flap suddenly opened again, and Juan stepped back inside. He looked at Marty with a little smile on his face.

"Juan! Juan, what is it?"

"You should have let me make love to you, Marty," he said, using her first name for the first time. "Now it is too late for me." Juan had been holding his hand over his heart, as if in a declaration of love. He lowered his hand, and when he did, the blood that had been trapped in the palm of his hand gushed down his side.

"Juan!"

Juan fell to the ground, and Marty leaned over him.

"Juan!" she called. "Juan!"

The tent opened again, and she heard the sound of a revolver being cocked. She looked toward the entrance and saw the man whose picture Eddie had drawn.

"Colonel Diaz?" she said.

Diaz was puzzled by her recognition. "Do I know you, senorita?" he asked.

"No. I just recognized you, that's all."

Diaz smiled. "You are a very beautiful woman, senorita, and while I am flattered to be identified by someone of your beauty, I fear recognition by a prostitute is bad for my reputation."

"A prostitute?" Marty gasped.

"You are half-naked. Colonel Alvarez was just leaving this tent. Surely you aren't going to tell me you are Colonel Alvarez's wife?"

"No, I . . .," Marty started; then, for the time being, she thought it might be safer for her if Diaz thought she really was a prostitute. "I'm not his wife," she finally said.

"I didn't think so." He stepped to one side and held the

tent flap open. "Cover your nakedness. You are coming with me."

"Why should I come with you?" Marty asked as she put the shirt on.

Diaz smiled. "If you can be a prostitute for Colonel Alvarez, you can be a prostitute for me. After all, what does it take but a little money? And with Alvarez dead, you will need *patrocinio.*"

"I need no one to sponsor me. Please, just let me go."

"I'm afraid I cannot," Diaz said. "Right now, you have two choices. Come with me as my private *puta* or stay here and be shot."

"Shot?"

"Yes."

"I don't understand. Why would you shoot me?"

"There was a raid against Santiago tonight," Diaz said. "Six of my men were killed. In order to stop this sort of thing, I am going to kill twelve rebels. Seven were already killed in battle. That leaves five more to be executed."

"But surely you wouldn't shoot a woman?"

"Why not?" Diaz replied easily. "Three of the seven who have already been killed were women."

Marty heard a shot fired, and she jumped. Diaz chuckled at her. "Make up your mind, senorita."

"All right," Marty said. "I'll go with you."

"Good, good. I'm glad you see it my way. It would be a waste to have to kill such a beautiful woman."

When Marty stepped outside, she saw the bodies of the people who had been killed. One of them was the young woman who had given her the water basin, no more than fifteen minutes ago.

Fifteen minutes? Had all this happened in just fifteen minutes?

"Can you ride?" Diaz asked.

"Yes."

"Bring the girl a horse," Diaz ordered.

One of Diaz's men handed Marty the reins to a horse, and for the second time that night, she climbed into the saddle.

Diaz barked an order, and the raiding party of Spanish

soldiers left the encampment. By now, Marty was exhausted, not only from the lack of sleep but also from extreme emotional stress. She hung in the saddle with dogged determination, purposely not allowing her mind to think beyond the next minute. The entire focus of her life was centered around staying astride the horse.

By the time they reached Santiago, the eastern sky was laced with red. The city had already come to life, and she saw thousands of soldiers in bright blue-and-scarlet uniforms as they prepared for reveille. Many of the townspeople were out as well, and several of them stared in curiosity as she rode by.

Diaz didn't break the gallop until they were in the center of the town square, in front of the church. There the party halted. Diaz returned the salute of someone who greeted him, then swung down from his horse.

"Who is the girl?" a soldier on the ground asked.

"You are a mere sergeant!" Diaz reprimanded him harshly. "The identity of this girl should not concern you."

"I'm sorry, Colonel; I meant no disrespect," the sergeant replied in a wounded voice.

Marty heard the conversation going on and knew that it involved her, but she was so exhausted that, for the moment at least, it meant nothing to her.

"You," Diaz said to Marty. "Come with me."

Marty swung down from her horse and followed Diaz across the square and into the church.

Inside the church, the pews had all been removed to be replaced with sleeping rolls and tables. There were accommodations for nearly one hundred soldiers.

"The church is our headquarters," Diaz explained. "It's a brilliant idea, don't you think? The bell tower is the highest point in the city, and it makes an excellent place for our lookout. Also, I have heard that the North Americans do not like to shoot at a church."

"Don't you think it's a blasphemy to use a church in such a way?" Marty asked.

Diaz chuckled. "You, a whore, speak to me about blasphemy?"

Marty walked up to the apse, and though the altar had been stripped bare, she genuflected.

"Ha!" Diaz said. "A whore who has religion."

"Our Lord welcomes all in His church," someone said, and Marty looked over to see a priest standing nearby.

"Father," Marty said as she looked around the church. "How can you let them do this to a house of the Lord?"

"I tried to stop them," the priest told her.

Suddenly everything began to catch up with Marty, and she felt herself growing dizzy. Her knees weakened, and she had to put out her hand to support herself on the railing.

The priest was beside her in an instant. "Are you all right?" he asked.

"I'm tired," she said.

"Tired? You are exhausted." The priest looked at Diaz. "What have you done to this woman?"

"I haven't done anything to her," Diaz said. "At least, not yet. If she is tired it is because of what went on in that rebel camp. She was a whore for Juan Alvarez."

"No," Marty protested. "I wasn't."

"You were in his camp. What were you if you were not his whore?"

Marty's eyes closed, and her head fell forward. "Please," she mumbled. "I'm so tired."

"Colonel, I beg of you, let this poor child have some rest," the priest implored. "It is inhuman to treat a person so cruelly."

"All right," Diaz said with an impatient wave of his arm. "Take her with you, Father. Let her have some rest. There is plenty of time for what I have in mind after she wakes."

"This way, my child," the priest said. He led her out of the church and into a small building that, at one time had housed the nuns. Now there was only one nun left, and she met them as they stepped through the door.

"This is Sister Theresa," the priest said.

"Has she been injured?" Sister Theresa asked, her voice showing genuine concern.

"I think she has been wounded in spirit," the priest replied. "Please see to it that she gets some rest."

"Of course, Father," Sister Theresa answered.

Marty went with the sister to a small room. There she saw a bed, the first real bed she had seen since coming to Cuba. Sister Theresa led her gently to it; then Marty lay down and was asleep almost the moment her head touched the pillow.

"Lieutenant, we have telephone wire strung all the way from here back to the beach," Captain Bigelow told Todd. "We're in contact with every unit of the expeditionary force."

"And?" Todd asked anxiously.

"No one has seen her," Bigelow said. "She seems to have disappeared."

"How can that be?" Todd asked. "One woman in the middle of several thousand men doesn't just drop out of sight."

"What about the fleet?" Bigelow asked. "Do you think she could have returned to one of the ships?"

"I don't think that's very likely," Todd said. He sighed. "But I'm willing to try anything to find her."

"Keep looking as long as you want," Bigelow said.

"Thank you, sir." Todd reached for his hat. "Permission to use one of the horses, sir. I'll go back to the beach."

"Permission granted."

Todd mounted, then rode back through the array of American fighting men and equipment. To Todd's way of thinking, the soldiers were not being properly utilized. Through his field glasses, he had watched the Spanish preparing for the upcoming battle. They were working energetically to strengthen their fortifications, and they were moving into positions in the hills so they could command the open country approach to Santiago. The Americans were not engaged in similar preparations. They were not reconnoitering, and they weren't cutting new trails through the jungle. They weren't interfering with the Spanish in any way. Instead, the Americans were spending all their time foraging about for local varieties of food to spice up their rations, and they waited eagerly each day for the pack trains that brought mail from home. Many of the soldiers were busy bartering with the locals for tobacco. No one seemed concerned about the battle that would soon take place.

When Todd passed through the narrow draw on the beach side of this hills, he rode over to General Shafter's headquarters. He had a friend there, a classmate from West Point. Second Lieutenant Tibbs was General Shafter's communications officer. If anyone had any idea what was going on, Todd figured, it would be the communications officer.

"Todd, it's good to see you!" Tibbs said. Then he smiled sheepishly. "Or maybe I should call you Lieutenant Murchison, since you now outrank me."

The disparity in their rank came from the fact that Todd had been promoted to first lieutenant when he agreed to take an assignment with the Tenth Cavalry.

"Don't give me that," Todd said.

"So, tell me, how are things going at the front?" Tibbs asked.

"What front?" Todd scoffed. "There's no fighting going on anywhere, so there's no front."

"You sound like Wood and Roosevelt," Tibbs said. "They've already been here, agitating for an immediate attack. I guess you agree with them?"

"I'm just a lieutenant," Todd said. "It isn't my place to agree or disagree. I do feel we should be conducting routine patrols, though. The Spaniards are awfully busy. It would be nice to know what's going on."

"You didn't conduct one last night, did you?" Tibbs asked.

"No, why?"

"General Shafter has been in a tizzy, all day, trying to find out just who did. Every commander in the field denies having anything to do with it, but our advance lookouts and listening posts tell us there were several shots fired in Santiago around midnight last night. You sure you don't know anything about it?"

"Not a thing," Todd said.

Tibbs laughed. "Good. If General Shafter ever finds out who it was, he is going to make it very unpleasant for the guilty party. I'm glad I won't have to be worrying about you." Tibbs got a curious look on his face. "What brings you to headquarters?"

"I'm looking for Miss McGuire," Todd said.

"Miss McGuire? Wait; you mean Marty McGuire, that female correspondent?"

"Yes. Do you know if she is here?"

Tibbs shook his head. "I'm pretty sure she hasn't come around here lately. Someone that pretty I think I would notice."

"Damn," Todd said, his voice edged with frustration.

"What is it?"

"She seems to be missing."

"Missing?" another voice asked. Todd turned toward the door and saw General Shafter standing there. "Where is she?" Shafter asked.

"I don't know, sir. I was hoping she might be here, at headquarters. She isn't with any of the other units; I've checked with all the commanders."

"My God, what a disaster it would be if something has happened to her. The newspapers in the States would crucify us, to say nothing of the grief we would catch from the War and State Departments."

"Yes, sir."

"Are you looking for her?"

"Most thoroughly, sir," Todd replied.

"Good. We must find her."

"With your permission, sir, I would like to visit the *Oregon*."

"All right, go ahead. Do you think she might be there?"

"I don't know," Todd admitted. "But as you may recall, sir, she did do a story from the *Oregon*; there is a possibility she may have gone back. I'd like to go out there and see."

"And if she isn't there?" General Shafter asked.

"Then I will ask Admiral Sampson to signal the entire fleet to look for her. If she is on board a ship, we'll find her."

"I didn't assign anyone to keep a particular eye on her, because I received word that you had that task. The rumor was that it was a task with which you were most pleased."

"Yes, General, I did assume personal responsibility for her."

"You want to tell me what happened? How did she get away from you in the first place?"

"That, General, is a perfect example of my ignorance and incompetence."

Marty wasn't on board the *Oregon*. Todd hadn't really expected her to be, but he was determined to track down every lead until he found her.

Admiral Sampson was on board, though, and he volunteered to make an inquiry throughout the fleet. He signaled under his own code, thus giving the search immediate priority. The admiral's flags, floating atop the mast, were picked up and relayed, ship to ship, along the entire twenty-eight miles the fleet stretched out along Cuba's shoreline. Then, from the last ship, came the reply message: "Miss McGuire is not aboard and has not been seen."

"Thank you anyway," Todd said when the message was given to him.

"I wish you luck in finding her," Admiral Sampson replied. "Oh, it is nearly lunchtime. Won't you join us? I think we have some fresh melon today."

Todd thought of the beans and salt pork his men were eating in the field. He couldn't dine so sumptuously while his men were stuck with their dreary rations.

"No, thank you, sir. I've got to get back to shore as quickly as possible," he said.

"Thinking of your men?" the admiral asked knowingly.

"Yes, sir," Todd replied. "I suppose I am."

"Good man," the admiral said. "Good man. Oh, and be sure and pass my regards on to your father when next you speak to him."

"Yes, sir, I will," Todd said.

As Todd rode in the admiral's gig back to shore, he couldn't get Marty out of his mind. Where was she now? Was she in danger?

CHAPTER 23

S enorita? Senorita? Wake up, senorita."
    Like a cork floating up from far beneath the surface of
a pool, Marty came back to consciousness. She opened her
eyes and saw a woman in a nun's habit. Where was she?

"Are you awake now?"

Marty blinked her eyes in confusion.

"I'm Sister Theresa. Don't you remember me? Father Damien brought you to me."

Marty remembered then. She had been captured by Spanish troops and brought to Santiago. She was in a small building behind the church, probably a cloister.

"Yes," she said. "I remember now."

"You have slept for twenty-four hours, senorita," Sister
Theresa said. "I'm sorry to wake you, but you must take
some nourishment."

"Uh, twenty-four hours?" Marty sat up in the bed and ran
her hand through her hair. "I've slept that long?"

"Si, senorita. I have some food for you. It is just a little
rice. I'm sorry there is nothing more. The soldiers have confiscated all the food, and we are on very strict rations."

"Rice is fine," Marty said. "Thank you."

Marty took the bowl and fork from Sister Theresa and
began eating. The rice had been seasoned with oil of some
sort, and either that or the fact that she was really hungry
made it taste exceptionally good.

"I think the Americans will come soon," Sister Theresa said.

"Why?" Marty asked. "Has there been fighting today?"

"No," Sister Theresa said. "But everyone says there are 1 million Americans camped outside the city."

"There aren't a million Americans," Marty said.

"How do you know?"

"Because I'm . . ." Marty stopped. The woman was in a nun's habit, and she had treated Marty kindly. But it was best to trust no one. Marty had nearly told her that she was an American. "I'm just sure, that's all," she concluded.

"That's a shame," Sister Theresa said. "I was hoping there would be enough Americans to drive the Spaniards away."

"You are not a supporter of the Spaniards?"

"No, senorita," Sister Theresa said. "I know you are the . . . friend . . . of Colonel Diaz, and perhaps you've no wish to hear me say such things. But I have no fear of speaking the truth. Spain is a Catholic country, and yet the Spanish soldiers have defiled the Church in every way they can. No, senorita, I am not a supporter of the Spanish."

"Neither am I," Marty said.

"But you are the woman of Colonel Diaz, are you not?"

"Why do you say that?"

"He came many times yesterday and last night to check on you. He was most concerned."

"I am his prisoner."

"His prisoner?"

"I was with Colonel Alvarez when he was killed. Colonel Diaz took me prisoner."

"Colonel Alvarez is dead?"

"Yes," Marty said.

Sister Theresa crossed herself. "It is a pity," she stated quietly. "Colonel Alvarez was a true patriot."

"Colonel Alvarez was a rebel who was lucky to be killed in battle," a stern voice said. "I wish I had been able to capture him so I could execute him in front of the good citizens of Santiago. Good morning, Sister Theresa. How is our guest this morning?"

"Good morning, Colonel Diaz," Sister Theresa answered. She excused herself and left the room.

Diaz laughed. "I don't think that one quite trusts me," he said.

"Can you blame her? You've made a mockery of all she believes in," Marty told him.

"Oh, you mean the Church? That monument to mankind's confession of servitude to the powers of superstition and ignorance? Yes, we have made a mockery of it. But the funny part is, we have done it all under the authority of a Catholic Majesty." Diaz laughed. "Don't you think that's funny?"

"I think it's disgusting."

"Oh, yes, I forgot," Diaz said. "You are the whore with religion." Diaz put his hand on her shoulder, then let his fingers caress her neck. "Give me the chance, my pretty one, and I will show you something much better than religion. I will show you what it is like to be made love to by a man who has no fear of God."

Marty pushed his hand away, and he laughed.

"You think I speak blasphemy? Well, never mind; I've no time for such diversions now anyway. I must inspect the final defensive positions." He brought Marty's fingers up to his lips and kissed them; then he smiled at her and turned to leave the room. Marty thought of what he had just said about inspecting the defensive positions, and it suddenly dawned on her that if she could escape, this would be good information to have.

"Colonel Diaz?" she called, trying to make her voice sound as if she were really interested in him. "May I go with you?"

Diaz looked at her with surprise. "You want to go with me to inspect the defenses? Why?"

Marty had to be careful with this. She smiled coyly at him. "Oh, I don't care about your defenses," she said. "That's your problem, not mine. I just want to test you, that's all."

"Test me? Test me how?"

"When you captured me, I recognized you. You said you were concerned about your reputation if it were known that a *puta* knew your name. But just now you told me you had no fear of God. Surely a man who has no fear of God has no fear for his reputation.''

Diaz laughed out loud. "So, you want all the men to see you with me, is that it?''

"Yes. If you want the pleasure of my body, you must pay for it. I am a prostitute, remember? I always extract payment from my suitors. The payment I want from you is your public acknowledgment of me.''

Diaz held his hand out toward her. "You are a sly one. Very well, come with me.''

Marty followed Diaz outside the cloister.

"Sergeant, get a horse for the senorita!'' he commanded.

"Sí, Colonel.''

Shortly thereafter, Marty was astride a horse and following Diaz through the streets of the city. They rode for nearly two hours, looking at trenches and forts and at the soldiers who were detailed to them.

The city of Santiago was bordered on the west by a bay. The Spanish defenses were arranged in a system of forts, interconnected by a network of trenches. The forts were heaviest on the eastern approaches to the city, and that was as expected, because the American forces were spread out to the east. There was a fairly sizable gap in the northeast corner of the city.

"Why is there so much space between these forts?'' Marty asked.

Colonel Diaz laughed.

"So, you are a military strategist, are you? Have you heard voices from your God? Are you Joan of Arc, come to save your people?''

"No,'' Marty said. "I was just curious.''

"Look,'' Diaz said, and with his riding quirt he pointed to a hill less than two kilometers away. "That is San Juan Hill.''

Marty looked at the hill, and she saw several soldiers on its crest.

"As long as we control that hill, we control the approach to the city. And we control the area here, between the forts. Don't worry; the defenses are quite well laid out. All the forts have interlacing fields of fire so that . . .'' He stopped; then he laughed. ''You have no idea what I'm talking about, do you?''

''No,'' she said. She smiled at him. ''But it pleases me to hear you talk of it.''

''Pleases you?''

''Excites me,'' Marty said. She thought of Juan Alvarez and how he had accused her of being sexually aroused by the raid. ''Do you know what I mean when I say it excites me?'' she asked huskily.

Diaz caught his breath, and Marty could almost see tiny red dots appear in his eyes. He ran his finger along his lip as he continued talking.

''The forts all have interlacing fields of fire,'' he said. ''If one of the forts is knocked out, then the area can be covered by another fort. All except San Juan Hill. We have no fixed forts there, but we do have a half-dozen field artillery pieces and twelve hundred men. The Americans will attack in a line from El Caney Creek to the Santiago railroad. Those who come near San Juan Hill will be cut to pieces by our troops who hold the high ground.'' Diaz looked at Marty and waved his finger back and forth. ''That is the secret, my dear,'' he said. ''To achieve victory, you must hold the high ground.''

''What if the Americans capture San Juan Hill? Then they will hold the high ground, will they not?''

Diaz laughed. ''Do not try and determine military strategy. You aren't prepared for it. We know that the Americans' primary objective is Santiago. They are bold, vain men. They will try to take the city head-on . . . and they will fail.'' Diaz took out his watch and looked at it. ''It's nearly time for lunch. Come; let's return to the city.''

At the moment, they were on the outskirts of Santiago, just behind the network of trenches. As they started back into the city, the road passed beneath a banyan tree with low-hanging branches. Marty grabbed a limb and pulled it with her as she rode. Diaz, who was behind her, was looking off to his right and didn't see her. When Marty pulled the limb as far as she could, she released it. It slapped into Diaz with the impact of a baseball bat, unceremoniously dumping him from his horse.

"What are you doing?" Diaz shouted in surprised anger.

Marty wheeled her horse around, then grabbed the reins of Diaz's horse. She raced straight for the trench.

"Stop her! Stop her!" Diaz shouted.

The soldiers in the trench were so startled that they had no time to react. By the time they turned around to see what Colonel Diaz was yelling about, Marty, still leading Diaz's horse by its reins, had already urged her horse into a graceful leap over the trench. When she was on the other side of the trench, she dropped the reins of Diaz's horse and bent low over her own animal. She was to the road now, and she was getting away. She was going to make it!

Suddenly her horse let out a little whinny, and down it went. Marty was thrown over the horse's head, and she hit the ground hard.

For an instant she didn't know what had happened. She lay on the ground with all the breath knocked out of her, looking up at the sky, trying to figure out where she was and how she got there.

Gradually the breath returned to her body, and with it came a sense of location and the desperation of her condition. She managed to pull herself into an upright position; then she looked over at the horse. It was then that she saw why the horse had gone down. It had been shot.

The horse lay very still, killed either by the bullet that struck it or by a broken neck from the fall. Marty wished now that she hadn't released Diaz's horse.

Slowly, groggily, Marty got to her feet, but by the time she was standing again there were six Spanish soldiers within easy shooting range, and they were all aiming at her.

"Stop, senorita, or we will shoot you right here!" someone shouted.

Marty sighed, then started back toward them. Her escape attempt had failed.

As it developed, the church that was serving as the military headquarters also served as a military courtroom, for less than one hour after Marty tried to escape she found herself facing a court-martial by military tribunal. It was all being done legally and properly. An officer was appointed to serve as Marty's defense attorney, while another officer served as the prosecutor. There were three senior officers, including General Toral, second in command only to General Linares, sitting behind a table. These officers were acting as both judge and jury.

Colonel Diaz was an interested bystander, but he wasn't part of the judicial proceedings. He had been the one who initiated the trial, however.

The prosecutor read the charges in a droning, unemotional voice.

"The accused female is charged with being a spy, in that she did ride with Colonel Diaz to observe all the defensive positions of our soldiers, then attempted to escape so she could inform the Americans of those defense positions."

"Objection," Marty's attorney said. Marty was a little surprised to hear him say anything. He had been appointed as her attorney, but, as yet, they had not even been able to conduct a private conversation.

"What is the objection?" General Toral asked.

"Colonel Diaz knows only that the prisoner was trying to escape. He doesn't know if she intended to tell the Americans anything."

"How do you respond to that?" the general asked the prosecutor.

"The prisoner is not Cuban, as Colonel Diaz had been led to believe," the prosecutor said. He looked at Marty and smiled broadly. "She looks Cuban and she speaks flawless Spanish with a Cuban accent. But this woman is Marty McGuire. She is an American. This we know from one of our spies who was present at Siboney, where Miss McGuire was asked to speak to a group of Cuban detainees."

There was a collective gasp of surprise from those who were in the courtroom watching the trial.

"Are you an American?" her own attorney asked her in surprise.

"Yes," Marty admitted.

"If it please the court . . ." Marty's attorney said, standing and bowing slightly toward General Toral.

"Yes?" Toral responded.

"Since the defendant makes no denial of the fact that she is American, then I can provide no defense of her activities. Therefore, I plead her guilty of spying as charged and ask only that the court be lenient in its punishment."

"Wait a minute!" Marty said to her lawyer. "I didn't tell you I wanted to plead guilty."

"I am your attorney, appointed by this court," her lawyer said. "I may plead your case any way I choose, and I choose to plead you guilty."

"But don't you have to consider what I want you to do?"

"No, senorita," her lawyer replied matter-of-factly.

"Excellency," the prosecutor said. "As the defense stands adjudged guilty by her own lawyer, the prosecution will present no further evidence in this case. We ask that you sentence the defendant to death by firing squad, but grant her the right to a final confession and absolution by a priest."

General Toral and the two officers with him bent their heads together in a brief conference. Then General Toral placed a handkerchief on his head.

"Senorita McGuire, it is the decision of this court that you are guilty of spying as charged. At dawn tomorrow, you will be taken from this place to Calavera Hill, where you will be tied to a post and executed by a firing squad. Do you have anything to say?"

"No," Marty answered. Her throat was dry and her knees were weak, but she was rather proud of her ability to maintain her composure.

"May God have mercy on your soul," General Toral said.

Two soldiers stepped up to Marty and took hold of her. As they started to leave the church, they passed by Colonel Diaz.

"So, now you will see if this God in whom you believe exists," Diaz said. "What a stupid woman you are."

"My one consolation, Colonel, is that I no longer have to worry about you putting your hands on me," Marty said.

"Whore!" Diaz replied, and he slapped her.

"Colonel Diaz!" General Toral shouted. "Leave this courtroom! Leave at once!"

Diaz smiled evilly at Marty. "Tomorrow," he said. "Tomorrow, I will be there at your execution. I will personally give the orders to the firing squad."

"I'll be dead no matter who gives the orders," Marty said. "Do you think your words mean anything to me?"

Diaz grew red in the face; then he turned and walked out.

The soldiers returned Marty to the same room she had been in the night before. This time, though, they stationed a guard outside her door.

"Is it true?" Sister Theresa asked. "Are you really an American?"

"Yes," Marty said.

"And a spy? What a dangerous thing for you to do."

"I'm not really a spy," Marty said. "At least, I didn't intend to be. As I told you before, I was captured by Colonel Diaz and brought here. Actually, I'm a journalist."

"A journalist who goes to war is as brave as a spy," Sister Theresa said.

"And, I have discovered, just as foolish," Marty stated. She lay down on her bed and closed her eyes. Tears streaked down her cheeks. "I should have stayed with Todd Murchison."

"Todd Murchison? Who is Todd Murchison?"

"He is an American army lieutenant in the Tenth Cavalry and the man I love . . . or loved. That's all past tense now." She laughed, a short, bitter laugh. "By this time tomorrow, my entire life will be past tense."

Todd dunked his head into the washbasin and scrubbed his hair with soap. He washed all the sand out, then rinsed his hair and was drying it when Private Bates approached him. There was someone with Bates. At first, Todd didn't see the other person, because it was dark and the person was dressed all in black. As they got closer, Todd realized that the other person was a Catholic nun.

"Lieutenant Murchison? We picked this woman up out at the advance post. She's been babbling somethin' in Spanish, but the only thing we could understand was your name."

"My name? She was speaking my name?"

"Yes, sir," Bates replied.

"All right, thank you," Todd said. "I'll take care of it. Oh, send Corporal Jackson to me, would you? He learned Spanish when he was in Arizona."

"Yes, sir," Bates said.

"Teniente Murchison?" the nun asked.

"Yes," Todd said. "Uh, si. Si, I am Lieutenant Murchison." He pointed to himself.

"Lieutenant, you want me, sir?" Corporal Jackson asked, arriving at that moment.

"Yes, thank you, Jackson. Find out what this sister wants."

Jackson spoke in Spanish, and the sister smiled happily at the prospect of being understood. She began speaking, and she spoke so quickly that Jackson had to slow her down a little so he could understand her.

"Sweet Jesus," Jackson blurted in English. "It's Miss McGuire, Lieutenant. The Spaniards are about to execute her!"

"What?" Todd exploded. "What in blazes happened?"

Jackson related the story of Marty's capture, then of her subsequent attempt to escape and, finally, her trial. "They say she was spying on them, Lieutenant, and tomorrow morning at dawn, they are going to shoot her."

"Where?" Todd asked in a tight voice.

Jackson relayed the question; then came the answer.

"That's why the sister's here," he said. "They are going to take Miss McGuire out of Santiago to the place where they execute all their criminals. I guess they figure they can get there, do the job, and then return before we find out what's going on. But the sister sneaked out after dark. She took a big chance in coming here, Lieutenant."

"Yes, well, tell her the United States Army is thankf— no, no, to hell with that. Tell her that I, personally, am very thankful to her for coming to me with this information. And tell her we are going to rescue Miss McGuire."

Jackson translated the information; then Sister Theresa smiled and replied to his remarks.

"What'd she say?"

Jackson smiled. "She said Miss McGuire is wise to love such a brave man as the lieutenant," he said.

"Yes, well," Todd said. He cleared his throat in embarrassment. "You, uh, don't have to tell everyone about the entire conversation," he noted.

"Don't worry, sir. She didn't say anything the men didn't already know," Jackson said.

"Thank you, Jackson. That'll be all. Oh, and please see if there is anything the sister needs, like food or water. I'm going to see Colonel Baldwin to get permission to take out a rescue party; then I'm going to see the sergeant major and have him call for volunteers."

"Lieutenant, I'd like to be the first volunteer," Jackson said.

"You can't be," Bates put in quickly.

"Why not?"

" 'Cause I done volunteered, you fool."

"Thank you," Todd said. "Thank both of you."

The sky in the east had lightened to gray, but, as yet, there was no real indication of dawn. Marty was sitting on a box in the rear of a wagon. The wagon was being pulled by a team of mules. Father Damien was sitting on the box beside her. There were two mounted soldiers leading them and four mounted soldiers following. They were the firing squad. Colonel Diaz was also riding along with them, though he kept a haughty distance. Whether he was keeping his distance from the firing squad or from her Marty didn't know.

"I don't know where Sister Theresa is this morning," Father Damien said. "It isn't like her to disappear. She should have been here to comfort you."

"I'm sure it was uncomfortable for her, Father," Marty replied.

"How generous you are," Father Damien said. "You are forgiving of Sister Theresa's shortcoming, even as our Lord forgave his persecutors from the cross. Think of our Lord, my dear. Draw comfort from the fact that he suffered and died and yet returned with the promise of eternal life for all who believed.''

"Yes, Father," Marty said. Marty didn't know how to explain to Father Damien that, though she was Catholic, she didn't need to hold onto that thought to comfort her. She didn't need comforting because, in truth, she wasn't frightened. She didn't know why. She knew she was going to die shortly, that this sunrise would be the last she would ever see, and yet, to her amazement, she had never felt more calm or composed in her entire life. It was as if all cares and worries had been reduced to one infinitesimal grain of sand. She had less than fifteen minutes to live. It was as if someone had just told her that she had fifteen minutes to catch a train. When one was faced with certain death, death lost its mystery and its sting. She thought of the line from Corinthians: "O death, where is thy sting?" The line comforted her.

The wagon stopped, and Marty looked up. The driver turned around toward her and made an apologetic shrugging motion with his shoulders.

"I'm sorry, senorita," he said. "We are here. Would you get down, please?"

Marty slid off the box and hopped down to the ground. It wasn't until then that she looked closely at the box she had been sitting on and realized that it was her coffin.

"Let's do it and be done with it," Diaz said.

Father Damien held up his hand. "Colonel, she was promised the right to have a final confession and to be granted absolution."

"If you have to do all that mumbo jumbo, do it," Diaz told the priest. "But be quick about it. I want her dead and buried before the sun is full above the horizon. We are in an exposed position out here, and I don't like it."

"Come," Father Damien said, and he and Marty walked several feet away from the wagon. They both knelt by a post, and Marty realized then that it was the stake to which she would be tied for her execution. The stake was pierced and torn by bullets from previous executions, and it was stained with the blood of other victims.

"Bless me, Father, for I have sinned," Marty started.

Before Marty could utter another word, gunfire erupted. Immediately upon the heels of the gunfire, Marty heard a battle cry:

"Eeeeeyoowwww! Buffalo Soldiers!"

"What?" Father Damien started.

"It's Todd!" Marty shouted as she saw Todd break out of the woodland and ride toward her, leading a riderless horse. "Father Damien, I'm saved!"

The Spanish who weren't felled by the first volley turned their horses toward Santiago and started running. The Buffalo Soldiers gave half-hearted chase, but the real purpose of their mission, Marty's rescue, had been accomplished.

Todd reached the stake; then he swung down from his horse and captured Marty in his embrace. They needed no words. They exchanged everything in a kiss.

Todd squeezed Marty so tightly she was afraid he was going to break a rib. Then, with a happy laugh, he swung her around.

"Where have you been, girl?" he asked. "How did you wind up here?"

"That's a long story," Marty said. "Do you really want to go into it now? How did you know I was here?"

"Sister—"

"Theresa!" Marty said. "So that's where she went."

"Sister Theresa?" Father Damien said, hearing her name.

Marty turned to Father Damien and explained to him what had happened and Sister Theresa's involvement.

"I am so happy," he said. "Sister Theresa has done a brave and wonderful thing."

"What about the priest?" Todd asked. "Does he want to come with us? It isn't going to be safe inside Santiago much longer. We'll soon be attacking the place."

"I'm sure I can talk him into coming with us," Marty said. "The Spaniards have taken over his church and converted it into their military headquarters."

"They have? That's good to know."

Marty smiled at him. "I've got a lot more information

that's going to be good for you to know,'' she said. ''I didn't keep my eyes closed while I was there.''

''I noticed that. It almost got you killed, too. I hope what you got was worth it.''

''When you take San Juan Hill, you'll know it was worth it.''

''San Juan Hill?'' Todd laughed. ''We don't plan to take it. We're going to attack the city directly.''

''I don't think so,'' Marty said with a knowing smile. ''I think when you learn how all the defenses are laid out you are going to agree with me. San Juan Hill must be taken first.''

Chapter 24

It was three o'clock in the morning on July 1. Colonel Baldwin, Colonel Roosevelt, Colonel Wood, and Col. Nelson Pickett were in General Shafter's command tent. General Shafter was very ill now, and he lay in his bunk as he spoke to the commanders.

"Gentlemen, I fear I won't be able to participate as actively in today's battle as I would wish. However, certain information has reached me that makes me realize how imperative it is that San Juan Hill be taken."

"General, I thought we agreed that the best approach would be to attack the city and leave the hill isolated," Roosevelt said. "We were going to approach the city from the east."

"That is precisely what the Spanish expect us to do," General Shafter replied. "They are most heavily fortified in the east and most open in the northeast quadrant, once San Juan falls into our hands."

"How heavily fortified is the hill, General?"

"My information is that there are twelve hundred soldiers and very little artillery on the hill."

"I hope your information is dependable."

"It is, gentlemen. It is. Now, I suggest you get back to your men and make all preparations to attack. I will establish the battle headquarters at the El Pozo house. Please supply me with couriers from each of your regiments so that I may transmit my orders to you."

The three colonels saluted General Shafter and returned to their own regiments. By the time Colonel Baldwin reached his camp, his men had already finished breakfast and were formed into battalions and companies, awaiting further instructions.

Eight thousand, four hundred American soldiers would be climbing the hill against twelve hundred well-entrenched, well-armed Spaniards. Though the Americans outnumbered the Spaniards, the difference in numbers would be more than offset by a very real military axiom. It is much easier to defend than to attack, and the Spaniards had the high ground. The Americans would have to expose themselves and climb the hill to take it away from them.

"Here comes the colonel," Sergeant Major Baker told the officers and non-commissioned officers who were awaiting final instructions. Captain Bigelow called everyone to attention. Colonel Baldwin swung down from his horse and gave them at ease.

"All right, this is it," he began. "We've been lying around here for days now, wondering when something was going to happen. We've been watching the Spaniards dig in deeper and deeper, and now the time has come for us to earn our pay. We're going to take San Juan Hill."

"What about Santiago?" Captain Bigelow asked.

"Don't worry about Santiago. San Juan Hill is the key to this entire area. Trust me, if we capture San Juan Hill, we will have effectively crushed the entire Spanish resistance in all of Cuba. Now, go back to your units and get ready. We want to be in position to begin our attack at sunrise."

The officers and NCOs saluted, then hurried back to their own units to relay the orders to their men.

As the sun rose, Todd could see the long line of American soldiers. They were all cavalrymen, but all were dismounted, and they would attack San Juan Hill on foot.

Todd heard a rumbling sound and looked around to see a battery of field guns being hurried into position on a small nearby hill. The horses strained against the load as the guns were pulled up the hill. The gun crews unhitched the horses, then turned the guns around and got them into position. Todd watched as one of the guns was loaded. The men around the gun stood back and put their fingers into their ears. The man behind the gun gave a quick jerk on the lanyard, and the gun roared. A bulging white cloud erupted from the muzzle, the wheels whirled back twice on the rebound, and the shell went hissing through the air. A few seconds later there was a puff of smoke on top of San Juan Hill where the shell burst. Immediately after the first gun was fired, all the other guns in the battery opened up, and great clouds of white smoke hung on the ridge crest.

There was a peculiar rushing noise in the air; then something burst high above Todd's head. After the burst there was a whistling sound, then the sound of something cutting through the trees.

"Shrapnel!" someone shouted. "The Spaniards are raining shrapnel on us."

Another shell burst right in the middle of one of the other regiments, killing and wounding several.

Artillery was particularly frightening to the soldiers, for very few of them—even the veterans of the western campaigns—had faced it before. The Indians didn't use artillery.

"They've been up there long enough; they've got the range of everything," one of the officers said. "It's not going to be an easy task to get them out of there."

"Look!" one of the men shouted. "We got us a balloon aloft!"

Todd looked toward the balloon.

"You ask me, that's not all that bright an idea," Captain Bigelow observed. "I tried to get them to use the balloon three days ago. Then we could've gotten some idea of the lay of the land. Now it's too close to the front and it's just going to draw fire."

As if fulfilling Captain Bigelow's prophecy, the balloon was suddenly hit by a bursting shrapnel shell, and it began fluttering down in full view of both armies. The Americans could hear the cheers of the Spanish soldiers as the balloon sank into the trees. Todd noticed that both the balloonist and his observer survived the descent, for they climbed down from the trees, then beat a hasty retreat.

However, the destruction of the balloon seemed to fire the Spanish into grater zeal and the bombardment from the top of the hill increased, raking the Americans with deadly accurate fire.

As the balloonists ran back toward their own lines, one of them was hit as he crossed the San Juan River. He fell into the water, then became a particular target of the Spanish riflemen. Bullets kicked up all around the hapless soldier.

"Help! Help!" he shouted.

Suddenly Sergeant Major Baker stood up, then started running toward the river.

"Sergeant Major! Sergeant Major, get back here!" Colonel Baldwin shouted.

Baker continued to run toward the river. By now the Spanish marksmen had seen him as well and they started directing their fire toward him. Baker splashed out into the water, then reached down and scooped up the balloonist. As it was the practice to use smaller, lighter men for the balloon ascensions, Sergeant Major Baker was able to pick the man up, toss him across his shoulder, then start back toward his lines.

"Give him covering fire, men!" Todd shouted, and first the Tenth, then the men of the Ninth and Seventh, as well as the Rough Riders and Lightning Cavalry, all began shooting. The firing not only helped keep the Spanish heads down; it also had a secondary unplanned but desirable effect. Because the soldiers were not yet equipped with smokeless powder ammunition, an immense cloud of gun smoke billowed forth from all the shooting. The result was to hide Baker and the man he had rescued from the enemy. It also hid Baker from the Americans and, for a long, anxious moment, they stared into the huge bank of smoke. Then they saw Baker emerge from the smoke, the balloonist still over his shoulder. An immense cheer went up along the entire American line as Sergeant Major Baker became an instant hero.

As yet, no orders had been given to start up the hill, and the Americans who lay under the heavy barrage of fire began sustaining heavy casualties. One of the first to be killed was

Capt. Bucky O'Niel of the Rough Riders. Captain O'Niel was the man who had jumped into the water to try to save Cobb and English, and when the men of the Tenth learned that he had been killed, all felt a sadness over the event.

Then word came down for the Tenth to go over a wire fence that crossed just in front of its position, then push through a thick, almost impenetrable brush, starting up the hill. With a yell, they started on their mission, thus becoming the first unit to commit itself to the attack. Todd ran to the front of his men, and a flag bearer joined him.

Seeing the Tenth Cavalry start its attack, Roosevelt could wait no longer, even though he was supposed to. Without specific orders to do so, he rallied the Rough Riders, and they started up the hill as well. Roosevelt was the only one mounted, and he rode to the very front of his regiment, then rode back and forth from one side of his lines to the other, all the while keeping his men moving forward.

In front as he was and mounted as he was, he made a very conspicuous target, and even Todd, when he looked over and saw him, felt a begrudging respect for the man. He might be vainglorious, but he certainly wasn't short of courage.

By now every regiment had committed itself to the attack, and the men ran up the hill, cheering and firing. They would run for several feet, then drop to their knees and fire, then stand up and run some more. All the while, the Spanish were raining a murderous fire down upon the attacking troops.

The attack had accomplished one thing. The terrible artillery fire the Spanish had been raining down on the men was now lifted. The Americans had run toward the guns, and the Spanish artillery couldn't depress the barrels quickly enough to be effective with their fire. The sudden and unexpected cessation of Spanish artillery meant that the danger to those back in the field hospital had been reduced.

In the meantime, the Americans were using the Gatling guns with devastating effectiveness. One blockhouse was completely subdued by the rapid-firing guns, and from the trenches near the blockhouse a dozen Spanish soldiers broke and ran. The battle was over for them.

Along the rest of the hill, though, the Spanish riflemen

stuck bravely to their posts, and their fire doubled and trebled in fierceness. The crest of the hill crackled and burst in roars and rippled with waves of tiny flame.

The Americans advanced on hands and knees, crawling on their stomachs at times, and, where the ground permitted, with a rush. On top of the hill was a huge iron kettle, of the type used for sugar refining. Todd and several of his men used the kettle for shelter as they continued to direct their fire toward the blockhouse.

Observing the battle through binoculars, Richard Harding Davis was already writing his story:

They had no glittering bayonets, they were not massed in regular array. There were a few men in advance, bunched together and creeping up a steep, sunny hill, the top of which roared and flashed with flame. The men held their guns pressed across their breasts and stepped heavily as they climbed. Behind these first few, spreading out like a fan, were single lines of men, slipping and scrambling in the smooth grass, moving forward with difficulty, as though they were wading waist high through water, moving slowly, carefully, with strenuous effort. It was much more wonderful than any swinging charge could be. They walked to greet death at every step, many of them as they advanced sinking suddenly or pitching forward and disappearing in the high grass, but the others waded on, stubbornly, forming a thin blue line that kept creeping higher and higher up the hill. It was inevitable as the rising tide. It was a miracle of self-sacrifice, a triumph of bulldog courage, which one watched breathless with wonder. But the blue line crept steadily up and on, and then, near the top, the broken fragments gathered together with a sudden burst of speed, the Spaniards appeared for a moment outlined against the sky and poised for instant flight, fired a last volley and fled before the swift-moving wave that leaped and sprang up after them.

By the time the attackers reached the top of the hill there was great confusion, the different regiments being completely intermingled, white and black infantry regulars, white and black cavalry regulars, and the two volunteer regiments, the Lightning Cavalry and the Rough Riders.

As a result, the soldiers were disconnected from their chain of command. That didn't matter; they fought shoulder to shoulder, infantryman with cavalryman, regular with volunteer, and black with white, until finally the last Spaniard was gone and the hill was taken. When the Americans realized they had won the battle, they let out a mighty cheer.

Sometime later, with the hill secure, the men, exhausted and gun-smoke–blackened, were sitting or lying around, and taking a much-deserved breather.

One of the men who had been separated from his own unit was Pvt. Eugene Butler of the Ohio Militia. Sitting beside him was Private Bates of the Tenth Cavalry. Both men took out their canteens to take a drink of water, but Eugene's canteen was empty.

"Want a drink?" Bates asked, passing his canteen over.

"Yeah, thanks," Eugene said automatically; then he hesitated. He and Bates looked at each other.

"You're that white son of a bitch we run into in Tampa," Bates said.

"Yes," Eugene said. The two men looked at each other suspiciously for a moment. "Maybe you don't want to share your water with a white man," Eugene suggested.

Bates laughed. "A white man? Man, you ought to see yourself. You got so much gunpowder on you . . . you as black as I am. Here, nigger, take the damn water."

Eugene laughed with him, then took the canteen. A moment later, one of the men with Eugene's company saw him sitting in the middle of several troopers from the Tenth.

"Hey, Eugene, what you doin' over there with them?" he called. "Why don't you come over here with your own?"

"These are my own," Eugene said simply.

Later that morning, General Shafter prepared a note to be sent to the senior Spanish officer in Santiago:

I shall be obliged, unless you surrender, to shell Santiago de Cuba. Please inform the citizens of foreign countries, and all women and children, that they should leave the city before 10 o'clock tomorrow morning.

> Very respectfully, your obedient servant
> William R. Shafter
> Major General, U.S.A.

General Wheeler called for a volunteer to deliver the message under a flag of truce. Todd immediately volunteered, and Marty announced that she wanted to go with him.

"No, not under any circumstances!" Todd replied.

"Why not? You'll be going under a flag of truce, won't you?"

"That doesn't matter. You aren't going."

"Wait a minute," General Wheeler said. "Miss McGuire, would you really go with him if you could?"

"Yes, of course."

"I think you ought to let her go," General Wheeler said.

"General, you must be joking."

"No, I'm very serious. If she goes with you, the Spanish will realize that we aren't trying to trick them. Besides, she does speak excellent Spanish, and you might need an interpreter."

Todd looked at Marty and shrugged his shoulders. "I guess I'm outranked," he said.

General Wheeler laughed. "You know, son, I'm not really sure you are referring to me," he commented.

Todd called for a couple of horses, and a few minutes later he and Marty started riding downhill, toward the city, with each of them carrying a white flag. They rode slowly, and soon two riders came out to greet them.

"Are either of you armed?" one of them asked in Spanish. Marty translated.

"Tell them no," Todd said. "Tell them we have a message for General Linares from General Shafter."

After Marty translated Todd's words, the two Spanish officers led them into Santiago.

Marty looked around as they rode into the town. There was a great difference between what she was seeing here and what was on the hill behind them. Behind them were the bodies and wounded soldiers of this morning's battle. Even those who hadn't been wounded showed the results of the fight. Here, though, there had been no battle. All the soldiers were fresh and unbloodied. And yet the Americans were asking the Spanish to surrender.

General Linares, it turned out, had been on the hill when the fighting started, and he had been wounded in the shoulder. The acting commander was General Toral. This was the same General Toral who been the senior officer in charge of Marty's court-martial.

"I see you managed to survive the sentence our court imposed upon you," General Toral said when Marty and Todd were taken to the church that was still being used as the military headquarters.

"Yes."

General Toral rubbed his hair. "I'm glad," he said finally. "I didn't feel good about sentencing a woman to die, but I had to do my duty. Now I can say I have done my duty, even though you did manage to escape. Honor has been served."

"I don't suppose Colonel Diaz is as happy about it as you are."

"Diaz is dead," General Toral said. "He was killed in this morning's battle. What message do you have for me?"

Marty read it to him, then handed him the paper.

Toral stroked his chin for a moment; then he replied to Todd. "This city will not surrender. I will inform the foreign consuls and inhabitants of your general's message."

"Very good, sir," Todd said, saluting. Toral returned the salute.

As they started to leave, Marty glanced toward the altar. She saw that it had been converted into an operating table. A thin, pale figure of a man was lying on the table, ready for the surgeon's knife. The man was naked except for a breech-clout, and for one dizzying moment Marty could almost believe that he had just been taken down from the cross. The impression was brief, but so intense that it illuminated all the horrors of war.

Refugees began pouring out of the city, but by the deadline the next morning the Spanish army was still entrenched in and around Santiago. As he had warned he would, General Shafter began his bombardment.

The ships of the American navy moved into the harbor and began shelling Santiago with their huge eight- and ten-inch guns. The army on San Juan Hill moved all their guns into position and began shelling from the other side. For two weeks the Americans rained death and destruction down from the skies. No one could get in or out. As the siege continued, the Spanish sustained numerous casualties from the heavy firing, and the food dwindled.

Finally, on Sunday, July 17, formal surrender ceremonies were held. Marty wrote of the ceremony:

> General Shafter and the other generals on his staff rode to a large field near Santiago, accompanied by a troop of the Seventh Cavalry. There they met General Toral, who was accompanied by 100 Spanish soldiers.
>
> General Shafter then did a splendid thing. He presented General Toral with the sword and spurs of General Vara de Ray, a brave Spanish general who was killed at El Caney. After that, the Spanish troops presented arms, and the flag that had flown over Santiago for 382 years was pulled down and furled forever.
>
> During this flag ceremony, the Americans also presented arms. After the ceremony, everyone rode into the city, where the Spanish army placed all their weapons in an armory, leaving themselves disarmed.
>
> By noon, thousands of spectators were gathered in the plaza to witness the raising of the American flag over the governor's palace. At the same moment, 21 guns were fired, and a band struck up the tune "Hail Columbia!"

An unexpected bonus resulted from the surrender of Santiago, a bonus that not only pacified the city but also effectively ended the entire war. During the final arrangements, General Toral asked General Shafter if the surrender included his entire command. General Shafter, who had negotiated only for Santiago, was surprised by the question. "What does your command consist of?" Shafter asked.

"I have 11,500 men here in Santiago," General Toral answered, "7,000 in Guantánamo, 3,500 at San Luis, and about 1,500 more at a field camp thirty miles from here."

"Certainly," General Shafter said quickly. "The surrender includes everyone."

Very well," General Toral said without argument. "I shall have them brought in so their arms may be turned over to you."

With victories in Puerto Rico and the Philippines, the Spanish-American War came to a close. The U.S. ambassador to England, John Hay, wrote a letter to Col. Theodore Roosevelt. At a dinner held to celebrate the victory, Colonel Roosevelt read a sentence from the letter aloud:

" 'It has been a splendid little war, begun with the highest motives, carried on with magnificent intelligence and spirit, favored by that fortune which loves the brave.'

"I'll tell you this," Roosevelt said in a few additional remarks. "It may have been a 'splendid little war,' as Ambassador Hay says, but it has forever changed the history of the world. The United States is now a world power, with possessions spread over half the globe."

"Colonel Roosevelt, surely you don't mean the United States is going to take Spain's place in Cuba?" someone asked.

Roosevelt stroked his mustache. "You mean annex Cuba? Well, there are those who think it wouldn't be a bad idea. But I happen to believe Cuba will be given her freedom. She'll be a new and independent country in our hemisphere, and 100 years from now she will be a close and strong ally."

"That will be 1998, T. R.," General Miles said. "A lot can happen between now and then."

"Perhaps so," Roosevelt agreed. He took off his glasses

and polished them; then he looked up and smiled. "Of course, the good thing about a politician making predictions for 100 years in the future is that no one here now will be around then to call him on them."

His audience laughed appreciatively.

At the same time the victory dinner was going on at General Shafter's headquarters, another celebration was taking place in the church in Santiago. There, with the men of the Tenth Cavalry gathered in attendance, Marty McGuire became the bride of 1st Lt. Todd Armstrong Murchison.

When they stepped out onto the front stoop of the church, Colonel Baldwin called the assembled officers to attention.

"Officers," Colonel Baldwin commanded. "Present, sabers!"

The officers of the Tenth Cavalry made an arch of their sabers, and this time, one of those officers was black. Sgt. Maj. Edward Lee Baker Jr., wearing the Medal of Honor he had won for "disregarding his own personal safety to rescue a comrade under heavy fire," had just been appointed a first lieutenant.

To the cheers of the men, Todd and Marty hurried through the arch and into their future.